THE ROSECLIFF RANKINGS

Devoni Kinney

HOWLING WOLF PRESS

St. Paul ~ Santa Fe

FIRST EDITION

ISBN-10   0692275037
ISBN-13   978-0692275030

10 9 8 7 6 5 4 3 2 1

1 JUDGES AREN'T PORK

Sophie Poe punches in the security code to the faculty entrance and ducks into the custodians' closet to adjust her elasticized clothing, away from the prying eye of the security camera. She considers this closet her personal refuge from the hordes of chain-smoking, phone-texting students waiting to corner her, including one who's been tracking her movements with a GPS device. As she tugs at the waist of her polyester skirt, Charles VandenDungen emerges from behind a cabinet, wielding a blue fluorescent tube.

"I'm not happy," he says, "with my overheads."

As Sophie jolts upright, the hem of her dress clings to her hip, exposing her slip from the waist down. She struggles to flatten it, but the wintry air of the closet, battling the seeping August humidity, creates such a massive imbalance of electrons that the skirt adheres to her palm as if glued there. Trying to smooth it down, she scatters a pile of student papers she's laid atop a bucket.

The Dean seems not to notice. "I realized this morning that I despise the color of my overhead lights," he says. "I can't get anything done unless the light is just right." His left hand with its assertive wedding and, as bold as a Super Bowl ring, looms into her field of vision as he stoops and begins collecting her papers.

"I've got it," she says, grasping fistfuls of student product.

Setting aside his tube, the Dean collects the assignments and hands them to her, his sidelong glance inspecting her indignity. She turns to escape.

"Sophie?"

She glances over her shoulder.

"I assume you received notice that I'll be conducting impromptu evaluations of all faculty members."

As VandenDungen speaks, his left hand flutters about like a wounded bird until at last it lands in his nest of disheveled hair.

"I'm curious," he says, "are you working on something?"

"Hmm."

"A major article? Something publishable?"

"Um."

"Because of all the factors that go into the mix," he continues, "of all the elements that combine to make this profession of ours both the pleasure and challenge it is, that's the most important piece, isn't it? The scholarship piece?"

Sophie considers the point. Didn't a recent National Law Journal article quote some employers saying that law faculty scholarship is a waste of time?

"I'm not sure about that," she says.

The Dean smirks. "You're not sure if you're working on anything?"

Oh, she's sure about that. "Some recent commentators question the importance of legal scholarship, don't they?"

His faded prep school demeanor exudes a sense of superiority. "Do you really think our colleagues at Harvard and Yale will stop publishing because some practitioners don't understand scholarship?"

"I thought we're supposed to pander to the employers," Sophie ventures. "Aren't they a market force? Like 'demand'?"

"So you're not working on anything, then," VandenDungen says.

"It's hard to juggle everything, especially when I'm teaching three writing classes."

"That just doesn't wash, Sophie."

"Writing classes involve an extra load," she says, "a huge, extra load. I'm grading 70 plus papers each assignment."

"On the other hand," the Dean says, "it's not as if you're the CEO of a Fortune 500 company, is it?"

VandenDungen loves Wall Street culture and all its tired power symbols, injecting a reference to a mega-corporation into every conversation. He identifies intensely with the corporate world, frequently citing his 13 months working in the office of the general counsel of Meyeth Industries and to his single publication, an essay — "The Essay," he calls it — in a 2004 book titled Cry, The Corporate Warrior.

"It's not necessarily easy, Sophie," he says, "but you just have to do it."

"I need to prepare for class," she says. "I'm running late."

"You didn't answer my question."

She blinks. "No, it is not like I'm the CEO of a Fortune 500 company."

He sighs. "The question is, are you working on a major publishable article?"

"Well, I have a concept," she lies, "and I've done some research."

"Good." The Dean's squinty eyes remind her of John Malkovich's when his fake charm evaporates and the ruthless butcher inside is revealed. "I need a promise."

"What?"

"You'll give me a preview of the project."

She opens the door.

"Promise?"

Murmuring noncommittally, she lets the door swing closed behind her, bolts for the stairwell and bounds upward, whereupon she stumbles and drops the papers again.

"Sophie!"

Standing in the hall by the closet, the Dean exhibits his over-whitened teeth.

"I need that promise!"

"Jeez," she murmurs, as the legal definition of promise spins

7

into her mind. A manifestation of intent, written or oral, reasonably interpreted as a commitment . . .

But the Dean and his impatient brilliance have moved on down the hall.

§

The closet paper-drop humiliation has stolen valuable minutes from Sophie's prep time. Seated in her tiny office, she forces herself into a cursory review of the distinction between restrictive and non-restrictive clauses. As one of two professors tasked with teaching legal analysis and writing to first-year law students, she spends the first weeks of each semester "revisiting" basic principles of grammar, punctuation, and sentence structure with adult students who claim never to have been taught them in their prior 17 years of education.

Next door, the toilet flushes, sounding as if it could suck down the entire building. Over the five years of her instructorship at Rosecliff, she's occupied as many offices, including one "shared space" in which she attempted to grade papers and prepare for class at one end of the room while the students of the Rosecliff Law Clinic interviewed their mentally ill criminal clients at the other. Her current office is a converted closet at the end of the hall, separated by a thin wall from the only restroom on the third floor. No, she tells people, she can't identify faculty members by the sounds they make in the bathroom. Not consistently anyway.

"Got a moment?"

Chaz VandenDungen's thick-boned frame fills the doorway.

"I'm pretty rushed," Sophie says.

"This new project you're developing, I'm intrigued."

Why is he harassing her about intriguing projects? Does he have her confused with a tenure-track sycophant? Or, worse, has he instituted a new requirement that everyone has to publish scholarship, even marginal year-to-year contract employees such as herself?

"I need to get going," she says. "My class is starting."

"Give me a hint." VandenDungen says, eyes squinting diabolically like the cynical eyes of a jungle cat pretending to doze as its body grows taut with anticipation of the taste of its prey.

"I'm kind of superstitious," she says. "I think talking about a project while you're working on it jinxes it. So I haven't really talked about it to anyone."

"Get over that."

Surveying the chaos of books, papers, food wrappers, and empty cans on her desk, her gaze rests on a week-old newspaper with a headline reading "Judges Aren't Pork." She can use that as a title. It could be about a modern judiciary . . . a judiciary that could be traded . . . in the market!

"Well," she says, clearing her throat, "the title is 'Judges Aren't Pork.'"

The Dean's head tilts sideways, his sheer cliff of a forehead pleating into furrows. His expression telegraphs conditional interest, implying that more in the way of a title is required. She needs a subtitle, something witty.

"'Judges Aren't Pork," she sputters. "Boxed Bellies on the Bench or . . . No, wait, that's silly, that's not—"

"Fascinating!" VandenDungen says. "I'm hearing a marketplace metaphor, the judiciary as commodity, perhaps the commodification of justice itself."

"Exactly."

"Justice as product," he says. "I'm loving it."

According to the clock on her wall, Sophie is now a minute late to class.

"You'll be refining it, of course," he says.

"I'm late," she says, pushing past the Dean's deep-freezer bulk. Slamming the door behind her, she rushes down the hall.

"Didn't you get the memo?" the Dean calls after her. "Don't turn off your lights anymore! The new Rosecliff protocol is, leave them on! It factors into the Rankings! Never mind! I'll flip them back on for you!"

2 Streams of Revenue

The first faculty meeting of the semester takes place in a storage room in the basement of the library because, the new dean explains, "Rosecliff Law has been in storage for fifteen years." Though stuffed with law professors, the room is as silent as a meeting of Quaker Friends. Perched atop a stack of boxes, Charles VandenDungen faces the gathering. The silence persists.

"Does anyone here even know what 'revenue' means?" the Dean says.

"I'm not sure I understand," says Mason Masonips, a recently recruited transactional law specialist. "Are you really asking if we have heard that term? Isn't it a rhetorical question?" He glances at his colleagues, seeking affirmation of the vaunted Rosecliff School of Law collegiality and support.

VandenDungen ignores Masonips. "Look," he says, "in my interview process for this position I heard a lot of comments about 'drift.' 'We have no direction,' you said, 'we need some leadership around here.' And I have to believe there was truth to those statements. After all . . ." He pauses portentously.

"We're in the Bottom Tier Toilet!" Barbara Kitchen pipes up. Kitchen, a Rosecliff Law graduate, is a veritable balloon of puffing

Rosecliff pride. Whipping around in her seat, she surveys the faces of her colleagues, her crown of beet-red hair absorbing the dim fluorescent light, her eyes wide and accusatory behind magnifying lenses. "I mean, come on, people! We can sit here and be offended all we want, but it won't change the fact we slipped in the Rankings! And, remember, that's what we said we wanted, a dean who could—"

"Wake up!" says the Dean, cutting off his biggest supporter. "You are in crisis! Our entire profession is in crisis!"

The bodies of the faculty collectively tense up, as the specter of the Crisis in Legal Education presses down on them. It cannot be denied. Enrollment is down, student debt up, employment prospects dismal. Most discomfiting, their own careers are threatened. Here they sit, in a claustrophobic room crammed with storage boxes, in the basement of the aging law school building—"in storage," while competing schools have ramped up their efforts not to go out of business.

Across the room, Manuel Delgado swings sideways, flaunting his bulging left bicep on his seat back. No one knows what to expect from the mercurial Latino. He could go any direction. He might let loose a fusillade of expletives. He might lecture the colleagues on their faults and propose an extreme remedy. He might marshal the force of his fellow ethnic minorities; certainly, VandenDungen's none-too-subtle attack on their institution could be interpreted as an assault on diversity on multiple levels.

"This man is here to help us," Delgado advises. "Let's listen to what he has to say."

Relief floats across the room. The absence of a maniacal outburst from Delgado vents the tension.

"Go ahead, Dean," says Barbara Kitchen, "talk to us about revenue streams!"

"In due time," the Dean says. "First, it's time to unpack some myths." Standing, he pulls forth an easel holding a pad of white paper. The Sharpie screeches as he writes.

<u>MYTHS</u>

11

1. Teaching is important.
2. We are professionals.
3. You matter.

"Let's bust this one." VandenDungen points to the first item. "The view you hold of yourselves here at Rosecliff Law is that you're all outstanding teachers, you all have wonderful relationships with your students, which provides a maximal learning environment, blah, blah, blah." With a red marker, VandenDungen draws a circle around the first myth and a slash through it. "That is irrelevant. What counts in today's environment is public perception, particularly that of anyone who might fill out a Rankings ballot. It's critical to deluge these persons with leaflets and postcards about our scholarly output. But we can't do it if we don't seem to be productive. So your orders, henceforth? Crank it out, make it cutting edge or cross-disciplinary, and place it well."

He pauses to let that sink in.

"Dean," says Manuel Delgado, "when you say 'place it well,' what exactly do you mean?"

Delgado's prompt is so perfectly timed and solicitous in tone that it raises the suspicion he and VandenDungen rehearsed this little exercise in spurious cooperation beforehand. It is hard to believe Delgado would align himself with someone so unoppressed.

"I'm referring to a law review at a Top-Fifteen institution," VandenDungen says.

"Wouldn't breaking into the top 75 be good enough?"

Newt King's mild inquiry is the equivalent of lobbing a sizzling tube of TNT at the Dean, judged by the defensiveness of his response.

"Sure," the Dean says. "Why the hell not? And while you're at it, why not change the name of this place to Good Enough Fucking School of Law?"

"Earth to Newt," Delgado says. "Lower than the Top 35 and your reprint won't even be remembered when the ballots go out."

Sophie glances at her watch. With mention of the Rankings, her mind wanders to the errands awaiting her. She needs to shop for groceries, drop them at her father Arthur's house, and get home; her goal is to grade at least half a dozen student papers tonight. She hopes the grocery stop won't take long. She's worried about her dog Buggles; he's spent the day outdoors in the backyard in humid, 95-degree weather and pugs don't do well in the heat.

VandenDungen points at the second item on the list of myths.

"'We are professionals.' This may be the single most harmful one," he says. "It is a sentimentalist, romanticist fiction that we are an intellectual elite, existing on a plane far above the cares and concerns of a materialistic world. Legal education is not a profession, it is a business with a product to manufacture and deliver, a consumer base, and a multitude of market forces at play." He sears them with an accusatory gaze. "And you are in trouble."

In years past, any self-respecting faculty would have vigorously rejected the suggestion that an institution of higher learning is a quasi-corporate entity ruled by capitalistic forces. Now, the room heaves with sighs of disgruntled resignation. The new dean has wasted no time in trotting out the first principle of postmodern academic theory, that rational self-interest and market forces hold the key to everything.

"And *why* are we in trouble, Dean?" Manny Delgado prompts.

"Has anyone in this room bothered to read *The National Law Journal* lately?" the Dean says. "Or *The New York Times* for that matter?"

How can one avoid it, when summaries pop up daily in faculty e-mailboxes, accounts of students duped by pervasive fraud in the legal academy?

The Dean lets his rhetorical question and its multitude of dire implications wriggle in the faculty's guilty conscience, as tentacles of unfulfilled capitalism reach for purchase in their brains—advertising, branding, increasing costs, falling value for the dollar, jobless graduates, reluctant donors . . .

"So, my fellow academicians," the Dean says, speaking in the cadence of a preacher leading his sinners to their moment of rebirth, "though most of you prefer to distance yourselves from such unattractive concepts as profit and loss, balance sheets, line items, and how the university manages to continue to pay your salaries, the truth is—"

"We are marketing our Ranking!" Delgado breaks in, hammering his thigh with his fist. "God damn it! This is what I've been trying to tell you motherfuckers!"

With the recent acceptance of his article by the *Harvard Journal of Minority Rights, Interests, Privileges, Prerogatives, and Concerns*, Manuel Delgado has undergone a transformation. Previously, he was a vocal opponent of dominant-class performance measures such as grade point averages, LSAT scores, and, of course, the Rankings. Now he examines the faces of his colleagues as if he can scarcely believe the lowly company he finds himself in.

With the mention of the *U.S. News & World Report* Rankings, Sophie glances at her watch. She feels her ambition for the evening's plans slipping away, replaced by a desire for margaritas. The Dean's myth-busting is sapping her strength, and he is just beginning to mine the second one. She raises her hand. VandenDungen scans the room, his gaze sliding over her without acknowledgement.

"Excuse me?" she says. "I was wondering about the third myth. How could we not matter?"

Others murmur agreement.

"That's simple," VandenDungen says. "No single individual matters when it comes to promoting a higher profile of the institution. It's about marketing an image of the total package. It's about selling our consumers and our competitors on our successes." He pulls a box off a table and opens it. "And that's why I waited until now to unveil the new brochure."

The faculty literally had been groomed for the publication. During the chaotic week before classes began, professional photographers invaded the school. Everyone was summoned from their homes or offices, sent to "hair and makeup," then ordered to assume the most unnatural teaching postures imaginable, and held until the Dean had signed off on the frames. Afterwards, all faculty members were asked to write a short description of their teaching philosophy and submit it to the Dean's office.

Printed on thick, glossy stock, the brochure's cover features a dreamy Photo-Shopped image of Manuel Delgado and two other minority male professors leaning over a dewy-eyed blond Caucasian female student seated at a library table, a textbook open before her.

Sophie scrutinizes the picture, noting that the book on the table in front of the student is exceedingly thick, even for a law textbook; in fact, she realizes, it is not a textbook at all, but a copy of the massive reference tome, *Black's Law Dictionary*. Did anyone else notice the implication—that at Rosecliff, it takes three male professors to help a female student understand a dictionary definition?

In a corner of the picture appears a symbol, something like a coat of arms, designed to lend class but also clearly meant to convey approval by official authority—an insignia akin, yes, to the sought-after yellow badge licensed to the USNWR elite, but here inscribed with the words, Sophie squints . . . "Always climbing . . . forever striving."

As the faculty members leaf through the brochure, jaws drop open, one after another. Sophie flips through her copy, page after page of soft-focus faculty photos next to blocks of bold text. Searching in vain for her entry, she realizes the skills teachers have been isolated from the "real" faculty and lumped together at the end.

As she spots her listing, a gasp escapes her lips. Her supposed "quote" bears no resemblance to what she submitted; it sounds ridiculous! "Law is language, and language is law. I'm passionately in love with the language of law and the law of language." Does it even make sense?

The ambient snarl of displeasure in the room increases to a roar.

"Calm down," VandenDungen says. "It's not important whether you actually said what we say you said. Remember, this is marketing. It's brand-creation."

Sophie pages numbly through the rest of the brochure. Pretty much everyone sounds simple-minded in their quotes. Perusing them, she realizes that below each member's statement appears a list of his or her recent awards, speeches, service activities, and publications. On the last line a work-in-progress is noted, complete with title and, in some cases, expected date of publication. It seems

15

as if everybody except her is working on something. Thumbing back to her entry, her vision flutters as she reads.

> Work in Progress: Sophie Poe, *Two Hundred Twenty-Some Years and Counting: An Imaginary Dialectic On Grammatical Inconsistencies in Concurring Opinions of the United States Supreme Court.* (tentative title)

"Dean," Newt King says, his flat face tilted like a spinning plate, "there seems to be an error here. I'm not working on anything right now, particularly not a piece called 'A Wistful Deconstruction of the Connection Between the Infield Fly Rule and the Doctrine of . . .' Where's the rest of the title? If I'm allegedly working on something, it should at least have a complete title."

The room erupts in angry asides as faculty members read aloud the titles of their make-believe articles.

"Listen," the Dean says. "For those of you for whom works-in-progress had to be created, and regrettably that's a lot of you, you'll note we've indicated it is *tentatively* titled. You can change it to anything you want! It doesn't matter! The point is simply to get the word out that this is a productive, working faculty."

"Mine is real!" cries Barbara Kitchen.

"Ditto!" says Manuel Delgado.

Many in the room seem to be struggling to comprehend the subject matter of their bogus articles-in-progress. The temperature of the cramped space has increased appreciably since the brochures were distributed.

The faculty meeting collapses into jagged, fretful clusters. Sophie leaves with Elliott Ramsey, a Torts professor with an office across the hall from hers. Shell-shocked, they amble past the seemly gas-conservers and shiny hybrids in Parking Lot A to the Parking Lot B, where the lesser lights of Rosecliff Law park their second-hand sedans and trashed mini-vans.

"What's your fake article about?" Sophie asks.

Ramsey faces her, a pained expression in his eyes. "There wasn't one," he says.

16

She laughs. "Lucky fuck. I mean duck."

"No," he says, his voice shaky, "I'm not even listed. I don't appear."

They stare at each other, mulling over the significance of the omission.

"It was just a mistake," she suggests. "He's rushing everything."

Ramsey shrugs. "It doesn't matter if it's a mistake or intentional. Either way, I'm of no consequence."

"Bullshit. You're the most popular teacher we have."

"You heard what the man said." Ramsey gets into his faded blue Mazda 280Z. "That means nothing."

§

The trip to the grocery store takes longer than hoped as Sophie's hunt for the brand-specific foods on her father Arthur's list becomes an arduous exercise in futility. In the six months since his stroke, when Sophie took over his shopping, she's learned that for Arthur Poe, brand-substitution is not an option. Absolute fidelity to every detail of the list as written is required.

The store has rearranged its canned goods section, so when Sophie finally locates the Dinty Moore products, she finds only chicken and dumplings, chicken stew, and beef stew in cardboard microwaveable containers. She studies the list. Despite the squiggly handwriting, the word "canned" before Dinty Moore stew is unmistakable.

Whereas cans are required for stew, they are unacceptable for the next item on the list, "plastic bottle, Campbell's tomato juice." Unfortunately, there are no plastic bottles on the shelf, only enough cans to supply a brunch bar for a month. Recalling her father's extensive remarks on the displeasing metallic taste of canned juice, she passes them up. She locates the desired half-and-half and chicken wings, but the economy-size Excedrin is sold out. Throwing caution to the wind, she tosses three regular-size bottles into the cart.

With one item to go, Sophie approaches the lunch meat case with a sense of foreboding. In years past just about any supermarket could be counted on to carry a bountiful variety of wieners, but according to her father, the "liberal flakes" have defamed the finest meat animal on earth, the bovine, thereby causing disruption in the supply of beef hotdogs. As feared, there is no beef to be found among the otherwise diverse selection of Oscar Mayer sausage products.

§

Arthur lives on a cul-de-sac lined with identical cream-color duplexes offering a spectrum of life-management assistance alternatives to senior citizens. In Arthur's case, that means prescription orders, light housekeeping, and twice-daily "wellness contacts."

Arthur suffered a "shotgun stroke" wherein a piece of plaque dislodged from the lining of his left carotid artery, then broke into smaller pieces that scattered throughout the brain. Though he lost some memory and capacity for language, as well as movement in his left leg, he remains exceptionally astute about certain details, particularly those capable of capture on numbered lists.

As she knocks on Arthur's door, Sophie hears Fox News blasting at the customary 100 decibel level. She jabs the doorbell impatiently; does her father not realize she has things to do? At last the door opens, and she follows Arthur's fragile, limping frame down the narrow hall to the kitchen. She hands over the plastic bags, whose meager contents confess her shortcomings as a grocery shopper. He gingerly removes and inspects each item, sets it on the counter, and makes checkmarks on his list. When he finishes, he goes through the list twice more, at which point he peers at her through the spattered lenses of his large aviator frames and says, "No wieners?"

She shakes her head. "Not beef."

"Fucking liberals." He sighs as his bony shoulders cave forward in reluctant surrender to the persistence of the anti-red-meat movement.

"I've got to get going, Dad," Sophie says. "I have a stack of papers this tall to grade."

He follows her to the door. "You're still on board for. . . uh. . ."

"The doctor's on Tuesday?"

"Is that when it is, Tuesday?"

She nods. Arthur turns and shuffles back down the hallway.

"It's Tuesday morning," she calls behind him. "At 8:30."

Arthur reappears, carrying a huge wall calendar decorated with pictures of kittens. "That's 8:30 a.m., correct?"

He fumbles with the calendar, which is turned to the month of June. She takes it from him, flips it to August, and points to the following Tuesday's date. "It's here. At 8:30 a.m. I'll pick you up at ten after."

Arthur scrutinizes the month of August as if searching for a small town on a big map.

She taps the date again. "Right here. I'll see you at 8:10."

He gazes at her as if he has just noticed her presence.

"See you then. And thank you, madam."

As she closes the door behind her, Arthur shouts, "You better make that 8:00 a.m. We don't want to keep the doctor waiting."

§

Pulling into her driveway, Sophie spots Buggles in the back yard, peering through the chain-link face. A year after moving here, she bought a small house at the edge of the flood plain so that Buggles would have a place to run. She's since discovered that "on the edge of" meant "in" and, while the occasional flood waters never reach her home's foundation, her yard is perpetually soggy, which has led her to nickname the place Mud Flat.

Once changed into a tee shirt and baggy shorts, Sophie abandons her plan to grade student papers. Her brain feels muzzy, her analytical powers equivalent to a squid's. She opts instead for a microwaved Lean Cuisine Panini with a side of Doritos and an evening watching medical oddities unfold on TV, with droopy-eyed Buggles nodding off on her lap.

Tonight, the challenge facing the team of skilled surgeons arrives in the form of a woman whose 178 pound tumor has coiled around her body like a boa constrictor. Watching the surgeons work, Sophie marvels at their ability to refrain from making derogatory comments about the patient, who is overweight even without the tumor and who's waited so extremely long to have it removed. Despite the easy target lying unconscious on the table before them, the doctors and their assistants remain completely professional, filling Sophie with admiration and gratitude on the patient's behalf. The operation is progressing well when Buggles begins to snore and Sophie feels her own eyes grow heavy. Her drowsy appreciation is replaced in the last moments of consciousness by the image of herself lying supine on a gurney, mouth open, needle hanging out of her arm, a snake wrapping its muscular length around her abdomen, its head replaced by a cheesy US-NWR badge, while a tight-lipped Chaz VandenDungen plunges a syringe of tomato juice into her vein.

3 TAKING IT FROM BEHIND

The next morning, Sophie notices a manila envelope slipped under the door of her office. Assuming it's a late assignment, she tosses it on her desk and turns her attention to grading a batch of student papers. The first one begins inauspiciously. "The issue here is weather the plaintive can recover $ from the owner of the dog grooming place, and, should she even try?"

The third paper is so impressive she stops to run her digital version of it through Li'l Copycat, the plagiarism software that is more a part of the modern law teacher's arsenal than the Socratic method. In a matter of seconds, LC has found 17 instances of word-for-word verbal theft. With copycatting detection comes Honor Code investigation, which in turn intensifies free-floating student hostility and aggression, occasionally impelling a helicopter momma of a 24-year-old student to call the Dean's office. Should she just ignore her findings?

Sophie glances around for diversion, spots the manila envelope, and opens it. She removes a folder with a note stapled to the front.

To Sophie, my Honeypot,

Crusades are crude.
Seeking votes, vulgar.

21

Public service serves no purpose
Compared to my lust for you.

The folder contains photographs and leaflets relating to a campaign for the state senate in Oklahoma, evidently undertaken some years before by a plump, middle-aged man who was a student in one of Sophie's writing classes last semester. He stalked her over the summer, showing up at grocery stores and restaurants when she was there. She finally figured out he'd attached a GPS tracker to the undercarriage of her car.

Opening her file cabinet, Sophie drops the entire business into a folder marked "James Yoder," filled with anonymous notes, peculiar and suggestive drawings, plagiarized poems, cards that accompanied unwelcome bouquets, and e-mails.

Behind the bulging Yoder file is a thin one labeled Publications, containing a copy of a fifteen-page article about Clean Water Act claims that Sophie banged out one weekend in response to an S.O.S. from her colleague Wallace Shane, who'd committed to write it for the state bar magazine, procrastinated, then was bitten in the leg by a brown recluse spider and hospitalized for a week. Sophie feels kind of proud of the piece, though in retrospect she might've chosen a more imaginative title than "Clean Water Act Claims."

Her moment of modest pride slides away, displaced by the swollen worm of incomprehension crawling through her consciousness named "An Imaginary Dialectic" — a what? — "On Grammatical Inconsistencies in Concurring Opinions of the United States Supreme Court. . ." Covering 200 "something" years? Have the old grayheads really been grinding them out that long?

She plops back down in her chair. Dialectics? Imaginary ones, no less! She used to be a real lawyer! How has it come to this?

For five years now, she's been plodding along the professional track of least prestige in the Rosecliff Legal Skills Program. It was the only position available in the area when she moved back home to help Arthur recover from the financial and emotional crisis brought on by her older brother Quinton's embezzlement of most of their father's considerable retirement savings.

She'd been humming along rather nicely as a civil litigator at the Justice Department in Washington when she received a call from Arthur. Something was wrong at his law office. Quinton had left without notice. The bank had contacted Arthur about overdue loan payments. He couldn't find the paper statements and didn't know how to access computer records. Would she be available to visit, just to help sort things out?

Arthur's office was a dusty den of chaos and neglect. All but one of his five associates had left the firm. Financial records had been falsified, Arthur's signature forged on documents and checks. Clients' files were missing. Sophie hadn't realized how far things had gone downhill since her mother's death from cancer four years earlier. Arthur alternated between depression and rage. For six months, she tried to fly back and forth but it didn't work, so she finally decided to quit her job and move back home.

She accepted a visitor's position at the law school, thinking it would be a one-year gig and she'd move on after that. But Arthur continued to need her help, and then came the stroke. Nothing better had come along and probably wouldn't in this small community. She'd upheld her end of the bargain, accepting a fifty percent pay cut while attempting to teach semi-literate adults how to write professionally. She'd spilled red ink over reams of barely readable student product, until her eyes crossed, her teeth hurt, and her nerves twanged. Nothing had been mentioned about producing an eighty-page law review article; that torturous task was traditionally reserved for the "doctrinal" teachers, the tenure-track elite of the law faculty. Until VandenDungen's arrival.

Rosecliff's "national search" for a new law school dean was a high-profile charade, illustrating with embarrassing perspicuity that it is the rare academician who wishes to trade the delicious autonomy and unaccountability of professorship for the frustrations of being an administrator who controls no one and answers to everyone—especially in the Bottom Tier Toilet. Despite ads placed in every conceivable outlet, not a single candidate applied. As summer arrived, the university president produced the CVs of two prospects. The first was an African-American female professor tenured at an obscure Appalachian institution known only for graduating a man summa cum laude who, it was later discovered, had kept four sex slaves in a storm shelter to "relieve his stress" during law school. The second résumé belonged to a man with a remarkable set of credentials—Duke undergrad, Yale Law, L.L.M. from Columbia—and a short but prestigious practice experience, followed by a concerning pattern of deanships at unaccredited law schools, each lasting four years. Red flags appeared during the obligatory reference checks of both candidates. Since receiving tenure, the female professor had given everyone in her classes As. Comments made about the male candidate were hard to interpret. "We could think only of the future, never the past," said one former colleague. "He was very focused on the small detail, very hands-on," said another. "His mind works overtime," commented a third.

Despite doubts among members of the Dean Search Committee, both candidates were flown in for interviews. The lady washed out when she refused to explain her "all A" grade policy other than to say, "I do it because I can." That left Charles VandenDungen, whose job talk on educational theory, punctuated with references to "constructivism," "orchestrated immersion," and other helium-filled verbiage somehow sealed the deal, securing him a five-year contract as Dean of Rosecliff Law.

Recalling the process now, Sophie considers how well the references' ambiguous remarks about VandenDungen dovetail with the unuttered phrase "mental disorder."

Her attention drifts across her desk to the newspaper from whence she stole the title for her grandiose article proposal, "Judges Aren't Pork." It actually sounds like a pretty interesting idea compared to the Dean's choice for her. Maybe the story contains a kernel of a concept worth developing, she thinks. As she picks up the paper, the complete headline is revealed: "Cattlemen's Association Judges Aren't Pork Fans." According to the article, the judges in question refused an invitation from producers of "the other white meat" to a swine and wine tasting.

As she moans, the phone rings; it's Christopher Paine, the Associate Dean. "Do you have a minute?" he says liltingly. At Rosecliff Law, the phrase "do you have a minute," originating in an administrator's office, is code for "bend over, you're about to take it from behind."

"Not exactly," she says.

"It's important," Paine says. "Do you want to come down here, or should I come up there?"

When given this choice, one always prefers to "go there." Choosing to battle on someone else's turf is counter-intuitive, except when one takes into account that law professors are superb upside-down readers. Nasty rumors have been started, article ideas stolen, and careers jeopardized because one professor surreptitiously inspected another's desktop papers while ostensibly conducting a friendly office visit.

Arriving at Paine's office, Sophie is surprised to see VandenDungen there. As she takes a seat by Paine's desk, the Dean closes the door and scowls down at her. She glances at Paine, who is smiling with sad-eyed compassion. Pulling a chair over, the Dean sits facing her, his grapefruit-size knees not a foot from her small, bony ones.

"Sophie," he says, "you're expensive."

"What?"

"You cost a lot. Too much."

"What's that supposed to mean?"

Paine breaks in. "What Chaz means is, given the fact you teach in the Skills Program, your salary is relatively high as measured against the salaries of those who teach courses like Contracts, Property, and Torts."

"Unacceptably high," VandenDungen says.

She can't believe what she's hearing. It dawns on her what this is about. VandenDungen wants to cut her income further, perhaps to poverty level. Under no circumstances will she agree to a pay reduction. She's having enough trouble covering her debts as it stands.

"Did you mean to say my salary is inadequate?" she says.

VandenDungen shoots Paine a dark look.

"It's high for skills faculty, Sophie," the Dean says.

"I disagree," she says. "As a writing teacher, my grading burden

25

is much heavier, and I spend many more hours meeting with my students one-on-one than any doctrinal teacher." She looks to Paine for support, recalling his boasting when she was hired that unlike other law schools, Rosecliff did not segregate its skills faculty or treat them like second-class citizens. That turned out to be a complete fabrication.

"It may come as a surprise to you, Sophie," VandenDungen says, "but the new guy in town is trying to run a business. The fact is, you're being paid far more than the market supports. By paying you at the level we are, for the job you're doing, we're utilizing our resources in the least cost-effective manner. We could hire skills teachers for half your salary and use the other half to fund programs that would measurably impact the Rankings."

"Not quite half, Chaz," says Christopher Paine, his tone annoying silky.

VandenDungen leaps to his feet. "No, no, Chris, listen, goddamn it! Where I came from, we could have hired Sophie's equivalent for a quarter of what she makes! In D.C., would-be legal skills teachers walk the streets, panhandling! Hell, I could probably find a dozen candidates who'd do it voluntarily, just to be able to put it on their résumés!"

Sophie pictures legions of street people with law degrees meandering through the streets of D.C., contentedly pushing shopping carts overflowing with unintelligible student product.

Paine sighs. "Chaz has a proposition for you, Sophie," he says.

"I won't work as a volunteer," she says. "I draw the line at that."

"No, no, you don't understand," VandenDungen says.

"Correct."

"I'm offering you a chance to become a real professor and even have a shot at tenure."

Sophie considers the incongruity between the Dean's implication that she is an overpaid, fungible paraprofessional and his offer of a position of higher status and lifetime job security.

"Why would you do that?" she says.

"I happen to know you're more capable than you've demonstrated," VandenDungen says. "I read your article in the *American*

Law Journal. It is excellent."

She almost blurts out, "But they made me write that!"

As a student she was selected for the law journal. Everyone on the staff was required to write an article on an assigned topic. She put in 482 hours and 635 footnotes writing "The Hermeneutics of Internormativity As Applied to the Pluralist Aesthetic." It was the most agonizing experience of her life. The concepts of hermeneutics and internormativity were like eels sloshing around in her brain; they wouldn't stop moving long enough for her to identify what they were. Astonishingly, her article was selected for publication. When the journal came out months later, she excitedly opened it and began to read her piece. To her vexation, she couldn't really follow it.

"Look," VandenDungen says, "this is your sixth year at Rosecliff."

She nods.

"If we use the seven-year rule, you'll have a year to make tenure. You could apply in the fall semester of your seventh year."

Sophie feels numb. VandenDungen's proposal is worse than a salary reduction. He is presenting a classic Hobson's choice—the appearance of a choice where, realistically, none exists. If she rejects his tenure-track offer, her contract will not be renewed, and he'll recruit her replacement from among the homeless of the nation's capital.

"To be honest, Sophie," VandenDungen goes on, "I began thinking about this offer after we spoke about your article. We've got to pump up our scholarly output, and I just can't get your idea out of my mind! The judicial system as market-driven machine, the judiciary as freely traded commodity . . . it's so law-and-economics! I suspect you've got dormant potential, and I'd like to give you an opportunity to capitalize on it."

She tries to read Chris Paine's reaction to the Dean's bizarre idea, but the Associate Dean, eyes closed, is evidently under the sway of one of his trademark spiritual pauses.

"I thought law-and-economics was over," she ventures.

VandenDungen watches her warily, as if she's a wild animal

he's trapped that he suspects might try to escape. "It will never be over," he says gravely.

"There's no way I can be ready for tenure in a year," she says. "How can I cram six years of effort into one?"

Stroking his chin, VandenDungen contemplates her. "No one was stopping you from writing before now."

"I wrote an environmental article," she says. "For the practitioner."

VandenDungen flips his hand. "Pfffft . . . doesn't count. But I'd be willing to recommend to the faculty and the president of the university that the traditional two-article requirement be waived in your case."

Paine's eyes pop open. "On what basis?"

"My belief that if Sophie fulfills the promise of her proposal, it will be an adequate tenure piece unto itself."

"Are you joking with me?" she says. How did her offhand remark in the custodian's closet morph into a proposal bursting with extraordinary potential? This is a spoof, she suspects, orchestrated to demonstrate how truly expendable she is, by advancing the most ludicrous proposition imaginable and letting it lie there helplessly like a fish baking on a beach.

"Look at it this way," VandenDungen says, his hands gliding in the air as if on currents of wind. "This could be a very impressive undertaking, requiring hundreds of hours of research, culling and organizing the sources, and then—the writing! Consider the possible scope! You can deal with the history of judicial selection, election versus appointment, separation of powers issues, and layered on top of it all, the classic precepts of laissez-faire analysis, with justice as the currency!" He slams his meaty palms together. "Oh, yeah! We'll set that fucking University of Chicago back on its ass!"

"Chicago!" she says, alarmed. "Chicago has been leading the debate in law and economics since the 1970s!"

By now, Sophie is watching the scene from outside herself, gazing down from the perforated, asbestos-clogged ceiling tiles. Why has this lunatic permitted this fantasy, with her at its center, to carry him away? She doesn't know where to begin to detangle the fat wad of delusion he has dumped in her lap.

"No wonder this institution slipped to the bottom Tier," VandenDungen says. "Do you think Chicago, or for that matter, Yale, or Penn ever wait for an engraved invitation to enter the debate?"

"Chaz," Paine says. "Let's examine this idea a little more closely."

VandenDungen stomps his foot. "I knew this was coming! I was warned about this! 'A school like Rosecliff,' they told me, 'they'll hire you to raise them up, they'll *beg* you for help, then they'll send you off in a boat by yourself with a single oar and sit back and watch you paddle around in circles.'"

Paine's gentle features assume a tragic cast. "Let's all take a deep breath."

"You just don't get it, do you, Chris? Deep breaths have landed you where you are today!" VandenDungen glares down at Sophie. "It's really your decision."

"I'd like to think it over."

"I'll need your answer in a week." VandenDungen is already halfway out the door. "Recruiting season is just around the corner, you know."

§

Sophie's closest friend on the faculty is Wallace Shane, a gnome of a man nine years her senior who has pressed a friendship on her against her will because they both graduated from the same law school (number nine in the latest Rankings), and because, as he frequently comments, "there just aren't a whole lot of folks on this faculty who've had the first-class education we've had, Sophie." To which she typically responds, "I feel so elite."

Wally Shane has taken the cliché of the cluttered professor's lair to a whole new level. He occupies one of the largest offices in the law school, but every square inch of surface area is buried under multiple levels of "mixed media." He teaches environmental law

29

courses and through the years has accumulated a lot of environment himself, so that in addition to the usual unmanageable collection of papers and books, Shane's collection includes sticks, dried grasses, glass containers of various colors of viscous sludge, his rock collection, and what appear to be the remains of once-living creatures. A carefully maintained eight-inch-wide path winds through the wilds to Shane's desk.

Shane meets her at the door as if he's expecting her. Sophie figures word of her imminent unemployment has preceded her in uncannily rapid fashion. Typically, Shane appears worried. While other male professors are mired in the depths of depression, or choking on inarticulate anger, or tediously tending their bloated egos, Wallace Shane perpetually swims the murky sea of concern.

"I was looking for you," Shane says. "The lights were on in your office, but you were gone. I was concerned."

"The Dean wants the lights on all the time for some reason."

Shane's face flushes beneath its freckles. "Apparently if we increase our utility costs, we can show a higher per student spending ratio and thereby improve our score in one of the key factors used in the Rankings." He gestures to the ceiling. "I'll be leaving mine *off* 24-7 from now on."

Shane clears a swath at the end of his couch, and she squeezes her butt into it, eager to spill her guts about the Dean's proposal.

"The reason I was looking for you," Shane says, eyes twinkling, "is that I saw my Rolfer yesterday. You know that place down here?" He gestures to his hip. "He took one feel of it and says 'What in bloody hell is going on? Did someone close to you pass away?' I couldn't believe it. All the pain I've experienced over Karla dumping me has apparently collected in an area about five inches long and yay-wide, and it's effectively pulling my whole left side inward, kind of like a black hole collapsing in on itself, which explains why my entire upper body has been listing to port for months. Well, he took hold of me, and I thought he was going to yank my groin through my ears, but goddamn if I'm not walking straighter this morning!"

"You do look a bit brighter," Sophie says. "And you're definitely standing up straighter."

"Did you notice?"

"Right away."

"I just hope it makes a difference to that weird thing going on with my prostate."

"I don't know," she says. "That might be a separate issue."

"Could be."

"I thought your internist prescribed some medicine for that."

"He did, but it's not working. The pinching feeling is still there. I can't sleep."

They sat in silence a few moments.

"If it doesn't improve," he says, "I think my next step is to see the herbalist."

She nods. "It might be dietary, I suppose."

He looks up at her suddenly. "What's going on with you?"

"Did the Dean assign you an article-in-progress?" she says.

"Yeah, but fuck him. I write what I want. I noticed he has quite a doozie planned for you." Shane chuckles. "What's the matter? The topic doesn't excite you?"

"It's worse than that." She recounts the whole story, starting with the encounter in the closet and ending with VandenDungen's threat to replace her with a destitute Washingtonian. The story sounds outlandish in the telling, and by the time she finishes, she feels relieved; it's too ridiculous to take seriously. But the longer she talks, the less amused Shane appears. Arms crossed over his chest, he regards her gravely over the top of his wire rims.

"You know, this guy is just fanatical enough to mean it," he says. "With that fake article bullshit he pulled yesterday, I'm starting to believe he'll do anything to make good on his pledge to central administration."

"The Rankings?"

Shane nods. "I hear he told Wickendale that if they met all his conditions, and they apparently did, he'd pull us up in two years."

"Isn't that impossible?"

"Who knows?" Shane says. "But without tenure, you're vulnerable. The Rankings formula puts a premium on permanent faculty.

So I say you consider his offer."

Sophie studies his face for a hint, the faintest glimmer, that he's kidding. She hoped that as a senior faculty member, Shane would offer to fight for her right not to be forced into tenure. As a teacher in the Skills Program, she's been reading semi-literate student output so others like Shane wouldn't have to. Where is the gratitude?

"How in the hell am I supposed to turn out a Chicago-style article?" she says, her voice whiny. "In less than a year!"

"You're smart. You can write. And there are few if any faculty here who've had the legal education you've had, Sophie."

"I feel so elite."

"Realistically, what choice have you got?" he says.

"But I couldn't care less about the Rankings," she says. "I'm adamantly anti-Ranking. I just want to teach my classes, grade my papers, meet with my students, and be left alone."

"You forgot something," Shane says.

"What?"

"You want to be employed. You *need* to be employed, unless you've come into unforeseen wealth you neglected to tell me about. Didn't you say something last week about being upside down with respect to Mud Flat? And with your dad's situation, your mobility is limited. If you look at it from a certain perspective, you could be considered lucky."

"How do you figure that?"

"He's already told two people in the clinic he's not renewing them next year."

"What!" The law clinic has been the cornerstone of the law school for decades.

Shane nods. "Word is he's planning to reveal a new clinic model."

"No way," she says. This is so much worse than she thought. "What kind of new model?"

"Guess."

The phrase "revenue streams" resounds in her mind.

"For profit?" she ventures.

"You bet."

4 REINFORCEMENTS

On Friday afternoon, Sophie glances up from her grading to see that across the hall, Elliott Ramsey is closing his tattered copy of *Billy Budd*, flipping off his office lights, and departing for the weekly soirée at The Chestnut, a pub two blocks west of the Rosecliff campus. Though Sophie seldom attends the get-together, in light of her pending dilemma, she decides to go. As the fourth week of the semester comes to a close, the Rosecliff law faculty has begun informally to divide into two camps: those who seem ready to sign on to the Dean's Rankings mission, and those who've begun to squabble among themselves about just exactly whose fault it is that VandenDungen was hired in the first place. Taking a poll at The Chestnut will indicate where things stand.

It's a humid afternoon, and a crowd spills out of the cramped cinderblock bar onto the patio and lawn, students sprawling on the ground guzzling beer, professors sitting on the cracked concrete benches or in tippy wrought-iron chairs.

Sophie spots Ramsey standing under a tree with a small cadre of faculty members. As she ambles toward them, someone grips her arm from behind. Turning, she comes face-to-face with a man who looks vaguely familiar. She squints at him, trying to place him.

"Hello, Professor Poe. Did you have a good summer?"

The voice is distinctive, but it doesn't match the face. The man's clothing clues her in—white shirt, narrow black tie, black slacks, and scuffed black lace-up shoes. She's labeled it the Jehovah's Witness uniform, and it is worn every day, season in and season out, by James Yoder, her stalker. He's dropped at least forty pounds since she last saw him, and his normally pasty complexion is camouflaged by an orange spray-on tan.

"What about your summer, James?" she says.

"I'm glad school's in session again," he says. "It's great to reconnect with everyone."

He stares into her eyes.

"James, did you put a tracking device under my car?"

"You noticed?

"The guy that changed my oil did."

"I want to be sure you're safe. I want to take care of you."

"You need to leave me alone," she says, turning to head toward Ramsey's group.

"Professor . . . Sophie, did you find an envelope in your office?"

She considers denying it, but realizes that if she does, he'll probably deliver another one. She doesn't need any more outdated political literature.

She nods. "You ran for office," she says.

He nods. "I lost."

"Why did you give me that stuff, James?"

"So you know who I am, what I stand for."

"I told you before, it's inappropriate for you to communicate with me in that vein."

"But I'm not your student anymore," he says. "And I can't help it if I love you. I can't get your shiny blue dress out of my mind. It's all I thought about all summer."

"I'm meeting some people over there," she says, gesturing toward her colleagues.

This time he doesn't stop her, though his exaggerated sigh of disappointment wafts after her.

Approaching Ramsey's group, she takes stock of the attendees.

Wally Shane. The Dean of Students, Victoria Enquist, best known for her oppositionist stands against any form of generalization and/or categorization about anything, except the white male narrative, which she categorically rejects. No one at Rosecliff Law realized how extreme and verbal she was until she was already hired and it was too late.

Also present, surprisingly, is the sole Mormon on the faculty, Be Van Krist who, despite the fact he stockpiles a year's rations and supplies in his basement in anticipation of End Times, can be counted on to display more common sense than most professors.

And towering above the rest—Xavier Michaud. At over six feet tall, Michaud looks as if he could be father to the other men, except of course that Michaud is African-American, and, as Victoria Enquist might say, the rest are representatives of the dominant hegemony. Michaud, dressed impeccably and too warmly as always, in his Irish-knit sweater vest and Welsh corduroy pants, stands enigmatically apart, as is his wont.

Her colleagues acknowledge Sophie as she joins the circle, but no one is able to complete a proper greeting because Assistant Dean Enquist is engaged in a denunciation of the Rosecliff Law Clinic's treatment of its African-American criminal clients.

"The underlying assumption in our representation of those individuals," she says, "the position that we *need* to defend them, posits there is something inherently immoral about lawbreaking. No one considers that their conduct is valid and progressive, that an act of, for example, robbery, and the subsequent expenditure of the proceeds of that robbery in the community, is a legitimate form of wealth distribution. Why should a young African-American male be punished for this form of social restructuring?"

The others glance at Xavier Michaud, who listens, nods, and scrunches his face in silent ruefulness, but doesn't speak.

"Hey," Victoria says, grinning at Sophie, "is that lover boy I saw you with?"

"I didn't even recognize him," Sophie says. "I couldn't figure out who he was."

"He's on the Water Diet," Victoria Enquist says. "He's fasting for you."

"I need a drink," Sophie says.

Shane goes to fetch her a beer while the rest of them stand around waiting for someone to bring up what they're all thinking about.

Finally, Be Van Krist says, "Did you get the latest e-mail?"

Ramsey groans. "We're going to be peer-reviewing each other's classes. It's part of the Dean's new accountability program. God damn it! My classroom is sacrosanct. Nobody comes in unless I invite them."

Be Van Krist rocks back on the heels of his cowboy boots. Van Krist couldn't look less like a professor of law. His unkempt hair, protruding stomach, and too-small plaid shirt suggest he should be delivering the 5:00 a.m. farm report, but beneath the rube's exterior lives a Renaissance man who's traveled the world.

"Now to be fair," Van Krist says, "you could interpret this as a positive idea." Here is the Mormon voice of reason. "We're never too old to learn, and I'm sure we could all use some fresh energy in our teaching."

"The Dean is trying to pit us one against the other," Sophie grumbles.

"That's possible, too," says Van Krist, laughing.

Shane returns with her beer, and she takes a long draw. As the mug comes down, she glimpses James Yoder standing solo on the other side of the yard, gazing at her. As their eyes meet, he waves. She turns away.

Wallace Shane's face zooms in, stopping inches from hers.

"She's here," he whispers, trying to point with his head by jerking it to the left. Peering in the indicated direction, Sophie observes that Jennifer Fairfield is indeed making an entrance to the front yard of The Chestnut.

"She never shows up to these things!" Shane croaks.

Jen Fairfield saunters through the sunlit weeds as if she is walking the red carpet at a Hollywood premier. Hips swaying, chin up, highlighted hair shimmering, she manages to attract attention from every man there except, Sophie notes, James Yoder. Jen is not a classic beauty, but she possesses an abundance of the "it" factor, "it" in her case being sexual magnetism.

Appearing surprised to see her colleagues, Jen tosses her hair and smiles glowingly, as if she's spotted a lover across a crowded room. The men in the group all grin back. Shane sucks in a deep, quavering breath. He's been in love with Jen for years but has made little headway with her.

Xavier Michaud speaks for the first time. "Reinforcements have arrived." His face scrunches into a wide, beaming smile.

"Hiiii, everyone," Jen says. "God, it's so hot my thighs are sweating."

"Jeez," breathes Shane.

Stepping into the center of the group, Fairfield pivots slowly, giving everyone a hug except Sophie. The men squirm with appreciation. Wally Shane turns his head away and rubs his eyes, looking as if he might weep.

"Gosh, I should do this more often," Jen says. "It's fun to see you all outside of the law school. Everyone looks more human somehow." She laughs melodically. "I didn't mean that like it sounded." The men chuckle along with her. "I mean it's nice to relax and have a more natural type of contact."

Shane, Michaud, and Van Krist all speak at once in a babble that roughly translates to "Please have sex with me."

Jen whirls around suddenly. "Sophie! I didn't see you!" She pulls Sophie forward for a soft, sweet-smelling embrace. How could anyone smell so good in 90 degree weather, at the end of a work day, at the end of a work week?

"Do you think we can sit down somewhere?" Jen says, face and neck flushed. Elliott Ramsey strides to a table and growls at a couple of students to leave. There are only two chairs, and Sophie, feeling light-headed, practically jogs in order to secure one. The men all hang back, watching Jennifer stroll to the table, delicately position her round rear end in the chair opposite Sophie, and fan herself with both hands.

"Don't you need to face away from the sun?" Shane mumbles.

"It's fine," Jennifer says. "Sophie wouldn't want to face the sun any more than I would."

The men eye Sophie, clearly expecting her to sacrifice her comfort for Jennifer's.

"You can't face the sun for some reason?" she asks.

"It's no big deal, really. I'm just genetically predisposed to melanoma. My mother and sister both barely survived it. But don't worry. I'm sure the sun is low enough it shouldn't be a problem."

"You might as well avoid the risk," Sophie says, rising.

"No, no, really, stay put."

"Sophie won't be about minding," Xavier Michaud says, slipping into his adopted Irish brogue. "She's a right lass, so she is." Four years ago, Michaud underwent a transformation. Before, he'd been an introvert who steered clear of conflict, remarkably apolitical for an African-American law professor. After spending a semester's sabbatical in Ireland, he returned speaking the language of dissidence, with an Irish brogue.

As the two women switch places, Jennifer hugs Sophie again. "Thanks, sweetie," she says. Sophie is grateful for the hug even if it is from a woman. No one has hugged her for too long.

The late afternoon sun spears through the trees directly into Sophie's face. Shading her eyes, she squints at Jennifer through the glare.

"What's your fake article about?" Sophie asks her.

"Oh, I so lucked out about that," Jen says, brushing her glinting bangs from her eyes. "Chaz says he doesn't think I need to write one this year because I'll be busy with my committees. He says he's made the committee assignments. I have no earthly idea what he's giving me, but believe me, I didn't question it!"

Sophie calculates the number of hours required to serve on two law school committees versus the number required to serve on two committees *and* write a double law review article. She exhales loudly.

"You've been speaking to VandenDungen?" Ramsey asks Jen.

"Not by choice, I assure you," she says. "He keeps dropping by my office. He plops into a chair and starts to pontificate, and before I know it, two hours have passed."

This piques Sophie's interest. Up until this moment, Sophie has assumed Jen Fairfield is firmly in VandenDungen's camp. As two untenured female faculty members, they're automatically thrust into competition for whatever the law school powers-that-be might be doling out in a given semester.

"So how do you think we break down on the Dean's agenda?" Ramsey says. "Who can we count on to help us fight him?"

They look at each other.

"Are we it?" Ramsey says. "If so, I might as well tender my resignation tomorrow."

Xavier Michaud sways as if he has lost his bearings.

"There are others," he says enigmatically.

"Who?" Victoria Enquist says.

"There are things happening," Michaud says. "Here, there." He moves his hands as if painting the air. "Things unseen, yet powerful. There is targeting, and there is resistance."

Everyone stands silently, awaiting additional information, but none arrives.

"Uh oh," Wallace Shane says. He nods, indicating the street in front of The Chestnut.

There, wearing his Revo shades, cruising along in his black Lexus, is Charles VandenDungen. He stops at the empty crosswalk and surveys the crowd in the front of The Chestnut, appearing to pause when he spots the faculty group.

As he drives on, the group releases a collective sigh of relief.

Within five minutes, however, the Dean rounds the side of The Chestnut and strides toward them. His mouth pinches up at the corners, simulating a smile, but those eyes, Sophie reflects, those eyes hold so much ruthless calculation she half-expects them to burst open and spray her with a toxic substance.

"Dean," says Be Van Krist, "can I grab you a beer?"

VandenDungen shakes his head. "I can't stay long. Lo Ming is flying in tonight." Lo Ming is the Dean's Big Pharma rep wife. Sophie hasn't met her, and maybe she's making too much of this, but it seems that whenever someone mentions Mrs. VandenDungen, they pronounce her name "loaming," like the dirt.

The Dean checks his Rolex.

"What time does her plane arrive?" Sophie asks.

The taut pinching at the sides of VandenDungen's mouth increases, appearing now as if small marbles are implanted below his cheekbones.

"I realize it's Friday, folks," he says, "but it's only 5:20."

A hollow silence ensues. All geniality is dead or dying.

"The law school is deserted," he adds. "It's like a morgue."

If there's an appropriate response to his observation, no one in the group knows it.

Elliott Ramsey makes a stab at humor. "It's the weekend," he says. "They're out getting baked like the rest of us."

"I'm not talking about the students. Why would the students stick around the building when the faculty can't get out of there fast enough? When there's no sense of activity or community?"

The questions are characteristically rhetorical, of course.

VandenDungen is wound up. Something about his twitchy body movements reminds Sophie of a taser victim.

"Research indicates that the schools that rank respectably all have in common the fact that their campuses are vital places, alive with extra-curricular activities that make the students *want* to hang around, not only after classes but on weekends. In a sense, the law school becomes the surrogate home for these young people, a place where they can develop a hyper-productive synergy between their academic efforts and the rest of their lives."

Sophie takes a long swig of her warm beer, eyeing the others over her glass. They all have the same blank-eyed expression of impending doom that she must also be wearing.

The Dean's face is mottled from the heat and possibly a simmering stew of disgust and anger.

"Have any of you taken even a few minutes to think about what we could be doing that we're not?"

Sophie wonders if she could stop him by collapsing to the ground, pretending to faint from the heat

"Elliott," the Dean says in his private school accent, "has it occurred to you to hold contract drafting clinics on the weekends to help students with issues they might have relating to their apartment leases?"

Ramsey looks as if he might throw up.

"Perhaps you haven't heard of it," the Dean continues. "It's called skills training."

Ramsey says "fuck" under his breath. If VandenDungen hears, he doesn't show it.

"And you, Sophie. What about holding writing camps on Saturday afternoons? You could make it a fun thing. We could hand out tee shirts to the participants, like they do at real camps. 'I survived the Rosecliff Writers' Retreat!'"

Xavier Michaud turns and leaves without a word.

"I need the weekends for grading," Sophie says.

The Dean seems to want to slap her face. "No more about your horrendous grading burden, please, Sophie. That's what professors do. They grade. And they teach. And they produce scholarship. And they meet with students. And they serve on committees. And they create opportunities for deeper teaching, deeper thinking, deeper interaction, and it goes on and on."

"But—"

He holds up a thick-fingered mitt to silence her. "I have to go. Don't worry. This will be a continuing dialogue." And with that, he is off to pick up Loaming.

5 IT'S JUST BUSINESS

On Tuesday morning, Sophie arrives at her father's to find Arthur standing curbside looking at his watch. He wears faded gray denim jeans, a white oxford cloth shirt with frayed cuffs, Hush Puppy boots, and a stained canvas jacket. After the embezzlement, when he sold the farm Sophie grew up on, he decided to "simplify," eventually disposing of all but this one set of clothing, which at the time was in pretty good shape. He did own several hats and always donned one when going out in order to keep his hairpiece from flapping up in the wind. Today he wears a puffy polyester foam ball cap bearing the name of his former law firm, Poe & Poe, L.L.C.

As they motor through town, Arthur leans forward, watching the passing cityscape intently, as if he's never before seen stoplights, storefronts, or moving vehicles. Every so often, he murmurs, "Fascinating."

After about ten minutes, he pe6ers over at Sophie and says, "Remember, I've agreed to nothing."

He has an appointment at the regional medical center with a respected cardiac specialist who's going to discuss with him the possibility of cleaning out his blocked left carotid artery.

"Don't get me wrong," Arthur continues, "I have nothing

against the man." His eyes widen, his eyebrows rise, and his ears wiggle in a trademark expression that has been likened to that of the late William F. Buckley, Jr. "He's simply an unknown."

"He's not the enemy," Sophie says.

"We don't know that."

"He's one of the top cardiac doctors in the region," Sophie says. "He's there to help you."

Arthur's eyes brighten. The colloquy is playing out as expected; they've had this conversation at least three times before. Leaning back, he stretches his legs to their modest length and squares his shoulders. The lawyer in him is poised to take charge of the argument.

"Exactly how," he says, "do we know that is his motivation?"

"What else could it be?"

"Doctors are businessmen first, of course." He gazes over at Sophie, the surface of his eyes pitted and sunken like overripe fruit.

"What difference does that make, if he can help you?" Sophie says.

"That is yet to be determined."

Sophie drops Arthur off at the entrance to the medical building and parks the car a block away. When she joins him, he's gazing at the building directory with a puzzled look on his face.

"I think we're at the wrong place," he says. "He's not on the board."

Sophie points at the name Dr. Sukesh Khoury. "Here he is. Second floor."

In the elevator, Arthur's finger hovers over the panel of numbers, then falls to his side. Sophie punches number two, and he says, "Why did you push that?"

"That's his floor."

"I don't recall it that way."

In the waiting room, Arthur fidgets non-stop, checking the time every few minutes and muttering under his breath. Sophie searches for a gossip weekly, preferably *People Magazine*, but settles on *Women's Health Weekly*, specifically an article entitled "The Skinny On Eggs." She hasn't eaten an egg in ten years because she thinks eggs are bad for people genetically prone to high cholesterol such as herself. The article puts that misunderstanding to rest, touting the considerable benefits versus the negligible costs of egg consumption, and Sophie reflects wistfully on the many omelets she could have enjoyed over the last decade.

After 25 minutes, Arthur stands and puts on his cap. "Let's go."

"We can't! We waited a month for this appointment! I rescheduled my class because of it!"

"He doesn't value my time," Arthur proclaims loudly. "I'm leaving." He starts for the door.

"We've waited this long. Let's give it a few more minutes."

"My policy is I leave at 30 minutes. There are no exceptions."

Miraculously, at that moment a woman materializes in the doorway to the inner sanctum and calls Arthur's name. He shuffles back, a self-satisfied expression on his face.

The first stop is a cubicle in which an aide asks him questions and enters data into a computer.

"You've had a stroke?" the girl says, her eyes trained on the screen.

"That's what they say. I've reversed the effects by making some changes. I'd say I'm about ninety percent back."

"When was the stroke?"

"Six months ago," Sophie says.

Tap, tap, tap. "And your reason for this visit? Carotid artery stenosis?" Eyes are still locked on the screen.

"No such thing," Arthur says. "Nothing has been decided."

"A consultation about the stenosis," Sophie says.

"Do you know your approximate blockage?"

Arthur looks at Sophie.

"About eighty-five to ninety percent," she says.

"*Before* the measures I put in place," Arthur says.

Tap, tap, tap.

"Did you note that?" Arthur says. "About my measures?"

"And so, a consultation about the stenosis?" The aide gapes at them blankly.

After being installed in an exam room, they wait another 20

minutes for the doctor. The door finally opens, and in sweeps a handsome foreign-looking man with shiny black hair combed straight back off his forehead. He sits on a stool with wheels and rolls right up to Arthur, stopping a foot away.

"Hello, Mr. Poe. Welcome. How are you?"

"Excellent."

The doctor flips open Arthur's file, scans it, and says, "What can I help you with today?"

Arthur frowns. "I don't know that you can help me."

"You had a stroke, I understand."

"Allegedly."

"Hmm. I see the sonographer reports a rather substantial blockage of the left carotid artery."

"It's been taken care of."

"Oh. You have seen another physician?"

"No," says Sophie. "He thinks he cured himself."

Arthur shoots her a hostile glance. "Please," he says. "I can speak for myself." He addresses the doctor in his most stentorian tone. "I've changed my diet. I've lost ten pounds. I gave up drinking alcohol. I'm ninety percent back mentally. Based on those measures, I believe I've reversed the problem."

"Those are good changes," the doctor says. "But, sir, the sonogram shows the blockage remains, which is what we would expect. The only effective way to clear the blockage and reduce the risk of another stroke is to perform a procedure called a carotid endarterectomy. We open the artery, clamp off the blood flow, and shell out the plaque. The operation carries a small risk, but without the procedure, your risk of having another stroke within a year is forty percent."

"What's the risk of the procedure?"

"One to two percent of patients experience a stroke during or shortly afterwards."

"Would I be under general anesthesia?"

"Yes, sir. But the procedure takes only an hour to an hour-and-a-half. It's not a major operation."

"Would I be required to stay in a hospital?"

"Probably just overnight, to monitor you."

"All right. Thank you." Arthur stands.

The doctor appears startled. "I would recommend you have the procedure, sir. You have a major blockage."

"I appreciate that. I'll think about it."

The doctor glances at Sophie, who shrugs. Welcome to life with Arthur Poe.

"Thank you for your time," Arthur says as he exits the room.

As they drive away from the medical complex, Arthur says, "He was pretty sharp, wasn't he?"

Sophie nods. "I thought so."

"Very slick indeed."

"So are you going to have the operation?"

"It bothers me that he never seemed to get my point about the measures I've taken, the improvements I've made. He missed the fact that I'm back ninety percent. He just kept pushing the operation."

Sophie sighs. "The blockage is still there."

"He needs to drum up business. It's in his self-interest to sell an operation. I wonder how much he makes for each one."

§

When Sophie arrives at her office, she is met with a line of nine petulant students waiting to discuss their papers with her. She holds regular office hours right after her Tuesday morning class; when she cancelled the class, she meant to cancel her office hours as well. Instead, she spends the next two and a half hours fending off attacks based on the premise that a lower than desired grade on a writing assignment is her fault and she should make amends.

When the last student leaves, she collapses in her chair, rests her head on her desk, and takes a fifteen-minute power nap. When she awakes, she checks her e-mail. A message from Dean VandenDungen awaits her.

To: allfac@rosecliff.edu
From: Chaz VandenDungen

Re: Change in meeting time

As you know, last week I initiated a peer-review program designed to reinvigorate us all in our teaching methodology. The program requires each of you to visit one class per week taught by a colleague of your choice (a different colleague to be selected each week). You are to write an evaluation of each class you observe and share it with the colleague you have observed. It was announced that we would meet as a faculty on Wednesday afternoons to share our observations about each other's classes.

Due to a scheduling conflict, the time of the weekly meetings has been changed to Friday afternoon, at 5:00 p.m.

See you then!

So. No more Friday afternoon get-togethers at The Chestnut. Sophie puts her head back down on her desk. She really needs more rest. Studies show that people who take naps live longer. She'd like to put a couch in her office, but it is too small. She lies down on the floor and closes her eyes

§

Within days after Sophie accepts his tenure track offer, Chaz VandenDungen announces he's hired a consultant from the World of Business to help develop a vision for Rosecliff School of Law. Her name is Ann Kulter, and reportedly she agreed to give up her exciting, sophisticated existence in Philadelphia to spend a year in a flyover state, helping Rosecliff claw its way out of the BTT.

The faculty first encounter Kulter when the Dean brings her to a Friday afternoon teaching-review meeting. They enter the conference room together, sniggering chummily over some scrap of private humor. They make a daunting couple, Sophie observes, with their striking verticality and bold facial features. Kulter isn't what she expected. The title of Business Consultant does not bring to mind a willowy blonde with the kind of anorectic figure that belongs on a modeling catwalk, yet here is such a figure in the person of Consultant Kulter. Folding herself into a seat next to the lectern, Kulter appraises the U-shaped grouping of Rosecliff faculty for the first time, grimly flicking her gaze from one to the next while nervously running her fingers through her hair, then sweeping it from one side to the other over the top of her head, all in a self-conscious and doomed effort, Sophie surmises, to make it appear voluminous.

"I know we're all delighted Ann accepted this appointment with us," VandenDungen says. "Some of you have asked why I decided to bring her in, since academic oversight is within Associate Dean Chris Paine's purview, and I was hired to be point man on the Rankings issue. Why did we hire this Yale dual-degree business and law graduate to improve our Ranking, you're wondering, and now he turns around and hires another party to do the very same thing?"

"Especially since we're paying him $325,000 per year," whispers Be Van Krist, seated one person away from Sophie, with Wally Shane in between.

"Let me tell you a little bit about her," VandenDungen continues. "Ann hails from upstate New York. She, too, earned law and business degrees at Yale. She has a distinguished employment history in the private sector. In fact, we met at Meyeth Industries." They exchange a fond look. "She was actually hired right out of school as an assistant to the Meyeth Triplets themselves. She's gone on to work at a number of Fortune 500 companies, all of them in the 'top tier,' if you will, right, Ann?"

Kulter nods emphatically. "All the companies I've worked for have consistently ranked in the top 100 of the Fortune 500 list."

"Her work at these companies involved the evaluation of company performance," the Dean says, "more specifically, appraisal of efficiency quotients for specific departments. Her specialty is value-added assessment, with a sub-specialty in measuring professional-level personnel profit margins."

"Shit," moans Wally Shane. "I *told* everybody when we interviewed this fucker he was too in love with the corporate business model!"

"What *is* a personnel profit-margin?" Sophie wonders aloud.

"Now," says VandenDungen, "I'll ask Ann to talk to you a little about what she'd like to accomplish here and what she sees as the challenges we face."

Kulter stands to address them, hands on narrow hips. "First, I want to tell you all how thrilled I am to be here." Her voice grates on Sophie's nerves, with its rolled r's and pretentious Locust Valley Lockjaw intonation. Her equine face remains static with the exception of her thin lips, a corporate gamer's lips, taut with calculation.

"Chaz VandenDungen and I have known each other for a number of years," the Consultant continues. "We've worked on several projects together, and I think a great deal of him. When he called, I told him I was willing to do whatever I could to help."

VandenDungen beams up at her.

"I won't sugar-coat it," Kulter continues. "Rosecliff School of Law faces an uphill battle, a battle for its very existence. You are down in all the metrics," she ticks them off on her fingers, "incoming scores and grades, resource issues, student enrollment, faculty output. Your peers, if they've even heard of you, don't respect you. There is much hard work to be done. And that's what we'll be trying to get a handle on in the next few weeks."

The Consultant sits down, her expression grave.

VandenDungen pops to his feet. "On that sobering note, we will—"

"Dean?" It's Raymond Holthaus, a visiting professor who's made it clear he hungers to join the faculty permanently. He is on leave from the general counsel's office at Sprint, where he spent years filing tariffs. At meetings, he routinely breaks a cardinal rule for visiting professors—shut up—recklessly jumping into the center of the dialogue as if he has a right to an opinion, oblivious to his provisionality, usually with a suggestion Wally Shane describes as "a quarter turn off." Holthaus gives Sophie the heebie-jeebies, ever since he asked her for a ride home one day and, noting

49

she had a stick shift, said, "Have you ever wondered how that shift would feel between your legs?"

Appearing irritated, VandenDungen acknowledges Holthaus.

"Have you considered changing the name of the law school?" Holthaus says.

VandenDungen frowns at him. "What do you mean?"

"It would be only a superficial improvement, to be sure, but you all seem so disturbed about the Rankings, and there *is* something demoralizing about appearing so low on the list. Since the Bottom Tier is in alphabetical order rather than ranked, if you change the name of the school to, for example, Aardvon or Abalilt, or even Abba, like the Swedish group from the 1970s, I mean that might appeal to prospective students in a retro kind of way, and—"

"Aaaarrgghhh . . ." Shane, never one to hide his frustration in a faculty meeting, growls like a wounded she-wolf.

" —anyway, something like that so we would appear as number one in the Bottom Tier, and, to pick up on Ms. Kulter's point, the uphill battle would not seem quite so steep."

This suggestion is greeted with guffaws. Sophie realizes she is the only person in the room other than Holthaus who thinks it is a halfway decent proposal. It *is* demoralizing to appear so low on the list, and it isn't a fair reflection of their school. USN&WR ranks over 180 law schools. The top 145 schools are ranked according to their relative merit under the combined factors. The schools in the Bottom Tier are dumped together unceremoniously, arranged not by their worth, but by that pedestrian sorting tool, alphabetical order. The message in this disparate treatment is: Why waste time and energy fine-tuning the dregs?

VandenDungen clears his throat loftily, like a man preparing to explain the facts of life to a child, groping for a way to bridge the enormous gap in intellectual and emotional maturity. "To imply the only weakness in your idea is that it's superficial misses the central fact that it would be a transparent, desperate attempt to exalt form over substance."

"So?" Holthaus says.

Barbara Kitchen shoots out of her seat. "I guess you don't know because you haven't been here very long, Raymond, and evidently you haven't taken the time to bone up on this place, but thanks to Oberg Rosecliff, this university has existed for one hundred and twenty-two years! The name is steeped in tradition! There are many, many influential alumni around this state and elsewhere who would take serious umbrage at your proposal!" She sat down. "And by the way, mister, it's a very cynical proposal!"

Chaz VandenDungen's face assumes an ominous expression, checks burgundy, small eyes narrowed into knife-thin apertures. He blows air from his mouth in a long, slow whistle. In contrast, Ann Kulter's complexion is ghostly pale, her visage morbidly still.

"We'd better get to the task at hand," the Dean says stonily, "which is our weekly teaching review. Chris, why don't you take over from here?"

"Wait just a minute there," Xavier Michaud says. "I want to put something on the table."

The Dean and the Consultant exchange a look that dooms to hell any point Michaud might assert.

"Why are we buying in and selling out?" Michaud asks. He rises to his full height, which for some reason, possibly the collected grievances of his race, seems more commanding than customary units of measurement imply.

Sophie assumes other tenured professors will join Michaud's objection to the tyranny of the Rankings system. It has been widely and negatively publicized for incentivizing deception and fostering a shallow and unbecoming competition ruled by money, status, and that most repugnant and lowbrow of influences, reputation among peers. But no one speaks up.

"This is all a regrettable fraud," Michaud announces.

Sophie worries he is about to exit; her heart pounds in her breast, telling her that now is the time to air this issue. She catches the eye of former Dean Beau Ranier. He signed a letter or something, she recalls, a few years ago. A protest, subscribed to by law school deans across the country, setting out the flaws and foibles of the Rankings system and the damage it inflicts on basic principles and values of professional education. But she can't bring herself to speak up.

VandenDungen plummets into his chair, the momentum from his bulk slamming it into the whiteboard behind him, sending a dozen markers clattering to the floor.

Exiting a spiritual pause, Christopher Paine startles back to consciousness. Sophie envies his ability to escape to a more comforting place. Invariably, he emerges looking sleepy and sated, as if he has just had the best sex of his life.

"All right, then," Paine says. "Back to our teaching reviews. We'll start with the assumption that we've all complied with the program and have observed two of our colleagues at work in their classrooms this week. The protocol is to select two names at random, and those chosen will share their reviews of the teaching they observed." Reaching into a Rosecliff Law ball cap, Paine removes a scrap of paper. "Our first reviewer is Newt King." Paine nods at King, whose head is positioned like a satellite dish.

"I had the great pleasure of observing Manny Delgado on Wednesday," King says, eyes shut. "I must say it was a very educational experience."

VandenDungen and the Consultant share a prolonged look of disgust over this softball remark. Manny Delgado has tilted back his chair, crossing his legs at the ankle and his arms over his buff, puffed-out chest.

"Let me see," King continues, his face pruney, "the subject of the class I observed was the effect of an intervening force on the chain of causation in negligence. Manny handled the class with fluency and grace. Congratulations, Manuel."

"Thanks to you, too, Cy," says Delgado. "And welcome to my fan club, amigo."

"Excuse me," says Ann Kulter. She glances at VandenDungen. "May I, Dean?"

"Please."

The Consultant sweeps her blond locks back, one shoulder at a time, places her forearms on the table, and hawkishly appraises the room. "The law school business is a highly competitive enterprise. But here, you are not competing to be the best. You are not competing to be almost the best. You are fighting to reach the awe-inspiring goal of *not being the worst*, and this is a war for your professional existence. Now start getting honest!"

An awkward silence settles over the room. The majority of the faculty members look abashed. A few appear angry. Among the latter is Manny Delgado, who lets the front legs of his chair bang the floor. Sophie expects him to swear a blue streak then stomp out, but he remains seated, fists balled, face contorted with fury.

Sitting a couple of people away from the Dean, lesbian-minimalist Karla Johansson raises her hand. She is a petite woman with youthful features whose Scandinavian heritage has blessed her with a milky white complexion and an inscrutable countenance. In her pre-lesbian days, when married to Wallace Shane, she'd worn her naturally blond hair long, like the Consultant; now it is sliced up in designedly discordant layers.

The Dean says, "Karla?"

"I visited Manny's class, too, and while I generally agree with Newt, I did have a discussion with a student afterward. This student is at the top of her class, ya know, and she was practically in tears when we spoke. She says the women in the class, see, they all feel as if they're routinely marginalized. They're made the butt of jokes, or they're dismissed." She looks around the room with her wide-eyed, owlish gaze. "I'm just reporting what I was told."

Shane whispers to Sophie, "I tell you, somebody has drugged that woman! A few years ago, she would've pinned Delgado to the ground and stomped on his face. Now she's just a reporter, just the facts, ma'am! Where's the passion?"

Delgado pounds his fist on the table. "I know whom you are talking about! It's Katie Ingram, isn't it? What would that blue-eyed little girl know about being marginalized?" He unbuttons his shirt cuff and rolls up his sleeve, then points to his arm. "See this?" he says. "This is commonly known as brown skin! The fuck does a little white girl from the suburbs know about brown skin?"

"Manuel," Chris Paine says, "the American Bar Association is calling for more civility in the profession."

"Now you are implying that I am not civilized? I do not go along

53

with your attempt to control me, so I am some rough beast just down from the mountains, throwing a brutish shadow on your garden party?"

The tension in the room escalates by the second, everyone on tenterhooks, awaiting the inevitable explosion that will blast Delgado from the room. How long will it take?

Sophie checks her watch, then raises her hand.

"Yes?" the Dean says.

"I also observed Manny this week. He's an imaginative teacher, quite entertaining. But I don't think it's appropriate for a law professor to lob the f-bomb every other sentence."

Delgado shoots up from his chair, pointing at Sophie. "You are so full of shit, lady!" He sweeps his arms to encompass the whole group. "What, did you all get together and say, let's go watch that stupid Mexican peasant Manuel, then cluster-fuck him?"

He storms toward the door. "Here's your fucking teaching review!" he says, flipping an index card over his shoulder. The card sails through the air, landing on the floor next to Bill Wu, who picks it up, reads it, then places it on the table face down.

"That man should be summarily fired!" Ann Kulter announces.

A number of people ridicule her suggestion. Everyone knows a tenured professor can't be fired unless he sells grades or rapes a student.

In contrast to most of his colleagues, Xavier Michaud appears unamused. Legs crossed at the knee, he glowers straight ahead as his head nods rhythmically, a characteristic "bobble head" tic that signals mounting irritation.

"Madam," Michaud says in a tight voice, "we have a little concept at this institution called academic freedom." He targets Ann Kulter with his lacerating glare. "We didn't choose to be a member of this profession to be told what we can say and do. Manuel is a friend of mine. You are not qualified to judge him. You're here only to advise us on the Rankings." He points a finger at her, as he lapses into his brogue. "And lemee till ye, lashy, we ahren ever gahn to poot up with your tryin' to rool us."

The faculty is in turmoil, as people shout across the room at one another. Sophie notices that though the Dean appears distressed, Ann Kulter wears an expression of smug satisfaction.

In a few minutes, the cacophony diminishes. VandenDungen nods at Paine, who draws another name from the hat. His eyebrows arch. "Manuel Delgado."

"Pick another one," VandenDungen says.

Chris Paine hesitates. "Dean, Manny observed me this week, and frankly, I'd like to hear what he has to say."

"He's not here!" VandenDungen says.

"I believe his card is though," says Paine, looking at Bill Wu. "Don't you have it?"

Wu looks as if he'd chewed an aspirin. "I'm not certain this is the best choice to make," he says.

Paine smiles empathetically. "It's okay, go ahead and read it."

"I'd prefer not to," Wu says.

Next to him, Barbara Kitchen snatches the card from the table and reads it aloud. "Uninspired. Boring. A pussy."

Paine blushes. "Naturally, I disagree with that assessment."

Sensing the end of the meeting nearing, Sophie breathes a sigh of relief. It appears her own teaching will escape public excoriation this week. She's been observed twice. In one case, she arrived six minutes late to class because she'd spilled coffee in her lap and, while attempting to rinse it off, had drenched her skirt and had to hold it in front of the hand dryer in the restroom for ten minutes. In the second instance, she became enmeshed in a protracted argument with a student about whether an appellate court would be offended if a litigant wrote "Just do it!" in the plea for relief at the end of a brief.

As the meeting breaks up, Elliott Ramsey gestures to her and mouths the words, "You coming?" Despite the Dean's blatant attempt to squelch the Friday sessions at The Chestnut, Ramsey has vowed to continue. It's six o' clock, and she's tired, but she hates to miss what promises to be a lively debriefing. She gives Ramsey the thumbs-up.

"Sophie?" She turns to see VandenDungen and Kulter hovering over her.

"Do you have a minute?" the Dean says.

§

The Dean and the Consultant herd her up the stairs and into the faculty lounge. VandenDungen signals for her to sit, and Sophie plops into the "slippery chair," a shiny, black leather throne with a wide seat and a high back where job candidates try to hold on to their dignity.

VandenDungen slumps on the couch, the picture of late Friday afternoon surrender with his oily brow, floppy hair, and wrinkled, untucked shirt. In contrast, the Consultant appears crisp and fresh as she leans against an antique desk. The desk was donated in memory of the founder of the university, Deacon Oberg Rosecliff, whose heirs insisted on attaching a brass plate to it bearing the Deacon's trademark slogan, "Get 'Er Done." A tent card atop the desk admonishes "Do Not Touch," but the Consultant nonchalantly rests her bony buttocks on the marble writing surface, stretching out her thin, tubular legs. Sophie, whose legs are short like the rest of her, grudgingly admires them.

The Dean rubs his fleshy palms together and eyes Sophie wearily. "I've been talking to Ann about your article," he says.

Kulter levels her gaze at Sophie. Her gray eyes are a couple of shades too light, bringing to mind the stock characters in horror movies whose weird, washed-out orbs suggest a combination of genetic abnormality and devil-possession.

"The premise is interesting, I suppose," Kulter says, "but I wonder if the topic is within your experiential paradigm. I told Chaz that if we're going to invest in you to the extent he's contemplated, I want to be sure it's a sound investment."

Sophie studies her a moment, parsing her words for both their literal meaning, which is obscure, and their underlying message, which is crystal clear—*You're too dumb to carry it off.*

"I get it," Sophie says. "You want to know if I can stream revenue."

"Please don't take this personally, Sophie," Kulter says. "It's just a business calculation."

56

Sophie had thought only Donald Trump could attempt to draw this murky distinction with such frowny solemnity and self-righteousness. She looks at VandenDungen.

"I've done a lot of research, and I have an outline," she says. "I plan to start writing next week. It's interesting how well my thesis is proving out."

"How do you mean?" VandenDungen says, appearing genuinely interested.

"It seems that judges *are* pork—in ways I hadn't imagined." She glances at Kulter. "For example, over the years, some of the big conservative organizations have bankrolled law and economics programs at the elite law schools. The schools in turn have hosted posh law-and-econ seminars for judges to steep them in the legal philosophy of rational self-interest, which they hope the judges will then apply to cases—especially antitrust cases against wealthy corporations." She smiled. "You can't get much more laissez-faire than that!"

"Interesting," says the Dean. "Actually, that's similar to our plan for the Clinic."

"Come again?" Sophie says.

Kulter cocks an eyebrow at him. "I need a word with you in private."

VandenDungen noisily hoists himself off the couch and trails after the Consultant.

Sophie closes her eyes, practicing square-breathing exercises, a technique she learned listening to a radio shrink. They are designed to steady the cardio-pulmonary system but today they make her hungry for air—fresh air, which has not entered the hermetically sealed law school building for decades. Overhead, the fluorescent bulbs flicker and buzz, creating a sensation that a fly is trapped behind her eyes.

At last the door opens, and VandenDungen saunters in, eyes downcast, hands stuffed in his pockets. Kulter follows, head imperiously high.

"We have concerns," the Dean begins. "With the Crisis in Legal Education, and the downturn in the legal profession, we think an article focusing on market forces and the judiciary is untimely."

"It's more timely than ever," Sophie says. "Because justice is for sale. In fact, I just read an article about the Meyeth Triplets and their donations to state judicial races."

The Dean and the Consultant exchange a meaningful glance.

"It doesn't fit into the overall vision for this institution," Kulter says.

She looks at VandenDungen. "You said you thought I had a fresh perspective."

VandenDungen runs his hand through his hair, which is tousled far beyond what fashion allows. "It conflicts with other goals we're developing."

"Such as?" Sophie says.

"My analysis shows Rosecliff needs to carve a niche for itself, to be known for something," Kulter says. "Reputation among peers counts for 25 percent of the Rankings calculation. This law school won't get respect unless it's known for something unique."

Sophie turns to VandenDungen. "I know you're not suggesting I dump the article," she says, her voice shaky. "I've already put in over a hundred hours of research! I've outlined! I'm ready to start!"

"Ann will tell you how to proceed," VandenDungen says, "so when you do start over, you'll still be able to get the article out there in time to apply for tenure."

"You'll self-publish on the Social Science Research Network, or SSRN," Kulter says. "We can bypass the laborious traditional publication process and get your work into the hands of your colleagues more expeditiously simply by posting it ourselves."

"What worries me about that," says VandenDungen, "is the demise of the traditional gatekeeper between author and publication. I mean, the debate is really all around the antinomy posed by Solum on the one hand, and Leiter on the other. Are we in the academy egalitarian, or justifiably elitist?"

Gatekeeper? Antinomy? VandenDungen's words rebound off Sophie's skull like over-inflated basketballs as she mourns the annihilation of her Pork article.

"We can't afford to worry about that hypothetical crap, Chaz,"

Kulter says. "With electronic self-publication, we can build reputation among the relevant constituency in a matter of weeks rather than years. One can post an article on the site, then track on a daily basis how many hits and downloads occur for that article. If you publish a really hot one, with a particularly catchy title, even a shocking one, that attracts immediate and widespread attention, you might get downloaded hundreds of times just within the first few days. The exposure is invaluable."

Sophie peers at VandenDungen through her fingers. "I think a lot of people would want to download the Pork article," she says. "The title is pretty catchy. And everybody loves to read about corruption."

Kulter shakes her head. "It's too alienating to the people who count."

VandenDungen gazes at the wall as he absently scratches his backside.

"What in hell am I supposed to write about then?" Sophie says.

"Consider that your challenge," Ann Kulter says brightly. "But the take-home message here? You'd be ill-advised to proceed with any articles that compare judges to farm animals."

If she says "thank you" in that phony tone of hers, Sophie thinks, *I'm going to puke!*

"Thank you!" Kulter says.

§

Before heading to the Chestnut, Sophie stops by her office to get some student papers and notices her message light blinking. The voicemail says, "This is Mac Higgins over at Frankfort. I have a problem I'm hoping you can help me with. My ground has been poisoned. Please call me as soon as you can, ma'am."

6 VODKA

The crowd at The Chestnut is thinner than usual for Friday evening due to the daylong downpour. The moisture seems to have seeped in through the cinderblock walls and up through the concrete floor, creating a tropical clamminess.

"So now, for tenure, I need a new article idea," Sophie complains to the small group gathered at a corner table, "an article yet to be conceived, a big, flashy article that will be heavily downloaded off the SSRN website." She's been trying to make light of the situation, but inside she's depressed. Why didn't they make it simple and tell her, as they had the two clinic faculty members, that her contract won't be renewed next year?

"This deal about the number of downloads," Ramsey says. "It's like you're running for office. You have to get enough votes online before Beef 'n' Bitch consider you serious." He chugs his beer. "That's fucked up."

Sophie sips her beer morosely. "Whatever I end up writing, maybe I can download it myself over and over, day after day, to see if I can achieve the numbers that way."

Wally Shane shakes his head. "Won't work."

"Why not?" Sophie says.

"First of all, we're talking about multiple thousands of down-loads, something on the order of four or five thousand, probably, if you want to make the top of the new articles list. Second, I heard some guy at Santa Clara did that and got busted. He hired seven research assistants and had them downloading around the clock. Somebody got suspicious, and they were able to trace it back to him. So, no, Sophie, that's not a good idea. Hi, Omar."

Sophie whips around to see Omar Patel standing behind her. He'd snuck up silently, in his typical mysterious fashion. He smiles down at her.

"May I join?" he says.

"What brings you out?" Shane says. "You never come to these things."

"After that meeting," Patel says, "I feel the need to drink and smoke."

As the only two bachelors on the faculty, Omar Patel and Wally Shane were once close friends, traveling and socializing together, but a woman came between them. Shane dated her first, but then Omar entered the picture, and she went that direction. Shane wore his insecurities on his sleeve, and he had an unfortunate tendency to share his medical issues at inappropriate times. Evidently the object of their desire chose between the two men after Shane took her to lunch at a fancy restaurant, then proceeded to discuss his recent colonoscopy.

When Sophie looks at Omar, she sees sheer masculine beauty—glowing dark skin, long, inky-black hair curling over his collar. He exudes such dangerous allure that she imagines he might be leading a double life, a law professor by day, and by night, the head of some drug cartel or, like the South Florida professor who ran a Palestinian jihad, the leader of a global terrorist organization. He pushes all the familiar bad boy buttons. It is this sort of fantasizing about long-haired men and danger that led her to marry her ex-husband Chester Zywicky, who turned out to be not only a brilliant chemical engineering student but an equally talented manufacturer and distributor of methamphetamine. Her therapist Dr. Sally interpreted her attraction to dangerous men as a form of self-destructive behavior stemming from her parents' subtle attacks on her self-esteem, specifically their questioning her capabilities as measured against her brother Quinton's. That's why she decided to become a lawyer, Dr. Sally said—to separate herself from her worst impulses.

Omar Patel pulls out a cigarette and strikes a match.

"I didn't know you smoked," Sophie says.

"On Fridays only," Patel replies.

Normally this group wouldn't tolerate a smoker in its midst, but Omar Patel does pretty much whatever he pleases without opposition. He's become something of a legend around the law school, both for his mastery of the Socratic teaching method and for his childhood, during which he survived the Russian incursion into Afghanistan, escaping with his family to Pakistan, bound to the back of a mule. If that alone weren't exotic enough to paralyze Midwesterners, he's hinted at a brief stint with the CIA before attending law school.

"What are we discussing about?" Omar says.

"Sophie's got a problem," Ramsey says.

"Yah," Patel says. "The Dean, I would imagine?"

Sophie nods.

"How can he be problem?" Omar says. "He is weak." During the dean search, Omar warned the faculty that hiring Charles VandenDungen would be a mistake. "He is mean," he cautioned, "and he is weak. A deeply regrettable combination." But Chaz VandenDungen ended up the sole candidate, and for a bare majority of the faculty, the issue was "anybody but Christopher Paine." Paine served as Associate Dean under Beau Rainer for ten years, helping oversee the Rankings decline.

"Have you observed how the female consult is bending our dean?" Omar says. "He is letting her do his thinking."

They all nod, not only because it is an accurate portrayal but also because Omar's pronouncements are delivered in a voice resonating with accented authority.

A waiter approaches and asks for their orders.

"This much vodka, chilled," Patel says, indicating two inches' worth. Thrillingly, he pronounces vodka "wodka."

"May I sit?" he says.

The others shift to accommodate him.

"What is problem, Sophie?"

Sophie gazes at Patel. Despite her attraction, she is wary of spilling her story to him because she doesn't know him well and has no idea where he stands in the developing political wars at the law school. On the other hand, he's here, and he is asking, and she's never figured out how to keep her mouth shut. So she summarizes her predicament.

"I think," says Patel after several moments of contemplation, "that your problem is not so difficult."

"It isn't?" Sophie says, school-girlish admiration in her voice.

"Not at all." Patel throws back his vodka. "Consider what happens when one goes to website like this, where there are many hundreds of articles contributed. How does one decide which to select, which to read?"

"If there's one by a major scholar in my field, I'll download it," puts in Shane.

"Of course," Patel says. "Are there any others that might pull your eyes?"

Sophie decides to play along. "I'd probably pick one based on the title," she says. "I'm not sure why, but I like titles, actually more than the content itself."

"Of course," Patel says. "But do you download the work based on title, or do you merely peek at it?"

"I probably wouldn't download it," Sophie admits, omitting the reason why: if she downloaded an article, she'd feel obligated to read some of it, and she prefers not to torture herself unless mandated to do so by a university administrator.

"So then." Omar surveys the group. "What is answer to Sophie's problem?"

"Well," Shane says, "she needs to write an article that not only grabs people's attention with the title but is about something that holds them."

"That is it," Patel agrees. He sits back happily, as if he's accomplished his mission.

Sophie feels deflated. Despite the promising exchange, Patel's idea as voiced by Shane does no more than state the obvious. Of course she should write an article with an interesting title and content. Big deal.

Patel slams his vodka glass on the table. "So? What will it be?" He sticks another cigarette in his mouth.

Sophie feels pitifully lacking in the brilliance Omar Patel expects of her. Absolutely nothing comes to mind.

"You might consider titling it 'The End' of something," suggests Be Van Krist. "You know, the End of . . . of Crime and Punishment, for example."

"The End of History for Corporate Law," says Shane.

"End of Cost Allocations," Patel says.

"Religion at the End of Modernity," says Van Krist.

"End of Empire," Patel says.

"I saw one the other day," says Ramsey. "The End of Bankruptcy."

"Is that really ending?" Sophie says. "What if I need it someday?"

"That's not what it means, Sophie," Shane snaps. He takes it personally whenever she doesn't know something he thinks she should because it embarrasses their shared alma mater. "It goes back to Marx."

"Hegel," Patel says.

"'The End' signifies a point in time when the contradictions of society are finally resolved in a social/political system that is believed to be the best humankind can conceive," says Shane.

"Oh, God," Sophie sighs, shaken by the level of intellectual depth being advanced.

"Don't use End," Omar advises. "It becomes cliché now. Today's hot topic is anti-rational choice theory."

Sophie's head throbs. "We haven't even talked about the worst part," she says.

"Worse still?" says Omar.

"They say I can't offend the people who count."

Everyone at the table knows these words spell the end of academic freedom, portending a brutal, dystopian landscape of oppression for the untenured and tenured alike.

Glancing glumly around the table, she notices Elliott Ramsey's shoulders shaking.

"What?" she says.

"I've got it," he says, laughing.

"Got what?"

"How you can get everybody who visits the site to download your article and avoid offending the people who count."

"So?" Sophie says.

"Name it 'Fuck.'"

Victoria Enquist laughs raucously, surprising Sophie. Doesn't the word "fuck" demean women with its ugly denigration of the vagina?

Shane scoffs. "That's absurd."

"That is perfect concept," Omar says. "Every person likes it."

Stunned and a little drunk, Sophie says, "This isn't funny. Am I supposed to write a porn article? And post it on a website?"

"Sure," says Omar Patel, gazing into space. He takes a long draw on his smoke. "Why not?"

"Not a porn article, Sophie," Ramsey says. "Name if 'Fuck' but make it scholarly."

"I refuse to participate in this conversation," Shane says, pushing back his chair.

The waiter shows up again.

"I think I'll try some vodka," Sophie tells him. "About two inches' worth, chilled."

"I'll take the same," Shane grumbles. "Make it a double."

"You can bring in the meta-narrative," Enquist suggests. "Everybody fucking everybody willy-nilly is a rejection of the hegemonic meta-narrative."

"Hegemony and meta-narrative are done," Omar says. "Put fresh twist on it."

"I know!" says Enquist. "You could title the article 'Aw, Fuck,'

65

and it could represent the universal exclamation for making the wrong, irrational choice!"

They sip their drinks. Shane drinks his double shot in one long gulp, then coughs fitfully.

"I think," says Omar, "you must write 'Aw, Fuck.' But should be broad scope, analyzing all shadings of word fuck, including sex of course in its fascinating variations. That is what people want."

The challenge of combining sexual intercourse and anti-rational choice theory into one article confounds the group into a prolonged silence.

"I wonder if there's a way to bring in free market theory, too," Sophie mumbles.

Omar blows a smoke ring. "Anything is possible, no?"

7 F**KED

Sophie has begun to think she's lucked out and will not be peer-reviewed again when VandenDungen and the Consultant show up at her afternoon writing class. A couple of minutes late, she descends the long run of shallow stairs to the pit at the front of the lecture hall, her attention divided between not tripping and the unwelcome presence in front of the teacher's lectern of James Yoder. What excuse has he manufactured to justify standing there? And in light of the fact his sallow skin is hanging on his bones like a soiled sheet, how much more weight is he intending to lose on her behalf?

"Can I help you with your stuff, Sophie?" he queries "Here, let me help you."

He pulls her textbook from her arms, brushing her breast with his fingertips in the process. She wants to slap his freakishly gaunt face, but 34 first-year law students are watching, so instead, she retrieves the book from Yoder's sweaty palm and tells him, "Git!"

"I just wanted to tell you how beautiful you look today, Sophie," he says.

Avoiding his smoldering gaze, she murmurs, "It's Professor Poe to you, James, and I told you, leave."

"That suit really accents your figure. I can't decide which I like better, the blue dress or this outfit."

It's then Sophie notices the two dour faces of her reviewers in the back row. She spends several moments in a humid zone of denial. This can't be happening. There is no way she's going to be observed by the Dean and Ann Kulter—not today, when she has to tell the class how bad their last set of papers was while at the same time try to compliment them so they won't trash her in their course evaluations.

Yoder is gone, and what remains in the overheated atmosphere are the Dean, his Fortune 500 business advisor, and a teeming mass of first-year law students supercharged into a smelly frenzy of fear and aggression.

As she surveys the group, a few students sit quietly, respectfully returning her gaze; the rest maintain the cacophony while hiding behind the screens of their laptops. VandenDungen and Kulter sit shoulder to shoulder in the center of the back row, leaning into each other, their elongated torsos and obversely shaped faces— one too wide, the other too narrow—blending into a two-headed monster.

At least she's well-prepared for today's class, having incorporated a PowerPoint presentation to illustrate the common problems she's seen in the papers. The Dean insisted on state-of-the-art media stations in the classrooms and has made it clear that the faculty is supposed to use them as frequently as possible "to justify the capital expenditure." Many professors believe their students are less rowdy if soothed with colorful illustrations interspersed by anthropomorphic figures, projected onto a mammoth screen, that the use of "an alternative information dispersal system" makes for a less contentious classroom experience. On the other hand, showing entertaining movies in class, the analogous tool employed in high school and undergraduate education, is frowned upon here.

As she flips on the computer and projector, Sophie notes the two-headed monster is sitting dangerously close to a thorn in her side named Justin Cherry, a deranged slacker who spends every class period entertaining himself with a sotto voce running commentary, punctuated by outbursts of high-pitched laughter. Several students have informed her that his monologues bother them so much they feel they are not getting their money's worth out of her class and might have to discuss a partial tuition refund with Dean VandenDungen if she can't shut him down. One student threatened to organize a group post on an internet site called sinkyourprofessor.com. Sophie talked privately to Cherry, and he blathered on about his First Amendment right to freedom of speech. Short of arranging to have him drugged and his mouth wired shut, the only remedy she's come up with is to dismiss him from the class. She raised the possibility with Dean Enquist, who was sympathetic but advised against it as it might prompt a lawsuit by Mr. Cherry under the Americans With Disabilities Act. Without question, Justin Cherry, as a savvy member of the Ritalin generation, could handily defeat her authority by threatening a generic claim related to ADD, ADHD, Tourette's syndrome, or some form of obsessive-compulsive disorder.

And lately Sophie realized there is more to the story than she imagined, not only regarding Justin Cherry, but also about James Yoder, and about the Afghanistan war vet last year who, instead of raising his hand, mimed gunning her down. Enlightenment has been a benefit, the only benefit, of membership on the law school Admissions Committee to which Dean VandenDungen assigned her, she can only surmise, to make it clear how much he truly detests her.

Admissions, she has come to understand, is the ugly underbelly of the BTT law school, particularly grotesque in these challenging economic times, when applications are down, but institutional costs—including administrator and faculty salaries—remain on a steady rise. Seats must be filled at Rosecliff just as they are at Harvard; tuition dollars must be borrowed and forked over. So applicants whose GPAs and LSAT scores fall well below generally accepted standards of aptitude, whose records include unfortunate clusters of criminal history or episodes of emotional instability— well, their applications hit the yes pile, and just like that they become seat-fillers, their tuition dollars as green as anyone else's.

They become the lawyers of tomorrow.

Before discussing the student papers, Sophie remembers to announce a slight change in the number of course points to be allocated to an upcoming quiz. During grading, she noticed that most of the students are not grasping basic case citation form.

"So I think we'll do more work with that," she says, "and the upcoming quiz will be worth 35 rather than 25 points."

The inevitable groans follow. Sophie notices that Jessica Forshee—perpetually unprepared and whiny—has slammed her laptop shut. She shoots to her feet. "You can't do that!" she shouts. "You said 25 points!"

Sophie notes that her syllabus reserves the right to make changes where appropriate, whereupon Ms. Forshee picks up a textbook and hurls it in her direction.

"You are totally fucking up my life!" she screams. She storms out of the lecture hall.

Sophie experiences a cottony sensation in her brain, while at the same time recognizing a nearly irresistible urge to follow the student out of the room and just keep going. She glances at the two-headed monster and, predictably, all four eyes are as intently judgmental as a panelist's at an Olympic event. Has she been set up?

Also: Justin Cherry's running commentary is now drawing the attention of the monster. In peer reviews, nothing invites more naked scorn than a professor who can't control her students, no matter how mentally disturbed, so he must be stopped. Luckily for Sophie, he turned in a particularly off-the-wall paper that she can exploit to her advantage.

"Mr. Cherry," she calls out, "what do you suppose was the most common error made in formulating the statement of issues in the memos?"

Justin Cherry appears not to have noticed the question. His pointy head with its black mullet is turned sideways, his mouth running nonstop.

"Mr. Cherry?"

His head snaps forward, his lips stop moving, and he glares in her general direction. "Yeah."

70

"Did you hear my question?"

"Nope."

If the monster weren't there, she'd drop an insult on Cherry for not listening—at any given moment, at least half the students in the class aren't listening, mostly because they're engaged in some form of intimacy with their iPhones—and move on, but with the Dean and the long, lean nightmare positioned next to him, Cherry could easily set her up for a claim based on some auditory disability. A student did that to Be Van Krist last year, resulting in the university agreeing to a seven figure settlement to avoid negative publicity.

She repeats the question.

"How would I know? You graded 'em, dude, not me."

Sophie is prepared for him. She clicks her remote, and the first PowerPoint slide flashes on the screen, depicting a warrior-type figure she captured off a video game, holding a sign into which Sophie has cut and pasted the worst example of an issue statement she found in the memos—one written, in the happiest of coincidences, by Justin Cherry.

"Mr. Cherry, will you please read this and tell me your opinion of it?"

Cherry squints at the screen, his lips moving as he reads.

"What do you think?" Sophie prompts.

"It's cool."

Sophie turns to the screen and reads aloud.

"The issue is can monies be reciepted in this mess."

Chaz VandenDungen and Ann Kulter exchange a look.

A few students are waving their hands in the air. Sophie's instinct is to call on one, but ringing in her head is VandenDungen's lecture at their last Friday afternoon peer-review meeting, in which he stressed "the importance of rigorous Socratic teaching" and "demanding the highest level of performance from our students." He accused the faculty of being soft—it was "the Rosecliff way" to let students off the hook in their "misguided struggle to be popular rather than effective."

"When you say 'it's cool,' Mr. Cherry," Sophie says, "do you

71

mean it fulfills the requirements we discussed in class?"

"Yeah, okay."

"How so?"

"I'm not really sure. I don't think you ever talked about it."

Again she's ready, with a tried and true technique for dealing with a dodgy student—feed him the information he claims to lack and drill him about how effectively he can use it.

"Mr. Cherry, if an issue statement is supposed to inform the reader about the rules of law governing the case, as well as the facts that are relevant to the application of those rules, then how does this one measure up?"

"It probably sucks."

"Explain."

"I defer to my colleagues." Cherry gestures to the hands waving in the air.

"We want to hear from you," Sophie says.

"Yeah, okay, it sucks because it doesn't say anything."

"Professor Poe?" It's a woman sitting in the second row, who starts fluttering her hand in the air at the beginning of every class period and continues until she is called on or can no longer contain herself. "This issue statement is totally lame because it refers to no law and it refers to no facts."

"And what rules of law should the issue statement refer to in this case?"

"The rules of contract law because when the guy took his dog to the grooming parlor, he and the owner made a contract to have the dog cleaned."

Justin Cherry is leaning sideways, gibbering at the Dean, who smiles and nods his head.

"Let's look at another example." Sophie clicks her remote, but nothing happens. The snarling warrior-beast holding Justin Cherry's issue statement continues to stare at the class with his buzzy, pea-green eyes. She repositions the remote and clicks again. Nothing. She jiggles the mouse on the podium with no luck. As she fiddles with the keyboard, the class grows restive. Of course the technology would fail on a review day. Of course! But, she thinks maturely, this will be a "teachable moment" anyway. She has a backup plan; with student input, she'll draft an effective issue statement on the whiteboard. She flips the switch to raise the video screen, which is in effect a giant shade drawn down in front of the board, but no whirring sound occurs, and the screen remains in place.

This isn't the first time technology has failed Sophie in the classroom, not even close. The worst part of the experience isn't the obvious discomfiture or the need to improvise on the spot. The worst part is the contempt displayed by the students: the rolling of eyes, the exaggerated, disdainful sighs, the disparaging snickers—all the hallmarks of student tech snobbery. As if they could make this shit work right! Any good will that might have been built over weeks of smooth, crisis-free instruction evaporates in the instant it takes to lose control of some pestiferous electronic device.

Sophie has little choice but to continue with the paltriest of modern teaching tools, the spoken word. She'll show these Twitter addicts what "interactive" means! But with many of the students already in tech-superiority malevolence mode, she must tread carefully. Glancing to the right side of the classroom, her gaze settles on Cleo Miller, who sits in his usual spot apart from the other students, quietly and courteously awaiting her next move. Cleo Miller, who is always prepared, always cogent, and who, in this case, turned in a near-perfect memorandum of law.

"Mr. Miller, can you help me out?"

"Yes, ma'am."

"What rules of law will we need to incorporate in our issue statement?"

Blushing humbly, Cleo Miller says, "Well, ma'am, we should start with the requirement of an agreement about the work to be performed and the terms the parties negotiated."

§

With the help of a handful of reliables like Cleo Miller, Sophie survives the class, then retreats to her office to check the current level of her retirement fund on the TIAA-CREF website. The stock market always held great allure for her until she actually invested in it, at which time it became her worst enemy. Behaving erratically. Falling prey to fat cats with fat appetites. At one point, she'd accumulated over $75,000; today her retirement fund stands at $39,422. If she withdraws the money now, she'll incur a ten percent penalty plus taxes. She punches the figures into her calculator. She'll have somewhere around $28,000. Will that be enough to start over when the two-headed monster boots her off the tenure track?

It's customary for the reviewers of a class to drop by the office of the teacher they observed to provide feedback before presenting their comments at the Friday afternoon meeting. As she waits for VandenDungen and Kulter, Sophie scans her research notes for "Aw, Fuck." Omar proposed she expand the scope of the article far beyond the limits of her ambition. He dropped by her house a couple of evenings ago, interrupting her standing date with the medical discoveries cable channel, which was tracking the perilous journey of an uninsured single mother of four suffering from a combination of lupus, multiple sclerosis, fibromyalgia, and Crohn's disease—and now the docs suspected a brain tumor.

When Omar knocked, Sophie neglected to turn off the TV. By the time his gaze drifted to the screen, the scene had shifted from the wide-eyed young mother being wheeled into the operating room, her head bolted to a steel apparatus, to a grossly obese man who'd been stuck in his bathroom for two months. A crew was removing an outside wall to free him. Omar's disappointment in her choice of leisure activities was painfully evident, and as if to rehabilitate her, he launched into a dissertation of thematic possibilities she might tackle in her article.

Perhaps it should focus on the political dimension of the word fuck, he proposed, with some decoding of racespeak and genderspeak thrown in. She could examine the belligerent use of the word by those in power, including the fusillades fired on a regular basis by Richard Nixon, Lyndon Johnson, Dubya Bush and Barack Obama during their presidencies. She could use Rosecliff Law School as a microcosmic study of the use of the word as a tool of control, incorporating as an example an identity-disguised Manuel Delgado, with his overuse of the word in his classroom as a symbol of the insecurity he feels around his minority status.

Or might she be better off, Omar wondered, concentrating on the capitalistic exploitation of the word—the marketability of the four letters, F, U, C, and K? After all, those letters in various combinations have been employed profitably throughout popular culture, in movies like Meet the Fockers, and by companies vying in the marketplace, such as French Connection United Kingdom, known to fashionistas as fcuk®, whose profits reportedly spiked 81% after adopting the logo. With this slant, she could reveal the triumph of profit-motive over moral hesitation—a theme bound to be well-received by market purists.

Or if she really wanted to "blow some mind," he said, she could analyze this most popular of expletives in the context of the new libertarian paternalism. But that assumed she understood what "libertarian paternalism" meant.

"Isn't that an oxymoron?" she said.

He looked surprised. "So? More meatiness."

"I have no clue how to fit fuck into it."

"You will read up on it, and you will construct separate schema for it within broader debate."

As he rose to leave, Sophie blurted out, "What about the sex part?" *Shouldn't we have it?*

Omar studied her inscrutably. Unfortunately, he did not seem to be undressing her with his eyes.

"You were saying before that I should include that because everyone likes to read about it," she stammered.

"Too obvious," he said. "You would be hard-pressed to squeeze scholarship from it." He turned to leave.

"Why don't you stay awhile?" she said, hoping she didn't sound too needy. "Let's have a cocktail."

"I think not," he said.

After he left, Sophie's mind whirled with confusion—not over the intricacies of "Aw, Fuck"; that subject immediately dropped from her mind—but regarding Omar himself.

Was the attraction really there, or all in her mind? Why would he drop by her house in the evening just to discuss an article? Such a visit reeked of pretext, didn't it? But when given the opportunity to slip from business into pleasure, he'd turned tail. Perhaps his formality and conservatism were related to his roots in Middle Eastern culture. After wasting too much time analyzing their interaction, she vowed not to be drawn into yet another non-relationship defined by ambiguity and mixed signals, her pattern since her divorce from Chester.

Now, reviewing her notes of their conversation about her article, Sophie is scratching her head over his comment about "schema" when the phone rings.

"Hey, Professor Poe, this is Mac Higgins over at Frankfort. How're you doing?"

"I'm a little busy."

"That is a great article you wrote, ma'am."

Sophie pauses. She hasn't written it yet. So how—

"Oh! You read my Clean Water article?" she says, astonished.

"It's fantastic!"

"Thank you."

"I've actually got a problem with that very thing."

"I got your message, but I'm afraid—"

"Do you know anything about Meyeth Industries, Professor?"

She suddenly feels as limp as one of her house plants. The Meyeths: they are everywhere. The Triplets head one of the largest conglomerates in the world, with interests ranging from baby powder to explosives. They operate secretly, avoiding oversight whenever possible. Governments and courts look the other way. Sophie recalls her father's trouble with Meyeth some years ago, when Arthur ran for the state senate. Though he ran as a Republican, the Meyeths supported his opponent, who'd crossed parties for the purpose of defeating Arthur because he supported teaching the theory of evolution. He always said it was ironic because if anyone should believe in the brutality of natural selection, it was the Meyeths.

"A little," she says.

"This land has been in my family for four generations. Come to find out, the Meyeths are ruining it."

She rubs her head. "How do you mean?"

"They built a refining plant, and they're poisoning the air and dumping all sorts of shit in the water."

"Have you talked to any local attorneys?"

Higgens is silent. Finally, he says, "I know you must be very intelligent if you're a professor."

"I guess no one's interested," she says.

"That's an understatement! One guy said, 'Do you think I want to be shot in the head?'"

Sophie recalls reading an article about a lawsuit filed in the Northwest by a former Meyeth Industries employee. The employee alleged the Meyeth Triplets kidnapped him and held him captive in a remote mountain cabin in retaliation for telling the truth about something they'd asked him to investigate.

There's a knock at the door. "I'm afraid I need to go. I've got a meeting."

"Real quick, is my understanding correct, that a company can't dump waste into a lake or river unless there's no life in the water?"

"Pretty much," she says. "I'd need to know the details."

"Those I can give you. I'll put copies right into the mail, if that's all right with you."

She hesitates. What could it hurt for him to mail something?

"Sure."

"Very much obliged, Professor. Thank you for your time." He hangs up.

The door opens. Instead of the two-headed administrative monster here to rip her a new one, it's minimalist lesbian Karla Johansson.

"Oh, hey, Karla," Sophie says, smiling with relief.

She studies her colleague's ageless face in its perfect Scandinavian creaminess. Karla's owl eyes peer back unblinkingly through glasses of the utmost Euro-sophistication, bold in line yet narrow and sleek, perfectly contoured to her fine-featured face. When married to Shane, Karla shunned fashion in favor of an image of frowsy cerebralism. After being joined in civil union to her fashion-forward partner Lily, she's become almost unsuitably hip for an academic.

"I thought I was about to be reviewed," Sophie says. "Chaz and Ann just sat in on my class."

Sighing, Karla plunks down in a chair across from Sophie's desk. "That's why I'm here."

"That's why *you're* here?" Sophie says.

"Yaaah, that's it." According to Shane, ever since hooking up with Lily, Karla's northern plains accent with its flat vowels and dropped endings has intensified to *Fargo*-like proportions.

"Where are Chaz and Ann?" Sophie says.

"Well, they had to leave, see, they had some other business to attend to, somethin' that couldn't be avoided, so the Dean, he asked me if I could talk to you about the class for him."

"But you weren't there," Sophie points out.

"That's right, but see, Chaz and Ann summed it up for me, and I understand pretty much what went on and all, and what the two of them have to say about it, so it'll be me talkin' to ya about the class. 'Cause that's the way they want it, see. That's the deal we made."

Sophie recalls Shane's comment during the faculty meeting about his former wife's change of personality, from outspoken feminist to mild-mannered fence-straddler. He's theorized that Lily has exerted some sort of psychological power over Karla, and VandenDungen is finishing the job. For her part, Sophie smells the influence of money.

Sophie says, "Go ahead then."

Karla scoots her chair forward, crossing her arms on the desk. "What I understand, it's an issue of lack of control there. You're not the first to have it, and you won't be the last, Sophie. There's no shame in it."

"I couldn't get the audio-visual stuff to work!"

Karla frowns. "Ah, no, I'm talkin' about your students being out of control. Justin Cherry. And the girl yellin' and throwin' stuff at you and all. You just can't let the knuckleheads take over the class,

Sophie, that's all there is to it."

"Cherry's a jerk," Sophie says. "And I can't kick him out because he might file an ADA complaint."

"Heck, now, don't get defensive on me here."

"And Megan Stillwell is an addict." Sophie tries to recall what her admissions file said. "Benzos, I think."

Karla stares at her, eyes shiny and round as new pennies. "I'm just tryin' to say, woman to woman, that we don't always project as strong an image as we really need to, see. And if a Mr. Cherry or a Ms. Stillwell is around to take advantage, well, that's what'll happen."

Women don't project a strong enough image? She sounds like a man! Moreover, Stillwell's personality disorder aside, Sophie is pissed at herself for making the mistake of going first to Justin Cherry. But she's also upset because in order to maintain Rose-cliff's "the student-consumer is always right" culture, faculty have been left with few effective tools to combat the rudeness and enti-tlement they see daily in the classroom.

"Whyja call on Mr. Cherry, anyways?" Karla asks.

"Why did VandenDungen spend half the class listening to him instead of telling him to shutthefuckup?" Sophie says.

"Well, matter of fact, that's another point Chaz wanted me to talk to ya about, Justin's side of the controversy. Seems after the class, a group of students, they followed Chaz on up to his office, ya know, and they all had a little sit-down. Evidently, there's a number of 'em, they don't like the way you're conductin' the class there, Sophie."

Leaning back in her chair, Sophie glowers at the ceiling. This form of extortion—students filing to the Dean's office with com-plaints about a professor and a list of demands that have to be met in order to keep them from transferring to a higher-Ranked school—has become commonplace at Rosecliff. The administra-tion tolerates it because, as Shane puts it, "it's about the tuition money, stupid. Butts in the seats."

"If anybody in the front office would give us the authority to dismiss them based on conduct, we wouldn't have this problem,"

Sophie says. "If I could tell Cherry, keep your mouth shut during class or I'm dropping you, problem solved."

Karla blinks at her. "Now just settle down there. I want ya to know, Chaz and Ann both think that with some genuine effort, you could be just a super teacher!"

Her wide, mechanical grin puts Sophie in mind of Jerry Lunde-gaard, the car salesman in *Fargo*, when he told a customer he'd been authorized to take a hunnert dollars off the Trucoat.

"Oh, and Chaz wanted me to tell ya he's assigned ya your second committee, Recruitment. We'll all be going over to Washington, D.C. together here in a few weeks. So there ya go!"

8 THE IDEAL CANDIDATE

The faculty recruitment committee meets in a conference room that was hastily constructed as part of the cosmetic improvement package negotiated by Chaz VandenDungen. An old classroom was divided in two, particle-boarded down the middle, and slapped with fog-gray paint. Half became a meeting room; the remaining space was converted to offices for junior faculty.

Those who've attended meetings in the room have commented on the lack of sound-proofing. Sophie notices it immediately upon arriving when, as she sits down, she hears Bill Wu's voice through the wall, saying, "They lied to me," followed by a pause, and then: "The Dean's a fucking freak."

Sophie eyes Christopher Paine across the conference table.

"This is awkward," she says.

He raises his eyebrows. "What?"

She giggles nervously. "I guess when they remodeled they should have stuffed some of that old asbestos batting into the wall!"

Paine stares at her quizzically. "I'm sorry," he says. "I don't know what you're talking about."

She gestures in the direction of Wu's voice. "You can hear Bill talking pretty clearly."

Paine frowns at her. "I make it a point not to eavesdrop on other people's conversations, Sophie."

Chaz VandenDungen enters, trailed by the other members of the recruitment committee. As they settle in, Wu's voice resumes, though at a lower pitch. Apparently he's heard Sophie talking and realizes he might be overheard to the same extent. Straining to hear, Sophie picks up the word "farce."

To get things started, the Dean gives a pep talk. "You on this committee have quite a responsibility," he says. "Your task is to bring faculty to Rosecliff who are better than any of you." He lets that sink in. "If you'll permit a bit of folk wisdom, it's like the old horse trader says: I never buy me a brood mare that's not better than the ones I have."

The committee chair, Paul Singer, who was born and raised on a farm, rolls his eyes.

"The point is," VandenDungen continues, "our peers in the academy rate us based in part on how we look on paper, and our Ranking won't increase if they don't notice some changes. So." He scans their faces. "What does that mean?"

The committee members shift about sluggishly, recognizing the tenor of a teaching exercise. No one wants to be called on.

"Diversity," Sophie blurts out. It's always an acceptable response in a meeting like this.

"Absolutely," VandenDungen says. "Very good."

"We damn well better focus on putting more color on this faculty," Thea Volley says. Volley is an African-American woman in her second year of teaching, and the most junior faculty member on the committee. "Our viewbook notwithstanding," she shoots VandenDungen a withering look, "we are still a white faculty. At meetings, when I look around the room, I feel as if I should be wearing sun glasses, the glare from all the white faces is so blinding. We need to reach out to disadvantaged groups."

"Well put, Thea," VandenDungen says. "But is it enough that a candidate is a member of a disadvantaged group?"

This question is so easy Sophie chimes in reflexively.

"I believe we're looking for someone with top credentials and a

82

significant practice background," she says. "A graduate of a good law school, and at least four to five years' experience."

"You've just slammed the door on the very people we're trying to attract!" Thea says heatedly. "What about the first generation college-graduate, who lacks the connections to get into your 'good law school'? And by the way, let's acknowledge up front that 'good law school' is code for 'school dominated by the Caucasian power elite.'" Thea presses a button on the arm of her chair, which emits an electronic whirring sound as the back angles down and the seat rises up. Adjusting her body to conform to the lounge position, she clasps her hands together across her belly. "Query: why does it have to be a 'good law school'?"

Though she vowed not to, Sophie finds herself resenting the special accommodations made to Thea Volley. No doubt Rosecliff is lucky to have her. She is a talented young woman, and there was a fierce "bidding war" over her. Schools on both coasts, as well as here on the "middle coast," as VandenDungen positively spins the Midwest, competed in an effort to woo her. Rosecliff emerged the victor for reasons not entirely clear, though rumor has it VandenDungen offered her a salary far above the other contenders—higher, even, than some of the long-tenured senior professors at Rosecliff. Now, here is this ergonomically-correct automated chair the school purchased for the newly pregnant Volley, so she can sit in the position of her choice and not inconvenience the fetus. Custodial staff are occasionally summoned to move the chair from place to place. Snide remarks have been made about "driving Miss Volley."

"Anybody home, Sophie?" Thea says.

The others stare at her expectantly. She's been wondering how much the chair cost and, in any event, considered Thea's question rhetorical. But evidently, Thea and the rest of the committee are waiting to hear Sophie's reasons for wanting the candidate to be a graduate of a good law school.

"Would you consider the school I went to a 'good law school'?" Thea persists.

Sophie struggles to remember what law school Thea attended.

Did they expect her to retain the details of her colleagues' résumés? Whatever school it was, she doesn't dare comment on it. Who is she to judge the merit of various law schools anyway? That is the purview of the *USN&WR, Special Graduate School Edition.*

She nods at Thea, hoping her noncommittal response will suffice to move the conversation forward, but the Volley is visually searching her in a way suggesting otherwise.

"I have an idea," Paul Singer says tightly. "Let's discuss our scoring of the résumés."

"Good," says Chris Paine.

After a fanfare of paper shuffling, discussion of the candidates begins. In preparation for the national law faculty recruitment conference, known as the "meat market," they've sifted through hundreds of résumés, ranking them from 1 to 4, with 4 being the "ideal" candidate to interview.

Sitting next to Sophie, Xavier Michaud drums his fingers on his stack. Peeking at his score sheet, she notices he scored every candidate on the list "1." She whispers to him, "What's the deal?"

He responds with a Mona Lisa smile but says nothing.

"Well," says Paul Singer, examining the table of members' compiled scores, "it looks like we've got a basic consensus on the top seven or eight high-scoring candidates."

"That statement's inaccurate, Paul," says Thea. "Xavier isn't in agreement because he didn't give any of them high scores. It can't be said the committee has reached a consensus."

"But he doesn't like any of them, I guess, and he doesn't like them all the same amount, so his scores basically wash out," says Singer.

"Wash out?" Thea says. "Is that code for saying that as committee chair, you're disenfranchising him?"

"He did it to himself by voting one, one, one!" snaps Singer.

Sophie is busy analyzing the subtext in this exchange. Paul Singer is still sensitive about something that happened during last year's recruitment season, involving a prospect that he particularly liked. The candidate, who applied for a position teaching corporate law, was a white Southerner, articulate and well-published, with some impressive experience working in overseas markets. Her job talk went well, up to the point when Thea Volley questioned her about a footnote in one of her articles that Thea asserted contained "racist code," specifically the word "angry," referring to an article written by a black professor. Michaud and Manuel Delgado joined in, and by the time the session ended, the candidate was in tears. The next day, she withdrew her application.

"I had no idea what I was getting into!" Bill Wu says through the wall,

"God, Chaz, can't we do something about that?" Thea says.

"I've got somebody looking into it," VandenDungen says. "I guess soundproofing is a complicated process, unless they just tear it down and start over."

"So do it," Thea says.

"What we always did up in Minnesota," says Karla Johansson, "when the wind would go to a' blowin' and a' whistlin', and we could feel it right through the walls, ya know, we'd tack up some heavy quilts, see, and that'd dampen it down just enough so's we could keep ourselves warm and toasty."

Everyone contemplates Karla, mentally trying to apply her quilt suggestion to the conference room's sound-proofing problem.

"The same approach could be tried here," Karla says.

Sighing heavily, Paul Singer fidgets with his onyx-studded cufflinks. He is too well-behaved to assert himself to the degree the situation—the aimless, tedious drifting of a committee meeting—requires. Beneath the GQ-esque exterior exist the heart and soul of a properly raised country boy, who was literally taken to the woodshed and had the uppityness beat out of him. His natural aggression thus displaced, he developed a raging entrepreneurial ambition and now operates a successful oil and gas consulting business out of his law school office, to the tune of half a million dollars a year, earning him the nickname Sir Poil. He's saved more than enough to retire but continues to teach at the law school because his work ethic lacks an off button.

The Dean impatiently jiggles his hand in the air, his signal for "let's get going."

Singer clears his voice. "It looks like we'll try to interview the top seven or eight from this first batch of résumés," he says. "We all ranked them either 3 or 4—"

"Not true," says Thea.

"—except for Xavier, of course," Singer continues, "so their composite scores are well above our cut-off point. But we need to add a few more from the rest of the group to fill our interview slots, so I've picked some I think we should consider.

"This first one is really strong." He consults the résumé. "Vanderbilt undergrad, Northwestern law. Look at his experience. JAG lawyer, federal prosecutor, then a private firm. He's been teaching three years as an adjunct." He smiles. "Looks good to me." He drops the résumé in his "yes" pile. "Any comments?"

Xavier Michaud mimes an elaborate response, gingerly picking up the résumé as if it might be contaminated with anthrax and isolating it in the center of the wide expanse of polished redwood. Closing his eyes, he shakes his head and waves his forearms, generating the kind of "X" signal ground crew use to stop an aircraft.

"Does diversity mean the same thing to you as it does to me?" Thea asks Sir Poil.

"We're already interviewing five minority candidates," Poil says.

"Quotas," Michaud intones. "Hmm . . . interesting."

Sophie feels for Sir Poil. She reaches into her pile and extracts the résumé of a woman who graduated from a top law school and worked as corporate counsel to several blue chip companies. She, too, taught for several years as an adjunct professor. "Here's one to consider," she says. "With her experience, she'd have a lot of credibility with the students."

Volley, Michaud, and VandenDungen triangulate a look that instantly kills the suggestion.

"She's a woman," Sophie says. "Doesn't that count for something?"

"Women are not a disadvantaged group, not by any measure," the Dean says. "They constitute 51 percent of the population."

"Not on our faculty!" Sophie says. "We're barely 20 percent, and most of us aren't even on tenure track!"

"Sophie's got a point," Karla says. "There's no denying the wage gap. DOL statistics show women earn 77% of men's wages for the same work."

Sophie smiles at Karla. Later, she'll relate Karla's support to Wally Shane as proof that his ex retains at least a modicum of her former devotion to the feminist cause.

"But, then again, Sophie, didja notice how long since she graduated?" Karla says. "It's been, ya know, about fifteen years there."

"Oh. Too old?" Sophie says.

"No!" Christopher Paine cries out. "Can't say that!"

"Can't say what?" Sophie says.

"What we need to say," VandenDungen explains, "is that this particular candidate wouldn't bring any age diversity to our faculty."

"Do the candidates have to be a certain age?" Sophie says. "I didn't know that."

"Of course not, Sophie," Paine says in a long-suffering tone. "There are no pre-set requirements. We are open to all things, to all ideas, to all people. We're committed to assembling a faculty that represents a breadth of characteristics in all categories and classifications."

Sophie and Sir Poil exchange a look of mutual frustration. Sophie calculates the difference between the candidate's age and her own.

"She's not that old!" she says.

"Sophie," Paine says. "Please understand this. You cannot say 'old.' It's a suspect classification. It's a protected status."

Now it's Sophie's turn to shrug and sigh resignedly, at which point her cell phone sounds, playing a Mozart piano sonata. How could a harmless little sonata be so annoying? Normally she wouldn't bring the phone to a meeting, but Buggles is at the vet having an ingrown dewclaw removed, and she's been waiting for word on how the surgery went. She removes herself from the room, flipping open her phone.

"Sophie Poe."

"Professor Poe! So glad I reached you. It's Mac Higgins over at Frankfort."

"Hey."

"Is this a bad time?"

"I'm in a meeting."

"Another meeting? My sympathies! Won't keep you a minute, just checking in to see if you got the stuff I sent."

Sophie rubs her burning eyes. The human eyeball simply is not designed to look at black letters on white paper beneath harsh fluorescents for hours at a time.

"I haven't had a chance."

"That's no problem at all. I completely understand."

"I'll try to take a look at it when I get back to my office."

"That would be perfect, Professor! I just happen to be driving your way today, and that's the reason I'm calling. I thought if you'd had a chance to look at the stuff, I'd stop in and see what you think."

It is a universal truth that people who live in the country speak three times louder than city dwellers, either because they are accustomed to shouting at each other over the noise of machinery or across great distances or both.

"If that doesn't work for you, I won't impose myself," Higgins says.

Sophie pauses. Her inner voice chants *don't do it, don't do it.* But he read her article. He thought it was good. And he is so polite.

"Can you be at my office this afternoon, about 5:00?" she says.

"I'll be there! And thank you very much!"

Sophie groans. Every time she's tried to help a cold caller, she has lived to regret it. And now she's opening the door again. But this case feels different.

As Sophie reenters the conference room, Thea Volley is holding up a résumé.

"Did you all notice this one?" she says. "Fleur Shortbeard? She sounds really interesting."

They all pull out the Shortbeard résumé. Sophie instantly recalls the candidate. Her initial excitement had turned to dismay when she noticed that despite Shortbeard's stellar educational background and publication of three decent law review articles, she'd held a series of brief, offbeat positions having nothing to do with the practice of law. Sophie had ranked her "2" based on her education and the diversity factor—she identified herself as one-fourth Native-American.

"Sophie, you'll note she graduated from one of your 'good' schools,'" Thea says.

Sophie bites her tongue as she reviews the candidate's employment history. *Docent at the Colorado Museum of Mines?*

Sir Poil squirms in his chair. Sophie sees he's trying mightily to stuff his reaction, which must be similar to hers.

"She's got some really interesting experience, I think," Thea says.

Dog catcher for the municipality of Mountain View?

"Plus she's queer," says Karla Johansson. She appraises the group. "She sure is. Look here. She spent a little time as a barista at the Cuppa Double D in Denver. That's a well-known hangout for queer women. I just wanted everyone to have that information."

"I say we interview her," says Volley.

"But she has no legal experience," Poil says with obvious restraint.

All eyes focus on the Dean. He doesn't vote in committee meetings except in the case of a tie, but it could well come to that.

"I'd just like to say, she's no Thea Volley," Sophie remarks. "If that's what we're looking for."

Volley glares at her. "I object to that on two levels. First, I didn't realize you were an expert on Thea Volley. Second, I don't like the implication that I am fungible with other minority candidates. African-Americans are no more like Native-Americans than a loaf of pumpernickel bread is like a loaf of rye."

Sophie mentally compares the two breads, both of which she enjoys immensely. In her opinion, they aren't entirely unalike.

"These distinctions are important," Thea says.

"I meant that you held three significant legal jobs before going

89

into teaching," Sophie says. "She hasn't had one."

"Correction," Volley says. "Four!"

"My suspicion," says Chris Paine, "is that Ms. Shortbeard either couldn't get hired because of her ethnicity, or she found the atmosphere of the traditional law office so hostile that she instinctively rappelled away from it."

Flapping his lips, Sir Poil buries his head in his arms.

"In either case," Paine continues, "I think we should give her the benefit of the doubt and interview her."

"I have to go with Chris and Thea on this one," the Dean says.

The result of the vote is three in favor of interviewing Fleur Shortbeard, two against, with Xavier Michaud abstaining, his finger in the air, indicating "one."

§

At 4:45 p.m., Sophie tears herself away from the students waiting to talk to her after class, runs upstairs, locates Higgins's envelope under her desk, and flops into her chair. As she removes the materials, she remembers she is supposed to pick up Buggles before 5:30 and berates herself for needlessly complicating her schedule. After glancing through the contents, including photos, soil tests, water analyses, and correspondence with a Meyeth lawyer—and a copy of her article!—Sophie realizes already she's out of her depth. She wrote the article as a favor to Shane, but her understanding of environmental law is shallow at best, and of science in general, disturbingly muddled.

Mac Higgins arrives on time and isn't at all what Sophie expects; she pictured an overweight man in worn jeans, a frayed work shirt, and a pair of Timberland lace-up boots smeared with manure. Instead, he looks like a piece of the beautiful earth itself—intense blue eyes, natural sun-tanned skin, green shirt, creased black jeans. He carries a Day Planner, and on his belt, a holstered cell phone that goes off as he enters the office, playing the theme song from Sex and the City.

"Ma'am, I can't thank you enough for agreeing to see me."

"My pleasure."

He explains that he, his father, and his uncle farm 2,000 acres in the western part of the state. They irrigate, drawing water from a tributary of the Ichiwaw River. For the last couple of years, despite consistent farming practices, their yields have diminished.

"The plants themselves look sickly," Mac says.

At first they suspected seed problems. They sent the seeds to the state university, which reported they were of normal quality and advised checking the soil and water. The test results showed a mixture of chemicals and radiation.

"That explained it," he says. "And we knew Meyeth Industries had started fracking upstream. Guess what?"

"They're by-products of fracking?"

"Bingo!"

As if on cue, the toilet next door roars. Sophie is beginning to feel like one of Mac Higgins's soybean plants, undernourished and unproductive. She considers potential claims, assuming his theory of what happened is true. Unfortunately, despite her article, there is a blank space in her brain where information about environmental causes of action should be.

"The thing is, I don't practice law anymore," she says.

"I didn't realize that."

"Since I started teaching, I haven't had the time."

His gaze lends the phrase "eye contact" new meaning. "Maybe you can give me the name of another lawyer who can help me."

"Hmm."

"Am I asking too much? If I am, say so, Professor. I don't want to be a burden."

At which point she explains the facts of legal life to him. Yes, he might well have a claim, but even if the law favors him, practically speaking, he has no recourse because international companies like Meyeth Industries protect themselves so well they're unassailable; lus, judges, especially judges in this state, love Business, especially Meyeth Business, and hate "whiny plaintiffs." Rumor has it some judges are on the bench because the Meyeths put them there.

Sophie is aware she sounds like a coward and an apologist for corporate America. Mac Higgins watches her as if she's delivering a grave medical diagnosis. Not only is she letting him down, she's taking away all hope. She's become the most cynical of cynics, worse than Chaz VandenDungen, worse than the Consultant!

"So the law is there but it's no good to me," he says. "Is that about it?"

"Pretty much."

Higgins's cheeks are crimson. She can almost feel the angry heat coming off his body. . . as well as that delicious manly scent—is it Axe Metal . . . or Rise Up? At last she's able to smell them on a man instead of in the Walgreens deodorant aisle.

"Try filing a complaint with the government?" she says.

He observes her pityingly, that she has been reduced to suggesting such an obviously inadequate solution to his problem.

"Thank you for your time, Professor."

"You can call me Sophie," she says. "And don't go away so fast. Maybe I can figure something out. Oh!" She jumps up.

"What's the matter?"

"How would you like to ride with me to the vet's to get my dog?"

"Great! I love dogs!"

9 CONNECTIONS

The annual "meat market" in Washington, D.C. provides an opportunity for legions of legal educators to size up desperate lawyers eager to escape the prospect of a lifetime of stultifying law practice. From the recruiter's perspective, the goal is to grade as much raw meat as possible as efficiently as possible, in the hope that the process will yield some prime cuts, to be bid on later at "auction." From the interviewee's viewpoint, the objective is to collect a maximum number of job offers, the higher the schools' Rankings, the better the ability to play one against the other.

Recruiters from law schools across the country flock like common conventioneers to a monstrous D.C. hotel, an awe-inspiring monument to functionality, uncompromisingly devoid of warmth and charm. The interviews are designed as "speed dates," with candidates shuffling from room to room for interviews every half-hour, eight hours a day.

This year, recruiting is way down because of the Crisis in Legal Education. Nonetheless, Rosecliff's committee is attending because since VandenDungen's arrival, several faculty members have given notice.

It is Sophie's first meat market, and she's been warned that as the interviews wear on, the candidates begin to blend together until by day's end, they are all but indistinguishable. She proposed taking along a camera to snap shots of the candidates in order to facilitate later identification, an idea that draws scorn.

"And then what?" demanded Thea Volley. "We rank the candidates on how well they satisfy our notions of conventional White beauty?"

"Thank you so much for that suggestion, Sophie," the Dean added, "you've just laid the groundwork for a discrimination lawsuit against the university. The second one since my arrival, I might add, following the 'tiny bladder' suit just filed, one I'm afraid we'll lose." The Dean is referring to the fact that Rosecliff professors have started to crack down on students casually leaving and returning to the room in the middle of class; the students struck back immediately, filing an action alleging discrimination against those with smaller-than-normative bladders, who couldn't possibly hold it in for fifty minutes.

Regarding the candidates' identities, she is advised, it is permissible to scribble "notes to self" about the candidates, such as "large mole on nose" or "cleavage exposed," on condition that the notes are later shredded.

The members of the Rosecliff recruitment committee fly to Washington separately, indicating just how tired they've grown of each other's company. Sophie arrives at the hotel an hour before the reception for recruiters, insufficient time for tourism. Collapsing on the bed in her room, she flicks on the TV. After briefly considering a documentary about a man whose right foot weighs 48 pounds, she settles on back-to-back episodes of Sons of Anarchy.

After running out of time-killers, she heads downstairs to the gargantuan hotel lobby, a coldly cavernous architectural distortion with no clear center, made all the more confusing by the dizzying, dotted blue carpet and mirrors lining the walls. In contrast, the reception is located in a shadowy, prodigiously utilitarian event room that can be reconfigured to accommodate any requirement, or so testifies the complex grid of ceiling tracks.

The room is already densely packed. Apparently everyone has

arrived early, either to get it over with or to suck down the free booze. Smacking into a sea of grim, pasty faces, she feels as if she's walked onto a set for a cheap indie film entitled *The Predatory Academic*. Never has she encountered so many nakedly judgmental expressions at a single event.

At the bar, she parks next to a wide-bodied SUV of a man dressed in black, and orders a glass of wine. SUV downs a bottle of beer in a single long swig like a frat boy. His name tag identifies him as a professor from the University of Arkansas, Fayetteville, third quartile in the latest Rankings. He slams his empty on the bar and growls out a request for another.

"I like the way you drink," Sophie says.

SUV pointedly stares at her breasts, or at least the right one. No, he actually is staring at her convention tag, which bears her name and law school affiliation. In a preemptive strike, Sophie offers her hand and introduces herself.

"Rosecliff Law," she announces.

SUV grasps her fingertips for an instant then turns away, never having made eye contact, and concentrates on his new bottle.

"Hiya, Sophie!"

Karla Johansson has crept up behind her.

"Where ya been anyways?"

Karla removes the glass of wine from Sophie's hand, links arms with her, and steers her away from the bar.

"We don't think of this as a social occasion, see," she explains. "We've got work to do here."

As they reach hors d'oeuvre central, Chris Paine and Chaz VandenDungen join them. Already feeling the effects of the half glass of wine, Sophie recognizes she is entering her "effusive enthuser" stage, in which imbibing alcohol in an ambience of social unease compels her to compensate for the bad time everyone else appears to be having.

Glancing up at VandenDungen and Paine, she blurts, "Well, at least no one can accuse Rosecliff of lacking diversity!"

The acoustics of the makeshift reception area intensify the dreary murmur of the recruiters, and it isn't clear that any of her

95

three colleagues have heard her. Karla waves at an acquaintance, while the Dean's vulpine eyes whipsaw the room. Only Paine appears to realize she's spoken. He looks down at her in charitable tolerance, eyebrows teepeed quizzically.

"We're diverse!" she shouts. "Height diversity!" She gestures upwards, indicating the men's tall stature, then pats her own head and Karla's. Paine looks hurt and disappointed over her poor taste; diversity is never a joking matter in the Academy.

Glancing across the hors d'oeuvre table, Sophie's gaze connects with that of a handsome black man with graying temples, wearing a sharply tailored navy suit over a pink shirt and shimmering paisley tie. He smiles warmly at her, holds up an unidentifiable morsel, and says, "These are quite good. Have you tried one?" His charisma and sartorial acuity combined with his friendliness, contrasting so sharply with the otherwise grim collection of law professors, stuns her into flushed silence. She scurries around the end of the table and inspects the squarish tidbit perched on a napkin in his hand.

"That does look good," she enthuses. "What is it?"

He laughs. "I have no idea. Some layered thing."

"Layers are good," she says. "If you don't like one, you might like the next." As he looks directly into her eyes, she anticipates the moment when he will check out her conference ID tag.

"I'm not sure my palate is that discerning," he says. "But the total effect is pleasurable."

She chuckles amiably. "To be honest, I'm not sure I even have a palate," she says, immediately regretting it. Everyone has a palate. She might as well have said "I'm born and bred Midwestern—we love chicken-fried steak!"

Appearing amused, he extends his hand. "Marlon Herrington. Nice to meet you." His tag states he is a Dean at . . . where? No. She squints at his tag. Yes! Top Five!

Accepting his proffered hand, she introduces herself.

"Ah," he says. "Rosecliff."

"That's right," she says defensively. "Rosecliff."

"I know several of your colleagues," Herrington says. "Good

96

people. And I know your new dean."

Sophie scrutinizes this striking man who so impressively didn't bolt at the name Rosecliff. She didn't anticipate that a recruiter with such a lofty affiliation actually would have heard of Rosecliff, much less that he'd know some of her colleagues.

She peers over her shoulder to see if Chaz VandenDungen is still standing on the other side of the table. He's disappeared, but Karla and Chris Paine remain. Even through the gloaming, Sophie can read the anxiety written on their faces, reflecting their complete lack of confidence in her ability to hold up her end of a conversation with a man of Marlon Herrington's caliber. But, really, she would ask them, is it possible to embarrass Rosecliff Law any more than its highly visible, almost-last place USN&WR Ranking already has?

"You know Dean VandenDungen?" she says.

"Yes, I know Chaz," says Herrington. "He's completely crazy."

Whipping around, she studies his expression. A restrained smile plays at his lips, sparkles in his eyes.

A huge, ear-to-ear grin invades her face.

"Yes," she says, "he is."

"Can I get you a drink?" Herrington says.

"Oh, please," she says. "White wine." He sets off toward the bar. How dull wine sounds, given the giddiness she feels! "No, no!" she calls after him. "A shot of vodka, chilled!" She jogs along in his trail, bumping into bodies as firmly rooted as ancient boulders.

She and Marlon Herrington stand side-by-side at the bar, arms touching lightly, as the bartender pours two shots of vodka.

Herrington lifts his. "*Célébrons donc le marché de la viande.*"

She has no idea what he's just said, but it sounds like French, the language her mother urged her to study but which she rejected in favor of Latin, a dead tongue she'd never be expected to speak unless she joined the Catholic priesthood. Clearly, though, it is a call to celebrate something. She raises her glass. They down the vodka simultaneously.

"What are we celebrating?" she says, trying to improvise a translation based on dim memories of Latin root words. "Going to war

97

over food?"

"Well, sort of," he laughs. "The meat market."

"So far it's pretty ugly."

"Wait till tomorrow. By afternoon you'll want to jump out the window."

Grabbing two more vodkas, they stroll the periphery of the crowd, a sea of dark, linty cotton with mostly white faces bobbing randomly to the surface.

"So how do you know Chaz?" she says.

"We were classmates at Yale," Herrington says. He shakes his head thoughtfully. "Don't get me wrong. He's a brilliant guy. But what I remember most about him is the mood swings."

"Especially when he's off his meds," she says.

He raises his eyebrows. "He's taking medicine for it?"

"For what?"

"He's bi-polar, isn't he?"

"I have no idea," she says. "All I know is he's very unpredictable. Sometimes he goes on these rants, then he's sorry. Some of us joke that we have battered professor syndrome. We always know another attack is coming, but we stay."

As she finishes her shot, she glimpses Karla Johansson, who's observed her swill the last drops of vodka. Johansson is joined by Paine, then VandenDungen. The assemblage suggests it is time for the Rosecliff contingent to take its leave.

"I'd better go," she says.

"Hey," says Herrington, extending his hand and, along with it, a buzz of chemistry. "It was fun talking to you. Maybe we could get together again before this chaos is over."

"Sure."

He is still holding her hand. "Perhaps tomorrow night," he says. "I'm sure we'll be having dinner with our respective committees, but maybe we could meet for a drink afterwards."

"Great," she says.

He turns, waving farewell as he retreats into the joyless throng.

The warm flush inside her transcends the effect of drink, she realizes, darting toward the door. He has so attracted her that she feels a little shaky on her feet. As she reaches the others, they move into the bright hallway, chatting among themselves.

"They gave Richardson tenure anyway," VandenDungen says.

Paine stares at him in surprise.

"You know the article he published in *Seton Hall*?" the Dean continues. "About the First Amendment and cultural references to excrement, analyzing whether the product of bodily function, presented in any form, whether written, filmed, or recorded, can ever lawfully be considered an obscenity?"

"It turned off a lot of folks," Karla says.

"He submitted it as his third tenure article," VandenDungen says, "at Tulane they require three, actually the trend is to require three to four articles, one school now requires five, something I'd like to move toward at Rosecliff, by the way, but in any event, they had no choice but to take this excrement piece seriously. The faculty gave it the thumbs up, and central administration followed suit."

Sophie's discussion with Marlon Herrington provides a new perspective on VandenDungen. She's assumed his talking so rapidly and flapping his hands in the air are affectations he acquired attending Yale, Ivy League code meant to communicate his brilliance without the need to drop names or cite credentials. Now she realizes it must be his mania at work, so . . . did he just say *five* tenure articles?

"Ya know what he titled the piece, don'cha?" Karla says.

"The title is 'Shit,'" says VandenDungen.

It hits Sophie like a punch to the gut. This fellow Richardson at Tulane is one up on her in the quest for instant elevation to the top of the downloads list via an offensive title.

"Why would he do that?" Paine says, looking puzzled.

"It's this galdurn competitive downloading!" Karla says. "Now we've got yet *another* criterion for ranking schools. The more downloads per article, the more noteworthy the article is considered from a peer-review perspective, and that spills right over onto the affiliated school, ya know, in the aggregate. A racy title attracts more downloads."

Chris Paine massages his temples. "That's deeply troubling."

"I agree," the Dean says.

Sophie stares at him in disbelief. This is the very technique he and the Consultant advocated as her shortcut to tenure!

"But Chaz," she says, "when we talked that day about the site, you and Ann said self-publishing is the way to go, that—"

VandenDungen holds up his hand. "Sophie, don't interrupt."

"—that I could get some credibility by posting my article on the site and getting it downloaded a lot, that it would help my tenure application, and ultimately it could affect Rosecliff's Ranking."

"Please Sophie," he says. "If you want to be Charles Vanden-Dungen, apply for it. Otherwise, I'll speak for myself."

"You couldn't pay me enough to be you!" she snaps. God, he rubs her the wrong way!

"Well, if it isn't the folks from Rosecliff."

From the lobby approaches a stocky white man with a glowing, tanned pate, wearing an ill-fitting gray suit and tropical-print bow tie, marching toward them in a short-legged peacock strut.

"How are we doing, my friends?"

"Hey there, Gary," says Karla. "What's up?"

As Paine shakes the man's hand, Sophie tries to place him. Everything about him is familiar—the poor physical proportions, the mincing Geisha-style walk meant to be a swagger, the steroid-enhanced biceps straining against the cheap fabric—everything, except for his gleaming bronze skull. A phrase suddenly pops into her mind: "Penis with a wig on top." She pictures him with a pale complexion and a mop of too-dark brown hair. Yes! He is Gary Krackenair, who worked at the law school for two years, then, with the help of an army of research assistants, leveraged himself to a Top Fifty school in the East. He evidently abandoned his mail-order toupee along the way. When he worked at Rosecliff, Sophie and Allison, a former slave in the Skills Program, speculated that beneath the choppy brown pelt there was a pale, purpley head, thus his nickname, which they shortened to "Penis." Well, be it natural or spray-on, Sophie mused, the tan certainly had laid that image to rest.

Stubby feet splayed, Krackenair insinuates himself into the middle of their group and rotates his torso side to side, his hands on his hips. Sophie remembers reading an article on body language in *Small Business Monthly*—a staple at Arthur's dentist's office—reporting that studies have shown that a person in a group can establish dominance by acting as a kind of flexible "hub," with imaginary spokes shooting out to each of the group members. The idea is to make the others back up, using understated yet assertive movements of the ribcage. She was fairly certain at the time the author had made the whole thing up; the present demonstration is proof. As Krackenair's elbows brush the bellies of Paine and VandenDungen, neither man appears the least bit submissive. Even the peace-loving Paine looks as if he might smash Penis in the face. Karla appears even paler than usual. The "ick factor" is rising from this misguided display like a cloud of sulfurous fumes.

"I hear we're interviewing several of the same candidates," Krackenair says, still swiveling, oblivious to the repulsiveness of his power maneuver.

"That so?" Karla mumbles.

"I'll tell you what," says Krackenair, "we've really got our eye on Rachael Green."

Sophie giggles. "She's taken," she says. "Don't you remember? She and Ross got back together in the end."

If anyone understands her *Friends* reference, they don't show it. Sophie reminds herself that it is a faux pas of the highest order to mention a television show among academic types. She shouldn't have had that second shot of vodka, she realizes, as she is at a complete loss to identify the non-fictional Rachael Green, whose résumé she must have read.

"She sounds too good to be true," VandenDungen says. "NYU Law, LLM from Stanford."

"And the experience abroad!" Karla says. "I don't think we've ever interviewed a candidate who served in the Israeli army."

"You might as well give up," Krackenair says. "We're offering her a package no other law school in the country can match."

With that comment, Sophie's consciousness splits into two foci.

The reference to the Israeli army has pricked to life a long-subliminated interest in fighting in actual rather than figurative combat. To carry an M249, to employ its fully automatic force against an enemy bent on suppression of freedom—particularly the freedom of women!—would be more gratifying than any endeavor she could imagine while parked at her gray metal desk at the law school. Dr. Sally explained that her fantasy is rooted in her anger at her father for asking Quinton to join his law firm instead of her. All Sophie knows is she likes guns for some reason. That was another thing that drew her to her former husband, Chester; he was an expert marksman. One of their favorite activities together was target-shooting.

The other half of her mind remains with Penis in the hope he'll brag in further detail about the offer his school has made to the sought-after Israeli war veteran, purportedly unmatchable—though blinking in her mind, as big and bright as the NASDAQ sign in Times Square, is the figure $926,000,000, the endowment of Harvard Law School as reported in the latest Ranking of the Top Twenty Law Schools by Size of Endowment.

". . . flew her out to our campus and put her up in the most well-appointed inn we could find," Krackenair says.

"Hold up there," Karla says. "You invited her to visit—*before* the conference?"

"Not only *invited*," Krackenair roars. "It's a fait accompli! She visited for three days, a month ago!"

A shock wave rolls over the faces of the Rosecliff recruiters. Even Sophie's mouth gapes open. The rules of the hunt are clear, and Krackenair's school has committed a flagrant violation. The protocol, as overseen by the Association of American Law Schools, has been well-established for years. Candidates upload résumés before set dates in the summer and fall, and recruiting schools contact those they are interested in to arrange interviews at the November convention. If that "first date" goes well, schools invite the candidate to their campus for a multi-day encounter, climaxing with a "job talk"—an event akin to the classic amusement park game in which an overzealous "hunter" pays three dollars to take potshots at a two-dimensional duck. Schools are not to summon a candidate for on-campus seduction before they've speed-dated in Washington.

"Before the conference?" Paine echoes.

VandenDungen peers down his nose at Krackenair at such an extreme angle that his eyes are all but curtained closed behind their thick lids. Sophie expects an outburst, if for no other reason than VandenDungen hates to miss a trend. If inviting prospects to campus early in an effort to cheat the process is the new way of doing business, he should be leading the way.

"That could backfire on you, Gary," VandenDungen says bitterly. "It could bite your ass."

Sophie suddenly remembers candidate Rachel Green. She was surprised to see Green's name on the interview schedule; the "dance cards" of many of the best candidates fill up quickly with schools higher-Ranked than Rosecliff. It makes her wonder what could be wrong with someone who looks so stellar on paper that would cause her to lower her standards.

"Hey," says Penis, "all's fair. And I have to say, Ms. Green showed pretty strong interest in us. So don't get your hopes up." With that he peacock-struts on his way, the seat of his pants shiny from wear, exacerbated by the skin-tight, butt-busting fit.

"Listen," says VandenDungen, ruffling his hair with trembling hands, "I'm not going to be able to stay for the interviews. I'm dealing with something of a personal emergency, and unfortunately I'm going to have to put out some fires tonight."

Paine and Johansson eye each other, and Sophie understands the point. The Dean frequently ducks out of important events, citing an urgent matter "at home" requiring his immediate attention. His references to domestic crises are euphemisms for demands made by Lo Ming, a skinny string bean of a woman with the deportment of a polar icecap. In her uniform of black stretchwear, she resembles Catwoman more than a damsel in need of rescue. By accepting the deanship at Rosecliff, VandenDungen disrupted their comfortable existence in their Capitol Hill townhome, and she isn't letting him forget it.

"Chaz," says Paine softly, "it's really important that the Dean be a part of the interview process."

"Chris is right," Karla says. "If the deans of other schools are here, but you're not, it looks like ya don't give a darn! No explanation we give is gonna repair that first impression."

The Dean's expression undulates as if several personalities are warring over which will be displayed to the world. Is VandenDungen bipolar, Sophie wonders, or do multiple versions exist?

"That's ridiculous, Karla," he says dismissively. "You all are the important ones, the people the candidates want to see and hear from. A dean is just the captain of the ship; the faculty are the oarsmen. My absence shows my faith in your judgment."

"The other deans—" Paine says.

"I don't give a flipping fuck what the other deans do, Chris. Do you honestly think that's what's required to pull Rosecliff out of the Bottom Tier? Stop the presses! Dean Chaz VandenDungen showed up at all the meat market interviews, how impressive! What an institution! Which Rankings factor considers the Dean's presence at candidate interviews? Can you tell me that?"

VandenDungen's rage burns so hot that Sophie feels as if her skin is melting off her face.

Paine, Karla, and Sophie watch VandenDungen storm off toward the lobby.

"Shall we go to dinner?" Paine says.

10 First Dates

The next morning Sophie awakens to a mixture of dread and regret—dread of the 16 back-to-back interviews to come, regret that she slammed down so much vodka the night before, then proceeded to stuff herself to the eyeballs with wasabi-pasted sushi washed down with sake at one of D.C.'s trendiest restaurants. She, Karla, Chris, and Chris's wife Marjorie taxied up Michigan Avenue to a Top Asian establishment. There, they met up with Karla's wife, Lily, and another woman who looked as if she'd stepped out of a Talbots display window, wearing a cream twin set, tailored gray slacks, and a heart-stopping pink pearl necklace. After years of conforming to the drab sartorial customs of academe, Sophie felt like a native of a remote Amazonian village who'd just seen a head of blond hair for the first time.

Sophie had met Lily a few times at law school functions and likes the petite, wiry woman with spiked hair and a gap-tooth smile. Where Karla is as icy, pale, and distant as the Nordic landscape of her forebears, Lily, with her dark, boyish looks, exudes warmth and openness. Karla introduced the pink pearl woman simply as "Puff," an old friend from high school. Puff presented the epitomic image of conservative social striving, yet studying her, Sophie's gaydar went off at high alarm. She couldn't refrain from examining Puff's smokily-shadowed, subtly-lined eyes for a hint of the muted despair one would expect in such an exquisitely closeted lesbian.

At the table, Chris and Karla sat across from each other, soberly discussing the résumés of the candidates to be interviewed the following day. Sophie pretended to participate—but really, what remained to be said about a one-page résumé that wasn't already thrashed out in excruciating detail in committee? Oddly, no one mentioned the Dean's earlier meltdown at the hotel, which begged for analysis. Paine and Karla are two bloodless customers, Sophie concluded, and soon found herself yakking away with Lily and Puff, who were in partying mode and kept daring her to eat more spicy this, spicy that, and wash it down with sake.

Though she longed to join the impudence on her left, Sophie maintained an expression of mild amusement, tempered by professional detachment and superficial attunement to the flogging of the dead horse continuing on her right. It was all good fun until she overheard Chris Paine say something about a "new Rankings system." With that, his voice dropped a notch, effectively excluding Sophie.

By then Lily and Puff's gaiety had escalated to the point that Sophie could no longer eavesdrop on the conversation among Karla, Paine, and Marjorie. She yearned for entry into that triangle of boring collegiality, *needed* it. The existence of a "new Rankings system" is just the sort of information tenured faculty liked to keep to themselves, the better to use it effectively against the untenured. Chris Paine's lowering his voice illustrated the great divide between the Rosecliff party line of egalitarianism, of "faculty democracy," of the munificent inclusiveness touted in recruitment, and the reality of an oligarchic body controlled by a ruling elite.

Sophie's ire rose as she considered that a faculty wife was included in this cozy impromptu meeting, her opinion sought, whereas a professor up for tenure the following year was treated as if . . . as if tenure had already been denied! Marjorie Paine, putative member of the Rosecliff professoriate! The blissful Paines, Sophie ruminated drunkenly, disseminating their aura of spiritual and moral superiority, whose every mundane contribution was delivered with the earnest righteousness of a lecture from the pulpit. Sophie recalled just such an incident involving Marjorie Paine. She'd been returning a book six days late to the public library and happened to meet Marjorie in the parking lot. "Thank God for the no late fee policy," Sophie had joked, prompting a rebuke from Marjorie, who scolded, "That policy is in place for people who cannot *afford* to pay late fees, Sophie. There are many people here who are in *genuine* need." Sophie wasn't proud of missing the due date, but did it really call for a Sermon from the Mount?

As if reading her thoughts, Marjorie Paine looked at her and said, "Is everything all right, Sophie? Is there something you'd like to share?"

"I'd like to know about the new Rankings system!" she spit out. "I think I have that right!"

Marjorie stared at her blankly. "What do you mean?"

"Chris said something about a new Rankings system, and you all seem to know a lot about it. The Dean's been telling me I need to gear my article toward certain themes that will improve our Ranking. If the standards might change, I deserve to know that."

"No one said anything about a new Rankings system to my knowledge," Chris Paine said. "Did they?" He glanced from Karla to Marjorie.

"For the love of Pete, Sophie," Karla said, "we were discussing Newt King's sister. Poor thing's been diagnosed with a rare form of cancer."

"Malignant meningioma," said Marjorie. "It affects membranes in the brain and spine."

"Oh," Sophie said. *Newt King's sister. New Rankings system.* Jeez. She must be more toasted than she realized. They didn't even sound that much alike!

"I'm afraid the outlook is bleak," Marjorie said. "She's really suffering."

"So is Newt," Chris added. "They live together, you know. They've been very close since Newt's wife died."

"I'm sorry," Sophie sputtered, "I didn't know."

"Don't feel bad, hon," Marjorie said. "No one knew till a few days ago. All we can do is pray for her."

"And for Newt," Chris said.

Marjorie and Chris bowed their heads. Oblivious to the silent vigil, Lily and Puff carried on raucously. Karla shot them a lacerating look. Lily snickered. Rolling her eyes, Karla joined the Paines in prayer. Elbows on the table, Sophie rested her head on her balled fists, praying it all would be over soon.

By the time they returned to the hotel, she was so wasted she crashed on the bed with her clothes on. That turned out to be her wisest move of the day. At 2:00 a.m., a foghorn of an alarm blasted from a speaker in her room, and voices up and down the corridor yelled "fire!" She bounded up, panicking, circled dizzily, yanked at the door about half a dozen times, unlocked the door, yanked it open, and groggily weaved down the hall to the stairs among dozens of other swerving bodies. As the throng poured down the stairs and out into the chilly air, Sophie noticed that unlike her, many of the other hustling bodies met the night in various stages of undress. There was a whole cadre of men wearing nothing but their tighty whities. A number of individuals were stark naked. Sophie subtly tried to check them out; it wasn't everyday an opportunity arose to view a bunch of nude law professors. She spotted a white whale beached behind a bush. Could it be SUV man from the reception? Yes! He looked a lot larger shed of his slimming black outfit. Catching his eye, she gave him a big thumbs-up.

§

"The heck, Sophie," Karla says as Sophie enters the interview suite. "Look at the size of that latte! Ya gonna be okay there?"

"I feel great," Sophie says, her voice gravelly. When facing 16 interviews in a smelly hotel suite, after a 90-minute dead-of-night fire alarm, is it such a sin to fortify oneself with a 32-ounce coffee drink?

All of the other committee members have arrived, except Xavier Michaud. Karla checks her watch and vents to no one in particular,

"We enable him! We do! We let him get away with this!"

Thea Volley, resting comfortably in her adjustable chair, says, "A man of color expresses himself by absentia and you all think you've *enabled* him in some sense? Explain that to me."

Sophie does a double-take, aghast that Rosecliff has shipped the adjustable chair 1000 miles. What must it cost roundtrip, a thousand fucking dollars? The woman is only six months pregnant! Approaching it, she perceives the chair is actually a relatively cheap model, upholstered in fuzzy black fabric rather than leather. So it's a rental—cold comfort indeed.

The committee chairperson, Paul Singer, is arranging the seats in a smiley semi-circle, with the hot seat where the nose would be. He checks his watch.

"We've only got a couple minutes. Should we set some ground rules before the first one arrives?"

"Meaning what?" says Thea.

"Just that from past experience, the time passes quickly, and it works best if we have some sort of plan as to how many people ask questions in a given interview."

"I'd prefer not to be told when I may and may not speak," Thea says.

"I agree with Paul on this deal," says Karla. "It always helps to organize."

There's a knock at the door. The committee members select their spots. Another knock. Karla eyes Sophie expectantly.

"What?" Sophie says.

"As the most junior member of the committee, you'll be the door person," Karla says.

"I'm not the most junior member! Thea is!"

Karla flicks her eyes at Thea reclining in her chair, fingers laced over her minimally swollen belly. Returning her attention to Sophie, Karla's expression is like that of a mother issuing a nonverbal threat to a child, a promise of punishment to be meted out later, in private.

Sighing, Sophie plods to the door and opens it. Thus begins the first day of first dates.

§

Predictably, Sophie soon loses track of the candidates, as the faces, questions, and answers run together in her mind. Was the female with bright red lipstick and a frilly blouse the candidate who admitted that she wants to go into teaching "to relax"? Or was that the young woman with a spot on her lapel that looked like baby vomit? After a few interviews, Sophie remembers to make notes, but upon review, they aren't very illuminating. On one male candidate's résumé, she has written "loves fixing cars" and "zit on chin." On another, "seems brilliant—small, eraser-shaped head." In the margin of a résumé she'd originally starred as exceptional, she's written, "wants to bring back hostages as security for debt???" and "pompous ass dullard."

One of the more entertaining interviews occurs mid-morning, when a woman named Tulip Young shows up exuding waves of energy so scattered that a double dose of Ritalin suggests itself. She wears a brown polyester pant suit, and as she fields questions, she relentlessly scratches her thighs. Every so often, a rough cuticle catches on the fabric, and she elaborately wrenches it free. Sophie observes that the slacks have taken significant abuse, not all of it confined to the thigh area. Nonetheless, Ms. Young is bright, thoughtful, and articulate. She and Sir Poil discuss a film produced at Fordham titled *Revitalizing the Lawyer-Poet: What Lawyers Can Learn From Rock and Roll.*

"Hey there, Tulip," Karla interjects, "I'm Rosecliff's resident dyke slash bisexual, and I just want you to know that we're a difference-friendly institution, so don't worry, you should feel comfortable with that."

The ensuing moments of silence last an eternity. Tulip frowns at Karla, then returns her attention to Sir Poil, attempting to pick up their conversation where it left off. But the insertion of a sexual-identity issue into the middle of an impassioned analysis of the practicing attorney as Bruce Springsteen has taken its toll, and Tulip Young leaves the interview early.

"Hey," Karla shrugs as everyone glowers at her, "my gaydar

went off, and I just wanted her to feel accepted."

Having received nothing whatsoever from Tulip on her own system, Sophie is left to wonder whether Karla's or her own gaydar is more accurate.

§

At 5:30, the last interviewee leaves, and the disheveled Rosecliff recruiters breathe a sigh of relief. Like a desert sojourner Sophie hallucinates succor—a keg of beer materializing on the "refreshments" table, which at this point offers a tub of melted ice, an overripe banana, and a bottle of generic apple juice.

"Maybe tomorrow's slate will be more impressive," Thea says through a yawn. "At least we'll get to meet Rachel Green."

The committee members are debriefing about the day's candidates—one in particular whose first question to the committee concerned the level of his starting salary—when there comes a knock at the door. No one moves to answer it.

"Let's pretend nobody's home," Sophie suggests.

Karla motions her toward the door.

"It's past business hours!" she protests. "My doorperson duties are over!"

Exhaling loudly, Karla deigns to open it herself, revealing Xavier Michaud, as fresh as the morning mist, wearing one of his precisely-tailored, three-piece Irish wool suits imported from County Cork, complemented by a sienna cravat. He beams at them.

"Don' know 'bout the rest of ye, but I've got a mouth on me!"

Karla turns her back on him. Paul shakes his head, communicating that it is just plain wrong to blow off a day of interviews.

All is forgiven, however, when Michaud announces he has scored a dinner reservation for the committee at a restaurant called Izakaya Seki. Sophie has never heard of it, but everyone else gasps, and just like that, Michaud goes from persona non grata to man of the hour. It's as if a cool breeze has blown in, re-oxygenating the fusty air, providing everyone a second wind. That is the kind of miracle Michaud can work while skipping work, and the reason his colleagues continue to enable him.

"Will there be enough room for Lily, ya s'pose?" Karla ventures.

Michaud grimaces. "I had to pull every lever at me disposal to get a table for five. I figured we'd just show up with six, and they'd have to add a chair. But I don't think they'll do seven."

Sophie is thinking no matter how great the restaurant, she can't spend even another hour with this same group of people, if for no other reason than the words "résumé" and "candidate" would surely be uttered throughout the dining experience, causing her brain to leak out of her ears. She'll just grab a burger at the hotel grill and call it a night.

"Lily can take my place," she says.

Sophie expects at least a token protest, but Karla and Chris look relieved. Who can blame them after last night's Rankings system/cancer ignominy?

"Okay, then," Sophie says, moving toward the door, "I'll see you tomorrow."

"Seven-fifty sharp," Karla says.

It isn't until she is in the elevator, heading up to her room to change, that Sophie remembers her date with the dean from the Top Five school. But is it a firm date, or was it just a suggestion of something that might happen if the stars align auspiciously? In any case, what sounds best to her at the moment is beef on a bun, a beer, and bed.

On the way down from the ninth floor to the third, the elevator stops, and the Talbots lady "Puff" gets on, her face flushed with good cheer.

"Oh, hi, Sophie! You all must be finished for the day!"

Sophie nods. How can this woman have so much enthusiasm left after the night before? Oh, right. She hasn't been present in the ninth floor torture chamber.

Puff studies Sophie's face with a bemused expression. Suddenly she reaches out and pats Sophie's cheek.

"You are so cute!" she says. "You want to come out with us tonight?"

Maybe it's the phrase "come out," perhaps it's the weariness numbing her senses, but Sophie hears herself snap, "Just so you know, I'm not gay."

Puff's joyful expression falls off her face as if she's been slapped. Can her disappointment that Sophie is straight be that profound?

"Just so *you* know," Puff says, "I'm not gay either. My husband and I are going to the theater, and I thought you might like a few hours away from the lawyers."

The elevator jerks to a halt on the third floor, and as Sophie steps out, she turns to apologize.

"Have a nice evening," Puff says, as the doors shut.

In retrospect, Sophie realizes how egregiously she's misinterpreted what was a fond, maternal gesture, not a sexual one. At least the question's been settled as to the reliability of her gaydar.

§

The relief afforded by the privacy of her room washes over Sophie the moment she opens the door and takes in the crisply appointed king-size bed with its six oversize pillows and buoyant down comforter. She dives through the air, landing face-first on the pillows, breathing in the delicious scent of clean linens, a scent she rarely experiences with grubby little Buggles rubbing his runny eyes on her pillow cases and stealth-crawling across her sheets on his belly. Here, they are so fresh her eyes water with gratitude. They smell as if they've been hung on a clothes line and sun-dried. Is it possible, though, that the bed smells *too* hygienic, that the odor she enjoys is actually a chemically-induced antisepticity like decontaminated hospital covers? She draws another deep breath. Who cares? It's heaven! She could lie here happily for days. Room service for tonight, she decides. And an in-room massage. On the Rosecliff credit card!

When the phone rings, she reluctantly rouses herself from her stupor. It's Marlon Herrington. Evidently the stars have aligned; he is calling to confirm their date. His voice sounds mellifluous, soothing. He suggests they meet in the lobby and "go from there." Sophie considers inviting him to her room. She could use some male company. They could just relax together on the fragrant bed and talk. But he's likely to misinterpret such an invitation, and

113

she'll misinterpret it along with him, and the last thing she needs, given her precarious professional position, is a reputation as an AALS recruitment conference slut, a title justly reserved for the candidates. And isn't she trying to turn over a new leaf, make healthy choices about men? A one-night stand between a Top Five Dean and a BTT untenured instructor has epic-fail written all over it.

"What do you have in mind?" she says.

"*Suivons nos caprices!*" he responds.

Has he no idea how unsophisticated she is?

"Let's meet downstairs at the Pub," she says. "I need to eat, and I hear it's got a good selection of microbrews."

He pauses. Obviously her suggestion doesn't resonate.

"You don't like the Pub?" she says.

"I was hoping to get out of this damn hotel," he says. "You know those research laboratories where rows and rows of cages are stacked from floor to ceiling, and they take the rodents out every once in a while, perform some vile procedure on them, then pick them up by the tail and shove them back in?"

She knows.

"That's how I feel," he continues, "and when I see a chance to escape my cage, I want to run like hell from the lab."

A kindred spirit. No wonder she's drawn to him. "When you bring in rodent analogies, I can't say no."

"Good."

"I'll escape with you on two conditions."

"Anything."

"Please don't speak any foreign languages. And don't say résumé."

§

Marlon Herrington's excellent interpretation of what it means to escape is a small establishment on U Street called Twins Jazz, offering Ethiopian and Caribbean food and "intimate jazz." On the way there, Sophie admits to being a "jazz skeptic," a label she invented to elevate her prejudice against music detached from melody to something that sounds like an educated judgment.

Chatting over their beers, they seem to hit it off as effortlessly as they had at the reception. So far, the only thing they disagree about is jazz. When she bemoans the endless, fruitless faculty meetings at Rosecliff, then describes Manuel Delgado storming out, not only does Marlon listen, he one-ups her with a tale of two professors who actually shoved each other in a faculty meeting brouhaha over disclosure to a student of a confidential faculty vote.

"But you must love it anyway," Sophie says. "You're a dean. You wouldn't be a Dean if you didn't love your profession."

Marlon looks pensive. Another refreshing thing about him: he pays attention to a conversation. He considers what he's heard, and is more concerned with saying what he means than with how he sounds saying it, how quick or witty his mind seems, how memorable his phrasing. She compares his style with that of the many arrogant fast-talkers she knows, the Chaz VandenDungens of the world, whose responses aren't responsive at all but rather ego-missiles of jabberwocky sheathed in calculated deniability, fired at you before you've even finished your statement.

The waiter lays down some savory foodstuffs—lamb Ethiopian-style for her, and spicy tibs for Marlon. Sophie's stomach is still giving her hell, and surveying the feast in front of her, she debates a question of dining etiquette. Should she make a trip to the restroom in order to chew some Tums, or is it okay, especially in a jazz place, to crunch them down right there at the table like hors d'oeuvres?

"I don't love it," Marlon says.

For a split second, Sophie thinks he's read her mind and is offering his opinion on chewing Tums at the table. But of course he's responding to her comment about his job. If he can risk such candor, she can certainly ignore etiquette, so she pulls three Tums from her purse, pops them in her mouth, and washes them down with beer.

He looks at her, displaying his beautiful lit-from-within smile. "Is your stomach upset?" he says.

"I guess I'm not used to the exotic food. To me, Olive Garden is fine dining."

Laughing, Marlon digs into his tibs with gusto, while she tentatively carves a small bite of lamb. The fake-fruit flavor of Tums mixed with Amstel Light has created a pasty coating on her tongue, making the chunk of meat taste like a giant raisin.

"I guess no one loves their job all the time" she says. "At least that's what my father always says. You take the good with the bad. You persevere."

"I'm not sure I ever love it," Marlon says.

"Really?"

He shakes his head. "Not anymore."

"What changed?"

Now he seems sad. "I got into this because I thought it would be exciting to develop a vision for our institution and lead it forward. I liked my colleagues. I liked the idea we were focused on educating young people, improving the profession. I didn't foresee how much pressure there'd be to dismantle everything that makes it a great place."

"Dismantle?"

"The same thing's happening at Rosecliff, Sophie."

She studies him, not sure she follows. She is so wrapped up in her personal narrative that she hasn't considered the issues at Rosecliff from any other perspective—especially a dean's. To the extent she's thought about VandenDungen's motives, she figures he bumbles along out of self-interest rather than any larger design.

"From what you said last night," Marlon says, "I guess I thought you were onto us."

Sophie sips her beer, hoping not to appear as clueless as she feels. "Not necessarily," she mutters.

"My bosses are looking for profit," he says.

"Oh, okay," she says. "Revenue streams."

"They've even got me playing this computer game called 'Virtual U'."

"What's that?"

"I guess it's a variation on something corporations use to train their executives," Marlon says. "It's designed to teach administrators how to budget, with the goal of boosting profits."

"But you're a public university," Sophie says.

"Doesn't matter. Virtual U says we're supposed to decrease tenure track inputs and increase cheap, casual worker inputs."

With the mention of "profits" and "inputs," a familiar drowsiness creeps up on Sophie.

"I'm not sure about inputs and outputs, but what's wrong with dressing casual?" she says. "I mean, short of wearing a swimming suit to work or something."

"Sophie, casual worker is a term for a part-time contract worker, like an adjunct, with a low salary and no benefits."

"Me."

Marlon nods. "Virtual U encourages high turnover of this class of worker because you can keep their pay at the same low level indefinitely. We're supposed to practice firing them. We're supposed to look at a picture of the person and press a button."

She pictures VandenDungen's wide, jungle-cat grille. It would actually be fun to push a button to disappear him.

"That's just ridiculous," she says.

"I've got a mandate to decrease the number of our tenure track people by ten percent within five years and grow the number of our casual instructors to compensate."

Now she's hearing echoes of VandenDungen and the Consultant's palaver.

"Enough about that," Marlon says. "What about you? Are you happy?"

"Not really. But I assumed deans of law schools—"

"Couldn't lead lives of quiet desperation?"

How can he glow like that, how could he look so knowing and in control, if he's so unsatisfied?

"I think I answered the wrong call," he says.

"What do you think you should be doing?"

"Digging for ancient runes. I want to live an adventure, make discoveries. Like Henry III's remains. Did you hear about that? A team found them under a parking lot at Leicester. Or Franck Goddio. A few years ago his team unearthed a bowl they believe might

117

bear the first known reference to Jesus Christ. Did you see a picture of it?"

Did he suppose she subscribed to *Archeology Weekly*?

"It looks kind of like a big coffee cup," he says excitedly, "and on the side there's writing, *Dia Chrstou O Goistais*. By Christ the Magician!"

"So he was a magician? That explains a lot."

"Can you imagine the thrill you'd feel coming across something like that? It *means* something. It's important."

With the jazz swirling around them and Marlon's feelings about academic life mirroring her own, the concept of social-sexual lubrication entered Sophie's consciousness. Could Marlon be employing the techniques of underground "schools of seduction," whose members claim to be able to read women's psyches, use subtle tricks to bed them, then enter their conquests' names and "rankings" on spreadsheets?

Amid this suspicion, she realizes she's forgotten to ask the most basic question of all.

"Are you married?" she says.

Marlon appears surprised. "No. Why?"

She concentrates on separating the food groups on her plate into neat piles like a child who won't eat them if they touch.

"Is this a date?" Marlon says in an amused tone.

As a flush climbs Sophie's neck to her face, the lamb she's swallowing sticks in her throat like a fat chunk of chalk. She coughs but can't dislodge it.

"Not necessarily," she manages to croak. As she gasps for air, the lamb goes down the wrong pipe, and she can't breathe.

"I wasn't sure," he is saying. "I guess with our age difference, I didn't really. . ."

She stands, grasping the base of her throat, trying to suck in air. The meat feels like a golf ball sealing off her windpipe.

Marlon leaps up, eyes wide. "Sophie!"

She points to her throat, mouthing the words "can't breathe."

He looks around frantically. "Waiter!" he yells. "Someone help! She's choking!"

The jazz is so ramped up no one hears. She stumbles around the table, backs up to him, grabs his hands, and places them at the top of her rib cage. She presses on his arms, simulating a squeezing motion. The next thing she knows, she's in the air, her boobs mashed into her nose, and the lamb chunk pops from her mouth and flies across the table.

Marlon flashes a dazzling smile. "Whew. That was close."

She nods, coughing between sips of water. Her throat feels as if it's been rotored with a bottle brush.

"Thanks," she squawks.

"I'm sorry if I squeezed too hard," he says. "I've never done the Heimlich maneuver. I've just seen it on TV."

He said TV!

"You did a great job," she says.

§

Curled up under the clean-smelling comforter in her hotel room, Sophie ponders her evening and experiences a little crawl of humiliation when she recalls Marlon's shock at her assumption they were on a date. She considers which is worse: a charming man who uses ploys to get a woman into bed, or a man who desires only to rent her time and empathy, her "listening skills," in order to complain safely to someone so far down the professional pecking order, so unthreatening, that it's like the CEO of a company unloading to the custodian. Unable to rank them, she falls asleep and dreams of riding a race horse, one of those magnificent Triple Crown thoroughbreds who leave the starting gate with outstanding odds only to break a limb and have to be put down on the track.

11 FAKING IT

Day Two of the candidate interviews might just as well be Day Twelve, judging from the expressions of blank-eyed resignation on the faces of the Rosecliff recruiters—with the exception of Xavier Michaud, who looks as if he's wandered into the wrong room and should be breakfasting on eggs Benedict with a group of Golden Parachuters. Surveying the faces of the others, Sophie wonders if she appears as washed out and defeated. Karla has lost her Fargo perkiness, Sir Poil resembles a hollow-eyed prisoner of war, and Chris Paine's cheeks are as sunken as if he were nearing the end of a hunger protest. These people have all been through the drill before and must know something Sophie doesn't. She thinks of the second day as the downhill slope and finds herself in an upbeat mood.

It isn't long before she understands the reason for her colleagues' grim faces. By the third interview, the day's freshness has evaporated, replaced by a stale monotony that makes her want to bite off a chunk of her tongue and chew it like gum. Apparently, few occupants of the ninth floor obey the No Smoking rule, as the interview room gradually fills with second-hand smoke fumes and the unmistakable odor of burning weed. Though the weather outside is unseasonably mild, in the low 50s with sparkling sunshine, the temperature in the vent-challenged suite hovers at a suffocating 80 degrees. Room service hasn't shown up. Yesterday's banana is black. All the committee can offer the candidates is a plastic cup of lukewarm tap water.

Despite the dreary atmosphere, Sophie clings to a sense of professional optimism. Yesterday's candidates were a disappointment, with only a couple of standouts, but today *is* a new day; morning sunrays slant fetchingly through the window, and a number of the interviewees show promise. Rachel Green is scheduled, as well as another woman, Grace Winthrop, who has Ivy League credentials and seven years' teaching experience but for some reason hasn't received tenure at Penn. Radcliff undergrad, Cornell Law, five articles published since joining the Penn faculty. Obviously she wouldn't be attending the recruitment conference, much less interviewing with Rosecliff, but for the denial of tenure, plus the fact she knows Chris Paine. Sophie thinks Winthrop could lend some sorely needed status to Rosecliff; her prolific publication rate alone would help inflate a major Rankings factor.

The committee plods through four interviews, then comes Fleur Shortbeard, the age-diverse, queer, part-Native-American woman whose job experience includes dog catcher and museum docent. She sweeps into the room wearing a hand-embroidered muumuu. Her jet black hair hangs to her waist in two thick braids, and her full, lumpy face betrays signs of cosmetic enhancement performed with modest skill. She's just arrived in town from "the City," she allows as she settles herself, and is still in the thrall of a visit to the Museum of Modern Art. The first ten minutes of the interview consist of an exercise in cultural one-upmanship, during which many obscure restaurants and charming out-of-the-way destinations are referenced and expertise in artistic achievement claimed. The only dropped name Sophie recognizes is that of bad boy John Currin, whose masterfully executed pornographic portraits prompt a weirdly bloodless debate between the freethinking candidate and Chris Paine, the closest thing on the committee to a moral authority. At one point, Sophie almost interjects a comment about a Currin painting that resembles the head of an ostrich, but then thinks better of it because if Currin has never painted anything resembling an ostrich head, the ensuing correction would be pointed, humiliating, and exceedingly tangential.

"So there, Fleur," Karla says, "what're ya interested in teaching?"

"I'd be open to anything," Shortbeard says, "but I'd like to take a stab at something akin to what Professor Bill Miller teaches up at Michigan—a seminar called Faking It."

Silence swells in the room. Wiping a rivulet of sweat from her temple, Sophie wonders if in her state of half-attentiveness, she's misinterpreted what she heard and the phrase "faking it" had popped spontaneously into her consciousness rather than from the candidate's mouth, like in TV shows where the point of view character pretends to listen to someone drone on but hears only his own interior monologue. There is no way this middle-aged flake could be suggesting, first, that a professor at a Top Five law school actually teaches a course called Faking It, and, second, that she, the art-obsessed former dog catcher and museum docent, could possibly be hired to teach such a course at a school like Rosecliff.

"Are you familiar with it?" Shortbeard presses, scanning the semi-circle of faces for validation. Her gaze lingers on Sophie.

"With faking it?" Sophie says. "Of course."

"I mean, have you heard of the class?"

"Why would anyone have to take a class in it?" Sophie says.

"It's really a marvelously honest notion," Shortbeard continues, looking to the others, "that a group of professional students should spend a semester analyzing the myriad ways in which we stand outside ourselves watching ourselves play the various roles in our lives, all the while wondering if our cover will be blown."

Thea Volley rouses herself from her glorious recumbence, heaves an impatient sigh, and says, "What in bloody hell are you talking about?"

"Yah, okay," Karla says, "maybe some of your better schools can afford to do the metaphysical type stuff and all, but at Rosecliff we don't have the luxury of pickin' lint from our belly buttons, we gotta teach our students how to make a livin'. We tend to stress the practical side of the profession, see, the meat and potatoes."

Xavier Michaud rocks in his chair, hand cupped thoughtfully over his mouth.

"Intriguing," he says, gaze locked on Shortbeard. "I like this lassie!"

The committee has mere moments to recover from Fleur Shortbeard's tour of the abstruse before Rachel Green enters. Based on the candidate's famous name and her service in the Israeli army, Sophie had pictured Jennifer Aniston in combat fatigues, but the woman who strides in wearing a black pant suit and white silk blouse exudes her own brand of star power. She is tall and slender, with straight brown hair and luminous black eyes, and, refreshingly, she has a secure grasp of the basics of the job interview. As she introduces herself, she makes full eye contact with each of the committee members, addresses each as "professor," pronounces everyone's name correctly, and shakes hands with a firm, dry grip.

The interview is less question and answer session than a fluid conversation with an articulate, worldly young woman. The subjects discussed ranged from the politics of the Middle East, to the merit of phonetics versus the whole language approach to teaching reading, to the finer points of the rule against perpetuities in property law. Astonishingly, she's done her homework on the committee members, and, among other deft maneuvers, engages Sir Poil on the liability of a manufacturing plant for pollution damage to downstream users.

It's Mac Higgins's issue.

"Wait," Sophie says.

All eyes turn to her.

"Did you have a question for Rachel?" Sir Poil says.

"I'm sorry, what did you say about whether the manufacturer is liable? Like for crop damage or something?"

Sir Poil smiled. "You mean for consequential damages, Sophie?"

Sophie nodded. "Exactly."

"In several recent cases in which the manufacturer has been held liable," Rachel Green says, "at least where the pollution levels were significant under EPA regulations."

"Interesting," Sophie says. She's filled with equal parts awe, suspicion, and envy. Rachel Green, candidate, is perfect. Even allowing for the possibility of such perfection, why has it shown up for a Bottom Tier interview? Sophie decides that if no one else is going to ask, she will.

"Why us?" she says.

"I have a very positive impression of Rosecliff," Rachel says. "It has a wonderful reputation for collegiality, and I love the emphasis you place on teaching and the faculty's relationships with students."

The committee members glance at each other uneasily, recalling the faculty meeting in the storage room in which Chaz VandenDungen circled and drew a line through the "myth" that "teaching is important."

"These days, that's hard to find," Green continues. "So many schools just want to know what your publication aspirations are so they can add you into their Rankings formula. It's all about how much prestige you can bring to increase the all-important reputation among peers."

Karla clears her throat. "Well, so, what are your teaching interests, then?"

"Property," Green says. "Of course."

Everyone laughs knowingly; single-minded devotion to one subject matter, the more narrowly specialized the better, is as venerated in academe as the principle of monogamy in Christianity.

Sir Poil perks up, no doubt imagining the creation of his long-awaited "property institute" at the law school, represented by a web site brimming with bells and whistles and featuring photographs of Paul Singer, farm boy made good, in one corner, and in the other, this striking, Ivy League-educated warrior. He perused the candidate's résumé.

"Looks like you're interested in intellectual property," he says, referring to an article Green wrote about digital media.

"Actually, I've moved on from there," Green says, rearranging her elegant frame in the chair. "I'm interested in founding a program centered on the law of property in virtual reality."

Paul's amiable expression dissipates; he is a farmer's son and an oil and gas man, and for him, there is only one kind of reality—the kind that reveals itself in the production of material wealth—and moving on from there is not an option.

"Well," he says.

"It's too bad Chaz isn't here," Paine says. "He's quite interested in cutting-edge stuff."

Rachel's eyes sparkle. "I want to establish the program in Second Life," she says. "I want to live and work there, to teach in virtual classrooms, invite virtual guest lecturers. I see my entire professional identity existing and growing in virtual space."

So that explains it. Only maladjusted fanatics spend hours, days, months of their lives establishing bogus identities and existences in "virtual space." Rachel Green, Yale graduate, former Israeli soldier, apparently has turned into one. It all makes sense now. Second Life, Bottom Tier.

"I searched for a Rosecliff presence in Second Life but didn't find one," Green says. "I was surprised."

"Call me stupid," Poil says, "but I'm not sure what Second Life is. I mean, I know it's an internet place, but . . ." He shrugs.

Sophie is familiar with Second Life only because a man she dated, Robbie Galfudd, was obsessed with it and wanted her to join so they could "live together" there. She tried creating an intriguing and sexy physical look but ended up resembling a teenage boy with a Mohawk. Her relationship with Robbie began to unravel when he changed his avatar from a Hulk Hogan look-alike to a busty blonde in a micro-miniskirt, and then wanted his avatar to simulate having sex with hers in public virtual space.

"Why do we need a presence there?" Poil says. "Why can't we just stay on campus where we are?"

"With due respect, Professor Singer," says Green, "no one will be staying 'on campus' for long." She glances around at the group. "In fact, I'm looking toward a near future in which all of higher education takes place virtually. We have the opportunity to create a society that's never existed before. Second Life offers a laboratory for social experimentation. New ways of co-existing, of planning, building, trading have to be created. It calls for a reinvention of the very concept of markets."

Xavier Michaud is grinning. "I'm sensing overtones of Stephenson's *Metaverse*," he says.

"Do you know it?" Green says with obvious delight.

Michaud nods as he leans forward in his chair, elbows on his knees, hands clasped together in prayer position. "I'm guessing you're interested in the value-added issues around limitations on creation of materials."

Rachel's hands fly up and cover her mouth. She scoots her chair forward. "That's the single most critical issue!"

Michaud nods. "Crafting versus creating?"

As always, the reference to "markets" falls over Sophie like a magic sleeping potion. Given this exchange, she wonders, how is it possible that law students graduate knowing anything about the actual law?

The interview with Rachel Green—an increasingly technical dialogue about metaspace between Michaud and her—goes long, and after the candidate leaves, Sophie feels as if it's time to catch a flight home, yet a half-day of interviews lies ahead. She opens her mental box of excuses and rummages through the file marked "leaving early—sudden onset." Food poisoning. Relative in accident. Migraine—unfortunately she's never laid the necessary groundwork for that one. Unexplained collapse—she lacks the energy for such an extreme measure and, in any event, doesn't relish the thought of being handled like a bag of fertilizer by her colleagues.

Karla springs alive. "She's wonderful! We've got to have her! Jeez, those credentials, ya can't beat 'em. And how about that ambition! Talkin' about starting an institute at Rosecliff and all!"

Sir Poil appears disgruntled. "We're looking for someone to teach the basics and maybe an upper level elective or two, not a novice obsessed with starting some weird program that no one understands and has no real world application!"

"Some do understand," Michaud intones.

"What do you think, Chris?" Karla says.

"Chaz would like her," Paine says. "She's cutting edge. We'll talk to him and see what he says."

Sir Poil paces and fumes. He's been the property expert at Rosecliff for a decade and has made clear his goal to start an oil and gas law institute.

"Screw VandenDungen!" he says. "We're not hiring some virtual candidate!"

In the corner, Thea Volley snores softly.

§

The atmosphere in the interview room remains tense throughout the afternoon. Despite his rural roots and primitive upbringing, Paul Singer has fashioned himself into a gracious, genial professional, not given to outbursts. His angry reaction bodes ill. Chris Paine's deference to the Dean's opinions on recruitment—especially a dean who has himself dodged the grueling process—confirms Sophie's worst suspicions that no buffer exists between an orderly agenda of change at the law school and the moody and manipulative Chaz VandenDungen.

The remaining candidate of interest is Grace Winthrop. Sophie has studied Winthrop's application more thoroughly than any other. Regardless of why tenure was denied, Winthrop's educational and scholarly accomplishments speak for themselves. Chris Paine's noncommittal mumbles about Winthrop have been impossible to interpret; evidently he knows both her and her husband, who's been tenured at Penn for years. Piecing that together with the atoms of information on the form, Sophie has postulated that Winthrop is a wife and mother who pursued a law career after her husband established his, raising the specter of what Sophie calls "ball of wax discrimination." Finishing school a little late, mothering children a little too long, sacrificing that precious "bloom" for the sake of the family unit—all balling up to brand her irreparably as a dilettante, perceived by her spouse's institution as past her shelf life. And then, when the candidate enters, a new bit of information comes into play, one that takes Sophie several minutes to

127

assimilate. The contrast between Rachel Green and Grace Winthrop couldn't be starker; they are both attractive women, but where Green appeared subtle and sleek, Winthrop resembles a polygamist's wife in her long blue dress, sensible black shoes, and hair poofed on top and braided in back, all prompting the question: could the Penn denial be a case of discrimination on the basis of style? An absence of sartorial acuity, even an aggressive anti-style, is one of the hallmarks of academe. Food stains on ties and lapels are common; holes, missing buttons, and various forms of unraveling fabric, routine. At Rosecliff, one male professor actually has a case of plumber's butt. But an outfit suggestive of a fundamentalist religious cult is seldom seen.

Winthrop greets Paine with forced enthusiasm and maintains it through the introductions. Sinking into the chair, she sighs heavily, bringing sympathetic smiles all around. Winthrop grazes the ring of Rosecliff interviewers with wounded eyes.

Chris Paine small-talks her about their mutual acquaintances. When that winds down, the room rapidly devolves into a vacuum chamber in which no living creature could survive for long. The collective exhaustion and the unusual predicament of the candidate make for seven people with flatlining affects. Since no one has asked a question, Winthrop looks poised to up and leave. Sophie studies Winthrop's résumé, straining to come up with something to ease the candidate's discomfort. Winthrop's record is so stellar, her accomplishments so much greater than the other candidates', that Sophie's impulse is to say, "You're hired."

Winthrop lifts herself in the chair with both arms, then plops back down, in marked contrast, Sophie muses, to Rachel Green's polished repositionings.

"Well, here she is," Winthrop utters loudly, as if performing a monologue on a theater stage, "the woman Penn rejected—rejected notoriously, I might add. Dragged like a fatted hog to market by the ill-will of her treacherous colleagues."

Chris clears his throat. "What's your theory about why, Grace? What happened?"

Winthrop smiles bitterly, making Sophie wince. Bitterness never sells, regardless of one's brilliance on paper.

"No need to theorize, Chris. Everybody knows why. It's because the über-cool Penn faculty couldn't bring itself to hire Mary Poppins." She snorts. "Make that Mary *Frigging* Poppins. I was too goddamn nice, too sweet, apparently. Not edgy enough. I didn't know that being nasty and profane was a tenure requirement. But see, I can be as cool and as nasty as I frigging wanna be."

Wow. This woman was screwed over! Sophie feels a sense of solidarity, yet . . . she wouldn't want to be the one to break it to Winthrop, but her liberal use of the word "frigging" does not make her less Mary Poppins-like.

"One thing we've discussed amongst ourselves," Karla says, "is what your husband would do when you find yourself a position. He's—"

"Hubert L. Nobly Professor of Administrative Law and Regulatory Practice," Paine supplies.

"He's a frigging dog," Winthrop says. "Against whom I've filed for a divorce, by the way. So the dual career/geography conundrum doesn't apply."

"I'm so sorry to hear that," Paine says.

Winthrop's disclosure gives rise to a question for all to mull: Is there a causal connection between the Nobly Professor's dogginess and the tenure denial and, if so, is it actionable?

"Is this something recent?" Paine ventures.

"Hell, no, he's been cheating for years," Winthrop says. "Guess who he's been doing lately?" She looks to Paine for a response. He begs off, shaking his head and pursing his lips empathetically.

Winthrop scans the group. "Guess!"

"His research assistant?" Sophie ventures, chagrined by the obviousness of her guess.

From the corner, a whirring sound indicates that Thea Volley has uprighted herself. Volley hasn't appeared this fully alert since the interviews began, which seems like a week ago.

"Your dean?" Thea says.

"That's right," Winthrop says.

"I thought I remembered you have a female dean now," Thea

says. "What's her name?"

"Karen Frigging Kiloton," Winthrop says. "She of the skunk-streaked hair and puffy muffin décolletage."

The committee members emit various sounds, attempting to strike the right chord, somewhere between sympathy and disgust.

"Well, anyways," says Karla.

"I'm sorry," Winthrop says. "I know how I'm coming off, but to find myself, at this stage of my career, at the goddamn D.C. meat market is just . . . it's just so . . ."

"Humiliating," Sophie says.

Winthrop stares at her lap. A stranger entering the room might think she's a devout Mormon leading the group in worship.

"I've taken up enough of your time," she says, standing.

"Not at all," Chris Paine says. "We really haven't had a chance to discuss what you're looking for."

"It's fine, I understand," Winthrop says. "This is absurd."

Xavier Michaud rises, approaches Winthrop, and extends his hand. She accepts it, and Michaud covers their clasp with his other hand. "Please. Let's talk."

The interview limps along, fueled by ruptures of forced earnestness until at last it fizzles out, and Grace Winthrop departs. Chris Paine exhales despairingly, while everyone else sinks into themselves like deflating balloons.

Sophie sucks in air composed mostly of carbon dioxide and secondhand reefer smoke.

"I liked that candidate," she says, coughing. "I think she'd fit right in."

§

Returning from her trip to the nation's capital, Sophie meets with a countenance so discontented, so grudging, that what should have been a comforting homecoming turns out to be a guilt-inducing ordeal lasting longer than the trip itself. Buggles's angry depression over being left in a cage at the vet rather than at home with a sitter, as was customary, becomes a crucible of sorts for Sophie. His drooping bloodshot eyes, his tucked tail, his worrisome, aimless circling prompts her to engage in an exercise Judge Richard Posner himself might approve: a cost-benefit analysis, a calculation of the advisability of alternative courses of action, albeit not of government intervention in the free marketplace, or of building a super highway through a wetlands, or of marketing commoditized infants. Rather, Sophie applies the template to her entire professional existence at Rosecliff.

Exacerbating her funk are two messages on her machine, the first from Omar Patel, alerting her to the appearance of Richard Richardson's article, "Shit," on the SSRN site.

"It is not 'Aw, Fuck,'" he advises, "but it is perhaps of same genre, similarly motivated. About implications for you we can speculate only. We must get together and discuss."

Sitting in her recliner, a downloaded copy of "Shit" in her lap, Buggles lying supine on the rug, chunky legs outstretched behind him, tail pointing at her accusatorily, Sophie ruminates over the notion of the Cage, a six-sided structure of confinement—a coffin for the living—designed to curtail, no, *obliterate* freedom. No wonder Buggles is pissed. Marlon Herrington compared the monstrous D.C. convention hotel to stacks of cages containing rodents existing for the sole purpose of experimentation—a cliché, of course, but one that strikes a chord of truth in light of Buggles's lingering despondency. His temporary ordeal pales in comparison to that of laboratory subjects whose brief moments of release come at great cost—injection of an experimental poison, insertion of a foreign genetic code, removal of sex drive or the capacity to stop eating. No sun, no rain. No contact with their natural environment. Were they so unlike cadres of corporatized academics circling their airless cages, shackled to their computers, repeatedly tapping at their keyboards like hungry mice in a Skinner box, endlessly shuffling stacks of paper, occasionally being jerked from their cages for a demeaning "review" by a frowning note-taker, then shoved back in, all in the service of Theory or, no! Commerce, as embodied by that shameless marketing gimmick, that closed-loop, carnival crapshoot known as the Rankings? At least lab animals sacrifice their dignity for a noble cause.

But in what possible way would the world be better because a human being spends 437 hours writing a paper entitled "Shit," whose theme is . . . well, she hasn't read much of it, but the first paragraph indicates the author has painted with a broad brush. The paper promises to draw a connection between the law's treatment of the subject of excrement in all its disparate contexts, from First Amendment jurisprudence around the word "shit," including the written word, the spoken utterance, and various works of art incorporating eliminatory functions, such as Andres Serrano's Piss Christ photograph of a plastic crucifix floating in the artist's urine, to environmental regulation of "solid waste," to the constitutional implications of the corporate "poop sniff" — testing excrement or pee for the presence of controlled substances. The ambition! But to what end?

The question is whether continuing with "Aw, Fuck" will yield sufficient professional benefits to justify the cost in time and effort it will exact, in light of this strategically similar piece by Richard Richardson at Tulane. She's checked Richardson's download ranking on the SSRN site; the article stands at number three in the Top Ten list in the "Recent Hits" category. Sophie notes that number 10 in Recent Hits is an article titled "Why Shit Ain't Shit," a hurriedly slapped-together response by an All Time Top Ten professor-author, examining the lightweight nature of the scholarship exhibited in Richardson's "transparent grab at bloated download numbers." How can she now post an article titled with another naughty four-letter word and not be perceived as a fraud and copycat?

No wonder the critics are calling for serious reform in Legal Education!

The second message on her machine is from Marlon Herrington: "Hey, Sophie, I tried to track you down this morning, but you'd left. I realize I probably offended you the other night with that wisecrack about whether we were on a date, but remember, I *did* save your life, and I did enjoy your company tremendously. I'm looking forward to talking to you again."

Marlon Herrington has a sexy voice, she has to admit, and she's definitely attracted to him. Age isn't a factor, but the 800-mile distance between them pretty much dooms any chance of romance. Plus, despite their chemistry, something's missing. In any event, Omar is a lot closer and has suggested they get together. She'll see if her crush on him leads to anything.

Something has to give; her romantic life has been on life support pretty much since her divorce from Chester. She's had plenty of dates, which have served mainly to educate her on the difference in men's minds between a divorced woman and one who's never been married. The distinction is as alive now as it was in the 1950s. A woman who's been married is perceived as used goods that doesn't require courtship. Carnally speaking, she is an insignificant step above a hooker who can be had with minimal expenditure of time and effort. Sophie's gone out with several men who thought because they'd treated her to a hamburger she owed them oral sex on the first date. She might have made a mistake marrying Chester—yes, he turned out to be a gun-toting meth seller—but other than that, he always treated her with love and respect.

She's had a couple of longer term relationships, one with a Jewish man who confessed after six months that she was his "transitional woman," to which she responded, "Well, you have a small penis and size *does* matter!" The other relationship involved a successful D.C. lawyer who really seemed to like her. Things had been going well enough until he mentioned one evening how hurt he'd been when his former wife wouldn't include him in her threesomes. He didn't directly suggest he wanted Sophie to pursue kinky sex, but when he added, "Please do invite me to participate in any encounters you might have," she decided to move on down the road.

Now, as she gazes at the manuscript on her lap called "Shit," she reflects how perfectly the title punctuates her reverie on the death of romance. She tosses it into the trash, flips off the living room light, and heads to bed, then lies there listening in vain for the sound of Buggles dragging his claws across the wood floor behind her.

133

12 MASKS

The next morning, a phone message from Mac Higgins situates Sophie at a crossroads. She knows she can't take his case and shouldn't have let it get this far. She's unfairly led him on by suggesting she'll figure something out. She never should have taken him along to pick up Buggles at the vet's after his toenail operation.

Mac offered to take them both through the Sonic drive-in for dinner, but knowing Buggles's limited patience, Sophie declined. He insisted on expressing his gratitude through some type of food purchase so Sophie reluctantly invited him to Mud Flat, where they ordered a pizza. He declined a beer, stating, "I'm Red Bull all the way." He was very talkative, explaining how his father, who'd farmed all his life, had been forced to declare bankruptcy, putting the family farm into foreclosure. He'd hoped to buy it back from the bank, but the sickly crops had cut into his profits so significantly he hadn't been able to.

Sophie enjoyed studying the clean angles of his cheeks and jaw as he spoke. He was quite a specimen. And his candor and openness was refreshing. By the end of the evening, they were sitting hip to hip on the couch, as close as lovers. She hadn't thought anything of it until this morning when the memory sends a warm flush through her. She reminds herself that it's common for people who've grown up in the country to sit close to each other on a sofa, even if it isn't technically necessary. The tendency traces back to the small size of traditional farmhouse living rooms; the purpose of real estate was to turn crops and livestock into profit, not to create areas for people to loaf around in. If you had a large family or wished to entertain visitors, all bodies were required to fit in the space provided, however modest. You made room, even if none was left. This undoubtedly explains why Mac had scooted so close to her that their thighs and shoulders pressed together.

But how in the world can she help him with his legal problem? She hasn't practiced law in years. She has no spare time. She's never had a good experience with a cold caller. Meyeth is unbeatable–plus, given the Triplets' generosity to Rosecliff Law, her involvement would probably be considered a conflict of interest. The whole thing is preposterous; she has to get rid of it.

She fishes on her desktop for his envelope and rereads the contents, noticing he's highlighted parts of her article. Maybe she *can* help him find another lawyer.

She fiddles around on the computer for a while, poring over the few listings of attorneys who represent plaintiffs in environmental cases. She picks up the phone and dials.

"Yes?"

"Dad, what're you doing?"

"Hello?"

"Dad, it's me. What're you up to?"

"Is this Soapie?"

"It's Sophie, Dad."

"I'm doing splendidly, thank you."

"Are you busy?"

"I'm working up some figures."

"Can I drop by and talk to you for a few minutes?"

There's a pause, then a clunking sound. Arthur has dropped the phone; a little jolt of panic shoots through her.

"Okay," he says, his voice as small and hollow as if he's lost in the Australian Outback, "try me again."

"Can I come over and talk to you?"

Arthur chuckles for what seems like too long a time.

"Why, certainly, ma'am. I look forward to it."

§

Sitting at the light a block from Arthur's street, Sophie checks the rearview mirror and is startled to see in the car behind her a man closely resembling James Yoder, only bald. And wearing a big hoop earring? She squints at the reflection. It *is* James Yoder; he's shaved his head, and he's inching his car up to her rear bumper.

The light turns green, and she floors it, hanging a left at Arthur's cul-de-sac. Yoder follows. Screeching to a stop in front of her dad's house, Sophie jumps out and watches Yoder's car approach. He resembles an old man with his hairless pate, textbook clutch on the steering wheel, and stiff, excessively cautious driving posture. He doesn't glance in her direction or acknowledge her as he passes.

"James!" she yells. "Cut it out, damn it!"

He drives on, trailing a stream of blue exhaust.

Arthur stands on his front stoop, frowning at her. As she draws near, he says, "To whom were you speaking?"

She strides past him, down the hall to his tiny living room where she flops into his threadbare orange recliner. Closing her eyes, she breathes squarely. She's getting too stressed out. She needs to take charge of her life, face challenges from a position of strength, blah, blah, blah. What a freak James Yoder is, with his orange skin and huge woman's earring!

With the sun streaming in on her, she finally begins to relax, only to realize ten minutes have passed and Arthur hasn't come in. She dashes outside. Her father remains standing in front of the door, looking out across the street at a duplex identical to his own.

"Dad?"

"Are those fields planted to beans? Can you tell?"

"You want to come inside?"

"I'm waiting for Quinton."

"He's not coming."

"You don't know that."

136

"Come inside."

"What for?"

"I need to talk to you." She leads him to the living room. It takes great effort for him to put one foot in front of the other, resulting in a choppy, robotic strut.

"Can I interest you in a beverage?" he says.

"I'm good."

"You won't mind if I get one for myself."

He hobbles into the kitchen and executes some elaborate movements toward removing a Diet Coke from the fridge and pouring it in a mug containing two used tea bags. Sophie glances at her watch.

"Dad, I wanted to ask your advice on whether I should take a case or not."

Arthur holds up his hand. "Let's not get ahead of ourselves." He totters back to the refrigerator and opens it, only to remember the soda can is empty and should be thrown out. Glancing at the trash can eight feet away, he sighs and gingerly places the empty can on the counter. Gripping the mug with both hands, he makes his way to the couch and, after an apparent attempt to locate a coaster, surrenders and places the drink down directly on the blemished surface of the coffee table, shuts his eyes, and free-falls onto the sofa.

Clasping his hands over his sunken belly, eyes closed, he says, "Now."

Sophie summarizes Higgins's case, then transitions into a detailed description of her mounting work responsibilities. Arthur listens patiently, his eyes popping open when she mentions "Aw, Fuck." When she finishes, he says, "What are you asking of me?"

"Should I accept Mac's case?"

"Do you want to?" Arthur says.

"He needs help, but—"

"Help him then."

"I can't."

"Of course you can."

"I've never practiced any environmental law."

"So?"

137

"I won't know what I'm doing."

"Get someone to advise you."

"I can't ask anybody from the law school," Sophie says, "and I really don't want to ask someone on one of my service committees. They're gossips, and it can't get back to the Dean that I'm practicing law instead of writing theoretical articles."

"I'll help you."

Sophie doesn't know what to say. How can she take on a real case *and* write some huge article *and* keep up with her classes? Moreover, even if she could handle everything, how in the world can she accept Arthur's offer? He's kept his state bar membership active despite his stroke because all it requires is paying an annual fee and attending a few continuing legal education sessions, which he enjoys. But he's in no shape to appear in court.

"You were joking, weren't you?" Arthur says.

She looks at him quizzically. "About what?"

"You talked about writing an article with a title that means copulation. Obviously you are joking."

"That's what I was advised. There's this internet site—"

Arthur waves his hand. "That's the stupidest thing I think I've ever heard you say, Soapie. I didn't know you could be that dumb."

She feels her face getting hot. "Dad, you don't know anything about the requirements for tenure."

"Tenure is one thing. Writing an article using an obscenity for a title to get attention is another. It's moronic. You can't defend it, so don't even try."

"It's different from when you went to school. The market is being driven by the Rankings, now."

Arthur gapes at her blankly.

"All the schools are trying to improve their Ranking so they can attract better students and more money, and gaining notice by faculty publication is a big factor in boosting our reputation. I won't get tenure unless I can prove I'm valuable Rankings material with star potential."

Arthur has never had much use for academics other than as a

means to an end. He attended a state law school and finished a semester early because he was in a hurry to graduate and start practicing. He set up an office in his small farming community and built a solo practice into a six-lawyer office, attaining a nationwide reputation as a litigator in the process.

Arthur yawns, ending with a loud, "Ahhhhh," and adding, "God!"

"So you think I should represent Mac, then," Sophie says petulantly.

Looking at his watch, Arthur glances around the room. Finally, he reaches under his butt, pulls out a remote control, and flicks on the TV. Scrolling through the channels, he peers at Sophie as if he's just realized she's there.

"It's time to check the futures," he says.

§

Pamela's Deli is about as trendy as it gets in town for lunch, and that's where Sophie and Omar are heading. Gliding along in Omar's black Mercedes, Sophie peers at the residential landscape through smoked windows, immersed in a fantasy that she's a shadowy Middle Easterner's unnamed female companion destined to be a witness to some nefarious transaction, tracked by a counter-terrorism unit of the FBI. She knows the FBI in fact maintains a field office in the area and that agents could be dispatched at a moment's notice because one of her students mailed a mysterious ticking package to Chaz VandenDungen, and two FBI men arrived within fifteen minutes of a 911 call placed by Beverly Bustamante. The package turned out to be shredded paper—from the Dean's own shredder—wrapped around a tiny recorder playing a continuous loop of some loud ticking thing. The two hunky FBI agents seemed competent and professional far beyond what the amateurish incident required.

Glancing at Omar, Sophie wonders if he purposely cultivates an image that plays right into the worst fears of Midwesterners. If only he'd visit the local Supercuts, buy himself a side-part trim like

139

a local Lutheran, trade the Mercedes in for a Ford Taurus, wear khaki Dockers, a brown and blue checked shirt, and a navy sport jacket, no one would give him a second glance. Instead, he outfits himself in pervasive darkness, from his shoulder-length black hair, to the tinted windows of his car, to his black slacks, charcoal knit shirts, and ever-present designer sunglasses.

Aware she's studying him, Omar glances at her and smiles. They haven't spoken a word since leaving the law school.

"It's kind of quiet," she says.

"You do not like quiet?" he says. "What is objectionable?"

She decides not to be intimidated by his relentless profundity.

"Going to lunch together calls for conversation," she says.

"You start," he says.

"I gather from your message you think it might be a waste of time to finish 'Aw, Fuck.'"

They pull into the small lot in front of the deli. "Of course it will be waste of time. That is very nature of beast." He steps out of the car. "Come. For this discussion, we must have sustenance."

Despite its pedestrian attempt at industrial-style interior design, Pam's Deli serves up some tasty offerings, and both Sophie and Omar eagerly dig into their meals. After a few minutes, Sophie again raises the subject of her article.

"Let us look at this within broader context," Omar says. "Sophie Poe aspires for tenure at Rosecliff School of Law."

Sophie nods, striving not to let her physical attraction to Omar overpower her sensibilities.

"Sophie Poe has been advised by figure of authority that she must produce single, bustin' article in place of customary requirement of two. This is correct?"

Again, Sophie nods.

"One drunken evening at local pub, Sophie and colleagues conspire to create article concept that will draw attention and pop the top of SSRN rankings with provocative title and lascivious subject matter."

"True."

"Now another professor, tenured, has used strategy similar to

140

this, and he is popping the top, and Sophie wonders if this kills her own chances." Omar leans back in his chair, chewing thoughtfully. Sophie anxiously munches on a dill pickle.

Finally, Omar shrugs. "Who can tell?" he says. "You might pop, you might not pop, this simply cannot be known."

Air flaps out of Sophie's mouth.

"What else will you bring to table?" Omar says.

Sophie stares at him. For a moment she thinks he's asking in his odd syntax if she's going to have more to eat.

"As surely you know," he continues, "traditional tripartite tenure application consists of scholarship, teaching, and service. How is your teaching?"

Sophie recalls the evaluation delivered by Karla on behalf of the Dean and the Consultant. "Karla says if I could handle assholes like Edward Cherry, I could be just a super teacher."

Omar smiled. "I know Mr. Cherry. He is total idiot."

Sophie laughs. "Shane told me he was admitted because his old man donated one hundred large to the endowment association."

"What about teaching evaluations?"

Just the mention of teaching evaluations, those anonymous missives of condescension, ridicule, and bile that professors are forced to solicit from their disgruntled students each semester, tightens Sophie's stomach into knots. She looks at Omar sheepishly. "I don't know."

"Don't know? Or would prefer not to say?"

"I don't read them," she says.

"You are kidding with me right now."

She shakes her head. "I read them my first year, then stopped. They depress me. I don't know who wrote what. Like when I read one that said, 'She should go back to the minor leagues,' I wanted to respond, 'I'm already in the minor leagues, fool,' but I didn't know who to respond to."

Omar appears bemused. "The tenure committee will read them."

She sighs in what she considers a Russian manner. Two years of studying Russian literature as an undergraduate planted a pecul-

141

iarly un-American pocket of defeated resignation in her.

"So be it."

"And service?" says Omar.

Service—the tenure requirement that really pushes the limits of Sophie's tolerance. As a skills educator, she already serves the needs of dozens of students a year. She meets with them individually until her voice is hoarse and her ears numb. She grades scores of student papers written by young women and men whose prior 17 years of education failed to instill in them the fundamental principles of literacy in their native tongue; her job is to close this enormous chasm while simultaneously teaching them research, reasoning, argument, and source citation. In short, she serves her students until they suck her dry. But that isn't enough.

She also serves on two to three law school committees—presently, recruitment, admissions, and curriculum—that require her attendance at meeting after meeting. She shows up and tries to be as mentally present as her theta-waves permit. She reads memos, writes memos, does research as requested, wracks her brain over various conundrums, taps her inner creativity. She reports back in a timely fashion, listens respectfully to the reports of others. But that's just "inside service."

Then there's "outside service," requiring her to accumulate as many professional affiliations, activities, and presentations beyond the hallowed halls of Rosecliff Law as she can possibly manage.

"I've done what I can," she tells Omar.

"Inform me please."

She reluctantly complies, summarizing her appointment to a few prestigious but tortuously tedious lawyer committees.

Omar studies her in a way that makes her want to check her face in the mirror to be sure no pieces of food are stuck to her cheeks or between her teeth.

"What?" she says, pulling out her compact mirror.

"Who are you, Sophie Poe?" he says.

"What do you mean?" She laughs uneasily as she checks out her reflection. Shit! She actually does have a tiny sliver of red pepper between her front teeth. Also, she is notably flushed; she might as well have written "I'm attracted to you sexually, Mr. Patel" on her forehead! She puts away the mirror and attempts to wriggle the pepper loose with her tongue.

"I am lately much fascinated in these faces we put on us," he says. "I am deliberating to produce book, picture book, with title *Masks*. It will show people in two ways. One, as presented to public, and two, as one really is, with mask off."

Sophie imagines Omar pulling off her facial skin to see what she looks like underneath her mask.

"Ouch!" she says.

"I see I have struck nerve," he says. "So what is your mask, Sophie Poe?"

Her mind goes blank. She's never given it a name.

"Mary Frigging Poppins?"

"Explain," he says.

"Actually I stole that from a candidate we met in D.C.," Sophie says, "but it's pretty accurate. The mask I wear is that I'm a cooperative, happy junior law professor striving for tenure."

"You are not?"

"Not at all."

D'Oh! Omar is a tenured faculty member who'll be voting on her application.

"Who might you be then?"

She considers the question for a moment. Who *is* the real Sophie Poe?

"I started out just wanting to lie around and read books," she says. "But one of my college professors advised me to be more specific in my goals."

"So you chose law books."

"That came later. I majored in literature. I think I went to law school to compete with my brother for my father's attention."

"Your brother is lawyer, too?"

She nodded.

"Interesting. What is he doing?"

"Serving time."

Omar's eyes widen. "Seriously?"

She reluctantly explains what Quinton did.

"Ah ha!" says Omar. "Quinton was forced to wear mask of conformity but he could not bear it. It suffocated him."

Omar's analysis does little to illuminate the complexity of Quinton's life arc. It's time to change the subject off the Poe family.

"I've been thinking about conformity a lot lately," she says. "I don't like it either."

"How do you mean?"

"Take this Rankings thing, for example," she says, pretty much making it up as she goes. "A magazine dreams up a strategy to reverse its declining circulation by starting a nationwide popularity contest based on reputation and a bunch of malleable numbers, cynically playing on people's insecurities and obsession with position and competitive advantage, and everyone falls into lockstep formation like the People's Liberation Army."

Omar strokes his chin thoughtfully. "I think not."

"What?"

"I am begging to differ," Omar continues. "I am seeing not so much rebellion against conformity in Sophie Poe as engagement in self-defeating strategies."

"That's what my therapist says!"

He studies her disapprovingly. Like Christians, she supposes, Muslims eschew paid analysts like psychiatrists and psychologists; people are expected to solve their own problems by following the guidance of their deity.

On the other hand, Omar himself is psychoanalyzing her!

"Have you been watching Dr. Phil?" she says.

"I am serious."

"You think I self-defeat?"

"Not reading student reviews. Showing up at meetings less than cheerful. That's not winning you the points."

"Less than cheerful?" Sophie says. "Since when do you have to be cheerful to get tenure?" She recalls candidate Grace Winthrop who evidently tried to be liked by all only to be rejected as a lightweight.

Omar reaches for her hand. "I am trying to help, not cause distress. Just perhaps there are a few issues you should consider. That is all I am suggesting."

Picking up her purse, she scoots her chair back from the table. In one fluid motion, Omar flicks his sunglasses down from his head, and they come to rest squarely on his nose.

"Shall we go?" he says.

As they exit, they're slammed by a blast of frigid north wind. Omar grips her arm, and they forge ahead toward the Mercedes. Wally Shane suddenly materializes in front of them in a green and orange Army surplus parka, his pale, freckled face encircled by "fur" that resembles the pelt of a rat. His small frame slants southward as he grasps the Mercedes's antenna to keep from blowing away.

"Did you hear what happened?" he shouts. "VandenDungen's e-mail screw up?"

The three of them clamber into the Mercedes. Shane flips his hood back and blows on his hands. "It's colder than Pluto out there."

"What did he do?" Sophie says eagerly. "Did he screw up bad?"

"He accidentally sent an e-mail intended for Manny Delgado to the entire faculty," Shane says, eyeing them grimly. "It's worse than we thought."

"How is that?" Omar says.

Heaving a sigh, Shane explains. The e-mail lays out a plan to address Rosecliff's revenue-stream problems by transforming the existing law clinic into a real law office, staffed by students and new graduates.

"Yah," says Omar, "that is newest trend."

Shane looks skeptical. "I don't see how that's going to help us financially. Won't the law school have to pay the new graduates?"

"That Dean is slick willy," says Omar. "There must be more to scheme."

§

On the way back to the law school, Sophie's mind churns with

145

Omar's critique of her self-defeating behaviors. From time to time, Arthur has suggested the same thing. He put in 70-hour weeks his entire career, and he couldn't understand why she didn't. When she worked at the Justice Department, she put in a 60-hour week occasionally and thought she was going to die; she had to hit the sheets at 8:30 p.m. for several nights to recover. Her boss complained when she didn't show up on Saturdays or skipped too many after-work social occasions. Looking around the law school, she saw people like her boss and like Arthur who couldn't get enough of work. Barbara Kitchen even had a sticker on her office door that says "I live and breathe the law."

Sophie has observed that the younger faculty members hired in the last few years are particularly hard-core in this respect. Sophie and Shane refer to the cohort as the Digitals. At social functions, they segregate themselves from their older colleagues to make clear that they constitute a New Breed of legal academic—on the one hand, driven, business-like, indistinguishable in appearance and work ethic from highly successful practicing attorneys; on the other, far too cerebral to be satisfied by such a ploddingly practical life.

She glances at Omar. Would he say they are wearing masks?

Snapping back to the present, she considers the attraction between herself and Omar; this thing with him, whatever it is, isn't going anywhere romantically. He's assumed the role of her mentor, and she's starting to resent his unsolicited advice. His enigmatic personality, which captivated her before, is getting on her nerves. Unfortunately, she seems to be falling once again into her Unfruitful Love Pattern—physical attraction, obsessive fascination, daydreaming and fantasizing, followed by a gradual realization that the object of her lust isn't someone she likes that well. If the past is prologue, she'll soon be going out of her way to avoid him. Hopefully before she's slept with him.

As they park at the law school, she thanks him perfunctorily and starts to get out of the car.

"Sophie," he says.

As she turns, he flips up his shades and says, "You are lovely."

146

He takes her hand in his, presses his warm lips to her cold fingers, and kisses them.

She has to admit, Omar *is* hot.

13 BAD TRIPS

That afternoon, the Dean calls an emergency meeting to discuss the e-mail mistakenly sent to all faculty. Ann Kulter is close at his side—very close, Sophie observes, as she wonders if the Dean, perpetually at odds with Catwoman, is seeking succor in the companionship of the willowy blonde. VandenDungen and Kulter are well-prepared for the so-called emergency, and VandenDungen launches into his introductory remarks before everyone is even seated.

It's clear from the outset that the Dean is not in an apologetic frame of mind. "You want to know what's going on?" he says. "I'll tell you what's been going on! Hard work!"

"What Chaz means," says Kulter, "is that we've been working overtime on a plan to rescue the law school."

"Is it true I wrote an e-mail to Manual Delgado, laying out a recovery plan for the school?" the Dean says. "Yes. Did the e-mail get sent to all of you by mistake? Yes. Is it now time to reveal the plan to all of you? I suppose we have to. We'll start with a snapshot of where we are with respect to inputs, outputs, increase in revenues, reduction of expenditures, and overall efficiencies."

The room is stuffy. To Sophie, everything appears preternaturally bright, yet there's a certain wooly texture at the margins. She realizes she is on the verge of passing out.

"Ann and I have been crunching numbers," VandenDungen says, "and we've learned some alarming things, haven't we?"

He smiles at the Consultant with atypical warmth, which Sophie concludes must be the product of recent sexual release.

"Indeed we have," Ann purrs.

"We've charted some of the data," the Dean says, "and thought it would useful for everyone to be able to see it for themselves. Where the fuck is Darren?"

The door to the conference room opens on cue, and in walks the IT guru, Darren Youngblood, who quickly sets up a portable projector and screen to which the Dean connects his laptop. As Sophie's head lolls forward, Darren flips off the overhead lights. With the darkness comes a sense of relief, and she manages to remain sentient only to be accosted by a giant purple and white graph illustrating the law school's projected income and expenses for the fiscal year.

The purple towers against the whiter-than-flour background can only be described as a bad trip. The first tower, Expenses, is nearly twice as tall as the second tower, Income. The Dean and the Consultant take turns commenting on the slide, but for some reason, Sophie has trouble hearing them. The Dean moves on to the next slide, which shows a pie chart breaking down the expenses. The pie is divided into six pieces. The largest piece by far, over fifty percent of the pie, is labeled Faculty Salaries, in bold red print.

The dramatic illustrations engage a majority of the faculty, many of whom can be seen through the faux twilight frowning in concentration, stroking their chins, or whispering to the person next to them.

The Dean then introduces additional catastrophic evidence in the form of another graph, illustrating the sources and level of income to the law school. The tallest tower, student tuition dollars, is not that tall.

"Now seems a good time to hear from the Admissions Committee," the Dean says. "Sophie?"

Sophie feels like a dog who's been contentedly sniffing the grass only to have her leash yanked savagely by someone with utter disregard for the power of a choke collar.

"What?"

"You're on the Admissions Committee, aren't you?" the Dean says.

"Yes."

"Will you give us a report?"

Sophie searches the room for Xavier Michaud, chair of the committee, but doesn't see him. Nor can she find the third committee member, Bill Wu.

"I think Xavier would—" she says.

"Obviously, he's not here," the Dean says. "You are."

Sophie experiences an intense sense of vertigo. Clutching the arms of her chair, she squeaks out a reply.

"The news isn't good."

The Dean and Kulter laugh mirthlessly. "Tell us something we don't know," the Dean says.

The Dean is in his favorite mode, Rhetorical. He already knows all of the bad Admissions news. The Admissions director reports to him directly. Why is she suddenly the messenger?

"Well," she says, "applications for this fall's entering class were down twenty-three percent from last year."

"And of course those were down seventeen percent from the year before," VandenDungen adds. He sounds almost gleeful.

The room has taken on the silence characteristic of faculty meetings since the Dean arrived. Tense, angry, ominous. Perhaps mournful, as harsh realities encroach on magical thinking. What *is* the sound of three dozen academicians being shoved out the tiny Ivory Tower window?

As if reading Sophie's mind, Ann Kulter says, "May I ask you all what you had imagined the situation to be? Your classes are significantly smaller than usual. Does it ever cross your minds to wonder where your salary dollars are coming from?"

Mason Masonips raises his hand. "Do you want an answer to

that, or is it just rhetorical? Because to be honest, I never think about where the dollars are coming from. I'm a salaried professional, and that's all I need to know." He shrugs at the rest of the faculty.

"Dean," says Newt King, "I think I speak for everyone when I say we'd love to hear about the rescue plan."

The Dean ignores the remarks. "Sophie, continue with your report."

"As far as the types of applicants we're getting . . . " Sophie pauses, trying to recall the various measures—the mean, the median, the top quartile, the bottom quartile, the average. "The numbers are down." Dare she comment on some of the other problems the committee has been seeing in the applications?

"That's concerning," says Wally Shane. "GPA and LSAT scores are central to the Rankings. If we slip on those, we aren't going to be able to get into the Top 145. It's mathematically impossible."

VandenDungen stands tall, shoulders back. "Why are you looking at me?" he says. "I just got here. This is the mess I walked into. Sophie, tell your colleagues about the kinds of applications we're getting."

Where to begin? With the C+ student from the local community college? With the violent felon with the 75th percentile LSAT score?

"We're getting a lot of diversity in our applications," Sophie said.

"Excuse me," says Thea Volley. "You're misleading this faculty by using the word 'diversity' when you mean 'crap.'"

"We're letting in unqualified and troubled students," Sophie says. She feels like hiding her face in her hands. "Many with little chance of passing the bar."

As an Ugly Truth is introduced, the room explodes with energy: professors leaping out of their chairs, some shouting profanities; others—the younger ones—huddling together, grousing about being victims of this and that. No one wants to be bombarded with the details of the conspiracy.

Rising, Manual Delgado joins the administrators at the front of the room. "Student asses in seats!" he shouts over the cacophony. "That is where your salary dollars come from. So, my friends, you see the problem, OK? Please. Sit."

The unrest continues for several minutes, until the Dean pig-whistles the group to order.

"The more unqualified applicants we admit," Delgado says, "the more dollars we have, but the lower our Ranking goes. How, then, do we avoid having to admit the unqualified student?"

The next slide appears, depicting a revised Income/Expenditure graph. This time, the Expenditure tower is much shorter. The faculty murmurs as yet another slide pops up. It's the revised pie chart, and the Faculty Salaries wedge has been reduced to a modest slice, a slice the size of those served in restaurants across America before the obesity epidemic.

As the message sinks in, one-by-one the tenured professors scan the room, gazes resting on their most expendable colleagues, starting with the Skills Faculty—the research and writing teachers, the clinic teachers—those fungible B-trackers who leech the school's resources as if they were real professors, causing the Dean to call "emergency" meetings. Fielding one nasty glare after another, Sophie senses the vaunted Rosecliff collegiality slipping into a coma.

A new slide appears: purple text against the glaring white background, blank except for the heading, Rescue Plan. No one says anything. The faculty awaits rescue.

"Let's make this interactive," the Dean says. "Participate in your own rescue, professors! What steps do we need to take?"

No one speaks up. But, Sophie thinks, isn't the answer obvious? Didn't the Dean tell her she was too expensive?

"Cut salaries?" she finally says.

"Wait just a minute, mister." It's Barbara Kitchen, who makes it known at every opportunity that she, unlike most of her fellow tenured professors, *earns* her salary by working harder than a dozen of the others combined. "I assume you mean cut someone else's salary?" She looks around the room as if itching to start a fight. "Not my salary? Because I earn every penny of it, I assure you." She looks at her watch. "Oops." Standing, she limps toward the door. She needs a hip replacement, everyone in ten counties knows, but can't find time in her schedule for one. "Sorry! Gotta go! I'm scheduled to make a presentation to Families Without Fear tonight."

Chris Paine stands. "Chaz, you can't cut salaries," he says. His face is pale, his hands trembling. Sophie feels sorry for Paine, who clearly loves being a law professor. He is a civil rights champion, a prolific author of articles on a variety of constitutional law topics. He feels strongly about social injustice. Moreover, he has just finished construction of a palatial country home. "Leave salaries where they are," he says, "for tenured professors. But consider reducing the number of professors . . . over time."

This prompts the untenured to wail "What?" in unison. Sophie notices that several of the tenured join the outcry, Omar Patel among them.

"This will mean, of course," Omar says, "a heavy load for remaining professors. They will be like undergraduate professors. Such outcome is not advisable."

Being among the most expendable, Sophie resents Omar's comment. Each semester, he teaches upper level electives that, even in the best of years, enroll an average of eight to ten students per semester. Do Midwestern law students really need to know about Identitarian Politics and Shari'a?

"You still don't get it," the Dean says. "The days of each person teaching only two courses per semester and fiddling their thumbs the rest of the time are gone. Gone, baby, gone!"

"Other ideas?" Kulter says. She's been yanking hanks of hair back and forth over her head. Now she's twisting one around her finger—her middle finger. "Dig deep."

Leaning forward, Newt King angles his face as if trying to catch some sun from the quivering florescent lights. "Dean, I would think we could get a gang of adjuncts to teach the so-called Skills courses. Sheesh, when I went to law school, no one worried about teaching us skills."

"Excellent point," says VandenDungen, as he clicks his remote. Onto the screen pops a fresh pie: "Percentage of First-Year Budget

Allocation, Per Course." This pie consists of two roughly equal pieces, one tinted green, the other red. The red slice says "Skills Program" and the green slice, "All Other First Year Courses." No words need be spoken; the vivid illustration says it all. Despite their individual low salaries, as a group Sophie and her fellow skills grunts *are* expensive.

Another visual aid appears. Here is Alternative Cost-Effective Skills Program, bearing the sub-heading The Adjunct Model. Its bar graph and pie chart instantly soothe the ambient insecurities; relieved laughter ripples across the room. Skills has shrunken dramatically, morphing into a stubby platform, a single stair-step, and the program's slice of the revised first-year-cost pie is so modest it would pass muster with the most assiduous diet coach. A smattering of applause erupts.

"As you can see," the Consultant says, "Skills is sucking—"

"Excuse me, Ms. Kulter," a female voice interjects. Silhouetted in the doorway, crown of honey-color hair glamorously backlit, Jennifer Fairfield inspects the seating arrangements, then saunters into the dusky chamber, grabs a stray chair, and insinuates herself between Mason Masonips and Newt King. Tossing her hair into a bed-heady muss, she says, "I'm sorry I'm late, but I have some information we'll need in order to discuss this knowledgeably."

"As I was saying," Kulter continues, "Skills is sucking the life-blood out of our first year budget, how do you like that?"

"Is there so little literacy among you regarding financial issues that no one can comprehend the ramifications?" the Dean says.

"Is it true what I've read," says Sophie, "that adjuncts in programs like the one you described get paid $1700 per semester?"

VandenDungen eyes Kulter.

"Excuse me, Dean." Jennifer Fairfield waves a manicured hand in the air. She's unpacked her briefcase and arranged stacks of documents on the table. "I'd like to pass around copies of a survey of practicing lawyers. They were asked what they thought is the biggest problem facing the legal profession. A huge majority said it's law graduates who don't know anything about practicing law."

Sophie admires Jennifer, who despite her provisional status at the law school fearlessly employs her sex appeal, brains, and organizational skills to stand up for her own interests.

"That's baked in the cake," the Dean says.

"What?" Shane says shrilly.

"Skills can be taught by the skilled," the Dean says. "Practitioners."

"Chaz is correct," Kulter says, crossing her arms over her chest—a chest that appears to have doubled in size since Sophie last noticed it, not that she looks at women's chests. "The full-time faculty model for teaching this component of the first year curriculum has been rejected by most institutions for the obvious reason that it is a waste of resources. Many schools are using adjuncts to teach skills courses."

Sophie perceives that perhaps the "wasted resources" Kulter referred to have not been wasted at all but were redirected—into the Consultant's breasts! She has trouble not staring at what appear to be two large oranges—small grapefruits?—straining the fabric of her sweater.

It's time to speak up, Sophie realizes. But Paul Singer, who's been doing a slow boil over in the corner, beats her to the punch.

"Most of our students come to us lacking proficiency in basic language skills," Singer says, "to say nothing of organizational, writing, and analytic abilities. These are fundamental. You can't practice law without them. Our students need instruction by experienced teachers."

"No, no, no!" says VandenDungen. "That's exactly why we need to change what we're doing! Let's face it. If a person hasn't learned how to write by the time he or she is 23 or 24 years old, they're probably not going to. That's the point! You can't fix an unfixable problem by throwing money at it!"

Behind VandenDungen, the Consultant scribbles something on the whiteboard. She whirls around, revealing "72%," and next to it, "Percent of professors who are part-time or adjuncts in USA."

"You see," she says, "the full-time tenure-track academic is going the way of . . . of . . ."

"Kirkland's warbler?" says Wally Shane. "It was near extinction.

But it was judged to be valuable, and the federal government set aside 150,000 acres of land for its preservation."

"Thank you for making our point!" VandenDungen says. "We can't afford to dedicate hundreds of thousands of acres of land to preserving a single species of law teacher!"

The Consultant makes a series of strange gestures in the Dean's direction.

"Now for the centerpiece of the Rescue Program," he says, clicking the remote.

"Shit!" whispers Shane. "Here it comes."

Worried eyes peer up at an architect's dreamy rendering of a familiar building with a fancy new sign out front. The sign says, "Meyeth Law Office at Rosecliff." The rendering depicts the current law clinic, with a new façade. More illustrations show the inside of the clinic, with new façades, and drawings of slick figures that look like no one who would be walking the halls of a law school.

"What you see is a potential profit machine," the Dean says.

A shudder travels across the room.

"That's impossible," Chris Paine says. "The university can't operate a for-profit concern."

"Thinking inside the box again, are we, Chris?" the Dean says.

"This design," says Kulter, "is cutting edge. It takes advantage of the friends you have in the Meyeth Triplets, and if successful, it will boost three separate Rankings factors. It's a win-win-win."

The duo explain the plan. The Meyeth Triplets will buy the clinic building and apply façades throughout. Rather than dealing with petty criminals and family issues, the new Meyeth Law Office at Rosecliff will specialize in representing corporations—"deep pocket clients," the Dean says gleefully. The office will be staffed by unpaid students and new graduates, who will be paid as apprentices for their first two years. The office's profits will be funneled by the Triplets to the law school in the form of gifts, endowments, grants, and scholarships.

"Nifty," Sophie says to Shane, who gives her a menacing look.

Everyone else has been stunned into silence. It's hard to find

156

something wrong with the plan, other than the involvement of Richard, Fred, and Lorne Meyeth, who stand for everything the typical law professor exists to oppose.

Paul Singer stands. Sophie expects him to speak in favor of the proposal; Meyeth Industries is slated to be a major sponsor of his Oil and Gas Law Institute.

"I'd like to think about this before I vote," Singer says.

The Dean and the Consultant appear startled. "Vote?" they say in unison.

"This isn't up for a vote," the Dean says. "Sale of the building is an executive decision."

Singer flushes. "What happens to our clinic isn't."

"Actually," says Kulter, "if you read your appointment letters carefully, you would've realized that in light of the financial crisis, extraordinary powers have been reserved." She picks up a paper and reads aloud. "Your employment is subject to change at the discretion of the Board of Regents if such changes are necessary due to declining revenues."

"So?" Singer says.

"We've decided to allocate resources to this proposal," the Dean says, "and President Hooghly supports us."

Jen leans over and whispers between clenched teeth, "Looks like I'm out of a job, and just when my home study's starting."

"Home study?" Sophie says

"I applied to adopt a six-year-old boy."

Jen Fairfield applied to adopt a kid? Competitive, flirtatious Jen Fairfield? Sophie has misjudged her, figuring she's in the market for a man, not a child. And Sophie was so smugly pleased with herself that the animal shelter had approved her application to be Buggles's mom.

"His name is Dalton," Jen continues. "He's got a couple of health issues, but he is *so* adorable. I doubt the state will approve the adoption if I'm homeless and on welfare."

"Did VandenDungen ever talk to you about moving to the tenure track?"

Jen shakes her head. "I'm such an idiot. I thought I lucked out,

157

not having to write some huge article in a few months like you. It turns out the prick was just setting me up to dump me."

"I don't get it," Sophie says. "Your teaching reviews are off the charts. The students totally dig you. Why would he offer me tenure and not you?

Jen chuckles. "You really are clueless, aren't you, Sophie?"

"Pretty much."

"I graduated from Rosecliff Law. You went to a Top Ten school. You have Rankings enrichment potential. I don't."

§

Back in her office, Sophie is grading student research exercises, trying to keep her eyes open, when the phone rings. She assumes it's probably Mac Higgins. She doesn't have the heart to tell him she hasn't found anyone to take his case, so she lets the answering machine take the call.

"Sophie? Are you there?"

It's James Yoder's voice. Sophie rolls her eyes. She hasn't seen him since the day she yelled at him in front of Arthur's house.

"Sophie, if you're there, pick up. It's your father. Something's wrong."

She grabs the receiver. "My father?"

"I found him lying in the grass next to his front door."

Sophie leaps from her chair, panicky. A few left-brain cells manage to wonder what Yoder is doing at Arthur's house.

"Is he all right?"

"I called 911. They should be here any second."

"Is he conscious?"

"His eyes are closed. He's breathing. It seems kind of slow though."

A siren wails in the background.

"I'm coming right now." Sophie says.

"Go to the hospital," James says. "I'll meet you there."

§

As they wait for the results of Arthur's tests, James explains that he helps care for his "adopted Gramma" who lives at the end of Arthur's cul-de-sac, and spotted Arthur on the ground as he passed by. He shows great benevolence in not calling her out on her profane explosion the day she thought he was following her. Sophie thanks him profusely for rescuing Arthur and is prepared to reevaluate her attitude toward him when he grabs her and hugs her tightly, squeezing her breasts to his chest.

The doctor surmises that Arthur either has suffered a transient ischemic attack or fainted due to his chronic low blood pressure.

The next day, Sophie picks him up at the hospital between classes. As she speeds away, mentally calculating how much time she'll have to prepare PowerPoint slides for her second class, Arthur says, "Please don't take me back."

"You don't have to go back, Dad. You're released."

"Don't take me back to the cracka box."

It takes a moment for Sophie to process "cracka box," a phrase Arthur hasn't used for years. After the embezzlement, when the farm house was up for sale and they were searching for a place for Arthur to live, he would remark to a sales agent or state worker, "my daughter is shopping for a cracka box." Sophie thought he meant cracker box—a residence that was small compared to what he was used to. One day he elucidated. "You're looking for a box you can crack open and drop me in."

"You need to go home," she says now.

Arthur shoots her a withering look. "It's not my home. It's a tiny corner of hell unfit for human inhabitance. Why do you think I passed out?"

Sophie's grip tightens on the steering wheel as she fights for composure. They chose Arthur's living arrangements only after looking at a dozen alternatives, every one of which he fought. The place he's in now is actually nicer than the apartment he lived in before his stroke, and has the benefit of medication oversight and twice daily wellness checks, though obviously those haven't served their purpose.

Beneath her irritation at her father's complaints simmer ques-

159

tions she's never put to him: Where is Quinton now? Who cleaned up the financial and legal mess and found you a place to live? Who walked into your apartment and found you lying on the floor naked, moaning raggedly, Gollum from *The Lord of the Rings*? Who is writing a stupid pointless frigging article about—

"Sophie?"

"What?"

"Will you please at least drive me by the old place?"

"No."

"Please? I need to check out a few things over there."

Sophie glances at the clock; her class starts in an hour and a half.

"I need to get back to work," she says.

Arthur takes a series of deliberate, deep breaths, finishing with a loud "Whew!"

"Is something wrong?" Sophie says.

"I lately find myself getting short of breath, but once I fill back up, I'm perfectly fine," he says.

He doesn't look fine; he looks pale and drawn, his veins protruding under his thin skin.

"I think I'd better get you home so you can rest," Sophie says.

Arthur's body draws taut. "Sophie, you may wish it were otherwise, but I'm not dead yet." He flashes an exaggerated smile causing his upper dentures to slip down so it appears he has a double row of teeth on the bottom, and a toothless gum on top.

"Please," he mumbles, "do not take me back to that crypt!"

Clicking his dentures, Arthur eyes Parking Lot B with a worried frown.

"Why are we at the doctor's office?" he says.

"I'll drive you by the old house," Sophie says, "but you'll have to wait until after my class."

Arthur blinks. "You're taking a class? In what?"

Sophie walks around to the passenger side and opens the door.

"Come on," she says, taking his arm.

"Bullshit!" He wrenches his arm free from her grasp. Laboriously extracting himself from the car, he brushes off his shirt, hitches up his sagging pants, and says, "I've had about enough of your tricks, lady."

Sophie decides to deposit Arthur in the faculty lounge while she prepares and teaches class. The recent remodeling has stripped the room of its former cluttery warmth, replacing the overstuffed furniture and book shelves with shiny tufted leather chairs and glass cases containing plaques of oddly recent vintage, interspersed with generic bronze sculptures of bewigged barristers. But it has a TV, and Arthur seems to be able to extract hours of amusement out of the stock market crawls on cable business channels.

Two-and-a-half hours later, Sophie returns for her father, halfway expecting to find him lying prostrate on the hard polypropylene carpet. Approaching the lounge, she hears excited voices. Inside, Paul Singer and Xavier Michaud sit forward on the couch, and across from them, in the slippery candidate's chair, Arthur is talking animatedly.

"He *had* to admit it, boys! We backed him into a corner, and either way he tried to run, he slammed into a wall!"

"Hey, Sophie," Paul says.

"Mr. Poe, shouldn't he have anticipated you'd pursue that line of questioning?" Michaud says.

"Of course he should," Arthur says, "but he was underweight."

Michaud appears perplexed.

"In the gray matter!" Arthur says. "Ha, ha, ha!"

Michaud rises and shakes Arthur's hand. "It's been an honor, sir."

Singer follows suit. "It's a good thing you're retired. I'd hate to meet you in court over some of our lease clauses."

Arthur waves at the two men as they leave, then releases the arms of the chair as if he's been holding on for his life. He slides down so his chin rests on his chest and his legs splay apart limply. The illusion of vigor has vanished. He appears as if he's dropped ten pounds in five seconds.

"Dad?"

"Hmm?"

"Were you talking about the Dunn case?" In its day, the case of Earl Dunn v. Medico Health Services was widely known among lawyers for its novel theories of liability and the tenacity of its plaintiff's team, led by Arthur Poe. The appellate report of the case is even included in some Torts textbooks.

Arthur's eyes droop shut, and his chest is still.

"Dad?" She jiggles his arm, but his body remains motionless. She grasps both his shoulders and shakes. "Dad!"

His eyes spring open, glazed with confusion. Breathing labored, he searches the room as if he suspects enemies are crouched behind the furniture. Sophie helps him up from the chair.

He brightens suddenly. "I was just about to tell them about my cross of that arrogant asshole, *Doctor* Gantesy." He glances at her slyly. "He wasn't a real doctor, you know."

"I know, Dad. He was just a Ph.D."

§

After the episode in the faculty lounge, Sophie has no intention of chauffeuring Arthur twenty-five miles into the country just to drive by an old house. He's tired and weak. She's tired and stressed. Her students handed in a batch of new papers today, and she's written only fifteen pages toward what within a couple of months will have to inflate into 150 pages of bloated scholarship supported by a minimum of five trumped-up footnotes per page, mini-essays unto themselves. Having been "scooped" by the Tulane professor's analysis of scatology in the law, she's reverted to her Pork article, to hell with overly sensitive judges and the brown-nosing instincts of the Consultant.

"If I may inquire," Arthur says, "why are you turning here?"

She disregards the question. Any response will incite an endless, circular discussion.

"If you will comply with my request," he says, "I promise I won't ask you to drive me anywhere for a year."

She ignores him.

"I'll pay you fifty dollars," he says. "Scratch that. I'll pay you a hundred dollars."

She concentrates on driving. Arthur falls silent, his head dropping back against the seat, eyes shut. Studying his profile, Sophie experiences a paradigm shift. Instead of an annoying, argumentative, demanding parent, she sees a robust, hard-working man who loves open spaces and the wild rural air, trapped in a brittle corporeal shell, with nothing to look forward to but returning to a claustrophobic, six-sided coffin with holes. Has she more sympathy for a lab rat than her own father? Isn't a failing body enough of a burden? Must she add to the torment?

§

A few miles west of town, the landscape sheds its monotony, becoming hilly and unpredictable. Haphazard commercial development and hulking McMansions give way to modest squares of tilled land sprouting whiskery crop stubble and a few miles farther out, glimpses of the russet-color winter grasses of the prairie.

Sophie follows a winding county road south of the interstate. It's been a long time since she's driven this route. New houses with shake-shingle roofs and matching barns have sprouted up, interspersed among modest, decades-old dwellings, hubs for an eclectic variety of outbuildings constructed per principles of utility rather than fashion. Sophie registers each familiar landmark—the 1890s limestone church whose roof was sheared off by a tornado, the unincorporated town consisting of a single intersection where a triple murder occurred when Sophie was ten, the field where the farmer was flattened by his runaway tractor.

Arthur dozes, his respiration tentative. Sophie lays her fingers on his wrist to take his pulse—55 beats per minute, a little faster than usual.

As she turns south onto the gravel road, heading toward the farmhouse, Sophie is struck by how little has changed here compared to the surrounding area. The road stretches for a mile, ending at a wide creek lined with untamed trees and choking, viney undergrowth. The old farmhouse remains the only dwelling on the road. As the Escort crawls forward, intense longing smolders in Sophie. Just beyond this hedgerow, the house will be visible.

Blinking in disbelief, she slams on the brakes, causing the car to skid sideways on the gravel, jarring Arthur awake. The grand two-story farmhouse with its southern-style veranda—her childhood home, the stuff of Arthur's wistful yearning—is in a state of wretched disrepair. Peeling, moldy paint. Crinkly stalks of dead crabgrass spear up between the buckled floorboards of the porch. Ivy stems, free of their tended trellises, weave dense mats that cover the windows and creep up the roof, reaching for the brick chimney. Even the For Sale sign in the front yard has been assaulted into submission by an army of belligerent bindweeds. And the old barn! Once a source of pride for its imposing size and handsome limestone foundation, it remains intact, but the boards have splintered, and the entire structure tilts north with a strange, rubbery uniformity, as if it were a picture printed on Silly Putty. The only decent-looking building left is the white brick workshop on the north side of the driveway.

"What in hell are we doing *here*?" Arthur says hoarsely.

Sophie has no idea what to say.

"You agreed," he says, "quid pro quo, if I stayed in that godforsaken waiting room and talked to those interns, you said you'd . . . " He squints at the house. Sophie watches as his rheumy eyes move from one pitiful sight to the next—the mailbox lying on the ground, peppered with pellet holes, the overgrown rosebushes lining the drive.

He stares at her with alarm. He hopes he's hallucinating, she knows, that he is "altered" as the docs put it, as he was right before his stroke when the cobblestones leading to the front door of his apartment appeared to grow quills like a porcupine's and glow with iridescent rainbow hues.

"Shit no!" Arthur says.

She nods. "Yeah."

§

That evening, with Buggles sprawled on her lap, she taps out a petition captioned Mac Higgins v. Meyeth Industries, alleging violations of the Clean Water Act. She reads through it a few times, making minor changes here and there while trying to shut off the voice in her head telling her what a moron she is for picking a fight she can't win. Saving the file, she closes her laptop, then sits stroking Buggles's bulbous head as she drifts into semi-consciousness. Sometime later, Buggles jumps to the floor, waking her. She opens her laptop, scans the petition one more time, and adds a claim for ten million dollars in punitive damages.

14 Schemes

The voice on the phone is warm, familiar, and inviting. It belongs to Marlon Herrington, who's just deboarded a plane at the metropolitan airport 60 miles to the west and is heading to a nearby hotel, where the American Bar Association Section on Law and Archeology is holding its quadrennial meeting. He wonders if Sophie might be free for drinks and dinner. He says he has some "big news."

As it happens, Sophie is already scheduled to make a trip to the airport that evening to pick up Rachel Green, who's arriving for her three-day on-campus interview. Her flight isn't due until 9:30, creating the perfect opportunity to accept Marlon's offer, yet Sophie hesitates, wondering what can be gained. Long-distance relationships don't work, and anyway, she's never sensed genuine interest on his part. While she could use an advisor in the matter of her sputtering career, she recalls with distaste her sense of playing the role of beneficent reflector of Marlon's tortured brilliance. Still, he offers interesting company, quality eye-candy, and a meal and libation at a four-star restaurant. She calls him on his cell. "Okay!"

With only a couple of hours before she has to leave, Sophie embarks on a cleaning frenzy. Because she's Green's faculty host, her office will serve as the candidate's home base, thus she finds her-

166

self on hands and knees picking up stray papers, bottle caps, squashed raisins, poorly aimed gum wads, and half a Tampax wrapper, and mashing stacks of paper into her already crammed desk drawers. Then on to Slosh 'n' Wash to make her car presentable. She clears the interior of food wrappers, cracked CD cases, spilled peanuts, and all manner of Buggles residue in preparation for driving it through the so-called "tunnel of waves," where the gap in the seal of the Ford's windshield mocks her once again, water drip-drip-dripping on the dashboard in its tentative yet unrelenting rhythm.

§

The Roasted Pheasant revolves atop the Airport Ritz-Carlton. Marlon couldn't have selected a more seductive dining spot, as Sophie harbors a fanatical love of rotating restaurants. She arrives to find Marlon and a dirty martini waiting for her. Heart thumping wildly, she extends her hand; he grabs it and pulls her into a bear hug. He smells so good she doesn't want to let go.

They spend time catching up. Marlon listens patiently to her accounts of Arthur's problems and the evolving agenda of the Dean. If there is one thing that bonds them, Sophie reflects gratefully, it's their shared view that Charles VandenDungen is a personality-disordered bully.

"Actually, I've talked to Chaz a couple of times recently," Marlon says.

"My sympathies."

"It looks as if we'll be collaborating on a project."

Sophie sucks on her martini, wariness tickling the nerves on her arms and the back of her neck.

"Which brings me to my big news," Marlon says lightly. "I'm changing jobs."

A nauseating mix of giddiness, jealousy, and anxiety agitate the vodka and vermouth pouring into Sophie's stomach. Lucky Marlon! Leaving the world of academe to pursue his dreams. Leaving her behind. But . . . collaborating with Chaz VandenDungen?

167

"I'll be working here," he says, "right down the street."

Sophie's mind races through the possibilities. Aircraft mechanic. Parking lot attendant. Hotel concierge. What nearby position could be related to archaeology? Maybe he's using "down the street" loosely.

"The Museum of Natural History?" she ventures.

"I've accepted a position at The Zeus Group."

Zeus. God of Sky and Thunder. Ruler of Mount Olympus. Father of Apollo. Sponsor of archeological digs?

"What is it?" she says.

"Executive VP and General Counsel."

"Where do they dig?"

"What?"

"Zeus Group."

Marlon chuckles. "They don't dig anywhere, Sophie. They own schools, including Avalerion University."

Gurgling in response, Sophie assumes she's misheard him. He couldn't have said he's going to work for the largest for-profit education corporation in the country. Not he who'd mourned the abandonment of the traditional mission of the university. Not he who'd complained about the offensive encroachment of free market ideology into the administration of higher education.

"You're joking."

"Absolutely not."

And there it lies for what seems like five minutes of gaping silence, as Sophie attempts to beat back a buzz-killing sense of betrayal, while Marlon, apparently oblivious to the explosion of disenchantment he's triggered, signals the waiter for another round of cocktails.

Did he say Avalerion University?

Sophie's brain stumbles along, at a loss as to how to restart the conversation. Normally, "good Sophie," Mary Frigging Poppins Sophie, would step in to rescue this crashing social interaction by offering benign, supportive comments. "Congratulations!" "How wonderful!" "That's fantastic!" In short, fake it.

But that Sophie has jumped off the train, tumbled through a

thicket of weeds, and emerged scathed, limping, and in no mood for pretense.

"So," Marlon says, smiling as easily as ever, exuding his imperturbable serenity, "I'm scheduled to start the middle of January, and I'll be headquartered just down the way. Have you seen the Avalerion Building?"

"How could I miss it?" Indeed, how could anyone? It's one of the few recently constructed office buildings lining the interstate that wasn't abandoned in the Great Recession. Perched in a nest of tangled landscaping, its startling, ornithologically-inspired architecture—dramatic, angled "wings," primitive, square "head" of a penthouse—visually abuses passing motorists who are having a hard enough time paying attention while negotiating the endless exurban sprawl. And the whole thing clad in silver reflective material such that it resembles a massive version of one of those aluminum foil "sculptures" upscale restaurants wrap leftovers in.

"It's really quite amazing," he continues. "The company commissioned J'aim Tyoug-choi to design it."

She decides to let the indecipherable dropped name drift on by. Who cares?

"Are you familiar with him? He's one of the most notable postmodern architects in—"

"Marlon, you said you wanted to do something that matters."

He appears amused. "And?"

"Avalerion University is a high-tech diploma mill."

"That's not fair."

"It's the Wal-Mart of education. Massive inventory. Cheap labor. Grossly inflated administrative costs."

The waiter delivers their drinks along with plates of seared foie gras and whiskey-steamed shrimp. Sophie checks her watch, wondering if she has time to metabolize out another martini before she has to meet Rachel Green at the airport.

"I suppose you've got a right to be surprised," Marlon says.

"Thank you!"

"I decided to step down as dean," he explains, "not really sure what I was going to do. Then out of the blue, the president of The

Zeus Group calls. He was a classmate at Yale."

"So?"

"I said yes."

The appetizers taste so heavenly she wishes she could undo the unpleasantness growing between them so they could just sip their martinis and enjoy the luscious flavors. The luscious, *expensive* flavors.

"What are they paying you?" Sophie says.

His face lighting up, Marlon can't suppress a grin. "With stock units, options, and bonuses, about $5.2 million."

She gasps.

But can she blame him for making such a bargain? If a former classmate of hers appeared from nowhere and offered a multi-million dollar position, would she decline? Could she *afford* to decline, when it could mean working for a year and living on her earnings the rest of her life? If it is so impressive, so desirable, though, why does she feel sick at heart?

"What project are you and VandenDungen collaborating on?" she says, trying to keep her voice dispassionate, at least until the hors d'oeuvres are gone.

"I'm glad you asked." Marlon pats his mouth delicately with a corner of his napkin, a mannerism that suddenly strikes her as effete. "Because it could possibly involve you."

She stares at him, anesthetized enough from the martinis not to yelp in pain at the specter of Marlon and VandenDungen discussing how to use her.

"It can't," she says.

He places his hand over hers. "Hear me out."

She removes her hand, and it forks another bite full of foie gras, so intensely flavorful her eyes tear up. She plasters on a smile so Marlon won't assume she's about to weep, which for various reasons she feels like doing.

"Chaz wants to outsource the Rosecliff Skills Program, and I told him we'd be interested in helping to fulfill that vision."

"Does chopping up an educational program into atoms and selling them to the lowest bidder qualify as a vision?"

"No call to put such a negative spin on it, Sophie. There's merit to trying to maximize efficiency in any line of work, including teaching. We're perfectly positioned to partner with Rosecliff on this. I was hoping we could enlist you to be the director."

"Am I being punked?" The last bite of shrimp consumed, Sophie rises. "What've you done with the Marlon Herrington I met in Washington?"

"I'm the same man, same values," he says, "but there's no place for me in today's world."

She can relate.

"So, between you and me, I decided to get rich."

§

An hour and forty-five minutes later, a sobered-up Sophie is guzzling Diet Coke, trying in vain to find a non-torturous position on the molded plastic airport chairs. Green's plane is late. When it finally arrives, the candidate emerges looking so extraordinarily beautiful, cool, and put-together that Sophie in her state of dejection considers fleeing the airport without the candidate. Reasons for her absence? The best her sluggish imagination can come up with is she was accosted in the parking lot of the Ritz-Carlton and her car stolen, then recovered a short time later. But Rachel Green has spotted her. Green doesn't even attempt to hide her disappointment that the committee has seen fit to send the likes of Sophie Poe to pick her up.

On the way back, Sophie works to fulfill her duty to "sell Rosecliff" by spouting a string of inanities about the traffic-free ingress and egress to the airport, mentioning that it was built on 10,000 acres of cow pasture, then segueing to the point that despite appearances, Rosecliff isn't located in the corn-fed hinterlands, it's a mere 60 miles east of a bona fide megalopolis and an "international portal to the world"!

Glancing at Green, Sophie struggles to reconcile the Dean's Rescue Plan with this recruitment effort. Her confusion grows as, after a half-hearted attempt to show interest in Sophie's lowly position at the law school, Green launches into a revised rendition of her professional ambitions, reiterating her desire to found a center, which has metamorphosed into a center for virtual learning of all kinds, with its own "engineering cell" of IT professionals who will guide faculty in designing video games of their courses. Within a few minutes, Sophie realizes with relief that Rachel is practicing her job talk, hence she'll be expected to contribute exactly nothing to the "conversation" save an occasional affirmation that she remains conscious, as the Escort hurtles through the darkness at 80 miles an hour.

§

The next day, Marlon's revelations weigh on Sophie. As soon as she hands off Rachel Green to her lunch group, she roams the halls searching for Jen Fairfield, happening upon her in the second-floor library ladies' room.

"I would *never* use the john next to your office," Jen explains. "You must get so sick of hearing everyone's sounds."

"We need to talk," Sophie says.

Back in her office, Sophie recounts the conversation with Marlon Herrington.

"Five point two million dollars?" Jen says.

Sophie nods.

"And all he has to do is conspire with VandenDungen to demolish my job?"

The color rises in Jen's cheeks, and with that, Sophie knows it's on.

§

It is the third and final day of Rachel Green's visit, and the faculty convenes in the conference room for her job talk. When Sophie arrives, her favorite seat is still available, the chair behind the pillar. With her vision blocked, her hearing is even more acute than normal. Green's cultured voice is resonant and clear. Sophie has little option but to listen, for the third time, to the candidate's extravagant aspirations. Green articulates her vision for The Rosecliff Center for Virtual Legal Education. Rosecliff would set up an alternative Law School in Second Life, virtually authentic, complete with administrative offices, library, and common spaces for shared learning and socializing. Students could elect to attend some or all of their classes in cyberspace.

Lacking a view of the candidate, Sophie's gaze wanders over the faces of her colleagues. After five and a half years, she knows these people pretty well, and while the personas in this room might appear stimulated by Green's flights of fancy, open to any and all progressive pedagogical methods, the educators within must be crying out, "*Why, why?*" Isn't teaching hard enough without injecting issues of bandwidth, megahertzes, gigabytes, lags, and crashes between teacher and student? What benefit could derive from professors and graduate students having to design idealized digital self-representations, then expend all their patience "running" themselves like robots in a two-dimensional graphical universe?

Rachel Green pauses to solicit comments or questions.

The first comes from Wally Shane. "What are the environmental implications?"

"That's a great question," Green says. "The laws of Second Life require all citizens to follow green practices. As a result, it's a very clean space." She smiles. "Green is as green does."

Shane frowns. "No. What's the impact on energy usage from all these computers running non-stop?"

Green looks perplexed.

Be Van Krist pipes up.

"I think I remember reading somewhere that the average Second Life avatar uses the same amount of power as the average Brazilian."

No one seems to know what to do with this information.

Karla Johansson speaks up. "The heck are we gonna keep all these computers running smoothly? Apologies to Darren Youngblood, but IT can't get to the routine problems we're having now in a timely manner. Students'll be lined up by the dozens, whining about how their laptops don't function right."

Green's back in familiar territory. "I propose a dedicated IT unit within the Center to keep everything running smoothly. They'll interface with digital design consultants, who'll create classrooms, research laboratories, even a private island with a virtual campus. Of course, we'll have to lease land if we want to work on that scale."

"Ka-ching," says former Dean Beau Rainer.

Several others echo the sound of money being blown.

"Be quiet!" Chaz VandenDungen says. "We're not going to discuss any budget issues here today. This is a candidate interview, and in any event, those matters rest exclusively within the purview of the executive."

Paul Singer, who had one dose of Green in D.C., still isn't buying it. "What do you mean, land? What you're talking about has no greater relationship to land than a light bulb does to the sun. Call it what it is. A bunch of color dots on a computer screen."

Rachel Green smiles indulgently. She really is so incredibly beautiful it's hard to take your eyes off her. But it is clear she thinks the Rosecliff faculty is a group of old-school rubes.

"And you're suggesting we're going to pay a bunch of money for maintaining color dots on our computer screen?" Singer persists. "What rational person would do that?"

"It's really just like any other MMORPG, Professor Singer, and of course they all charge monthly fees for participation in their virtual worlds. The difference with Second Life, and what makes it unique and valuable as an educational tool, is that users create their own worlds. The fee is for leasing the space to build and maintain those worlds."

Paul Singer exchanges glances with Beau Rainier; Midwestern-born and raised, the two men are mutually averse to being toyed with by a smooth-talking, East Coast female, regardless of how attractive.

"Don't you think this plan might be just a little grandiose, Rachel?" says Barbara Kitchen. "Especially because, no offense, but you haven't even taught a class yet! I'm not sure you realize that we have to actually train lawyers at this place!" She looks around the room as if they've been assigned to a group project and she is doing all the work. "Recruitment committee members? Hello? Aren't we looking for someone to teach basic property classes?"

"Barb!" says Rainer, the only person capable of taming the snarling beast that is Barbara "Law is my Life" Kitchen when she gets up on her hind legs. "This is neither the time nor the place."

"Time? You want to talk about time? Well, I don't know about the rest of you," Kitchen roars, "but I'm *busy*, God damn it, *extremely busy*! Unlike some people." She peers around the room, clearly searching for someone in particular. Fortunately, Sophie is hunched behind the pillar, out of Kitchen's sight line. "I mean, do I have to *list* the committees I serve on?" Heads across the room shake "no," but a mind-numbing enumeration of committee names and titles assault whatever decorum remains. "Chair, the Drug Offense Committee of the State Bar Association . . . ranana ranana ranana . . . of the city bar committee . . . ranana . . . ranana . . . ranana . . . pro bono counsel to . . . ranana ranana . . ."

Sophie no longer hears words. She tries to hear them, but she can't. She hears only indecipherable noise. Panic rises in her. She thinks about Chris Paine, whose hearing loss, caused by his oversize lawn tractor, makes him appear perpetually bewildered. She thinks about the Korean man at California Nail who does her manicures; he awakened one morning deaf in his right ear, never regained hearing, and has never smiled at her since. She thinks about her best friend from high school, Lucy, who shortly after graduation lost the ability to understand language only to discover she had an inoperable brain tumor.

"Ranana, ranana . . ."

Eventually someone manages to flip off the Barbara Kitchen switch, and the next thing Sophie knows, Dean VandenDungen shoots up out of his chair, exclaims something, and begins to clap. Assuming the presentation has ended, Sophie too stands and claps. VandenDungen and she are the sole applauders. Green remains at the lectern. Sophie's hearing returns.

"That's exactly what I've been talking about!" the Dean says, scanning the faces of the faculty. "Creativity. Vision. Innovation. Big thinking. Setting the bar high." He turns back to Rachel Green. "Was that excruciatingly hard to do, Rachel?"

"No, sir."

"Was it brain surgery?"

"No, sir!"

"Was putting it together an unassailable peak that only highly trained, exceptionally gifted athletes could scale?"

"No, sir!"

"Kudos." With that, VandenDungen sits down.

Simultaneously, Ann Kulter stands up. After swinging her mane around a few times, she says, "I hate to burst any bubbles, but that's what bubbles do. They burst." She turns to face the candidate. "You're not exactly on the bleeding edge with this concept, Rachel."

Sophie observes how remarkably the two women counterpoise each other, from a physical standpoint. Light against dark. Feminine against non-specific-gendered.

"Have you heard of State of Play?" the Consultant demands.

Unruffled, Green says, "Of course."

"Perhaps you could enlighten the rest of us," Shane snarls.

"The Ivys have been holding annual conferences on the status of virtual learning for years," Kulter says. "The purpose is to assess the progress, development, and challenges to virtual learning, and, despite all the hoopla, the latest commentaries indicate not much headway has been made. Rosecliff needs New, Ms. Green. Rosecliff needs Different. In order to accomplish its Rankings mission, Rosecliff needs Wow!"

Rachel Green remains as cool as if ice packs are strapped beneath her clothing. "That's exactly what I'm proposing. WOW, an acronym for World of Warcraft, is the most successful MMORPG in existence. Its graphics and interfaces are state of the art, while at the same time completely accessible. The Center for Virtual Legal Education would employ similar technology, but with more user proactivity."

Kulter scowls. "I've lost you. You're not addressing my point."

Facing the faculty again, Green ignores her. "I envision creating a universe comprised of dozens, even hundreds of law schools, in which student avatars from all over the country and world interact, attend classes at each other's schools, hold debates, socialize, eat communally, etcetera, thereby breaking down the competitive barriers among the institutions and replacing them with collaborative opportunities."

Sophie imagines avatars eating together. They could be made to "eat," no doubt. Animated figures have been eating for decades, from Popeye squeezing a can of spinach into his mouth to Homer Simpson stuffing down Marge's pork chops, but what would be the point of it between law student avatars?

"I don't see how any of this relates to our primary mission, which is Tier-climbing," Kulter says.

"If successful, I believe my Universe would make real-world games like the Rankings irrelevant and obsolete," Green says. "It's all about the institutional outliers taking back their power."

"I doubt anyone from Columbia or Stanford would be interested in attending Rosecliff classes, not until we're at least Top 25," Kulter says.

"With due respect, Ms. Kulter," says Green, "that would be the case only if what Sophie Poe told me was untrue."

Sophie's mind jolts to attention. There is no time to figure out what she might have said to Rachel Green; there is time only to register that it was probably a lie, and now the viability of this lovely lady's entire proposed Universe rests on her own cramping shoulders.

Green smiles at her. "Remember, Sophie?"

"We talked so much," Sophie lies. "I'm not sure what you mean."

Green has control of the room and takes advantage of it. She paces leisurely yet confidently, commanding the attention of a roomful of seasoned questioners of received wisdom.

Green nods in Sophie's direction. "You said that despite where Rosecliff places in the Rankings, its faculty is exceptional enough you'd be willing to put your best professors up against any in the country."

Sophie has no memory of such a comment. Meanwhile, her colleagues are staring at her with expressions ranging from pleasant surprise to incredulity.

"And I told Sophie that if she was serious," Green says, "and if her claim is valid, then I believe we can offer incentives to students at other law schools to sample our courses, show the world what we can do."

Sophie has no memory of hearing Green say anything of the kind.

"I have no idea what incentives you're thinking about," Kulter tells the candidate, "but in my opinion, you're in a dream world, and we need real solutions."

"So here's a real solution for you," says Green, glowing. "I've actually saved the best for last."

VandenDungen squirms with excitement. "Bring it on!"

"I propose bringing MOOC to MMORPG," Green says.

Shane howls like a lonely coyote. "God damn it! Stop this shit!"

The lovely lady from the East has taken it one step too far, acronym-wise.

"With due respect," Green nods to Shane, "Rosecliff can be a pioneer in this. We can offer a variety of online courses in our Second Life school. But we will buck the trend toward free courses by charging a modest fee, on top of our tuition for entry to our virtual campus."

VandenDungen is on his feet again, clapping rousingly. "This is the most thrilling thing I've heard uttered in these halls since I arrived!" he declares. "It's the sort of big, out-of-the-box idea I've been hoping for—frankly, what I've been prodding you all for." His disappointment is palpable that the Second Life Rosecliff scheme hasn't been conceived by one of the law school's existing faculty members. He sidles up to Green. Arms crossed over her hard fruit-breasts, Ann Kulter eyes him stonily.

§

Jen develops a theory about VandenDungen that she intends to exploit in a scheme she claims does not constitute blackmail. According to Jen's research, Catwoman has yet to move permanently from D.C. to live with the Dean, despite the fact he's invested over $700,000 in a faux chateau with six bedrooms and an elevator to accommodate the wife's extended family of origin, including a disabled uncle. Lo Ming occasionally pops into town to make official appearances, her pubescent-shaped wisp of a body sheathed in a black unitard and platform boots. Jen thinks—and she is not alone in this—that Lo resembles a bony male in drag, as her feminine characteristics, though believed to be genuine, are subtle at best.

Furthermore, in the months since his arrival, Chaz VandenDungen has undergone a physical transformation that Jen contends reveals a soul in turmoil. His wife's refusal to join him, his obvious attraction to the Consultant, who's also been compared to a drag queen, his notable weight loss, and his wild mood swings even while medicated suggest a man on the edge, prone to reckless acts, who might, just *might*, be caught in an indecorous act by a diligent investigator.

Though an eavesdropping device would be preferable, tracing VandenDungen's movements is all Jen and Sophie can afford. The plan is to attach a TrackStick to the undercarriage of the Lexus, where it will remain three weeks, logging data, at which point it will be removed, plugged into a computer, and analyzed. Because Jen has done the thinking, Sophie volunteers to place the gadget, but Jen will hear nothing of it.

"There's no *way* I'm going to let you expose yourself to that risk," Jen says. "You've got a shot at tenure. I don't. I'm hash unless I can get rid of VandenDungen and his outsourcing fetish. I'm the one who has to do this."

"But I'm more sneaky," Sophie says.

"Not *more* sneaky," Jen says, "a different kind of sneaky."

They toss that one around for a while, drawing some super-fine distinctions in duplicity, which causes The Consultant to pop into Sophie's mind.

"Kulter," Sophie says.

"What about her?"

"I hear she has a two-year renewable contract."

"Hmm."

"Shouldn't we have a plan for her?"

Jen processes the question. "I'll put one in development," she says.

15 Hearing

The law firm of Fiori & Fiordimondo is one of the few large regional firms that will still consider hiring Rosecliff Law graduates. Beyond that, Sophie knows little about it, so when the phone rings, and an earsplitting voice shouts the name "Cleve Fiordimondo," Sophie, who's been pounding away at her article, draws a blank.

"Eh, Professor Poe, I'm sure you meant to have your petition served on me but you made a mistake and had it served on Ed Lassiter, however, he's not designated for service of process for this company. Frankly, I haven't seen this kind of error in years. I guess you haven't practiced in our state, or, if you have, you're as green as a raw soybean. I *could* file a motion alerting the court to the improper service, but I suppose in the long run that would only delay the proceedings and wouldn't be in the best interests of my client, so I won't. I'll accept it as served and waive all objections."

As Sophie's mind abruptly shifted gears—out with the Pork, in with the pollution—she realizes the shouter must be the attorney for Meyeth Industries.

"You're fucking with my head, right, Professor," the voice continues, "with this punitive damages bullshit? You know, when I found out you teach at Rosecliff, I knew I was in for pain and suffering. We all roll our eyes when we get slapped with a professor lawsuit. It's a joke but a costly one. You people have nothing to do over there but harass honest business people with spurious claims. You can pour a hundred hours into a case just for the quote unquote learning experience. We can't afford to do that in the real world."

"What was your name again?"

There was a pause during which Sophie is forced to listen to Fiordimondo's strident, snorgley breathing. If he is being asked to state his name again, his whistles and snuffles indicate, the earth must be off its axis.

"Cleve Fiordimondo!"

"What are you calling me about?"

Another pause, with sound effects.

"Did you file a lawsuit against Meyeth Industries?"

"Yes."

"That's what I'm calling about!"

"I'm busy right now."

She hangs up. Her right ear rings with the tinny aftermath of Fiordimondo's rant.

She forces herself to return to the article. At 63 pages and 258 footnotes, it is way behind where it ought to be. The spring submission cycle is fast approaching. But it isn't going to write itself, so she revs her engines and taps away. "For decades, lobbying groups with pointed agendas have sought to influence the selection of judges by a variety of means. They have funded lavish getaways at resorts for appointed judges and contributed directly to the campaigns of elected judges. For example, the Foundation for Research on Economics and the Environment (FREE), an anti-environmental group, regularly solicits federal jurists to attend 'seminars' at privately-owned Montana ranches, where the invitees enjoy 'blue ribbon trout streams,' horseback riding, whitewater rafting, and hiking through 'millions of acres of pristine wilderness'."

As Sophie compiles footnote references for the statement, Manny Delgado materializes in her doorway as if by divine fortune; her conversation with the Meyeth lawyer is knocking noisily about in the back of her mind, and Manny possesses an encyclopedic knowledge of prominent litigators.

"Do you know a lawyer named Fiordimondo?" she says, hoping the question didn't prompt any associations with "brown skin."

"Cleve Fiordimondo? Of course."

"What can you tell me about him?"

"He is an asshole," says Delgado, "and he is one of the best defense attorneys in the region. The man is in his late 60s, early 70s, and he puts in 15 hour days, six days a week. He'd work seven but his wife won't let him work Sundays. She is a Christian woman."

Sophie sighs.

"Why do you ask, *chica*?"

Sophie describes what she's gotten herself into.

"You are totally fucked," Manny says. "Meyeth never settles and—"

"Meyeth always wins," she says.

"What the fuck are you doing anyway? Aren't you up for tenure in the fall?"

She nods.

"You need to have your head examined, *tonta*."

"Tanta?"

Manny eyes her pityingly.

"*Tonta*, Sophie. It means 'fool.' But of course you gringos can't be bothered with learning even the most basic vocabulary of another language. Fuck, no! Instead, we now have 30 states—30 states!—that have in effect adopted English as their official language! Do you have any idea how that poisons the atmosphere of communities against Spanish-speaking citizens?"

"To what do I owe this visit, Manny?"

Delgado takes a deep breath, his pigeon-puffed chest straining against his shirt. Sophie steels herself for another blast of hair-trigger hostility, but fortunately the tension seems to seep out of him, and he sinks into the chair across from her.

"Well, as you probably know," he says, "I'm chair of the Internal Affairs Committee."

Not only doesn't she know, she's never heard of the committee. Since when do the pastoral groves of academe have divisions for investigating corruption like gritty inner-city police stations?

"According to the Dean, it is a new trend among law schools," Manny says, "part of the internal accountability movement that's sprung up since the student blogs started ripping us a new one. Chaz says many schools are instituting such controls."

"I bet he just made that up," Sophie says.

"Be that as it may, I am here to inform you of a matter that has come to our attention."

"I don't have time for any new matters!"

"A lady from Oklahoma called the provost yesterday," Delgado continues, "who in turn called Chaz. She identified herself as the aunt of one of our students. She was very upset about her nephew. He told her he is involved—*sexually* involved—with one of his professors, and she fears the professor is harming her nephew. Apparently this student's health and mental well-being have always been precarious, and she claims he's suffered a great deal as a result of this relationship. The aunt says she believes he will need psychiatric care."

The blood whooshing rhythmically in Sophie's ears would have to substitute for a drum roll build-up to the inevitable.

"The aunt identified the professor who is sexually involved with her nephew as you, Sophie."

"James Yoder is not my student!" she cries out. "I had him last spring!"

Manny Delgado's eyes bug out. "You are admitting to it? What the fuck were you thinking, taking a student as a lover?"

"What? No! He's not my lover, he's my stalker! He's psycho!" She forces herself to square-breathe, but manages only three sides before righteous indignation takes over. "And by the way, Manny, you had a student lover, and you married her!"

The Delgado temper flares. Muscles bulge all over his body like The Incredible Hulk's, threatening to split open his clothes.

"Tina was not my student when I married her! She was a former student, and not a single person expressed concern about our relationship. Here, someone has called—from out of state!—about an improper sexual liaison—"

"Why is his aunt calling, Manny? He's middle-aged!"

" —leaving me no choice but to follow up on it."

Sophie speaks as evenly as she can. "James Yoder is unbalanced. He stalked me all summer. He leaves me notes." She removes the Yoder file from the cabinet. "Look at all this crap! It's been going on for months."

Delgado flips through the cards, poems, and drawings, getting obvious pleasure from inspecting Yoder's cartoons of tiny-headed figures with overlarge genitalia.

"Why did you not report this?" he says.

"Victoria Enquist knows. I think she's written him a few e-mails telling him to stop."

Delgado jots some notes. As he rises, Sophie says, "He really needs help."

Delgado appears surprised.

"Think about the university's potential liability," she continues. "What if he acts out in some serious way? If it's shown we knew he had problems, Rosecliff could have some serious exposure."

"Sophie, the Dean is going to want to have a hearing on this matter."

"On James?"

"And you."

"Damn it!"

Manny squares his shoulders and adjusts his waistband, which in turn requires repositioning the tight fabric squeezing his thick thighs and on down his legs until he is fighting with the hems of his slacks, which are clinging to his socks.

Huffing as he straightens up, he says, "We'll be getting back to you."

§

The hearing on the Yoder Internal Affairs matter is shaping up to be the kind of adversarial proceeding in which the allegation itself demolishes the presumption of innocence, and the accused is placed in the untenable position of trying to prove a negative. A paper has appeared in Sophie's mailbox bearing three names: James Yoder, Victoria Enquist, and Hannah Roark. Manny Delgado denies it's the prosecution's witness list. "This is a fact-finding mission only," he said. "You have nothing to worry about." But then he added, "You are free to call whomever you wish on your behalf." He's also informed her she could bring along a "representative," a transparent euphemism for "defense attorney." Sophie's choice was a no-brainer: Jen Fairfield.

Fifteen minutes before the hearing, Sophie has worked up a nervous sweat and is blasting herself with a hair dryer she's purchased to keep in her office for the purpose. Resentment boils up in her, prolonging the drying process. How can it be that an institution whose very *raison d'être* is the principle of constitutional democracy is forcing her into the equivalent of a trial based on a random, unsupported assertion of illicit sex. Sex? She hasn't had sex in almost three years!

The hearing room turns out to be VandenDungen's office—an unexpected site. The Dean has enlarged the original and decorated it in the style of a Wall Street player's inner sanctum, complete with an egg-shape, glass-top conference table, two TVs tuned to business news stations, and a live stock ticker with glowing red symbols and numbers scrolling along beneath the crown molding.

On the way there, Sophie meets up with Wally Shane, who's been experiencing shooting pains beneath the right side of his ribcage; preliminary tests showed his liver enzymes are elevated. The doctor assured him this was common, but Shane is convinced he has liver cancer. As they appear to be headed in the same direction, Sophie asks where he is going.

"To your hearing," Shane replies.

"Is Jen going to call you as a character witness or something?" Sophie says.

"I'm on the committee."

Sophie feels hurt he hasn't mentioned it and says so.

When they arrive at the Dean's office, Jen is already present, decked-out as if she's scheduled to argue a case of uncommon importance before the United States Supreme Court. At the confer-

186

ence table sits the Dean, Chris Paine, and Manny Delgado. As Sophie seats herself next to Jen, she senses an imminent explosion of hot air from the other side of the table.

"We are gathered here today—" begins Chris Paine.

"I'm chair of this fucking committee," Delgado says, fists balled, "and I'll say what we're gathered for."

Shane sighs loudly.

VandenDungen studies Sophie with his heavy-lidded eyes. "Let me begin by saying I'm extremely disappointed to see you sitting here today, Sophie. I had a choice to make among the B track instructors at this law school. Actually, I didn't *have* to make a choice, but I chose to make a choice. I chose to select a person who I believed has the potential to jump track so to speak, the individual with tenure potential. And I selected you for reasons that, frankly, I'm not sure I can remember at this moment. But one thing is clear. The person sitting before me today is not the person I selected."

Sophie glances at Jen, who eyes the Dean with a distinctly feline expression, sweetness underlain by contempt. She removes a tape recorder from her briefcase.

"I'm sure you gentlemen realize the importance of due process—Chris, you teach it!—as well as the value of an accurate record."

VandenDungen stares at the small recorder as if it's a rodent he'd like to flush down the toilet.

"The purpose of this hearing," Manny says, "is to explore if Visiting Assistant Instructor, um, Assistant-Associate . . . what *is* the title of your position, Sophie? Do you even have a professional rank?"

In walks Victoria Enquist, trailed by James Yoder and a gray-haired woman wearing a baggy dress and carrying the Holy Bible. The woman glowers at Jen, assuming the voluptuous lady with the honey hair must be her nephew's paramour; it can't possibly be the tomboy next to her wearing a suit that looks as if it's been fished out of a lake and dried "natural" on the deck next to the day's catch.

A kerfuffle ensues. Weirdly, no one seems to have planned for

187

the group's arrival. As the Internal Affairs Committee and Dean Enquist debate procedure in an inharmonious tangle of lawyer babble, Sophie loiters in the reflected fury of the Oklahoma menace, until she suddenly realizes that James is trying to burn a hole through her clothes with his projectile lust.

At length it's decided the parties already situated will remain where they are. The new arrivals will wait on VandenDungen's aniline leather couch until called, at which time each in turn will be seated at the small end of the egg. Enquist and the aunt sink onto the couch. James stays put.

"I love you, Sophie," he says.

As far as Sophie is concerned, the matter is over. Exhibit A: the accuser. Exhibit B: her nephew. Case rested.

Victoria Enquist rises, pulls James to the couch, and punches his chest until he falls back onto it. "Shut up," she says, "until you're asked to speak."

"We'd like to hear from Hannah Roark first," Manny says.

The primly-attired woman totters to the witness chair, her gaze flitting suspiciously between Jen and Sophie.

Manny wastes no time getting to the heart of the matter.

"As I understand it, señora, you allege that Ms. Sophie Poe is fucking your nephew James Yoder."

Jen doesn't object, so Sophie elbows her, whispering, "That's inappropriate language at my hearing."

Tears leak from Hannah Roark's downcast eyes as she sniffles and hiccups.

"You might want to rephrase your question," Chris Paine says.

"And you might want to go fuck yourself, sir, since you have never litigated a single case," Delgado says.

"Jesus Christ!" Shane says. "Mrs. Roark, why do you think your son and Ms. Poe were involved?"

Hannah Roark peers at him gratefully. "Jimmy and I are close, has been since my sister died. He tells me everything. And last spring he calls, says he and one of his lady professors was having an affair. I knew he never should have went out of state to school but it's the only one who'd take him."

188

"Did you and your nephew have additional conversations about this matter?" says Delgado.

"Once it started, he didn't talk about nothing else, seemed like."

"What else did he tell you?" Delgado says.

"Says she was the most beautiful woman he'd ever seen." Roark cast a sideways glance at Jen. "Looked like a princess. He mentioned quite a little bit about a blue dress."

"With due respect, ma'am, did he provide to you details regarding their sexual relationship?" Delgado says.

The waterworks sputter on, accompanied by a chorus of blubbers and snivels.

"Answer the fucking question!" Delgado pounds his right fist on the table. As his wedding ring strikes the surface, a sliver of glass shoots off, striking Hannah Roark in the forehead.

"Oh, my good Lord!" she cries.

With that outburst, Sophie again ceases hearing words. Jen, Victoria, and Chris all jump up to comfort the witness. Jen produces tweezers and tries to remove the chip of glass embedded above Roark's left eyebrow. The old lady knocks her hand away, then spits out some words that sound to Sophie like "ranana . . . ranana . . .ranana," but which she's pretty sure is some biblical admonition.

After Chris Paine removes the tiny shard, and a Band-Aid has been applied to the wound, testimony resumes. As Vanden-Dungen worries over the flaw in the table, Paine takes up the questioning, and back and forth it goes, with both questioner and witness emitting unintelligible sounds. At one point, everyone looks at Sophie, who turns to Jen and gestures to her ears, mouthing the words "didn't hear." Jen scribbles something on a legal pad and shoves it toward her.

Q: Did he tell you anything about their lovemaking?

A: Best lover he ever had.

Simultaneous urges to nap and vomit hit Sophie. Crossing her arms on the table, she buries her head in them.

The next thing she knows, Jen's poking her in the ribs. James is seated in the witness chair, and Sophie's hearing has returned.

After some preliminary questions, Paine says, "You've been present during your aunt's testimony, so what we need to know is, did you in fact have a sexual relationship with Professor Poe?"

James's face is as emaciated as that of a death camp prisoner. His gaze meets Sophie's. She attempts to telepath to him: *Tell the truth, tell the truth.*

Finally breaking eye contact with her, James looks around at the others at the table.

"I did not have sexual relations with that woman," he says.

Sophie jumps up. "That's right! Thank you, James, thank you!" Sitting down, she grins at Jen. "It's over!"

Jen leans toward her and whispers in her ear. "Sophie, that's one of the most famous lies in history. I'm not sure it will be believed."

"I never told anybody to lie," James adds. "Not a single time. Never."

16 SO WHAT?

A week after the hearing, the Internal Affairs Committee issues its judgment. Jen presented a killer defense, cross-examining Hannah Roark about James's history of mental instability. It turned out that as an undergraduate, he was accused of breaking into females' dorm rooms and, when called out about it, claimed he was inspecting their refrigerators for deadly molds. Additionally, Jen had entered into evidence key documents from Sophie's Yoder file, including an e-mail Sophie had sent Victoria Enquist stating, "Please make him stop!" As for evidence of Sophie's own behavior, there was only James's description of her "jumping up and down like a crazy person, screaming at me, when I was driving over to take care of my adopted Gramma." But that was tempered by his comment, "she never looked hotter."

The committee found insufficient evidence of professional misconduct. Not exactly the rousing declaration of innocence Sophie had hoped for, but at least the issue was laid to rest.

No sooner does Sophie learn of the decision than Cleve Fiordimondo slaps her with a four-inch-high stack of discovery in the pollution case, a harsh reminder that in civil suits, all the "action" takes place on paper. Fiordimondo also files a motion to strike her punitive damages claim, asserting she'd included it in her petition without securing permission from the court as required by the civil code. Face burning, she looks up the code section. He is right, of course; it was passed by the state legislature last session and went into effect in the summer. She feels like someone who should be working a twelve-step program; she acknowledges her life is unmanageable and only a greater power can restore it to sanity.

§

A winter storm, the second ice storm in a week, is wreaking havoc. Sophie creeps along, gripping the steering wheel as she gazes at vehicles that have skidded off the road, been rear-ended, are facing the wrong direction, and in the case of one truck, ended up in a ravine by a creek, standing vertical on its front grill.

When Sophie knocks on Arthur's door, he answers immediately, wearing his old canvas coat, an orange fur-lined hunter's cap with ear flaps and a chin strap, and green rubber muck boots.

"Good afternoon, Sofa."

"Dad, are you going out?"

He squints at her. "When you said you were stopping by, I assumed we were going for a drive by the old place."

"The weather's terrible."

He peers into the thick, wintry air. "What's it doing out there?"

"Sleeting. Or maybe freezing rain. Is it the same thing?"

"No, ma'am, it is not." Stepping past her, he extends his hand. "We've got some sleet here."

"Let's go inside," she says.

His condo is dark and smells like burnt waffles. He offers her coffee. After several minutes of opening and closing kitchen cabinets, he withdraws the offer.

"I guess I don't have any," he says.

"You should have." She made a grocery run and stocked him up three days ago. She removes a can of Folgers from the corner cabinet, noting it hasn't been opened. "It's right here."

"I wondered what in the Sam hell that was," Arthur says.

Her heart sinks. She can no longer ignore the fact he is getting worse. "Dad, have you been confused a lot lately?"

"No more than usual."

"Do you feel kind of down?"

He blinks at her. "What do you mean by that?"

She makes coffee. They sit in the tiny living room and drink it in silence, watching the ice-pocked air through the narrow window.

"If we're not going for a drive," he says, "then why are you here?"

In view of Arthur's condition, Sophie feels ridiculous bringing up the pollution case.

"Dad, I'm wondering if we should change something."

"Like what?"

"I don't know. You seem depressed."

He scowls at her. "Why are you going into these matters?"

"I'm just asking, are you okay?"

He slams his coffee cup on the table. "Hell, no, I'm not okay!"

"What's the matter?"

"Don't you remember anything at all?" He spits out the words. Saliva drops spray the air. His mouth protrudes as his thin lips draw taught over his dentures. She hates this expression of his. It often precedes some biting remark.

"I remember everything," she says.

"Why won't you do anything for me? You won't help me. You won't drive me anywhere. You want me to die."

She attempts to restrain herself. She wants to yell at him. She wouldn't mind throwing something at him.

"That's not me you're talking about," she says. Her voice is shaking. "It has nothing to do with me."

"The fuck it doesn't!"

"I didn't abandon you. That was Quint."

"You're not supposed to say that. It is never to be mentioned!" He scoots forward on the couch as if preparing to stand but his fury is sapping his meager supply of energy.

"He was your chosen one, and he screwed you over."

"He's a scum-sucking fuckhead. A bottom-feeding piece of

193

shit!"

"So why are you yelling at me then?"

"Who's yelling?"

Though they both fall silent, the words they shouted seemed to ricochet around the room like ping pong balls. Time ticks away as they glare at each other. Arthur gets up and goes into his bedroom. She considers leaving but makes no move to do so. She hears him urinating, then running water in the sink. He returns to the living room, glancing at her tentatively. He's removed his orange hunter's cap and is patting his hairpiece.

"Is that all for today?"

"You need to have that operation," she says.

"What one?"

"Where they clean out your artery. You're not feeling well because you're not getting enough oxygen to your brain. You could have another stroke at any time."

He clicks his dentures.

"You could end up a vegetable."

Click, click, click. "So what?"

"Dad!"

"Ten percent die on the table," he says.

"Two percent."

"Not acceptable," he says, swaying woozily. "Unless there's something else, that's all the time I have right now."

She could raise his level of care from Wellness, Level 2, to Caring Hands, Level 1, which would increase the number of home visits from two to three per day, as well as provide food preparation assistance. The cost would double, but Medicare would pick up a portion.

He's halfway to the front door to see her out.

"There is something else," she says.

He wiggles his eyebrows and ears.

"I wondered if you could give me some advice on the suit against Meyeth Industries."

"What kind of advice?"

"All kinds."

"Well." He studies his feet, wobbling and jerking as if buffeted by the wind. Puttering back to the living room, his face tense with concentration, he struggles to summon his lawyer mien. He lowers his body gradually, straining against the pull of gravity and the prospect of collapse.

"Downstream pollution claim, if I recall," he says.

She nodded. "I've got Cleve Fiordimondo on the other side."

He stares at her.

"He's burying me in paper."

"What do you think Meyeth pays him for?"

"Do you know him?"

Eyes closed, Arthur rubs his gray stubble. "Good lawyer. Loves the spotlight."

"I already embarrassed myself." She explains that she included a punitive damages claim in her petition, and before she even gets to the embarrassing part, Arthur interrupts.

"Section 26-5212 of the code states the plaintiff must move the court for leave to file a claim for punitive damages and the petition may be amended to include such a claim only if the pleadings, when taken together with such other evidence as the court may in its discretion consider, shows there is a probability it can be proved the defendant acted willfully, wantonly, or with reckless disregard for the rights of the plaintiff."

Sophie stares at Arthur. "How did you know that?"

"How did you not know it, Sofa?"

"It's Sophie, Dad. Just plain Sophie."

"The legislature has been considering limiting punitives for years. Finally got it done last term."

Sophie is awash in despondency for several reasons, chiefly how far she's in over her head and how seriously she is malpracticing.

"The court will strike the claim," Arthur says.

"I know."

"But you can always file the motion again after discovery."

Arthur has flicked on the TV and is watching a commercial for an electric wheelchair. An elderly lady is spinning in circles on a mountaintop.

"How in hell did she get up there on that chair?" Arthur says.

"Dad, I was thinking maybe you could be co-counsel on this case."

Arthur continues to watch the commercial. Now a man with a full head of wavy gray hair is sitting on the beach in one of the chairs.

"Did you hear what I said, Dad?"

Eyes trained on the screen, he says, "According to you, I'm confused."

"I could use you, Dad. I'm overwhelmed."

"With your paper about intercourse?"

"I could give you the file, and you and the client could get together and draft answers to the discovery, plus round up all the documents they're asking for."

His eyes shine brightly from the hollows in his sunken face.

"Do you have a decent claim for punitive damages?"

"You tell me."

"Would I get a cut of the fee?"

She nods excitedly. If this works, *if* it works, she will feel tremendously relieved.

"Bring me the file," he says. "I'll take it under advisement."

§

It is customary for a professor working on a scholarly article to present it in draft form to the Rosecliff Law bi-weekly writers' group, wherein one's peers can publicly question the writer's intelligence and eviscerate the article's thesis. Sophie's Pork article now stands at 93 pages, 419 footnotes, about two-thirds complete. But she is more worried about the content than the length. It made sense as she wrote it paragraph by paragraph, but leafing through the bloated manuscript, she has serious doubts about its coherence. Worse, she fears she has nothing new to say on the subject of the inadequate system of selecting judges. But is it really necessary to say anything new? Conventional wisdom holds that merely synthesizing existing authority and commentary, a "descriptive" piece, is insufficient; a worthy article must be "prescriptive," break new ground, suggest a creative solution to the problem addressed, however impractical or even ludicrous. But in her research, Sophie has learned that many prominent professors argue back and forth with each other for years about the same issues.

Though the article is infused with her cynical attitude toward the judicial marketplace, she hasn't reached the point where she can make suggestions for reform, assuming she has any when the time comes. She hopes the workshop will generate some, as the professors compete among themselves to prove whose intellect is broader, deeper, most inventive. In the best case scenario, she'll be able to finish the article with a bang, using everyone else's ideas, post it on SSRN, rack up some downloads, then send it out to law reviews.

But first she has to face the firing squad, unflinchingly endure whatever comes, and convince her colleagues that even though she came to the Rosecliff faculty via the "back door" of the institution rather than through the "front door" as a result of meat market recruitment, she has the makings of a tenure-track star.

A few days before the workshop, Sophie contracts a bad cold, which begins with a sore throat, then progresses to painful, phlegmy bronchitis. Reason enough to put it off, she thinks, heading to the office of Barbara Kitchen, the leader of the writers' group.

A prolific writer, Kitchen is known for her no-nonsense bent. Most of her articles are descriptive how-to pieces aimed at the practicing lawyer. She gives lip service to the importance of theoretical scholarship, but her disdain for abstraction rips apart that pretense at every meeting.

Kitchen's office rivals Wally Shane's for the sheer mass of paper stacked on paper stacked on more paper. The kinetically charged Kitchen is bouncing around when Sophie arrives. The dramatic difference in the two women's energy levels is palpable, inducing guilt in Sophie. Why isn't she more of a go-getter like Barbara Kitchen? Why does she feel near death around this woman?

Kitchen barely acknowledges Sophie when she enters. Leaping

from behind her desk to a box of books on her couch, she almost knocks Sophie over.

"Excuse me," she mumbles. "I'm busy. What do you want?"

Sophie explains she isn't feeling well and needs to reschedule her article presentation.

"You're not prepared, are you?" Kitchen says.

"Of course I am. But I have a sore throat and bronchitis."

Reaching into the center of a leaning tower of paper on her desk, Kitchen extracts a single sheet and dangles it in front of Sophie's face. Sophie tries to read it but Kitchen is leaking kilowatts, and the paper vibrates like a twanged rubber band. Sophie snatches it from her fingers.

> To: allfac@Rosecliff.edu
> From: Chaz VandenDungen
> Re: Sick policy for faculty

It has come to my attention that some faculty members are under the misapprehension that the sick day policy in place for staff also applies to them. For obvious reasons, this is false. After researching the issue, I discovered that before I arrived, there existed no policy on sick days for faculty. Consequently, the following policy is hereby instituted, effective immediately:

As professionals, faculty members are not entitled to "sick days." Faculty members must meet their obligations, including teaching their classes, attending committee meetings, etc., unless they are hospitalized or produce a written report from a physician that they are physically incapable of attending to their duties.

The reference to "professionals" hits a sour note with Sophie. Didn't VandenDungen bust the myth that "We are professionals."?

"It doesn't say writers' group," she points out. "Which is a voluntary activity, not an obligation."

"If you're not ready, Sophie, just say so." Kitchen coughs fitfully. "I've had the flu for two years, but do you hear me complaining about it? Do you think I try to escape my obligations because of it? No. I show up rain or shine, day or night."

Sophie bites her tongue to keep from making a snarky remark about Kitchen's postal service slogan.

"I'm just not feeling well. My head's stuffy, my throat hurts, and I'm coughing up green slime. I'd prefer—"

"Not to show up. I get it. But per the Dean's policy, the workshop will go on, with or without you."

"Isn't my article the only one scheduled?"

"Life is all about choices, Sophie. And if you choose not to hear our feedback, so be it. We'll discuss it in your absence."

As Sophie steps into the hallway, Barbara Kitchen mutters, "Personally, I don't think you can afford to miss it."

§

It takes Sophie 45 minutes to present her article. A few people ask questions along the way, but for the most part, it goes smoothly despite her antihistamine-induced sense that her scalp is crawling off her skull. When she finishes, she asks for comments.

Omar Patel raises his hand. "So what?" he says.

"What do you mean?"

"You are at pains to describe this marketplace of judiciary," he says, "the buying and selling of judges, the injustice resulting, most especially to more disadvantaged consumers. But, I guess one might say, big whoopee. That is byproduct of the messiness that is our sausage democracy."

"I agree!" says Kitchen. "Would you rather have a dictatorship like in Iraq before the war? Let's just select judges like Saddam Hussein did!"

"What?" says Sophie, feeling as if her brain is hovering like a cumulus cloud just above her head.

"I think you've done a splendid job laying out the case against election of judges," Newt King says. "Congratulations, Sophie."

"Thank you."

"I have to wonder, though, and I'm sure you've thought about this, and it will be coming in the final section of your article, but what's the solution to this problem? Because the only other alternative to election of judges is appointment, and as you yourself note, that is vulnerable to politics as well."

"I was thinking the same thing, Newt," Xavier Michaud says. "Is there a third way?"

Michaud's question sends a shock of electrical current through Sophie's vertiginous brain. *A Third Way?* That's it! The seed from which she can grow a Solution to the Problem. Why has she not realized it on her own? When there are two ways that don't work, one has only to invent a Third Way, a new path out of the dense forest of confusion, repetition, and revisitation that is the perpetual state of legal scholarship.

"Yes," she says, "there is. And it will be forthcoming, in the final section of my article."

"Tantalizing," says Michaud.

"Give us a preview," says Kitchen.

Sophie points to her ears. "I'm sorry. I'm having this problem. With my hearing, off and on. And with this cold, it's much worse."

"What's the Third Way, Sophie?"

"What?"

Kitchen mouthed the words. "*What is the Third Way?*"

"I can't hear you."

"How convenient."

"What?"

17 JEOPARDY

Mac Higgins is scheduled to meet with Arthur on the pollution case the same Saturday VandenDungen picked for "the first annual Rosecliff Law Inspirational Retreat." The Retreat is to take place in the Comfort Room at the Alumni Center, about 200 yards west of the law school. Sophie has instructed Mac to meet her and Arthur at her office, figuring she can run over and check on their progress during breaks.

Sophie arrives at the law building with Arthur in tow at 8:25 a.m., five minutes before the retreat is to start. Fifteen minutes later, Mac still has not appeared. As she paces nervously behind her desk, Arthur sits in one of the visitor chairs, calmly perusing the case file. She hasn't seen him look this good in months.

He looks up at her. "What's wrong?"

"He's not here," she says. "And I need to leave."

"What for?"

"I told you. I have to go to a retreat."

"Go on." He smiles at her. "Retreat."

"I can't."

Exiting her office, Sophie trots down the stairs to the first floor and walks briskly to the front door. She peers out to the parking lot. No sign of Mac's truck.

The building is quiet, all the office doors closed.

"Sophie, what are you doing here?"

She whips around to confront an equine visage emitting a pretentious patrician voice.

"Nothing."

"The retreat has begun," Kulter says. "Why aren't you there?"

"I have to take care of something first."

"What could be more important than the retreat?"

The front door opens noisily and in bustles Mac Higgins.

"Hey, Professor!" he says. Removing his cap, Mac strides to them, grabs Sophie, and gives her a big hug. "It's so great to see you!" He extends his hand to Kulter. "Hello, Miss. Mac Higgins from Frankfort."

Kulter stares at Mac's hand as if it were a cow pie.

"We gotta go," Sophie says, grabbing Mac's arm.

On the way up the stairs, Mac exudes a cool, fresh smell. Sophie glances at him. He seems more handsome every time she sees him. And today, given the tingly feeling spreading throughout her body, he is giving off some major sexual pheromones.

When they enter the office, Arthur, who is wearing a coat and tie, stands.

"Mac Higgins, Frankfort."

"Arthur Poe, Blister."

Mac cocks his head. "Blister?" He looks at Sophie. "Why didn't you say so? Blister has some of the finest soil in the state!"

"Sophie tells me you farm," Arthur says. "I would imagine if you're up around Frankfort, you irrigate."

"No, sir. We dryland farm, but tell you what, if the next couple of years are as drouthy as the last two, we'll have to change something."

"I'm leaving now, okay?" Sophie grabs the glossy two-pocket folder containing the retreat agenda. "You two can take it from here?"

Both men nod.

"I'll check back at the break."

"So you got yourself some dirty water," Arthur says to Mac.

"You bet I do!"

202

§

Sophie opens the door to the Alumni Center at 9:05. As she enters the Comfort Room, the attention of her colleagues shifts from the wiry man who is addressing them to her, clearly grateful for the diversion her late arrival provides from whatever the speaker is saying as he strolls around collecting note cards from them.

Mouthing the words "sorry I'm late," Sophie tiptoes around the circle, searching for a place to land. The only empty spot is against the wall next to the Dean, who has tilted back his chair and is rocking zealously. As Sophie approaches, intending to move the spare chair to the circle, VandenDungen slaps its seat, commanding her to sit next to him. Pretending not to notice, Sophie grasps the seat back, only to find the Dean has wrapped his meaty digits around a chair leg and is torqueing it.

"Ow!" The unexpected motion wrenches Sophie's left elbow. "Let go!"

"You let go!"

"I'm trying to join the group!"

"This chair's designated for a specific purpose!"

"What I'll do," intones the speaker, shuffling through the note cards he's collected, "is keep these for two months then send them to you. By that time, you'll have forgotten all about them. They'll alight in your mailboxes like little birds, reminders of promises past, forcing you to ask yourselves, have I followed up on what I pledged to do during the retreat? Have I invigorated my teaching in creative ways, or is that just something I wrote down because Dewiddy made me do it?"

Sophie releases the chair. The Dean bangs it back against the wall. Dewiddy approaches Sophie and hands her an index card.

"The assignment is to write three new teaching methods you pledge to try out in your classes in the next month or so."

Sophie stares at the card, then at Dewiddy, whose eyes brim with the passion of a true believer in the retreat process.

"Where am I going to sit?" she says plaintively.

"Right here of course." Omar Patel's warm fingers brush her right wrist. She gazes down to see his stunning brown face floating saucer-like above a field of brilliant white; in a traditional kurta over pajama pants, he looks as dressy and spotless as a virgin bride. He's created an eight-inch space for her on his chair seat. How can her butt possibly look that small to him?

She shakes her head absently, preoccupied by the contrast between Omar's immaculate threads and the sea of dingy denim comprising the rest of the slouching circle.

Elliot Ramsey stands. "I'm leaving. Take mine."

"Thanks," Sophie breathes, and slides into Ramsey's seat, grateful for its lingering warmth.

"Wait!" VandenDungen booms. "This is classified as mandatory professional development."

Ramsey proceeds to the door and exits. Rushing after him, VandenDungen can be heard jabbering about professional obligations while Ramsey shouts something about a "dance recital."

Sophie stares at her blank index card, trying to summon up three innovative teaching methods to submit on the spot. She needs to make a bold affirmation that missing the lecture hasn't affected her resourcefulness.

Scribbling three ideas, she hands the card to the facilitator.

"Awesome!" he says. "Look at you, bypassing the dialogue and innovating on your own! I'm impressed." He contemplates the card. "Fascinating! Share with us what 'Punctuation Jeopardy' is, Sophie."

"Well, obviously it's based on the TV game show, but the categories all relate to punctuation issues. For example, 'Apostrophes and Possessives.' Another could be 'Comma or Semi-Colon?'"

"Wow!" says Dewiddy.

"Today's students know next to nothing about the semi-colon," she adds. "Anyway, I'd choose five categories, then divide the class into three or four teams. Representatives from each team would take turns playing Jeopardy. I'd be Alex Trebek, and I thought I'd even download that tick-tock Jeopardy theme and play it. It would be a lot of fun. And educational, of course."

"Cute," says Manny Delgado.

Sophie looks at him sharply.

"In the best sense!" he says.

He sits forward on his chair, the textured plastic seat submitting to the pressure of his buff glutes. "Sophie, that is the most adorable idea I have heard here today. Of course, you have some stiff competition. You missed Bill Wu's suggestion that we all use clicker remotes so we professors can keep our tech-addicted consumers as happy as members of a studio audience in an infomercial. And then we had Ruth Ribidium's concept of letting students self-select into groups with the goal of transforming case reports into play scripts to be acted out during class so the students can truly *feel* the material in case they didn't *feel* like reading it. How inventive!"

Having returned from chasing Ramsey into the parking lot, Dean VandenDungen stands in the doorway, breathing laboriously and baring his teeth. He's packed on fifty pounds in the month since Catwoman relocated from D.C. and moved into their mansion. She is rumored to be skeletal; he appears to be eating for both of them.

"I don't mean to pee on your Grape Nuts," the Dean pants, "but that's not exactly an original idea, Sophie."

"I just now thought of it!"

"It's been floating around the legal writing community for years," he says. "I'm surprised you didn't recognize that."

Sophie shrugs. "I never heard of it until I thought of it."

Ann Kulter slips in past the Dean. "Which in itself says something," she comments.

Sighing despairingly, VandenDungen shakes his head; less than a year into his five-year contract, his expression announces, he's had about all he can take. Well, thinks Sophie, then he shouldn't have told Ruth Ribidium he hopes she'll retire soon as he needs to assign her plum corner office to someone with fresh potential, code for "young."

"Dean," Kulter cuts in, "we have an issue over at the law school."

VandenDungen's face assumes the boiled look that invariably

precedes a pressure-release.

"The definition of retreat is refuge, Ann, asylum, getting away from it all," he rumbles.

"A couple of gentlemen have taken over the faculty lounge," Kulter says tightly "and they appear to be practicing law. They have papers scattered everywhere. When I asked them to leave, the older gentleman told me to stick it."

VandenDungen squeezes his eyes shut and, with hands pressing the sides of his head, seems to be trying to keep his skull from exploding.

"Can I trust you to handle nothing on your own?" he says through gritted teeth.

"*Trust?*" Kulter shrieks. "You dare to talk to me about *trust?*"

Which reminds Sophie she hasn't heard anything about the results of the Trackstick Jen planted on the Dean's undercarriage. It must be about time.

Sophie tries to brush past the Dean and Kulter unnoticed, but as she reaches the outdoors, Kulter calls behind her, "Sophie, if you're involved somehow with those men suing Meyeth, you need to stop it."

Sophie freezes for a moment, then walks on.

"Remember, Meyeth is on tap to fund the new clinic!" Kulter shouts.

§

Back at the law school, Sophie finds Arthur and Mac in the faculty lounge, chattering away like old friends.

"Did you ever meet Ralph Menken?" Mac says.

"I knew a Stephen Menken," Arthur says.

"That's his dad. You know how Stephen has that one front tooth that sticks straight out?"

"Yep."

"You'd know Ralph was his son if you ever saw him. He's got that same one front tooth that sticks straight out, just like his old man!"

"Isn't that something," Arthur says, "how a thing like that passes down."

Sophie assesses the scene. Kulter was right; the two men are drowning in a mass of disorganized paper.

"Have you guys accomplished anything?" she says.

"Hey, who was that skinny broad who bothered us 'while ago?" Arthur says. "She busted in here and went on about . . . let's see . . . she was all uptight about . . . " He glances at Mac. "What was she saying?"

"Some horseshit about are we working on a case, and if we are, we have no right to use the facilities for private gain," Mac says.

"I reminded her that Rosecliff is a public institution," Arthur says, "funded by taxpayer dollars, and we have as much right to use the room as she has to use the toilet at an Amtrak station."

Mac guffaws. "It was awesome."

"She tried to look at the file," Arthur says, "but I put a stop to it."

Mac studies Arthur admiringly. "He said he'd sue her for intentional violation of attorney-client privilege."

"Whew," sighs Sophie. "My ass is so—"

"Guess what!" says Arthur. "Mac went over the heads of the public relations people and talked directly to the Meyeth regional rep. The bastard told him the plant has never dumped any waste into the Ichiwaw River, and if the crops don't grow, it's because the farmer's stupid."

"He really said that," Mac affirms.

"Was there a witness?" Sophie says.

"My hired man was with me. They came out to my place, and we were standing there looking at the shitty corn."

"They?" Sophie says. "How many Meyeth people were there?"

"They sent three people!" Mac says. "They flew in from headquarters in a Lear 35, stayed about an hour, ate lunch at the local café, and flew out again. That was a day of work for them."

Sophie glances at her watch. She begins collecting the papers strewn about the lounge.

"What are you doing?" Arthur says.

"You need to find someplace else to work."

"Leave everything alone," Arthur says. "We have a system going here."

Sophie is holding a ten-page interrogatory containing 20 questions, some with several sub-questions. "Nothing's filled out," she observes. "These are due in less than a week."

Grinning, Arthur points to his head. "It's all up here," he says.

§

After dropping off Arthur, Sophie meets Mac for brunch at what he confesses is his favorite restaurant, IHOP. She feels as if she's packed on ten pounds just by walking into the place. As he wolfs down samples of every item that could possibly be categorized as "breakfast food," she salivates while picking at her fruit plate, reflecting on one of the great unfairnesses of life, at least hers: the drastic variance in metabolism rates between males and females in their age group.

"Things are going pretty well, aren't they?" Mac says.

Holding up a finger as she finishes chewing, Sophie attempts to reconcile the blank pages scattered about the floor of the faculty lounge with "pretty well."

"Your dad is something else," Mac continues.

She nods.

"Who'd have guessed I'd end up having a lawyer like him in my corner? He's more intelligent than three of my B-school professors combined!"

"B-school?" she says.

He laughs. "Don't sound so shocked. We're not as stupid as Meyeth thinks."

"I didn't mean—"

"I decided to get my MBA when I quit hog farming. I'd made quite a bit of money in it, and I wanted to grow crops instead."

"Because hogs smell so bad?" Sophie ventures.

"You get used to the smell. It was really that I wanted a new challenge, and dad was retiring. I kind of wanted to keep things going."

They finish off their meals simultaneously. Sophie glances at the bill and unzips her purse.

"No, ma'am." Mac snatches up the check. "This is on me. But let's not rush off. How about another cup of coffee?"

Mac's eyes seem to be speaking to her about a whole host of subjects that aren't routinely discussed at IHOP.

"Well, sure," she says.

After the waiter refills their cups, Mac brings up his hog farming days again, adding this time that his wife leaving him was another reason he decided to make a change.

"I tried everything I could to make it work, but she said she just had to go," he says.

"Because it smelled so bad?" Sophie says. It's inappropriate, but, if there's one thing she knows, it's that pig farms smell worse than just about anything else on earth, and she wants Mac to admit it.

He looks at her much more searchingly than her snide comment deserved.

"Well, yes, she did hate the smell," he says.

"Okay."

"But she also had a fondness for the electrician who rewired our barns."

"Ouch," she says. "I'm sorry."

"She's a girl with problems. I knew that going in."

"Nobody can really understand how complicated marriage is until they go through it," Sophie says.

"That's true." He sips his coffee as his eyes process her marriage remark. She sees he's surprised that she considers herself qualified to comment on marriage.

"I was married for six years," she says. She describes her love-at-first sight with Chester, their elopement, his increasingly secret-ive behavior, and her discovery of his extra-curricular activities.

"Did he do meth?" Mac says

"No, he just made it and sold it."

"Why?"

"He says he wanted us both to graduate debt-free."

"Hmm."

"I still loved him even when I divorced him. But I was going to sit for the bar exam. How could I be the wife of a man serving time for manufacturing drugs?"

As they reach their cars, he says, "This was fun. Maybe when all this is over, we can get together. "

A time when "all this" would be over seems so remote, she doesn't even consider it a possibility.

§

Jen Fairfield uploaded the data from the TrackStick onto her computer and, with help from Darren Youngblood—one of many moths to her flame—decoded and interpreted it, producing a log of the Dean's movements over a three-week period. Based on VandenDungen's apparent attraction to women resembling skinny men, Jen theorized he might be frequenting a club on the interstate called Tinker Bell's, featuring all manner of variously gendered persons expressing themselves on platform dance floors. Costumes are de rigueur, the only requirement being that each incorporate at least one element of the original Tinker Bell's look.

But Jen's theory isn't proving out. Instead, the data reveals the Dean regularly visits an apartment building some 77 miles away, in a tony area of the metropolis.

"The building's right across from Maple Creek," Jen says. "It's called Yachtkeepers. It's one of the most exclusive addresses in the city, so whoever she is, she's loaded."

"Maybe he's keeping her."

Jen thinks for a moment. "Why are we assuming it's a she?"

"Maybe he's keeping it, then," Sophie says.

Further investigation is indicated, and Sophie volunteers. Jen protests, but Sophie insists, pointing out her experience in identifying her brother's whereabouts after the embezzlement as well as the identities and locations of his girlfriend, two current wives, and a "business partner," who turned out to be the former proprietor of a defunct strip club.

The most straightforward approach would be the best; at least it had worked in Quinton's situation. Get a phone number, get a name, make a call. People love to talk, particularly when they should keep their mouths shut. In her brother's case, she sorted through numerous caches of hidden and discarded bills, discovering recent unopened phone statements in the manger of one of the farm's stock trailers. The bills revealed a pattern of compulsive phoning, with the overwhelming majority of calls being placed to two numbers, one traditional and the other a cell number. The land line number was unlisted. A quick search online and $39 later, Sophie had the unlisted person's name, one Meshell Pickett. Yes, Meshell Pickett said, she knew Quinton Poe; she was engaged to him. They were supposed to have been married two weeks before, but she hadn't seen him in three, and not only that, he'd slipped the engagement ring off her finger while she was asleep. The cell phone belonged to a Peter Unbar. Yes, said Peter Unbar, he knew Quinton Poe. They'd agreed to put up $10,000 each toward the purchase of a gentlemen's club, but he hadn't seen the fucking prick since he'd made the moronic mistake of giving Quint ten grand, trusting him to make the down payment on the deal.

But the Dean's case is different. They have a location, but it's a condominium building with 50-some units. In the old days, the names and apartment numbers of residents would be listed at the entrance of a building. But now, a different approach is needed: a criss-cross directory that includes apartment buildings. Darren Youngblood from tech services helps her out with that one, but unfortunately, no one listed as living at Yachtkeepers sounds familiar. Should she give in and do old-school surveillance, Sophie wonders—sit in her car night after night, drinking cold coffee out of a paper cup, until she eyeballs the Dean arriving at the building?

As she mulls over the possibility, a voice in her head, sounding very much like Arthur's, admonishes, *this is the stupidest thing you've ever done, Sophie, even dumber than naming a legal article after the act of copulation! Pretending to be some cheap private eye? Who are you kidding? And what about the pollution case? Is it going to prosecute itself?*

True enough, she admits. But what about Jen's job? The Dean has made his objective clear regarding the existing Skills Program; it's slated to be outsourced beginning next year. Even if Jen applies and is hired as one of the instructors, no judge will approve an adoption when the prospective parent is pulling down a trifling $8,200 per year.

The TrackStick data shows a pattern of twice weekly visits to the Maple Creek building, usually on Monday and Thursday evenings, with VandenDungen arriving between 7:00 and 8:00 p.m. and leaving within two to three hours. Seems simple enough. Show up at Yachtkeepers fifteen minutes or so before 7:00 on a Monday or Thursday evening, and wait for VandenDungen to arrive.

But then what? How will she know what unit he visits? She can hear Arthur laughing at her. *What are you planning to do, Jamie Bond, wear a disguise and slip into the building behind him, before the door closes?* What's wrong with that idea?

Guilt pulls at her from the corner of her desk, where her swollen, malnourished porker of an article squeals for attention. At 117 pages, cluttered to the hilt with 601 footnotes, it awaits its final, thundering climax: a brilliantly original resolution to the intractable dilemma of judicial selection. Spring submission season, during which thousands of similarly overweight and under-important opuses hit the inboxes of stressed-out student editors across the country, begins soon. Sophie had planned to submit ahead of the curve, but now that's out of the question, chiefly because she hasn't yet manufactured an earthshaking "Third Way" of judicial selection.

Her mind skirmishes over which activity is less appealing: thinking about the conclusion of her article or embarking on a surveillance of VandenDungen.

Fifteen minutes later, she's speeding west on the interstate toward the metropolis, attempting to brainstorm a Third Way. As she pops the top on a tube of bacon-ranch Pringles, the number three flashes in her mind in various colors and fonts, preceding a blank to be filled in by a burst of inspiration. *Three wise man, three makes a crowd, three on a match, three blind mice, baby makes three, three branches of government! Whoa!* There we go! Appointments by the executive branch—no good; she criticizes them in her article as being subject to cronyism. Judicial—she can't very well argue that judges should select themselves; talk about a good old boys' club of entrenched interests. That leaves the legislative branch. To her knowledge, no one has suggested that judges be selected by legislatures. That's it! But how would it work? A commission could present a slate of candidates, and both legislative bodies, house and senate, would hold hearings and vote on them. What a ridiculous mess! Oh, well. What did it matter? As Omar Patel might say, the messier the idea, the better; more meatiness that way.

§

Sophie arrives at the Yachtkeepers condominiums at 6:40 p.m. twenty minutes before VandenDungen's earliest arrival time. Parking for the condos is located beneath the building, protected by a barrier arm, so she spends a considerable amount of time parallel parking the Escort on the street. Donning a ball cap she's brought along as a disguise, she approaches the front of the building via a winding sidewalk lined with benches and small trees. As she suspected, the front entrance to the building requires a code.

Then it dawns on her. If the TrackStick data is accurate and VandenDungen really is a regular visitor here, he might well have a key card to the parking garage, permitting him to enter the building via an elevator from an underground level.

She can cover only one entrance. Which one?

This really is a preposterous idea.

She decides to check out the underground entrance to the building. The lot is a brightly lit, single-level affair, with an elevator located where she expected it, but with a better hiding place than anticipated—a dim, truncated hallway to nowhere next to the elevator that offers a decent vantage point from which to view the garage.

A couple minutes later, the barrier arm lifts, and a dazzling little emerald-green coupe enters the lot. She squints from her bunker as it buzzes around a corner. *An Aston Martin?* Cute, but, not being VandenDungen's Lexus, irrelevant. Tires squeal as its driver searches for an empty spot.

Sophie glances at her watch; it's 7:07. She flips through the newspaper to the "Ask Dr. Gott" column. Today, a woman from Ohio wonders if Vicks VapoRub really is an effective treatment for toenail fungus. The doctor responds that he is unaware of any controlled studies investigating that treatment for onychomycosis, though anecdotal evidence, including some from his own readers, supports its efficacy. Certainly, it could do no harm.

"Sophie? Is that you?"

She looks up into the face of Marlon Herrington.

"No," she says, the newspaper shaking in her hands.

He laughs. "What are you doing here?"

"Waiting for a friend."

"Who?"

"Just a girlfriend."

"What's her name? I might know her."

"Vicksy. Vicksy Pringle."

Marlon cocks his head. "Vicksy? There's a Vicky on the third floor, but I haven't heard of a Vicksy."

"Are you visiting someone here, too?" she says.

"I live here."

The possible implications of his answer bombard Sophie's mind, which fizzes with static.

He punches in a code and the elevator wheezes into action.

"One of the perks of selling out," he says with self-mocking irony. He lacks his usual aura of serenity, however, seeming agitated as he glances toward the parking lot. She tries desperately to think of ways to prolong the conversation.

The elevator door opens. "Great seeing you," he says as he steps inside.

"Maybe we could have a drink," she says, "catch up."

"Let's do it," he says.

She sticks her arm between the closing elevator doors, and they rebound. "I mean now. I could use a drink. Hard day."

Marlon frowns. "I have a previous engagement." He presses a button, and the doors begin to shut again.

She sticks her foot between them. "Do you mind if I wait for Vicksy in the lobby though?" she says.

He hesitates. "We're not supposed to let in people we don't know."

"You know me."

"I mean only our own guests."

The elevator doors are clenching and unclenching her foot.

"Please? I'm cold. I promise I won't get you into trouble."

Marlon glances over her shoulder as another car enters the garage.

"All right," he says, "come on."

Grabbing her arm, he pulls her into the elevator and pushes the lobby and fifth floor buttons.

She grins at him. "So do you miss academe?"

He checks his watch. "Sometimes, I guess."

Exiting at the lobby floor, she says, "It was great seeing you again. Let's have that drink sometime."

"Sure," he says. "Call me."

"What's your . . ."

She stares at her reflection in the brushed steel of the closed doors. Her ball cap looks stupid, perched high on her head, and her sweat shirt is dusted with Pringles crumbs. Pushing the Up button, she boards the elevator and selects the fifth floor.

In the minutes that follow, Sophie vacillates between thinking she is an amazingly astute investigator and realizing that pursuing a highly paid executive to his condominium is a fairly creepy accomplishment. If Marlon happens to pop his head out his apartment door and see her, he could probably have her arrested. But she's determined to wait it out until 8:00 p.m.

Installing herself in a cove next to the exit door on the fifth floor, she passes the time reading the want ads and listening to the occasional whir of the elevator responding to a call for service. And smelling . . . well, pot. She follows her nose up and down the hall, determining that the smell is strongest at the far north end. She returns to her newspaper. As she considers phoning about an item in the For Sale listings, "king-size mattresses, still in their plastic! $235," the elevator stops and disgorges a recession-proof couple— trim, flawlessly groomed, moving along the carpeted corridor fluidly, cloaked in an air of financial invincibility. As they approach, Sophie moves forward, intending to walk purposefully toward the elevator, but she winds up jigging in place in a puddle of crumpled newsprint. The scrutiny she endures is haughty but devoid of fear. As their door whooshes closed behind them, she decides her surveillance is over.

As she gathers up the newspaper, the elevator doors open again, and out strolls Charles VandenDungen. Turning left, he continues to far end of the hall and knocks on the last door—the pot door. He appears deep in thought, oblivious to her presence. She's paralyzed by the fatefulness of the moment. After all the planning and the waiting, she has no idea what to do.

He knocks again, impatiently. The door opens, and Marlon Herrington appears, wearing a shiny smoking jacket. Sophie reaches into her pocket. Aiming her cell phone, she snaps a picture.

18 SURLY BONDS

Sophie forwards the photo of Herrington and VandenDungen to Jen, and the next morning, it appears as Jen's computer desktop background.

"Take it down!" Sophie says. "Nobody can know about it."

"Everybody's going to know. That's the point."

In truth, they aren't sure what to do with it.

"You think the Dean is gay?" Jen says. "Not that there's anything wrong with that."

"Nothing in the world wrong with it," Sophie says. "Let's not even label it. Let's just say he enjoys meeting a man in a condo two or three times a week, staying a couple of hours, smoking weed, then leaving."

"Maybe they're discussing the outsourcing plan," Jen says.

"Could be."

They mull over their next step.

"What if we e-mail him," says Jen, "attach the picture and say something like, I understand the Board of Governors is scheduled to meet in three weeks?"

"That's blackmail," Sophie says. "You said we weren't going to do that, remember?"

"We have to do something," Jen says heatedly. "They've already interviewed me for my home study. I'm obligated to notify them if there's a change of circumstances. If something doesn't happen fast, I have to disclose I'm not being renewed."

Sophie's been thinking about her conversation with Marlon at the revolving restaurant. "I think we have a better use for this than blackmail."

Jen leans forward, all ears.

"According to Marlon," Sophie says, "he and the Dean talked about using Avalerion University as a feeder for the outsourced Skills Program."

Jen sputtered. "Avalerion? You mean that . . . that . . . monstrous internet thing where they steal students' money and pay the instructors minimum wage?"

"VandenDungen is going to sell it as cutting edge sophistication, and anyone who opposes it will be labeled a lazy, out-of-date technophobe. And don't forget."

"What?"

"Rosecliff steals students' money, too."

Jen appears thoughtful. "I think I see where you're going with this."

"VandenDungen has an obvious conflict of interest," says Sophie. "He demolishes a program the faculty just built, then replaces it with a 'product' purchased from his special friend."

They study each other ruefully, aware of the daunting distance between this fleeting moment of triumph and actually winning the battle.

"How are we going to expose it?" Jen says.

"It has to be done by tenured faculty," Sophie says. "I've got a couple in mind."

"Sophie, you shouldn't be doing this. If it doesn't work, you're finished here."

"Just take that picture off your screen. And wish me luck."

§

Amazingly, Arthur not only retains Mac's answers to the interrogatories, but he also manages to dictate them into proper form, and even arrange for his former secretary Marilyn to type them up and prepare the responses to be sent back to Fiordimondo. Sophie can't square the flawless performance with the man who thought they just planted a field to soybeans across from his townhouse.

Sitting in Arthur's living room reviewing the document, she reads over Mac's personal information. With his education, he'll be impressive on the stand.

Arthur bangs cupboard doors in the kitchen. "I'd offer you some pretzels if the little bastards would just reveal themselves to me," he says.

"Dad, you did a great job on these. Thank you."

"I guess you're over hating me," he says, "at least for the moment."

"What?"

"The day you were trying to convince me to go under the knife," he says. "You just spewed hatred."

"Oh, my God!"

"Here're the little pricks." Arthur dumps pretzel sticks into a bowl and shambles into the living room. He hands the bowl to her. "You do like pretzels, don't you?"

"I spewed hatred? Isn't it the other way around?"

He looks down at her, his eyebrows rising and falling like flippers in a pinball machine.

"You've always been so paranoid, Sophie. Thinking your mother and I loved Quinton more."

"You did."

"That's silly."

"Dad! After Quint left, when we were in the office that one day, you said, 'Quinton was my favorite.'"

"I didn't mean anything by it."

"You urged him to go to law school, but when I mentioned it, you discouraged me."

Arthur flops on the couch, lies down, and stares at the ceiling. "Ah, that's better." He closes his eyes.

219

"You said you didn't think I could do it. You said I'd never stick with it."

"Your track record was questionable. You were married to a criminal."

She sighs. It's clear that delving any deeper into the psychological aspects of their relationship is pointless. If she raises the possibility that her choices might be related to the Poe family dynamics, it would ignite another round of bickering. Arthur is in complete denial of his role in how Quinton turned out. In Arthur's eyes, Quinton was always a golden boy—smart, handsome, athletic, and mechanically inclined enough to serve as part-time hired man on the family farm. The other aspects of Quint's personality—his mild manner, his passive nature, his avoidance of conflict—were either invisible or unacceptable to Arthur. The pressure to follow in Arthur's footsteps and attend law school began early, was brought to bear often, and was met with little overt resistance—though Sophie, inveterate snoop that she was, once came across evidence of what her later research indicated was "psychological displacement": diaries filled with Quinton's florid penmanship describing elaborate fantasy adventures starring characters with names like Habeas Corpuscle, detailed sensual experimentation, and accounts of his own participation in school sporting events in which he referred to himself as the Third String Retard.

He attended a state university and law school, making mediocre grades and graduating a semester late after dropping out of school and disappearing for four months. His performance at the law firm was marked by what Arthur later characterized as "extreme disorganization," resulting in one client filing a complaint against the firm with the state bar. Despite firing him twice, Arthur couldn't shake the conviction that buried somewhere inside his dreamy, quirky son was a razor-sharp litigator capable of living up to the promise stenciled across the glass storefront: Poe and Poe, L.L.C. Hired back a third time, Quinton lasted six weeks, leaving behind the disaster that Arthur never recovered from.

"You've got yourself quite a plaintiff there," he says.

"His level of education is definitely a plus."

"That's not what I mean."

Wearing a sleeveless undershirt and boxers, Arthur shuffles over to the coffee table, looking like someone who has slipped the surly bonds of a nursing home. Hands trembling, he picks up a manila envelope and removes several sheets of lined paper, handing them to her.

"Look what he sent me."

Sophie scans the pages filled with Mac's chicken-scratch penmanship. He's written a list of 19 names and addresses, with notes under each entry. As she studies the notes, her pulse quickens.

"Is this what I think it is?" she says.

Arthur nods. "He told me he heard about other farmers whose crops have been affected. Typical thing a plaintiff says. Usually doesn't amount to anything. But I told him to see if he could find some. I didn't think he'd really come up with anybody."

Sophie jumps up. "This is unbelievable. This could really be something. Right? This could be—"

"Potential class action, correct."

Sophie hops and blithers unintelligibly for a few moments.

"He says he was going to bring us more plaintiffs. Something about catching them in a net."

"He's got an internet site for this?" Sophie says. Her mind conjures a scenario in which a convoy of 1,000 farmers riding tractors storms the federal building in the metropolis, led by her, roaring along on a Harley, and Arthur on one of those versatile little machines from The Scooter Store that can be obtained by Medicare recipients at little or no cost.

"I'll call him," she says excitedly. "I'd like to talk to him about the site."

"Now let's not get ahead of ourselves," Arthur says. "We're still at an early stage. In fact, we're behind. We haven't even served our request for admissions. Our deadline's coming up." He goes to his wall calendar. Tilting his head back, he squints.

Sophie waits. As sharp as he's been lately, he'll come up with it.

"Let's see now." Arthur's index finger bobs laterally from square to square, day to day; is he mentally counting? After he's gone through the equivalent of a month of squares, Sophie joins him at the wall.

"Dad, that's last December."

"True. Your mother's birthday is here." He points at a black star that marks the 16th.

"This is March," she says.

"I didn't say it wasn't. I was simply pointing out her birthday."

"I've got the case dates marked on my office calendar," Sophie says. "I'll call you when I get there and you can make a note of them."

Arthur faces her. Though he'd once been a good six inches taller, they now seem nearly eye-to-eye. She feels relieved that her father gives off no discernible body odor; he must be bathing regularly, cleaning his dentures.

The muscles of his jaw twitch as he glowers at her.

"What is today?" he says.

"The twelfth of March."

"As I recall, the court order gave us until the March 25th to complete all written discovery. You better get to work."

She returns to the living room, slips the interrogatories back in the envelope, and gathers her stuff.

"Do you have a calendar for this year?" she says. "I've got extras if you need one."

"The day I need a calendar on my wall is the day they shovel dirt on my carcass."

Arthur does possess a phenomenal memory and has been known to carry around an enormous amount of information in his head, including court schedules for multiple cases. But he doesn't realize what an essential backup Marilyn was all those years.

As she opens the door, Arthur calls out, "Would you be planning any stops at the market, Soapie?" Scooting up behind her, he hands her a scrap of paper. "If I could bother you to pick up a few things . . ."

The list looks more like a paragraph of prose than a column of discrete items.

Juice, orange, Minute Maid small frozen (no substitutes!)
Pepperidge Farm Oatmeal bread (squeeze to test freshness pls, if not <u>very</u> soft get Toasting White)
½ doz. brown eggs, cardboard carton if possible, if not, Styrofoam acceptable, must be large or extra large, no <u>cracked</u> ones
Kraft American cheese slices individually wrapped, beware of generics & cheese "food product" and other like synthetics
Sure Fine Premium Overnight Disposable Absorbent Underwear, Medium size

Her eyes linger on the last item. Sighing, she closes the door behind her.

19 BRUTAL HONESTY

Thunderheads crowd the horizon on the morning of the Rosecliff Law graduation ceremony. Faculty members don their regalia and line up according to seniority for the procession across campus. Sophie and Jen assume their positions at the end of the line, behind the new hires, as befits instructors with their conditional status. Sophie glares at the four Digitals ahead of her, all of whom joined the faculty after she did and now regard her with an exasperating blend of pity and superiority. Ten feet behind her, students grouse about anything and everything that crosses their minds: the cost of renting their robes, the oversize raindrops plopping on their velvet tams, their mountains of debt, their anemic employment prospects.

Sophie makes the mistake of glancing back. Jessica Forshee sneers at her. "This is bullshit," she announces. "We should be ahead of the faculty. The professors should kiss our asses." Beyond Forshee, toward the end of the line, James Yoder stands several feet to the right of the formation, looking like a walking skeleton. Sophie turns away before he can acknowledge her.

In the cavernous hall, the graduates' families and guests are already in their places. The faculty members seat themselves in the front rows in orderly fashion, and the students do the same on the opposite side of the aisle.

On the dais sit Dean VandenDungen, Christopher Paine, the Consultant, and Judge Tammy Franklin from the state Court of Appeals, an alumna of the higher-Ranked law school in the western part of the state. VandenDungen introduces the judge, who was selected by student vote to make the commencement address because of her conservative views, which appeal to the majority of Rosecliff's students. Sophie plans to escape to the recesses of her mind during the speech.

Judge Franklin is an imposing figure, nearly as broad and solid as a college linebacker, with close-cropped black hair. The students welcome her with an extended round of applause. Unlike the faculty, she has their respect. She's a real-world professional, they think; a genuine attorney, in a powerful, prestigious and well-compensated position, something they fear is out of their reach as Rosecliff Law grads. Their eyes light up as the judge straightens her papers and adjusts the microphone. She peers at them over her reading glasses.

"Good morning, losers," she says resoundingly. Pause. "Have I got your attention?"

Hell, yes. Even Sophie is alert and attentive.

"And now," the judge continues, "I suppose you expect an apology. Guess what? It's not coming."

Jen looks at Sophie with wide eyes. Sophie glances at Shane, who is in the front row. His pinched expression is painful even from twenty feet away.

"I'm known for my honesty," the judge says, "and I assume that's one reason you invited me to speak to you today. Some call it brutal honesty." She pauses for effect. "I call it doing you a favor."

The students erupt in laughter; this is what they expected from the tough-talking, independent-minded spirit—she's a libertarian after all—who managed not only to survive but to thrive in the sparsely populated part of the state where none of them wants to end up.

"So . . . congratulations, graduates. Today you enter a ruined profession. That's right; the legal profession is ruined. It's trashed. Hashtag: law sucks. It's been bought and paid for by the rich and powerful. They own the system. And they skim their talent from the top."

Oh, my freaking god, Sophie thinks. *My article is true!* She stares at the Dean, but he is stone-faced, eyes fixed on the judge.

"Rosecliff Law School has let you down. No doubt about it. The generations of lawyers who have come before you have let you down. That's a given. You came to law school with a dream. That was a mistake. Give it up. Get over it."

I like this, Sophie thinks, feeling philosophical and totally in sync with the judge. *All dreams must die. Why not theirs? Who made them special?*

"I realize you feel entitled to reap material rewards based on your education. Let me correct that misunderstanding. You are entitled to nothing."

The graduates fall silent. Some are frowning. Others appear dazed. In contrast, the families and friends of the graduates shift about noisily; a couple of babies are crying. Some of the older folks look traumatized.

"You didn't have to attend law school," the judge says. "You chose to. You didn't have to borrow a truck load of money to pay tuition and fees to Rosecliff University. You decided to. All the data was there for you to see. So you can't get a job? Suck it up. Go volunteer somewhere."

The Dean sits forward on his chair, appearing poised to leap up and tackle the judge. Kulter lays a hand on his arm.

Sophie is thinking that for all the truth the judge is telling, she isn't going far enough. She should add something about how students expect to be paid inflated salaries . . . like tenured professors.

"I have some advice for you," the judge says as she wraps up her remarks. "Forget the big firms in the big cities. You'll never get hired there. Seek the blue highways, go off the beaten paths. Go to the people who need your help—the little people. That's what will make you happy in the end."

Someone in the faculty section applauds. It's Mason Masonips, the transactional law specialist. Masonips graduated from Columbia University and worked as an associate at Gibson, Dunn, & Crutcher, one of the largest law firms in the world. Though his clients were corporations bent on hostile takeovers, he evidently feels it is important for someone to serve the masses who are denied meaningful access to the justice system.

As Judge Franklin sits down, a hissing noise emanates from the area where the students are seated. It continues as the Dean starts calling the graduates to the stage to receive their diplomas. As they cross the podium, they stop in front of Chris Paine and Kulter, who arrange a hood on each graduate's neck. Everything goes smoothly, and some of the students even smile as they move their tassels from one side of their tams to the other. The hissing dies down, and harmony appears to be restored until one of the graduates makes a show of tossing his diploma into a trash barrel as he returns to his seat. Though a few others follow his lead, the ceremony ends without completely blowing up.

§

Sophie receives word that a prestigious law review has accepted her Pork article. That takes a load off her mind. It means she should qualify for tenure—if the Dean honors his word. What are the chances? She has a witness to the Dean's promise, Associate Dean Christopher Paine. Paine has the backbone of a fish, but it's all she's got. In any event, she's done all she can in that arena, so she'll be able to face summer break with the single focus of getting a handle on the law suit against Meyeth Industries.

She has spent most of the day with Mac Higgins. They decided Arthur would work on the petition to join the new plaintiffs, while she prepares the admission requests for Meyeth. After the run-in with Ann Kulter the morning of the retreat, she couldn't very well meet with Mac at the law school; she has no choice but to have him come to her house, which means she's spent the evening before endeavoring to erase all traces of a life lived without regard for even the most basic principles of cleanliness and order.

Arriving home, she forces herself to take a searching and fearless inventory of her home's interior. The first thing she notices is that the rooms have all but lost their separate identities. Clothes, dirty and clean, folded and unfolded, lie on kitchen counters and the dining room table. Plates of half-eaten food and glasses lined with the scum of their former contents rest on the tables and floor of the living room and bedroom. Student papers carpet the bathroom. Files relating to Mac's case are strewn across the couch. And scattered among the clutter, of course, are Buggles's spiky black hairs, vomited mushes of grass, and dusty paw prints. Four hours and three glasses of wine later, Sophie collapses on the couch, surveys the results, and gives herself a thumbs-up. He'll never know.

At 10:00 a.m. Saturday, a gargantuan red pickup truck pulls into the driveway at Mud Flat. Its sidestep wheel wells overhang the edges of the crumbling driveway. Excessive and politically incorrect though it seems, the truck's lustrous enormity attracts Sophie in some indefinable way, bespeaking a heedlessness to fashion, a freedom of spirit, that the cramped and cautious energy savers of the Rosecliff law parking lot lack.

Sophie watches Mac approach her front door with his purposeful, forward-leaning stride and determinedly optimistic expression. Boots, blue jeans, white shirt, crisp sleeves following the curve of his biceps. He carries a plastic grocery bag.

As she opens the door, his soulful eyes meet hers. He steps inside. He exudes the same clean smell she remembers from their first meeting. "Nice place."

Buggles's toenails can be heard scrabbling on the wood floor. Hurtling around the corner from the bedroom, he skids to a stop, spots Mac, and explodes into a grating bark.

Mac squats down. "Hey, Bud, remember me?"

Buggles doesn't. His bark intensifies. Sophie tries to quiet him, but as usual he ignores her.

"No problem," Mac says. "I thought he might not remember." He removes a bag of pork rinds from the grocery sack and feeds Buggles a half-dozen or so. Buggles crunches them down, slobbering onto the couch cushions. Soon his eyes droop, his head sags, and he surrenders to snoring slumber. Sophie removes him to the recliner.

"I don't get that sleepy when I eat 'em," Mac says.

Dumping the rinds in a bowl, Sophie hands Mac a Red Bull, which he holds up, smiling.

"I like a woman who remembers a man's favorite drink."

A thrill passes through Sophie over his reference to her as *a woman*. Not that there is any doubt, but it's the way he says it.

Buckling down, they speak at length about the facts leading up to Mac's crop damage and his visit from the corporate suits. They'd been so condescending to him, using his complaint as an excuse for a trip away from the office in the private jet. It makes for quite an ugly picture. Plus he's brought her information on four more potential plaintiffs.

"Wait until you talk to Phil Rafferty," Mac says. "He documented everything with pictures.

As they wind down, Mac exhibits no sign of getting ready to leave.

"So, what have you got planned for the day?" he says.

She explains there's a party at the Dean's house that evening because, as he announced, "Lo Ming and I have never been properly received." Mac notes that Sophie doesn't appear to be in a partying mood, which prompts her to present an overly long and tedious narrative of the events trigged by VandenDungen's arrival at the law school. Mac listens attentively and asks questions along the way. At the end, he says, "You shouldn't have to put up with that."

"Thank you!"

"You're cute," he adds, then leans in and kisses her. Shocked though she is, she returns the kiss. He really knows how to kiss. He massages her lips with his, then steers his tongue in, gently opening her mouth, just a little. What a welcome relief from the all-too-common technique where a man opens his mouth wide as if he's eating a cheeseburger.

As they draw away from each other, she locks eyes with him and says, "I just violated the state and federal Code of Ethics for Lawyers."

He smiles. "Oops."

"No, really, kissing a client is about as improper as it gets. It's a major conflict of interest."

"But I have no problem with it," he says.

A knock on the front door rouses Buggles, who wakes up grouchy, and whose panicked, maniacal yaps shred their ear drums.

Standing on the front stoop is none other than Omar Patel. He is dressed, as he has ever since the retreat, in traditional Muslim pajamas; today, teal and black.

"Good morning, Sophie. Today is beautiful day, and one wonders if possibly you want to come out to play, but I see from monster truck perhaps you have guest."

Stepping out, Sophie closes the door behind her. She's certain it wouldn't be a good thing for Omar to know about her involvement in the dirty water litigation.

"You do have guest?" he says.

"It's just a friend visiting from out of town."

"He is man friend?"

"He's actually my cousin. We're kind of busy right now."

Omar flips up his shades. "Busy with cousin?"

"He's an accountant. He's helping me with my taxes."

He studies her with his penetrating, unmasking eyes. "Doing taxes. Good Sophie. Good citizen taxpayer." He frowns. "But, taxes due in April, and now is . . . after that."

The door opens. Mac extends his hand to Omar.

"Mac Higgins, Frankfort."

Omar introduces himself. "So, visiting for taxes? Good for you."

"Texas? No, Frankfort, about a hundred twenty miles northwest of here, up in Butler County."

"I mean good to help Sophie. Nice."

"She's the one helping me. I wouldn't have a hope without her."

Omar glances at them back and forth.

"You're a lawyer, right?" Mac says. "You must know how tough the big boys are."

"Okay." Omar taps his sunglasses back down into place. "Good luck with big boys." He walks away in a flash of color, a musky scent flowing behind him.

"When I first saw him," Mac says, "I thought he was some kind of sheik! That's why I came out! I never met one!"

§

The VandenDungens reside in a newer subdivision of tract castles on the south side of town, in which a decade ago, many mansion-size homes were erected in very quick order on tiny lots, with disproportionate attention paid to a mishmash of cosmetic detail and not enough, it's come to be known, to construction fundamentals such as soil testing, structural reinforcement, and sewer tie-ins. Thus, a few had begun to list, sink, or stink, but, as luck would have it, not the Dean's.

Despite the fact Sophie's been to his house once before, she has trouble picking it out without reference to the house next door, an immense three-story pink stucco with window balconies, owned by the proprietor of Bajahi Nail, a wispy Vietnamese-American slave driver by the name of Viet Cho, who goes by "Victor." In comparison, the Dean's gray two-story with Queen Anne turrets, colonial windows, and portico-on-stilts appears malnourished.

Because the houses are allotted so little land, and the driveways, designed to accommodate three or four cars, are so wide, parking space on the street is at a premium. There's room for only about two and a half cars to park on the street in front of the Dean's residence. Sophie arrives 30 minutes late to find the street lined solid with vehicles, many parked with bumpers touching or half their lengths blocking someone's driveway access.

She leaves the Escort what seems like a mile away and finally makes her sweaty entrance, to find the Dean and his wife looming in the foyer, tensely monitoring several matters—he, the number, identities, and arrival times of attendees; she, the complaints of various neighbors coming in on her cell phone, alternating with staticky messages from caterers in the distant kitchen, blaring out of a walkie-talkie.

Sophie attempts to dodge the duo, but the missus unexpectedly drops everything to greet her with the chilliest demeanor Sophie has ever encountered in the host of a party. Having met Lo Ming at various functions, Sophie knows her to be a master of the double-edged compliment. At an alumni celebration, she took Sophie's hands, looked her up and down, and said, "You look so much better! You've lost weight!" Now she exclaims, "I'm so glad you managed to get here before dinner service!" As usual, Lo Ming wears a form-fitting black outfit, accessorized by a massive pewter contraption around her neck that does violence to the concept of a necklace.

Sophie makes her way through a great room and down a hallway to the kitchen, drawn by tantalizing cooking aromas. She enters a room that is like no kitchen she's ever seen, a complete house unto itself, containing its own living room with fireplace, media bay, dining area, breakfast bar, and restroom.

Predictably, the drinkers among the faculty cluster tightly at the open bar, lubricating themselves at breakneck pace in preparation for pretending to be enjoying themselves as they "receive" the Dean and his wife. Sophie heads toward the group, where Wally Shane and Paul Singer are conversing intensely about the Dean's recent job offer to Rachel Green

"Meta my ass," Shane whispers harshly.

"Now he's talking about funding her with soft money, to the tune of $500,000," Singer says. "Supposedly from the profit he's going to make off our new Rosecliff law office."

"Meyeth Law Office at Rosecliff," says Shane. "So fucking pretentious."

"According to Bev, he's already prepared the press release," puts in Elliott Ramsey.

Sophie notices that the Digitals, congregating around the reclining Thea Volley, have already separated themselves from the rest of the guests. Not one of them holds a beverage in hand, lest they be mistaken for weak and cowardly academics who, unable to make it in the real world, drown their insecurities in alcohol. So superior they don't even need hydration!

Pouring another glass of wine, Sophie sidles up to Wally Shane, who's reporting to Manny Delgado on the condition of his large intestine following a worrisome touch of rectal bleeding.

"The doctor says he didn't see anything significant," Shane says, "but what does he mean by 'significant'?"

"I'm glad to find you two gentlemen together," Sophie says. "Does the Internal Affairs Committee still exist or was it just thrown together for my stalker case?"

Shane and Manny look at each other and shrug.

"We haven't had any business before us since your case, *cariña*," Manny says. "Is he bothering you again?"

She shakes her head. It occurs to her that except at the graduation, she hasn't seen James Yoder for a while. That should be a positive thing, but for some reason it gives her a creepy feeling.

"I'm requesting an investigation into a different matter," she says. "This goes all the way to the top."

Manny laughs. "Like Watergate, eh?"

Shane appears concerned, and a little excited. "You know something about VandenDungen?"

She begins to describe the events leading up to the snapshot of Marlon and VandenDungen at Yachtkeepers. She's in the middle of recounting their dinner at the revolving restaurant when the Dean steps up on the raised hearth and clinks his glass.

"I have an announcement to make," he says. "We're going to have a surprise guest join us for dinner."

Sophie has a sick feeling in her stomach. The dean's surprises are spirit sinkers.

"He ought to be here any minute," the Dean continues. "It's one of our benefactors, Lorne Meyeth. I don't need to remind you of his importance. Be sure to give him a warm welcome when he arrives."

A chill runs down Sophie's spine, as if the Dean has announced the imminent arrival of Jeffrey Dahmer for dinner. It's one thing to think about the Meyeth invasion of Rosecliff in the abstract; it's another to have one of them under the same roof. Sophie has seen the Triplets only in web pictures. She can't tell them apart. They blend together into a single generic whole: jowly, Caucasian male senior citizens in the Dick Cheney mold.

Just as she's about to finish telling Shane and Manny her story, a commotion at the front door draws their attention. Lorne Meyeth has arrived.

"Fuck this!" Shane says. "I'm leaving." But he stays put.

Manny makes a beeline for the hubbub. Sophie can see Lorne Meyeth's silver hair, serious face, and flat, dark eyes. She expects to feel a jolt of fight-or-flight adrenaline, given that a representative of the Enemy has entered her zone, but her senses are wine-dulled. VandenDungen's arm is around Meyeth's shoulders. Manny shakes his hand and chats him up, managing to draw out a rigid smile that barely masks the sour countenance. Meyeth glances around at the faculty members. Perhaps Sophie is projecting her own feelings, but she intuits that Lorne Meyeth isn't thrilled to be here. She wonders what he really thinks of the present company, particularly in light of the recent, ubiquitous bad publicity about law professors.

Before long VandenDungen is back up on the hearth, clinking on a glass.

"Dinner is served," he announces. "Please be seated in the dining room."

§

Six long tables fill the room to capacity, placed so close together that persons seeking to sit anywhere other than the margins face a daunting challenge. The spaces between the back-to-back chairs barely permit one average-size person to squeeze through. The two-story room fills with a cacophony of grunts, scrapes, screeches, and the clattering of wood against wood. At one point, the corner of a table punches a hole in a Sheetrock wall.

Sophie manages to slip in next to Wally Shane. The chair seat is too low, such that the table's edge presses at top of her rib cage, giving the impression that she'll be dining on her own breasts. Shane grumbles non-stop about the ill-conceived arrangement.

Across the table, Barbara Kitchen shrieks her displeasure, launching into a homily about the basics of entertaining—"Sufficient space for one's guests is rule number one!"—then declaiming at large, "this is the worst party the law school has ever given, I can assure you." Behind Sophie, the Digitals quietly critique the VandenDungens' home, commenting on the "outdated ostentation."

"Anyhow, as I was saying," Sophie whispers to Shane.

"Yeah, yeah, yeah," Shane replies irritably.

"What would be the proper way for me to report a situation to the Internal Affairs Committee for investigation?"

Shane peers at her over his wire rims. "I'm not sure what the problem is. You were talking about a restaurant moving around and some guy who works for Avalerion University."

Sophie picks up where she left off, recounting that Marlon Herrington and VandenDungen discussed a partnership between Rosecliff and Avalerion to replace Rosecliff's current Skills Program with adjunct distance instructors, paid at poverty level.

Shane chokes, spraying gin and tonic out his nose.

"Who does VandenDungen think he is?" He coughs, then slurps some more gin and tonic.

Catering staffers are passing plates of food from the ends of the tables. Swearing abounds, as elbows collide and brown sauce spills.

Clink, clink, clink. The Dean is up again, this time beneath the arch between the dining room and foyer, poised to speechify about the honored guest and the institution's gratitude.

Sophie decides to finish her story. As she describes her surveillance, Shane appears skeptical. When she tells him about the photograph, he snorts with disbelief, prompting Sophie to pull out her cell phone and show him the picture of the Dean and Herrington, which so startles Shane, he shoves himself away from the table, ramming into the back of Thea Volley's chair. A wail goes up, climaxing in an outright scream.

"Oh my God, oh my God," Volley howls, clutching her belly.

Bedlam ensues, as all who are able leap up and rush around

helplessly since the tables block access to the lady in distress.

Still holding her phone, Sophie notices the Dean glaring at her as if she is responsible for the chain of events. Strictly speaking, she is, but talk about blowing something out of proportion!

Shane leans over Thea Volley, his face gray with worry. Sophie studies the position of Shane's chair and the angle of Volley's. At most, Shane's sudden movement jarred Volley and the fetus; it couldn't possibly have caused harm to either party.

"Shane," she murmurs, "it's okay."

Feeling an alien presence, Sophie spins around to find the dean close behind her. His head seems massive and inhospitable to lifeu. She studies its landscape, searching for the now-familiar signs of imminent rage. The fundamentals are there—the pinched grimace and the angry squint, the burgundy blotches winging out from the nose, darkening as he stares down at the picture on her phone of himself and Marlon Herrington. She can feel heat coming off his body. She shuts down the picture.

Someone yells, "Quiet!" Lorne Meyeth stands in the archway, looking surprisingly nondescript for a billionaire. He begins speaking, but in such a quiet voice that no one can hear. He continues mumbling away, apparently not caring whether he's heard.

"God damn it!" Delgado is on his feet. "Have you no respect? This man is saving our asses! Shut up and listen to him."

Meyeth persists in his quiet speech.

"Speak up, sir!" Delgado says.

". . . not my cup of tea. But despite public perception, we do try to give back," Meyeth says. "And my brothers can be very persuasive. So we offered to start the law office at Rosecliff, to create a pipeline of revenue through which we can funnel needed funds to the law school, while still making a buck for ourselves, of course." He scans the faces of the professors. "Are there any questions?"

There is only one question on the professors' minds; in matters such as this—billionaires privatizing academic law clinics—they think as one. What will it do to their Academic Freedom—code for doing as they please, when they please, answering to no one? But they cannot ask that question to Lorne Meyeth because he and his brothers believe in another kind of freedom: the freedom to maximize wealth at any cost. The two concepts are not compatible.

So the room is silent.

Finally, Christopher Paine raises his hand. "My understanding is you intend for the new clinic to represent companies. As you know, our clinic has traditionally represented a different type of client: indigent criminal defendants, poor families in crisis, etc. I'm wondering if the law office will be providing those kinds of pro bono services."

"I guess you didn't hear what I said before," Meyeth says.

Paine shakes his head, along with everyone else. Barbara Kitchen says, "None of us heard what you said because you were barely speaking aloud!"

"I *said* . . . is this loud enough?! I *said* that I don't have a whole lot of respect for academia or the professors who make their living in it. I *said* that I take offense at the elitists who emotionally waterboard students into caring about nothing but getting abortions and legalizing marijuana. Supporting this treacherous agenda is not my cup of tea, but—"

"Your brothers talked you into it!" Sophie exclaims, startling herself. But she prided herself on being a good listener.

"So, again," Meyeth says through gritted teeth, "are there any questions?"

No, none.

20 GIRL PROBLEMS

"We are pioneers," the Dean proclaims at the last faculty meeting of the semester. "We are plowing raw ground here. While others are following the old models, we're taking a quantum leap. Is our model guaranteed to be successful?" He regards his audience with something like affection or, at least, a new kind of tolerance. "Yes! It is! Does that surprise you? That I can say success is guaranteed? When does that ever happen?"

Sophie *is* surprised, that a plan that seemed dubious at best is now scheduled to become reality over the summer. Perhaps she should revise her article's scope to include a section titled Professors Are Pork.

"It's guaranteed," the Dean explains, "because the Meyeths will funnel to the Law Office as much business as it can handle and, hurrah, hurrah, the resulting revenues! How can it not be a winner? Especially when we are going to have leadership of the caliber of Cleve Fiordimondo!"

A squawk involuntarily escapes Sophie's lips. "What?!"

"Lorne Meyeth called me this morning. He's arranged for the Clinic to have top-drawer management."

The clouds are dark on the horizon, casting shadows over her future. It looks probable that Arthur, with her support, will be pitted against the Meyeth Law Office at Rosecliff.

§

"Arthur Poe for Plaintiff Mac Higgins, your Honor."

Hippolytus "Hippo" Kotsiopoulos squints at them from the bench, resembling the portly mammal for which he was nicknamed. Kotsiopoulos is a senior federal judge; he's semi-retired but available to sit for cases assigned him by the chief judge of the district. Several of Sophie's students have clerked for Kotsiopoulos after graduation so she knows things about him that are less than encouraging. Reportedly he can sleep with his eyes open. In addition, or perhaps in connection with this trait, Kotsiopoulos decides many of his civil cases without considering any evidence. When petitions are filed, his law clerks peruse them, condense them to a paragraph or two, and read the summary to the judge, whereupon Kotsiopoulos responds with his "gut reaction," labeling the case as a "loser," a "winner," or "manure."

"Is that you, Arthur?" he says.

"It is, your Honor."

"I didn't know you were still alive."

Today they're in court on their motion to certify Mac's case as a class action. Meyeth contends there are too few plaintiffs and not enough common issues of law and fact to support the class.

Rising, Cleve Fiordimondo barks out his name. "I'm still alive, too, Judge."

"Whaddaya know," Kotsiopoulos says.

Next to Cleve Fiordimondo sit two recent Rosecliff Law graduates. One of them is Jessica Forshee, the slacker who accused Sophie of fucking up her life by changing the number of points possible on a quiz.

Hands splayed on the counsel table for support, Arthur mutters, "Idiot!" He pats the Kleenex wad stuck to his cheek. When Sophie stopped at the duplex to pick him up, he was standing in the bathroom wearing only a towel around his waist, pressing a washcloth to his face in an attempt to staunch the bleeding from a shaving nick.

"The fucker won't stop!" he shouted.

When he removed the cloth, the wound spurted blood out of proportion to its miniscule size. Sophie realized the bleeding wouldn't stop because Arthur had been taking blood thinners since his stroke.

"I don't understand it!" he said. "I've never bled like this before, God damn it! This is bullshit!"

On the way to the courthouse, he squirmed and cursed, checking his reflection and dabbing his cheek. Just when he thought he'd conquered it, the stream would start trickling again, and a new round of swearing would begin.

As they pulled into the parking lot, he shouted, "I can't go in like this!" He fretted and steamed awhile, until Sophie told him she was going in alone since their hearing was in ten minutes. He tore off a piece of tissue and pressed it to the wound till it stayed, then exited the car with surprising speed and agility, catching up to her easily with a speedy, stiff-legged strut.

"Arthur," Kotsiopoulos says, "what's the matter with your face?"

"Fiordimondo punched me in the parking lot," Arthur says. "He told me to drop this case or else."

Sophie freezes. She hoped that Arthur could handle himself in court, but what an inappropriate thing to say!

Kotsiopoulos looks more alert than he has since the hearing began. He stares at Arthur a moment then chuckles.

"Why didn't you hit him back?" he asks.

"I didn't want to overpower him, Judge."

"Is that all you've got to say?"

Arthur throws back his bony shoulders.

"Your Honor, in Reardon versus General Motors, the court made clear it would not countenance attempts by large companies to force individuals with the same injury to sue the companies one by one. The benefit of the doubt is to go to the claimants. We've got 73 plaintiffs who've experienced the same type of pollution on their farms, resulting from Meyeth Industries' dumping of waste

240

into the Ichiwaw River. We ask the court to certify this group as a proper class."

"Hmm," the judge says. "Does that little girl with you have anything to say?"

"Judge, this is my daughter Sophie. She's not a little girl, she's a law professor. Do you have anything to say, Sophie?"

"No." Sophie's face feels hot with embarrassment over her father's mistake. "Year-to-year provisional instructor" is nothing like "professor," but her father doesn't care. He's proud of her.

"Your turn, Cleve," the judge says.

Fiordimondo stands at the lectern and smiles at Kotsiopoulos with big, perfect teeth. Sophie wonders whether his real teeth were as large and protruding; it doesn't seem as if the false ones fit his mouth, but why would a person choose replacements bigger than the originals?

"Judge, we've outlined our position thoroughly in our brief," Fiordimondo intones, "but the sum and substance is if Mr. Higgins believes he's been wronged, he needs to prove that on his own and not try to throw dirt on the molehill by piling on with a bunch of disgruntled folks he rounded up on the internet."

Leaning back in his chair, Judge Kotsiopoulos stares at the ceiling. The minutes tick past. The judge's clerk picks up a magazine and leafs through it. Cleve Fiordimondo busies himself organizing files in his briefcase. His two young associates are texting on their phones. Arthur sits completely still. Sophie can hear his shallow breathing. Every few breaths, he attempts a deep, relaxing one but more often than not fails.

Sophie isn't sure what they're waiting for. A court wouldn't rule from the bench on an issue like class certification. The judge's clerks will read the briefs, talk to the judge about how the motion should be decided, then draft an opinion for the judge's approval. She stands, planning to interrupt the judge's reverie to request permission to leave. Clasping her arm, Arthur pulls her down.

After thirty minutes, the judge jerks forward, appearing startled to see the lawyers. He sips from his coffee cup.

"The court grants plaintiff's motion to represent the class. Let the record so reflect. Written opinion to follow."

§

Flush with victory, Arthur chatters the whole way home. They stop at Dairy Queen for a celebratory milkshake, and Arthur calls Mac to tell him the news. He hands the phone to Sophie. "He wants to talk to you."

"Sophie, thank you!"

"My dad did most of the work on the certification."

"It never would've gotten this far if you hadn't listened to me. You're just a terrific girl!"

Sophie ponders the fact she's been called "girl" twice in two hours. Feminists fought for decades not to be called "girl." Though Judge Kotsiopoulos ruled in their favor, his reference to her as "little girl" sticks in her craw, not that it is anywhere near the first time she's been condescended to by a judge. Conversely, Mac's use of the word makes her smile, bringing the label back to pleasant neutrality and beyond. To her chagrin, her brain spontaneously sings out "I enjoy being a girl" from *Flower Drum Song*.

§

As they turn onto Arthur's cul-de-sac, Sophie notices a car parked in front of the duplex. "Looks like you have a visitor."

Arthur focuses on the street ahead.

"Ah, it's James. He said he'd be stopping by."

At that moment, James Yoder, with his bald head and emaciated frame, emerges from the car and watches them approach.

Sophie's heart skips a beat.

"He's such an interesting fellow," Arthur says. "You know, he's the one who found me when I passed out. He's been a great help to me."

"What?"

From behind his car, Yoder stares at her. His eyes, enlarged by his cadaverously thin face, burn into hers like those of a dying man trying to stay connected to the living.

242

She slams the car into park and turns to her father.

"What do you mean he helps you?"

Smiling, Arthur waves to Yoder, then frowns at her.

"What's the matter with you?"

"Does he stop by a lot?"

Opening the passenger door, Arthur gingerly grasps each leg and lifts it out. James comes to his aid, offering his arm for Arthur to hold to pull himself up, then guiding him with a light touch on his shoulder as the two men cross the lawn to Arthur's front door.

By the time Sophie enters, James has settled in the old recliner with his feet up, as Arthur searches for something in the kitchen. She finds herself in a rare state of speechlessness. While Arthur putters around, describing the hearing, James trains his feverish gaze on her. The urge to flee is so powerful she has to root herself in place by force of will, to consider her options rationally. She can't just walk out, leaving this mental case alone with her father.

"Got it!" Arthur shouts, holding up a red canister.

"Awesome," James says.

"Dad, could I talk to you a minute?"

He doesn't seem to hear her.

"Dad? Do you have your hearing aids turned up?"

Arthur scoops coffee into the basket and sprinkles something on top. She joins him in the kitchen.

"What is that?" Sophie says.

"My special blend," Arthur says, "a little cinnamon, a pinch of saccharin, maybe a bit of nutmeg."

"That was red pepper."

"What?" He peers closely at the label. "Shit! That's impossible! I always keep my cinnamon right there! Who moved it?" He glances over his shoulder. "Did you by chance move the cinnamon, James?"

Sophie feels light-headed. Her stomach seems to float up to her throat. "Why would he move your cinnamon?"

Rising, James approaches them, his shoulders hunched forward. "You ran out," he says. "I bought you a new one." Reaching behind Arthur, he removes a bottle of cinnamon from the shelf.

"Here it is."

Squeezing his eyes closed, Arthur rubs his forehead. He leans against the counter for support.

Up close, James's skin resembles a peeling yellow onion.

"You've been buying him groceries?" Sophie says.

"He says you've been busy. I was trying to help you out."

Sophie slaps his face as hard as she can. "Get out of here."

Eyes still shut, Arthur murmurs, "I don't remember running out of the cinnamon."

James stays put. Sophie attempts to read his expression. It seems like a mixture of gratitude and . . . revulsion? He raises his chin, as if daring her to hit him again.

She smacks him on the other side of his face.

"Get!"

"Sophie!" Arthur says. "What in the hell is wrong with you? Stop it!"

She raises her hand again. James backs away doubtfully, like a dog whose owner has turned on it.

"I'm reporting you to the police," she says as he scampers out the door.

"The *police*?" Arthur says. "What are you doing? He's been of great assistance."

She runs outside. "If you ever come here again, I'll . . . I'll shoot you!" She reenters the condo, slamming the door behind her.

"Jesus Christ, Sophie! What in the name of God has gotten into you?"

Arthur is pale and shaky. She leads him to the chair and sits him down. "I was making coffee," he says weakly.

Sitting across from him, she fills him in on James Yoder. He's reluctant to believe there's anything wrong with his helpmate.

"I was thinking about making it official," he says, "putting him on the payroll."

When she mentions the poems James sent her, Arthur says, "You never could take a compliment."

"Dad, he drew genitals on them."

It takes her half an hour to convince Arthur that Yoder is using

244

him as a way to get close to her.

"I did wonder a couple of times why he wanted to hang out with me so much," he admits.

"Hang out?"

"He's been coming over to watch TV in the evenings."

"Why didn't you mention that?"

Arthur looks at her levelly. "Why would I? It's my life."

They sit in silence. Arthur's sagging demeanor makes him look a decade older than he did in court. He is clearly devastated that his new friend has turned out to be an imposter.

"He did ask a lot of questions about you," he says. "I thought he was just making conversation."

Sophie rises. "Should I make some coffee, Dad?"

"I'm tired."

She takes the hint. "Please let me know if he comes over here again," she says at the door.

Clicking on the TV, staring dully at the crawls, Arthur does not respond.

21 I WANT MY MEAT

Shane had told Sophie he planned to talk to other senior faculty members and take Herrington/VandenDungen conflict-of-interest issue to Vice President Wickendale, but weeks have passed since the Dean's party, and she's heard nothing. In fact, the entire law school building seems to be enveloped in a hush. As the sky darkens, even the rumbling thunder sounds muted, as if filtered through cotton.

Sophie decides to pay a visit to Shane. She knocks on his office door and gets no response, so she peeks in. Shane sits on his couch between two stacks of paper, hands on his knees, staring vacantly at his bookshelves with bloodshot eyes.

"What's wrong?" Sophie says.

"My father died."

"Oh, no!"

"I just got back from visiting him. He seemed okay, a little weak, maybe, but he's been worse. His next door neighbor went over this morning and found him in bed. Dead."

Moving one of the paper towers to the floor, Sophie plops next to him. She puts her arm around his shoulders, and he leans against her.

"I should have stayed another day," he says.

"He would have died anyway," Sophie says.

"We can't know that. He seemed pretty happy to have me around. I leave, then he dies."

"It was his time."

"Bullshit."

They remain together on the couch as the minutes pass. Shane's ticking clock sounds as loud as a hammer striking a nail. As she pats his shoulder, Sophie's thoughts wander to Arthur. A series of scenarios run through her mind's eye in which she discovers his dead body, first in his front yard, then in the recliner, then on the kitchen floor. James Yoder suddenly pops into the picture, and the scenes replay; this time, James stands over her father, regarding her with his searing, desperate gaze.

"The arrangements are already made," Shane says. "But I need to go back down and get everything organized."

"What can I do?"

He thinks it over. "Would you be able to come to the viewing Thursday? I could use the support."

"Of course."

At the door, she hesitates, remembering why she came. She tries to weigh the importance of busting the dean against the gravity of Shane's loss, but that doesn't work; they are two unrelated things. The question is whether Shane will be offended if she brings up the subject. She decides he'll understand.

"Have you talked to anybody about the Dean?"

"Oh, shit. I meant to tell you. I talked to Chris Paine."

Sophie's heart sinks. Paine doesn't have the acorns for the job. Being a conflict avoider himself, he'll find a way to deflect the problem, possibly by blaming Sophie.

Shane produces an anemic chuckle. "He seemed more concerned about you than the Dean. He was all about how obsessed you are, following VandenDungen and taking pictures."

Granted, it does seem kind of obsessive. That's why context is so important.

"Did you talk to anyone else?" she says.

"Kitchen and van Krist."

Whenever she hears the name "Kitchen," Sophie's hackles go up, and her fight-or-flight response kicks in. If there are sides to be chosen, Kitchen will never be on hers. Be van Krist is a different matter—fair, open-minded, and unafraid.

"Why'd you pick Barbara?" she asks. "She hates me. And she's leader of the VandenDungen cheer squad."

"She's a pit bull when it comes to protecting the reputation of the law school. She didn't believe the story when I first told her, but I told her you have a photo of them, and that caught her attention."

They discuss the potential fallout from VandenDungen seeing the picture at the party. Shane brushes it off.

"In the chaos of the moment, he probably didn't even know what he was seeing."

"If you were having rendezvous with someone and you saw a picture of it, wouldn't you know?"

A red tint crawls up Shane's neck and spreads over his freckled face.

"*Are* you having rendezvous with somebody?"

A smile wriggles his lips, fighting against the pain tugging at the corners of his mouth.

"Two people, actually," he says.

"You're dating *two* women?"

The smile wins out, even as his eyes pools with tears.

"I've been spending some time with Jen and Dalton."

Sophie can't hide her surprise, recalling Jen's negative comments about Shane, especially his "neurotic preoccupation with his health." She wonders what's changed.

Shane's droopy visage lights up as he talks about Dalton.

"He's an unbelievable kid. Bright. Funny. For some reason, we just hit it off. And he loves rocks!" Standing, he removes a reddish fist-size rock from a shelf. "We found this last time we were out." With his shining eyes and high color, Shane looks like a kid himself. "Dalton knew what this is! Sioux quartzite!"

As he studies the rock, his face falls. "Well, I guess I need to get going."

"So what are Kitchen and van Krist going to do?"

"They're going to try to get together and decide this week."

"Are they planning to talk to Wickendale?"

"I assume."

When Sophie returns to her office, there's a message from Vice-President Wickendale's secretary on her answering machine, saying Wickendale wants to meet with her. Perfect! She calls his office and sets an appointment for first thing the following morning, then heads for van Krist's office. A note taped to his door states his classes are cancelled due to a family emergency. Her sole remaining option is to pay a visit to Barbara Kitchen, but she'd rather cut off a finger. She decides meeting with Wickendale alone might be the best way to get her story across anyway.

§

The office of the Rosecliff University president is a hornet's nest of complacency and conflict avoidance. The president, Calvin Hooghly, enjoys being off campus on frequent "fund-raising tours," visiting alumni who reside near one of *Golf Digest*'s Top 100 Greatest Golf Courses, preferably one in the top quartile. Resolution of faculty issues rests with the vice-president for academic affairs, Donald Wickendale, an avuncular walrus who manages to combine exemplary accessibility with a peculiarly catatonic affect. He possesses a variety of facial expressions calculated to convey he is listening attentively, but it's well known he maintains surface affability by gliding along on automatic pilot, routinely excreting all memory of a visit after it ends.

Never having been to the Vice President's office, Sophie is unprepared to negotiate the maze of administrative checkpoints required to gain entry to the inner sanctum of Donald Wickendale. In fact, she notes as she takes one right angle after the next, she hadn't realized that running a university as poorly as Rosecliff has been run requires this multitude of administrative layers identified on bracketed plastic name plates tacked up in the corridors.

In the reception area that leads into Wickendale's office, she notes the luxuriousness of the new-smelling plush carpet beneath her feet. What happened to the institutional linoleum tile that was supposed to be standard issue for public universities? And what's with the fancy oil paintings on the wall where cheap generic prints should be? Between two such paintings hangs a framed newspaper article from four years ago whose headline proclaims "Rosecliff University Ranks In Top Fifty of Small to Medium Size Midwestern Universities." High-end carpeting and original artwork? With that dubious Ranking?

Ten minutes later, sitting across from Wickendale, Sophie decides he doesn't resemble a walrus so much as a miniature Jackie Gleason—same bloodhound countenance, same pear-shaped silhouette, but compacted. The flesh ringing his middle is so massively packed and inflexible he's like a late-term pregnant woman unable to bend at the waist; he leans back against his chair rather than sits in it, so that in order to look at a visitor, he has to crane his head forward, but this is impossible due to the circumference of his neck. Sophie is put in mind of a strapped-in Hannibal Lecter riding the wheels of a hand truck like so much human cargo.

Fortunately, the Vice President knows precisely how to swivel his chair sideways so he can see her out of the corner of his eye.

"How are you doing, Sophie?"

"Pretty well."

"Looks like a beautiful day out there."

Sophie follows Wickendale's gaze; he's right, the weather has cleared. The early morning sparkles, sunlight glinting off the freshly washed leaves of the oak and walnut trees.

"That was some storm yesterday afternoon," he says.

Sophie nods.

"I'll bet we got two inches of rain. Maybe more. We sure needed it."

As Sophie formulates a statement that might jump start the conversation, her phone rings, the ID indicating it originated at the law school. With Wickendale eyeing her sideways, she excuses herself and answers it.

"Sophie, it's Elliott. I'm sitting here with Beverly. I thought you'd want to know that Ann Kulter just left the Dean's office. Are you with Wickendale?"

"Mm hmm."

"She's headed over there. I overheard them saying something about fracking."

Sophie's mind races as she realizes this little tête-à-tête has nothing to do with the VandenDungen/Herrington conspiracy.

The door opens and Ann Kulter enters, a lockjaw smile pasted on her face.

"Ms. Poe," Wickendale says, "I asked you here because it's been brought to my attention that you are spear-heading a legal campaign against our most generous benefactors." In the struggle to keep her within sight, the VP's eyes jiggle in their sockets as they hit their absolute leftward limit. "I find it hard to believe you would betray Rosecliff like that."

"I'm withdrawing from the case," Sophie says. "Continuing would be a conflict of interest."

"Well, that's the right thing to do," Wickendale says.

"Ron," the Consultant says, "the lawsuit isn't the only issue we've had with Miss Poe."

Wickendale's eyebrows shoot up.

"I'm here today," Sophie says, "to discuss a serious matter that goes to the highest levels of the law school."

She addresses Wickendale. "I believe you're aware of Dean VandenDungen's proposal to dismantle the Legal Skills Program and to outsource the classes to contract workers."

"Ugghh," says Wickendale, as his eyes spring back to dead center, resulting in him staring at the transom over his office door. "I'm aware the Dean is responding to budgetary restrictions in a variety of ways."

Kulter leans over to whisper in Wickendale's ear. Unmistakably, she means for the Vice President to look down her shirt at her gel-filled chest baubles. Which he appears to enjoy doing.

"You hit a student in the face?" Wickendale says to Sophie. "When he was getting into his car?"

"Actually, he was in my father's living room."

Sophie recognizes she's being led away from her point by gameswoman Kulter. She feels her anger grow, even as she digs deep into her stored files on the psychology of assertiveness. She recalls a vignette she read in an old self-help book, about a man who bought some steaks and ground beef at the grocery store; when he got home, he couldn't find his meat purchases. Returning to the store, he explained the situation to the check-out clerk, meeting with skepticism, excuse-fabrication, and generally non-responsive and guilt-inducing reactions. The strategy suggested by the author was the Broken Record approach, which involved repeatedly asserting what you want without getting irritated or angry. Every dodge by a store employee was to be countered with a pro forma acknowledgement of the employee's statement, followed by a simple, direct mantra, *I want my meat*. In an illustrative mock dialog, one assistant manager says, "You'll remember later where you put your purchases. Come back tomorrow if you can't find them," to which the assertive role model says, "I understand why you feel that way, but I want my meat." Another suggested the customer had left the purchase in his car, to which the response was, "It is not in my car, and I want my meat." And on and on for several pages. *I want my meat*.

As Kulter continues whispering in Wickendale's ear, Sophie says, "I want the dean investigated."

"You assaulted a student!" Kulter says.

"I understand how you feel, but I want the dean to be investigated. He is being improperly influenced."

Kulter discharges one of her panting laughs. "I guess you didn't hear me or if you did, you were unable to process it."

"I want VandenDungen and Herrington investigated for conflict of interest. They have a personal, perhaps an intimate relationship, and VandenDungen is throwing business Herrington's way."

Wickendale manages to sit forward somewhat, though at any moment he might pop back like a bent tube balloon. "Did you say *intimate* relationship?"

"That's just stupid," says Kulter.

"I did say intimate relationship, and I think it should be investigated." Sophie opens the envelope she brought and removes an 8" x 10" print of the Yachtkeepers photo. What she's lost in clarity by enlarging it, she's gained in implication of impropriety, stemming chiefly from the juxtaposition of VandenDungen's business suit against Herrington's shiny pot-smoking jacket. She hands it to Wickendale, who studies it.

Sophie watches the Consultant, whose puzzled expression parallels the VP's. A new emotion—shock, sadness, distress—attempts to break through her Botoxed countenance but remains trapped like a swarm of insects beneath the plasticized flesh.

"So?" Kulter sputters. "All I see is Chaz standing in the hall and another man opening a door. This is supposed to mean something?"

Sophie smiles; the Broken Record tactic has worked. She's succeeded in refocusing the conversation on VandenDungen.

"The man in the photo is Marlon Herrington, an executive at Avalerion University," she says. "Herrington told me he and the dean are working on outsourcing the Skills Program to Avalerion." She removes a sheet of paper from her envelope and hands it to Wickendale. "This is a spreadsheet that puts the photo in context. It shows the visits the dean made to Herrington's address over a three-week period and how long he stayed."

Kulter's lips tremble as she takes in the data. Wickendale's labored breathing fills the silence.

"Are you suggesting Dean VandenDungen is trading the outsourcing contract for sexual favors?" he says.

"I don't know what they've been doing, but these meetings seem to be personal."

Wickendale picks up the phone. "Donna, can you bring me the memos I got from Dean VandenDungen on the budget cuts?"

A few minutes later, the Vice President is flipping through papers in a file, discharging a series of noises involving flapping lips, batting eyes, moist snorts, and one outburst customarily associated with the bathroom. Finally, he looks up.

"I'll need time to study this," he says.

"Before I go," Sophie says, "I want to explain what happened with James Yoder." She relates the events involving Yoder and Arthur. "I was scared when I found out he'd infiltrated my father's life."

"I don't blame you," Wickendale says.

"Put *that* in context," Kulter says. "There's a history of exploitation here. Or should I say sexploitation."

"I was acquitted!"

Wickendale addresses Kulter. "Yes, wasn't that matter resolved?" He toddles to his chair and leans back into it. "So, Sophie, I've heard about your article. I'm interested in your solution to the problem of undue influence of judges."

"Well, actually, I suggest a Third Way . . ."

22 MORE HEARING

Following her cage fight with the Consultant in Wickendale's office, Sophie assumes that she's successfully handed off the VandenDungen/Herrington matter to the proper authorities. So when one Remy Terwilliger phones her and prattles in a British accent about being chair of a university committee undertaking an investigation, she experiences a senior moment.

"So when would be a convenient time?" he says.

"To do what now?"

"Meet with the committee, of course."

"About what now?"

He replies with an exasperated grunt.

"I'm sorry," she says, "I have a bit of a hearing loss."

"Oh, well then. The Vice President has requested that the university Conflict of Interest Committee look into a matter involving Dean VandenDungen. I believe you are the complainant."

The way he says the world "complainant" makes it sound as if she's bothered the FBI by filing a grievance about somebody's beagle peeing on her petunias.

"I don't know about being a *complainant*," she says, "but I did provide information to Vice President Wickendale about the Dean's relationship with—"

"Yes, yes, I know all that, which is why I'm calling. Would two weeks from tomorrow at 1:00 work for you?"

"But this really has nothing to do with me. It's about the Dean and Mr. Herrington. They have all the facts you need. Anything I could relate would be hearsay."

"Ha! Spoken like a true lawyer, Professor Poe. Unfortunately for you, the formal rules of evidence don't apply to our committee hearings. So 1:00 Tuesday, the 16th? Room 207, Scott Hall. See you then."

Hanging up, she flips through the pages of the University Directory. Remy Terwilliger is a professor in the Department of Applied Research at the School of Pharmacy. Drat! At first blush, one would suppose a scientist would be the perfect leader of such an inquiry, drilling down for facts devoid of bias, sifting through evidence with a discerning eye, immune to the charm or spin or intellectual sleight of hand that are the stock-in-trade of men like VandenDungen and Herrington. But in Sophie's opinion, Wickendale could not have made a worse choice. Believing themselves to be especially brilliant and important, with needs that cannot be met through ordinary channels, research scientists share a central characteristic with the very subjects of the Committee's investigation.

§

The morning of the Conflict of Interest hearing dawns hazy, hot, and humid. Sophie has learned that the Committee consists of five members drawn from a cross-section of university departments. It goes without saying they all have in common a deep antipathy towards the Law School, which by definition is filled to the rafters with lawyers and also happens to be housed in the most recently remodeled building on campus. Not to mention the salary differential. On average a law professor makes 30% more than those in other disciplines and teaches half the number of courses. Sophie understands the resentment. On the other hand, as a legal *skills* teacher, she is treated nearly as poorly as they are.

Sophie has no idea what to expect when she walks into Room 207 at the appointed time, but it definitely isn't a Salman Rushdie look-alike, who introduces himself as Remy Terwilliger. She recognizes one of the other committee members as the university writer-in-residence, a minor celebrity with five self-published novels under his belt who goes by a single name, Twig. The committee members scarcely acknowledge Sophie's presence as they pore over materials laid out in front of them.

After some introductory remarks about the purpose of the hearing, the chairman says, "Professor Poe, we've heard testimony from Dean VandenDungen and Mr. Herrington, as well as several other faculty members. We have some questions for you, but before we get to them, why don't you tell us your side of the story."

At that moment, Sophie realizes she has in fact harbored certain expectations about the proceeding, including that Chaz VandenDungen would be the defendant while she would be respectfully or even gratefully treated as the prosecution's star witness. But it isn't shaping up that way.

With five sets of skeptical eyes trained on her, she summarizes the events culminating in her trip to Yachtkeepers and the now infamous photo of Herrington greeting VandenDungen.

"I find this very disturbing," Terwilliger says.

"I agree," says Sophie. "That's why I took it to Vice President Wickendale."

Terwilliger exchanges a look with Twig, whose scraggly Fu Manchu moustache is braided in two plaits that dangle from his chin to the table top, where they coil like a pair of snakes.

"You misunderstand," Twig says. "What concerns us is *your* conduct. The attachment of a tracking device to the Dean's car. Following him to his destination. Hiding in wait. Using false pretenses to gain entry into a private residential building. Taking unauthorized photographs." Twig glances at the other committee members, who nod in agreement. "These are classic stalking behaviors, Professor. They are criminal acts."

In retrospect, her actions do seem over-the-top, even to her. But why has the focus of the inquiry shifted from the impropriety of the Dean's actions to hers?

"But isn't this hearing about the Dean making decisions based on his own interests rather than the law school's?" she says. "About the impropriety of steering business to a personal acquaintance?" She searches their faces.

All eyes shift from her to Terwilliger. "Candidly, Ms. Poe, the issue we're most troubled about at this point is your own conflict of interest."

"What?"

"This lawsuit against Meyeth Industries. You and your father are the plaintiffs' attorneys."

"As I explained to Vice President Wickendale, I'm no longer acting as counsel in that case."

Terwilliger reaches beneath his stack of papers, retrieving a newspaper. "Apparently that isn't public knowledge."

He drops the paper on the table in front of her. It's the local daily, which she seldom reads. The date is . . . today. She scans the material above the fold; a story about the state legislature defunding core programs in K-12 schools. She glances at Terwilliger. What is she missing?

Clearly irritated, he flips over the paper. On the bottom half of the front page, there's a photo of Arthur and Sophie walking in a parking lot. The headline: *Father-Daughter Team Takes On Meyeth Industries.*

Sophie feels as if her entire body is on fire. Her heart is thumping so crazily she can actually see it beating through her skin like a cylinder head pumping in the center of her chest. She actually looks pretty good in the picture. Pretty cool and professional.

She fights to keep her voice steady. "But this is supposed to be about the Dean."

"The Dean has provided a reasonable explanation of his activities," Terwilliger says.

"What did he say?"

"Thank you, Professor," Terwilliger says. "The committee will issue a report with its findings."

§

On the way back to the law school, Sophie runs into Vanden-Dungen himself, who is heading toward the central administration building. She wants to ignore him, but he plants his bulk squarely in her path.

"I don't get it, Sophie," he says. "I gave you the opportunity to succeed here, and you screwed it up."

She tries to push past him, but he remains rooted in place, so she goes around him. She glances back over her shoulder. He's watching her, shaking his head. Was he born with that unctuous smirk as a permanent feature?

"I hope you enjoy disappearing me on Virtual U!" she shouts.

§

Two weeks later, the Conflict of Interest Committee issues its report, concluding that the charge against Dean VandenDungen is unfounded. "The committee could find no evidence of impropriety on the part of Dean VandenDungen. To the contrary, the evidence demonstrates that he diligently explored options for reducing costs of certain programs within the Law School, a worthy goal given today's challenging economic climate and an activity well within his purview as academic and administrative head." Shortly afterward, Vice President Wickendale and President Hooghly sign off on it.

§

When Sophie shows the report to Shane, he hits her with some harsh truths.

"This isn't about conflicts of interest," he says, "not Vanden-Dungen's, and not yours."

"What the hell is it about then?" she says.

"What's it always about?"

Sophie considers the question. What *is* it always about?

"It's about the Rankings, stupid," Shane says. "He vows he's going to pull us up to the Top 145. That's all they care about across campus."

Opening her briefcase, Sophie removes her faculty handbook. "It says here, 'It is the duty of every dean to avoid entering into transactions in which—'"

"Sophie, you're not listening."

"So he can violate the rules with impunity because some magazine monkey crunches some numbers and gets everyone in Higher Education worked up into a nonsensical frenzy?"

Shane shrugs. "I'm just giving you a reality check."

Sophie stews in her own juices for several minutes, considering the implications of Shane's words and her own choices.

"I'm toast," she says.

Shane doesn't disagree.

With the Skills Program demolished, replaced by Herrington's outsourced adjunct scheme—not to mention the Meyeth suit— she is headed for unemployment. She feels dejected, depleted.

"You're not giving up, are you?" he says.

"He's won. He's a dean. His pal is a former dean, now a CEO of a huge company. And everyone's owned by the Meyeths. So there you go."

She rises to leave, her mind whirring with visions of her and Arthur's dire futures. They'll both have to move, but where? She'll have to begin a job search immediately. Will she be able to supply any decent references? Will Salman Rushdie-Terwilliger's "disturbing" conclusions regarding her stalker-like behaviors plague her?

She opens the door.

"Wait," Shane says. She perceives that the wheels of his self-described "considerable intellect" are turning. "You know, there is an appeal process from the findings of any university committee."

She doesn't know.

"It goes to the Board of Governors."

She isn't feeling better yet. To her mind, the Board of Governors is just another body composed of people with mainstream bona fides, status quo head-nodders who'll buy into the dean's Rankings mission and who'll view her as some minor player in a drama of her own creation, as off-her-rocker as James Yoder.

She stares numbly at Shane, whose eyes have begun to twinkle, always a hopeful sign.

"Do you know who the chairman of the Board of Governors is?" he says.

She shakes her head.

"Ralph Bozeiden."

She draws a blank.

"Oil and gas."

She still doesn't understand the point.

"I don't know him," she says.

"But someone does," Shane says. "Think."

"Oh, for God's sake, Wally, what are you trying to get at? Just say it."

"He's funding Singer's Institute. Paul is practically a member of the family. Bozeiden treats him like a son. We'll talk to Paul."

Is Shane suggesting they engage in influence peddling?

Perfect.

§

Two weeks before the fall semester is to begin, Sophie receives a letter informing her that due to budgetary restrictions, her contract to teach at the law school is not being renewed.

23 Hope

The trial of Mac Higgins vs. Meyeth Industries is fast approaching. Trial preparation requires more work than Sophie imagined, much of it in unfamiliar territory. They need expert witnesses to explain the complex process of fracking as well as the economic impact of the dirty water on Mac's crop yield, but the Meyeth influence is making it difficult. Sophie finds one expert at the state land grant university, but when she tries to hire him to testify, he begs off; Meyeth helps subsidize his department, he explains. He could lose his job.

Luckily, Arthur's name still means something in legal circles. He reaches out to his many contacts and they are able to find the experts before they've even figured out how to pay for them. When the bills for initial consultations come in, Sophie is alarmed. These hired guns charge $200 per hour and up. When she worked at the Justice Department, she never had to pay her witnesses! She didn't have to pay for anything! They paid her!

"Shouldn't Mac take care of these?" she asks Arthur.

"No, ma'am. It's customary for the plaintiff's lawyer to advance these costs."

"I don't have the money."

"You should have considered that before taking the case."

Sophie glares at him. "You should have said something. You know how tight I'm stretched."

Arthur shrugs.

"I pay for half your groceries!"

He appears surprised. "Nobody asked you to."

Sometimes she wonders if Arthur's sporadic cluelessness is a symptom left behind by the strokes or something he adopts when it's convenient.

"Let's go into the accounts," he says, "move some money around.

She doesn't bother to remind him that the days of "accounts" and "moving money around" are long past. She is sure if Mac realized what was going on, he'd offer to cover the expenses, but she also knows the farming operation is in debt, and he'd have to draw down further on his credit line, assuming any remains. Instead, she takes the funds from her retirement account, trying not to think about the heavy penalty for early withdrawal.

§

After a stressful meeting with the fracking expert one afternoon, Sophie exits the interstate in search of soothing pastoral scenes. Rolling past fields where cattle and horses graze, she fondly recalls Sherwood Anderson's observation about livestock, that "they eat grass, make love, work when they have to, bear their young. I am sick with envy of them." Is she really so alienated from her own life that cows making love strikes her as an attractive alternative?

She decides to drive by the old farmhouse. With the ice storms a distant memory, she's unprepared for the damage the house sustained. The front porch is barely visible through the tangle of broken tree branches in the front yard. Closer inspection reveals a perforated roof, cracked windows, and, worst of all, the collapse of the barn. The only structure left unscathed is the brick workshop.

Sophie wonders why she decided to torture herself with this misguided detour to Melancholy Manor. Perhaps she can move in and become the Edith Bouvier Beale of the Midwest. As pitiful as her childhood home looks, though, it touches a chord deep inside her, providing a measure of comfort despite its dilapidated state.

Clearing a spot on the porch, she sits down. Within a few minutes she hears gravel crunching. A gray pickup pulls into view. The two men inside peer in the general direction of the house.

"Ho there!" The man in the passenger seat waves as the truck pulls into the driveway, parking behind the Escort.

Emerging, they glance around hungrily, taking her in as just another feature in the landscape. They walk the property, murmuring back and forth as they duck between two barb wire strands and scuff out into the back pasture. When they return, they circle back to the front of the house, appearing surprised she is still there. They are obviously related, Sophie notes, though a generation apart in age; they have the same face, long and thick-jawed with a prominent mouth, and the same narrow, sloping shoulders. The older man must be pleased about how effectively he reproduced himself.

"Is this your house?" Junior says.

"No."

They glance at each other, clearly wanting to know who she is and what she's doing there, but she feels no obligation to tell them.

"We were going to try to lease this ground," the older man says, "but we heard it's in foreclosure. Do you know anything about it?"

She shakes her head, disliking the direction this is going.

"If it's cheap enough," says Junior, "we might buy it."

"Course we'd knock the old homestead down," Papa says. "It'd all be cropland."

"It's native grass!" she says.

"Ain't no good to us that way," Junior says. "We don't have no cattle."

They both eye her expectantly.

"Well," she says, "I might buy it, too."

"Oh, really?" Papa says. "Do you run cattle?"

"No."

Papa chuckles. "What would you do with all this land?"

"Maybe I'd buy some cattle," she says petulantly. "Or maybe I'd start a big hog farm."

The men share an amused glance. Dragging their booted feet through the thick, waist-high stalks of grass, they head back to the truck.

"Take care now," Papa calls over his shoulder.

She frowns at him. Thanks to them, her stomach is in a knot. She was doing her best to escape for a couple hours; she was actually finding the crude dilapidation, nature reclaiming its space, something of a tonic. Then up pops the specter of her distressed childhood home being sacrificed so one more field of government-subsidized corn can be planted.

On the drive back to town, she imagines herself in a bank applying for a loan to buy Melancholy Manor. The callow loan officer is all smiles until she submits her balance sheet. His gaze skips down the assets column, which includes her diminishing retirement account, her Escort, and $950 in savings, then lingers on her liabilities—six overused credit cards, a sizeable student loan balance, an 88% mortgage on Mud Flat. Then he gets to the anemic income column and bursts out laughing.

§

The Rosecliff Board of Governors is meeting. The agenda is posted on the university web site. Sophie studies it in vain for mention of her appeal of the decision of the Conflict of Interest Committee. She filed the necessary paperwork but has serious doubts it will succeed. The Governors could well consider her appeal moot as she's no longer employed at Rosecliff.

And even if it goes forward, will anyone understand the significance of Marlon Herrington's smoking jacket?

Her only hope lies with Paul Singer. She and Shane didn't even have to ask him to intervene; he volunteered. Like everyone, he was aware of the compromising Yachtkeepers photo, but he didn't know the whole story until Sophie explained what had driven her to "stalk" the dean. Singer is a straight arrow, and no one has greater loyalty to the university. Singer expressed his disgust over

VandenDungen's unilateral management style, his lack of transparency, his reliance on the Consultant, and especially his disrespect for the democratic traditions of the institution.

"Let me see what I can do," he said.

But Sophie has heard nothing since then. She imagines the worst. She can't accept that she lost the battle with VandenDungen. A kind of paralysis sets in, as if the events of the last year have deadened the nerves required for soldiering on.

Then Paul Singer calls her. "The investigation into VandenDungen has been reopened," he says.

"No."

"The Board determined the committee's investigation was too narrow and lacked the proper focus."

Hope lives! "Are you serious?" she shouts into the phone.

"Ralph has met the dean on several occasions and doesn't like him," Singer says. "Ralph really dislikes being condescended to."

She laughs. "So what's going to happen?"

"The Board has directed the President to appoint a new committee—ad hoc, specifically for the purpose of examining all facets of the Dean's decision to partner the law school with Avalerion."

24 BETRAYAL

The days whiz by. As Sophie and Arthur prepare for trial, they put up with each other to a greater extent than either of them thought possible. Sophie continues to withdraw her retirement money to support them. She decides to take advantage of the lean times to buy fewer groceries and thereby lose weight but ends up spending the surplus on wine.

As the trial nears, Sophie receives a phone message from an editor at *People Magazine*, which happens to be her favorite leisure-time periodical. The message says the magazine is interested in the David-Goliath story of her and Arthur going against the powerful Meyeth Triplets. They want to do a story on the case.

Under normal circumstances, Sophie would be over the moon about being featured in *People Magazine*. Who wouldn't? But when the message arrives, she feels so overwhelmed that it seems like just one more thing she has to deal with. Meyeth has flooded them with motions and demands. Arthur has remained surprisingly sharp about legal matters, but he tires easily. They sorely need another lawyer on the team, but so far, they haven't found anyone willing to help. When Sophie describes the case, eyes glaze over, and no one's calendar will allow such a big commitment. It's pretty clear everyone thinks they'll lose.

Surprisingly, Arthur urges her to do the *People* interview. She figured he'd disparage it as so much pop-culture frivolity. But he says, "This is national exposure, lady. Unlike your professor activities, it might actually lead to something."

Stressed though she is, she relents, and the magazine schedules a reporter and photographer to visit their town. The reporter is pretty much what she expected: a hipster twenty-something man, Jesse, who could not possibly relate to her situation. But it's all been arranged, and it's too late to back out. He spends half a day with her, including a "tour" of Mud Flat, introduction to Buggles—of whom many photos are taken—a visit to Arthur's, and a "meet" with Mac at Arby's, which seems mostly like a photo op. Jesse seems quite taken with their cause against Meyeth Industries. When they leave, Sophie feels more disappointed than relieved. Is her life so tedious and banal that a few hours are sufficient to capture it?

"You're assuming that you are the story," Arthur tells her. "But you're only half of the story."

That gives Sophie pause. To her, there is only one story, the one they're preparing to tell to a jury.

"I'm pretty sure Jesse gets it," she says. "He knows who the good guys are."

"You are being naïve," Arthur informs her.

§

Sophie learns just how naïve she is the day before the trial, when the *People* issue containing her story hits the stands. At first glance, it appears to be what she hoped for: a photograph of Arthur and her, back to back with their arms crossed over their chests, looking serious and tough opposite a composite of photos of the expensively-suited Meyeth Triplets individually and together in various combinations—a collage of thin lips, ruddy jowls and reptilian eyes. But the text betrays her. Jesse has betrayed her! He spoke to a bunch of Rosecliff people, as well as . . . James Yoder! The reader could well have the impression that she is a temperamental, unattached lady with an inappropriate fixation on a middle-aged student. And Arthur—oh my God!—Arthur, thanks to James, sounds like a doddering old has-been who wouldn't know a courtroom from a bathroom. "He was confused about even the simple things," James is quoted as saying. "To tell the truth, he can barely function. I can't imagine how he can pull this off."

Sophie feels like breaking down, but she can't afford to. She can't tell Arthur about the article. He'll find out about it at some point, but he's planning on making the opening statement in their case; he's had it memorized for months. She won't let his confidence be undercut by Jesse's duplicitous slop.

§

On the first morning of the trial, the scene at the courthouse isn't exactly as Sophie once imagined it—a parade of disgruntled farmers riding into town on tractors, led by her on a motorcycle and Arthur on a scooter chair. Instead, the parking lot and front stairs of the courthouse are swarming with reporters. Sophie and Arthur push their way through, as if this were a perp walk, and they are the perps. The reporters charge, shouting insulting questions such as "Do you think you can stand up to the Meyeth lawyers, Mr. Poe?" and "Are you sure your law license is still good?"

Walking swiftly as always, Arthur says to Sophie, "I didn't know I look so ancient."

"You look good," Sophie says truthfully. "Ready for battle."

Inside, in the courtroom, the atmosphere is subdued. The scenario strikes Sophie as a bit incestuous. At the defense table is Cleve Fiordimondo, the Supervising Attorney at the Meyeth Law Clinic at Rosecliff, along with three recent Rosecliff grads and two Rosecliff interns. Sophie recognizes a couple of law school administrators milling about. Of course, the Rosecliff team is flanked by high dollar lawyers from some white shoe firm.

Jury selection goes well enough. The defense uses strike after strike attempting to drain the pool of people who've expressed in one way or another that they are fed up with corporate America. With a jury seated, Judge Kotsiopoulos calls it a day; opening statements will begin the next morning.

Sophie drops off Arthur and Mac, who is staying at a motel, then heads home. Mac is scheduled to come by in a couple hours so they can go over the major points in his testimony one last time. Fifteen minutes before he's due, Sophie is finishing off a half-gallon of coffee ice cream when Buggles ruptures into croaking spasms. She thought she'd broken Mac of his very uncool habit of arriving early "just to be on the safe side." She rushes around picking up stray clothes and dirty plates, then checks herself in the mirror, as the doorbell rings.

"Come in," she shouts.

As Sophie emerges from the kitchen, the door swings open, revealing Jesse, the *People* reporter. His presence is so unexpected that both she and Buggles are speechless. Random thoughts fly through Sophie's mind, the oddest being that Jesse is there to sexually assault her. Then she notices he's carrying an open laptop, and she realizes that probably no one would do that if they intended a sexual assault.

"Sorry," he says.

"You should be," Sophie says. "You made me and Dad look like idiots in your story."

"I meant sorry for barging in."

"Well, you're here."

"Can I sit down?" Jess says. "It's been a long day." He plops on the couch.

"It's not over for me," Sophie says.

Jess pats the cushion next to him. She accedes, curious about what's on his screen.

He turns to her. "When I was researching your story, I spent a little time talking to folks in Montana."

"Why?"

"Background on the Meyeths."

"Okay."

"Yeah, they own land up there. Anyway, during that when I

270

was there, this guy contacted me. He's a real estate agent. He sent me an e-mail, but I never followed up on it." He clicks on the laptop and places it on her lap. "Take a look."

Sophie leans forward to read it.

> I heard you're doing a story on a lawsuit against Meyeth over fracking. I'm sure you know they have a family compound near Boise. I sold it to them. But I bet no one is telling you that when they were looking to build they were very worried about environmental conditions. They wanted to make sure there was no oil drilling or HYDRAULIC FRACTURING by any company going on nearby that might DEMINISH THE VALUE or disturb them in some way in the use and enjoyment of their property. Now there is a lawsuit in progress here to stop a proposed FRACKING site not far from their compound and guess who is one of the plaintiffs? FRED MEYETH on behalf of TRIPLE M RANCHES, LLC, the company that owns the compound.

A warm flush of excitement runs through Sophie, tempered by a note of caution inspired by the writer's use of capital letters and the possibility he might be unhinged.

"Who is this guy?" she says.

Jess shrugs. "Some real estate agent."

"But why is he doing this? What does he get from it?"

"I don't have any idea."

Sophie stands. She feels like twirling around. She takes the laptop from Jesse and rereads the message.

"We need to contact him," she says.

Jesse's eyes bulge. "There's no 'we' here."

"We both want to get to the bottom of this, don't we?"

Jesse looks up at her. "I just thought you'd want to know about it."

It strikes her that if Jesse had wanted to "get to the bottom" of it, he already would have followed up. Jesse moves to the door.

"Wait," she says. "I didn't even write down the guy's information."

"Clay Umshied. Latimer Real Estate."

As the door closes behind Jesse, Sophie realizes why he put such a disappointing spin on the article, why he came tonight, and why he just flew out the door. He is basically a good guy, but neither he nor his magazine is interested in a real exposé of anything to do with the Meyeths.

Headlights shine through the front window, meaning Mac is here. Sophie feels paralyzed. If true, Umshied's tip could change the entire shape and tenor of the trial. But it's 10:42 the night before opening statements.

"Hey," Mac calls out as he shoulders the door open.

Grabbing her coat, Sophie turns him around and says, "Come on. We gotta go."

§

Arthur listens to Sophie's news with his eyes closed.

"So how should we proceed?" she asks him.

"I'll handle it," he says.

"Let's call him," she says. "We need to talk to him right now."

Arthur holds up a hand. "Hold on there. Slow down."

Sophie sighs. "We don't have time."

"Of course we do. Don't worry."

"But I need to know what will be happening tomorrow."

Arthur looks up at her with cloudy eyes. "You will observe Cleve Fiordimondo crawling on his knees, begging us to accept a settlement."

Arthur's grandiosity does nothing to quell her nerves. She pictures Fiordimondo and the other expensively clad Meyeth attorneys as they appeared in court that morning, robust, impeccably groomed, and supremely confident, then she looks at her father, all 144 pounds of him, thin-skinned with blue veins protruding everywhere, sitting there in his pin-striped "court shirt" and his threadbare boxer shorts. She rises to leave. Arthur shuffles after

272

her, with Mac bringing up the rear.

"Sophia," Arthur says as they reach the door.

"Huh?"

"I've been thinking about something."

There follows an extended pause during which her father's breathing sounds uncertain and rattley.

"Thinking about what?" Sophie says finally.

"I never favored your brother."

"Dad," she says, feeling embarrassed. "It's okay."

"In the world I was raised in, a man went into business with his son. It was nothing personal against you."

He reaches out and jerks her forward by the neck and scrapes the side of her face with his beard stubble.

"You're a good daughter."

25 PUNIES

Arthur stands before the jury, his face gaunt, his tie knot off-center, his gray suit looking three sizes too big.

"Not in their backyard," he says, his voice strong and clear. He pauses, looking at the jurors one-by-one, making the kind of eye contact with strangers that helped him become a winning plaintiff's attorney for decades. "Oh, there's no problem with tearing up the earth to make a profit—just make sure it's done near other people's homes. Water pollution? Air pollution? Earthquakes? No problem! That's just collateral damage, so long as it's someone else's damage. Just the cost of doing business. The price that must be paid—by others, of course— to fuel those private jets and infinity pools."

Sophie glances at the jury. They are engaged. A couple of them are smiling. They like Arthur. One of his greatest assets is authenticity, and juries like authentic.

At the defense table, Cleve Fiordimondo is clearly disturbed. He hadn't expected to hear anything from Arthur about jets and pools. Now he's on his feet with an objection, and the judge calls the attorneys forward for a bench conference. Fiordimondo complains that the Meyeths' lifestyle is irrelevant to the issues in the case. Arthur argues that it shows knowledge of the potential harm and is pertinent to their punitive damages claim.

Judge Kotsiopoulos considers their arguments, then shakes his jowls, turns to the jury, and advises them that he'll allow reference to in the plaintiffs' opening statement but to remember that what the attorneys say is not evidence.

The attorneys return to their places. Arthur resumes his position behind the lectern. He glances at Sophie, a puzzled look on his face. She gives him a thumbs up, trying to urge him past whatever is bothering him. Flipping through her papers, she pulls out the text of his opening. He didn't take a copy to the lectern, but she could easily slip it to him. He smacks his lips several times, then closes his eyes. Sophie clears her throat, but he doesn't respond.

"Arthur?" It's Judge Kotsiopoulos. "Continue, please."

No response.

"Arthur? Are you all right?"

The faces of the jurors show concern. The faces of the defense team look a bit smug. They're already counting him out? Sophie evaluates a scenario in which Arthur is subtracted from the equation. The case could go forward. She knows it inside and out.

"Well," Arthur says. His eyes remain shut.

"We'll take a break," the judge says. "Bailiff? Take the jury for a break."

Arthur's eyes snap open. "A farmer doesn't have the luxury of . . . of . . ." And with that, he collapses to the floor. Flat on his back. Mouth open.

Sophie and Mac leap up together. Sophie blinks rapidly and hyperventilates while Mac crouches over Arthur, making a series of deliberate movements with his hands that Sophie recognizes are the steps to assess whether CPR is needed. Next, he's ripping open Arthur's court shirt, pumping his hands on Arthur's chest.

As Sophie gazes down at her father, his eyes open, and he winks at her. At least she thinks that happened. But did she imagine it? Mac is still pumping on his chest. That means he's trying to start Arthur's heart. So Arthur couldn't have winked.

Someone has called an ambulance. The paramedics lift Arthur like so much kindling, and he's gone. Mac's arm rests across Sophie's shoulders.

The bailiff has removed the jury.

"Counsel?" It's Judge Kotsiopoulos, motioning to the lawyers to follow him to his chambers.

The chambers are surprisingly cramped, and Sophie is squished up against the nearest of a plethora of Meyeth attorneys. The judge rolls his heavy-lidded eyes, signaling disgust with the over-representation.

"So?" he says. "What's going to happen here?"

Fiordimondo says, "Defendant moves for a mistrial, Judge."

The judge's fleshy features reposition themselves into a sleepy semblance of a grimace.

"On what grounds?"

Sophie wishes the judge hadn't asked Fiordimondo such an open-ended question because it prompts a tedious lecture on the law of mistrials. He winds it down with, "Given today's dramatic event, my client cannot receive a fair trial." He glances at Sophie. "I would think Ms. Poe would want a mistrial, too. She's lost her lead counsel."

In truth, she kind of does. Handling this trial with its scientific complications, alone, is an intimidating prospect. But there's no way she's going to admit that.

"Absolutely not, Your Honor. We're ready to proceed."

Eyes shut, pumpkin head resting on the chair back, the judge softly snores. The attorneys shuffle their feet impatiently. No one wants to wake him up, drawing disfavor. Sophie is in no hurry for the ruling; she is worried he'll grant the mistrial, if for no other reason than he prefers sleeping to acting like a judge. The fancy out-of-town lawyers do not understand Judge Kotsiopoulos and his laid-back style. They don't like it, and, Sophie observes, they are preparing to make that known. A Young Turk steps forward, raps his knuckles on the judge's desk, and says, "Your Honor, we need a ruling on our motion."

The judge shows no sign he heard.

Turk raps again. "Your Honor –"

The judge leans forward. "Motion denied." His eyes are open, doing an odd swirly dance. "And you should know, Cleve, that if the plaintiffs can prove what they claimed in their opening, I will grant the motion to add a punitive damages claim. So we'll extend the break till after lunch so the two sides can have a conversation."

26 SETTLEMENT

The biggest disagreement between Sophie and Arthur is whether Buggles will remain an indoor dog. Arthur dislikes dogs; he's always preferred large animals, particularly the female bovine. "She's the most impressive creature on God's earth," he says to her for the gazillionth time. "She lives her entire life in the open, withstanding the harshest conditions nature can dish out. Temperatures ranging from below zero to 120 degrees. Sleet, hail, dust storms, lightning, tornadoes. Meanwhile, turning a diet of grass, salt, and water into food for human beings, she bears calf after calf, year after year, nursing them to a weaning weight of over 500 pounds."

Pointing at Buggles, he declares, "What in the hell does that freakish thing contribute to society?"

They compromise on a plan permitting Buggles to access the utility room, Sophie's bedroom, and the living room on his pillow if Sophie is present. "And of course you're free to let it destroy your office," Arthur allows. "That's entirely up to you."

Setting up an office in the front of the workshop was the easiest part of their move back to the farm. Sophie power-washed the outside, removing about two-thirds of the flaking white paint, leaving a weathered brick exterior a New York designer would appreciate.

Inside, she painted the walls, sealed the concrete floor, laid down a rug, and moved in some old library bookcases she found at a flea market.

The house is another matter, and still a work in progress. Luckily, the limestone structure remains sturdy, but most everything else has to be replaced, including the roof, windows, and plumbing. The front porch has been rebuilt. Since the weather turned nice, Arthur has taken up residence there, reading the *Wall Street Journal*, listening to CNN on his new satellite radio, and producing endless tapes of various calculations.

Spraying Round-Up along the foundation of the workshop, Sophie glances over at him. He is studying his calendar.

"Aren't we expecting Mac this morning?" he calls to her.

"Tomorrow morning," she says. Mac is a regular visitor to the farm, helping with the restoration and keeping the pastures mowed. Sophie's pretty crazy about him, except for his loud voice. She made the mistake of complaining to Arthur.

"He also chews loudly," she added.

"Get earplugs," Arthur said.

This morning, the still air is filled with the sweetness of spring combined with the acrid odor of grass fires; landowners of all stripes, from the exurban lord of ten acres to ranchers who own thousands, are burning away last year's dried weeds and thatch.

Crunching gravel announces the arrival of Karla Johansson; she and Lily are making their first will together. Since opening her law office, Sophie has drawn a surprising amount of business from her former colleagues at the law school. Evidently lawyers don't practice on themselves any more diligently than doctors do.

Karla wears the coolest Euro-style sunglasses Sophie has ever seen. It makes Sophie feel successful to have a client with such an outstanding sense of fashion. Karla hands Sophie a package wrapped in brown paper; it feels like a framed picture of some sort.

"What's this?"

"For your new place of business," Karla says. "A few of us got together."

Inside the office, Sophie tears open the paper and turns over the frame. It is an enlarged facsimile of a check from Meyeth Industries made out to Sophie Poe, in the amount of $12,250,000. Beneath it, in bold letters, appear the words

MEYETH SETTLES *** SOPHIE DOESN'T.

Sophie is speechless; some of her former colleagues actually *do* like her.

Of course, most of the money went to her clients, but she pulled in enough in contingency fees to purchase the farm and rehabilitate the house.

Half an hour passes before she and Karla get around to talking about the specifics of the will. As a communitarian, Karla explains, she feels an obligation to promote information balance regarding Rosecliff, and Sophie is hungry for gossip, whatever it's called. Kara breaks the news that Chaz VandenDungen has just been selected as the new dean of a provisional New England for-profit law school named Standard Law Academy and will be leaving Rosecliff at the end of the spring semester.

It isn't exactly good news. How can one celebrate the misfortune of a whole new batch of victims?

"Oh, and did ya hear about the new Rankings?" Karla says. "They just came out."

Sophie feels as if Karla has mentioned the name of someone she went to high school with and barely remembers.

"What?"

"The *U.S. News* Rankings."

"What about them?"

"We made it into the Top 145."

"No."

"Yah. Ya know Rachel Green?"

Sophie nods. Sure. The beautiful wingnut.

"She sent a pamphlet to all the law schools in virtual space or some kinda thing, and anyways, the pamphlet invited everyone to attend Camp Rosecliff. 'Law, Raw,' was the slogan, and believe it or not, that somehow boosted our reputation enough to move us up."

After they discuss what she and Lily want in their will, Karla and her Euro-style sunglasses depart.

Sophie finishes killing the weeds around the workshop and barn foundations, then heads for the porch. She has about fifteen minutes before her new client arrives. Ming Qi is a farmer that Mac met at an implements show. He claims that he bought a defective planter from the Jack Buck Company. "It just lays the seed on top of the ground," he told Sophie on the phone. "I could have done that without spending $40,000." He said he'd contacted the Buck Company numerous times, but it refused to make good on the planter's warranty.

Mounting the steps, Sophie glances at Arthur. He is slumped forward in his chair.

"Dad!"

Heart in her throat, she rushes to him and slaps him on the back. His breathing is ragged, the inhalations too far apart.

"Dad! Wake up!"

She grabs hold of his bony shoulders and shakes him as hard as she can.

His eyes pop open.

"Dad? What happened?"

"What in the hell are you talking about?"

"You were hardly breathing!"

He smiles at her, dentures loose, face as gaunt as one of those dying people in a Colors of Benetton ad.

"I love you, Sophie," he says, "but you never could take a joke."

"Damn it, Dad!"

She turns as a car approaches and pulls into the drive.

"Is that our new client what's-his-name?" Arthur says. "Minky?"

She nods.

"Let's get to it," he says.

Sophie takes his arm, and they head down the stairs.

"Fill me in again," Arthur says. "What's his problem?"

"He's been given the shaft," she says. "Bullied and bullshitted.

He needs our help."

Arthur's eyes sparkle. "He came to the right place, then, didn't he?"

"Yep," she says, smiling at him. "He came to the experts."